Empire and Tyranny

By Michael G. Bergen

The Rutherford Chronicles

A tumultuous family journey through the 20th Century

Part 3

"...we shall fight on the beaches, we shall fight on the landing grounds, we shall fight in the fields and in the streets, we shall fight in the hills; we shall never surrender..."

— British Prime Minister Winston Churchill, in one of his most famous speeches to the House of Commons on 4 June 1940.

"The enemy wins their battles from the air! They knock out my panzers with American armour-piercing shells."

— German Field Marshal Erwin Rommel, The Desert Fox.

"That's impossible! The Americans only know how to make razor blades."

— Reichsmarshall Hermann Göring, a German World War I fighter pilot ace, politician, military leader, and convicted war criminal. He was one of the most influential figures in the Nazi Party, which ruled Germany from 1933 to 1945.

"We could do with some of those razor blades, Herr Reichsmarshall."

— Field Marshal Erwin Rommel.

"Defend Paris to the last, destroy all bridges over the Seine, and devastate the city."

— Adolf Hitler—August 1944

"The fruits of victory are tumbling into our mouths too quickly."

— Emperor Hirohito of Japan, 29 April 1942

For my late grandparents and parents,

who lived through trying times,

and for all their descendants.

Contents

Prologue

My repeating theme is why warfare captivates each generation's youth, motivating them to join conflict? Is it the proud military uniform acting as an attraction to the opposite sex? Is it because military service offers global travel and adventure? Or is it the pride of protecting one's country?

I knew my father had fought and survived WWII in Europe. I also learned that my British grandfather fought in the South African Boer War and WWI. He spent four years as a prisoner of war in Germany. Why did my grandfather join two destructive wars? Why did my father eagerly join the Canadian Army at the start of World War II and witness the horrors of that war in the hard-fought Italian Campaign? As a 7-year-old, I met a cousin in England who was a sailor in the Royal Navy during the Korean War. He became my hero and role model, setting me on a course to join the Sea Cadets, the Royal Canadian Navy, during the Cold War.

Does this sound familiar? Has your family lived through such historical events? Have you had relatives who followed similar painful paths, possibly more recently? I suspect many of you have.

So yes, I became such a young man, fascinated by my heritage and military history. I'm a student of conflict. Similar to those who came before me, I was eager to put on my uniform and join the war.

Empire and Tyranny

That is long behind me now, but my interest didn't wane. So, later in life, I embarked on a project to understand my forbear's challenges. They had left no written record or diaries and were loath to talk much about their war experiences. Driven by a desire to understand their lives and experiences, I undertook research into major 20th-century conflicts. That research provided the historical framework for this series. I found historical records and books that followed every step they made in three 20th-century wars. My imagination filled in the blanks they had left by not recording their personal journeys.

This book is the third of four, describing a tumultuous family journey through the violent 20th century. The heart of the story revolves around Joe's struggle to reconcile his wartime experiences with the desire for a peaceful life. An underlying theme is the resilience of the human spirit, as exemplified by the Rutherford family. Despite facing many challenges, including war, poverty, and personal tragedies, they persevered and maintained a strong sense of family and community. This theme evoked in me a quiet admiration for their determination and a deeper appreciation for the importance of family bonds. Their ability to find joy and hope amidst adversity was inspiring.

Another prevalent theme is the cyclical nature of history. The story highlights how quickly societies can forget the lessons of the past, leading to the repetition of conflict and suffering. The parallels between World War I and World War II, experienced by Joe, resonated strongly and left me with a sense of unease about the future.

In this quest for my family history, I learned that war is frightening, painful, and undesirable. The Center for International and Security Studies in Maryland has documented all the wars and conflicts of the twentieth century that resulted in 231 million deaths. So, why do we keep falling into its dangerous trap? Why allow warmongering politicians to send each generation's youth into battle? What accounts for our enduring captivation with war heroes, and why does each generation seem to ignore the previous generation's blunders?

Those are the questions I seek answers to in **The Rutherford Chronicles.**

This third book in the series begins in the weeks following WWI when Joe returns to his young family after his four years of incarceration in German PoW Camps. He was a virtual skeleton, a survivor of the war and the Spanish Flu, but alive! Joe, his family, and England's Northwest industrial struggle went on through the hard interwar years. The workers of many of England's traditional industrial areas face an increasing battle with layoffs and company closures through the Great Depression. Joe and his family moved south to Croydon, South London, in 1936 and gradually rebuilt their lives until Adolf Hitler launched World War II. The Canadian forces arrive, and one of them marries a Rutherford daughter. The rest of their story follows...

1
The Interwar Years: 1919 to 1939

Recovery and Remembrance

Joe Rutherford found his way that January night in 1919 to Hawthorn Leslie's shipyards in Hebburn on the River Tyne, where he had worked before the war. Joe and others from his regiment had endured 1,479 days of hunger and anguish in captivity. The Germans captured them in October 1914, and four years of prisoner-of-war camps in Germany had left scars on his mind. His years of confinement left him haunted, his mind in turmoil. He had lost friends, too, friends the enemy had shot on the Western Front or when escaping from the POW camps. Others became ill and died before they could experience the sweetness of the freedom he was now enjoying. There had been too many days when guards were watching his every move, blocking any attempt to escape. But he was fortunate to have survived the Great War that killed or maimed millions of people, including two of his closest friends and three brothers-in-law.

It was a chilly night on Tyneside[1], the shipyards, factories, and workers' terrace houses enveloped in fog and

---

[1] The industrial and urban areas on both banks of the River Tyne, historically part of the counties of Northumberland (north bank) and County Durham (south bank) including the urban areas of Newcastle upon Tyne, Gateshead, Tynemouth, Wallsend, South Shields, Hebburn and Jarrow. This busy region is extended south in County Durham to Wearside on the River Wear and Teesside on the River Tee.

hoarfrost. Joe recalled the Vehnemoor Celle VI POW Camp in the peat moss bogs of northeast Germany. He and his marras[2] had attempted an escape on just such a night. The camp was thirty-odd miles from the Dutch border, and they had almost made it. However, that occurred in January 1917, more than halfway through the 'Great War', which was later referred to as World War II. After that, they spent nearly two years as POWs at Germany's largest POW camp, Soltau.

The constant rumble and hammering of the yards and factories of Tyneside reminded him of muffled guns and rifle fire. And the smoke rising from dozens of factories created an acrid smog[3] like the battlefields. Joe soon dismissed that analogy from his mind as unpleasant memories. He had survived a month of hell on the battlefields of the Western Front early in the war, too. "It doesn't sound much," he thought. "In that month, my battalion lost 1,000 officers and men. They had trained together and travelled to the battlefields of France together. 800 fellow Durham Light Infantry marras had lost their lives, limbs, or freedom within one month of arriving at France's River Aisne on the Western Front. Joe had read that three-quarters of a million British soldiers had died or were missing in

---

[2] A friend, pal, buddy or mate in the north of England, especially among the working classes.

[3] "*The morning fog*," Santa Cruz Weekly Sentinel, 3 July 1880. It is really not fog at all, but cloud of pure white mist. warmer and much less wetting than a "Scotch Mist," not differing entirely from the true British fog, facetiously spelled "smog" because it's always coloured and strongly impregnated with smoke, a mixture as unwholesome as it is unpleasant.

action in that war. And the enemy wounded another one and a half million men in that 'war to end all wars.'"

"Many of those men were only boys," thought Joe. "The war had also disabled many who could never again work or lead a regular life." In silence, he thanked God for not suffering the same fate.

Tyneside was one of the leading industrial regions in the world for coal mining and shipbuilding since the Industrial Revolution when Britain produced most of the world's ships. Along with Clydeside, Merseyside, and Wearside, they had built more ships in the last century than anyone anywhere else. Besides the collieries, Jarrow and Hebburn had two primary employers in 1919. Palmers Shipbuilding and Iron Company was by far the largest employer in Jarrow, and the smaller Hawthorn Leslie and Company was in Hebburn. Between them, they provided a living for 90% of the workers in this part of Tyneside. Joe had worked for Hawthorn Leslie before he left for the Great War in 1914. He had worked there before he left for the Boer War in South Africa in 1901.

At Hawthorn Leslie's Hebburn yards, Joe found his old marra, Mike O'Brien, meandering in the darkness, too. Joe and Mike were lifelong friends who had fought in two wars together. They had endured the Great War side by side in the battles on the Western Front and three POW camps in Germany.

"Aalreet[4] Mike, what are ye doing here at this time of night?" he called out in his best shipyard-Geordie[5] livened up with a touch of Irish brogue?

"Aalreet Joe, I suppose the same as ye," said Mike, winking. They both laughed and embraced.

"They are still hard at work," said Joe while surveying the yard. "Look. There are at least a dozen ships in different stages of building in our old yard, including destroyers, cargo ships, tugs, and a large passenger-cargo ship. And Palmers? They look busy, too. I visited there yesterday."

"Aye, lots of work. We must get in there again," said Mike. "With the war over, they will not get as much work."

"How are ye doing, Mike?" asked Joe. "Getting any stronger?"

"I guess so. And you, Joe?" said Mike.

"Aye, getting there; Mary is doing a fine job of looking after me. And I'm home with my little family again!"

"Aye," said Mike. "It's such a pleasure to be back home. Ruth is looking after me, too. And my little Michael is such a fine laddie."

Joe and Mike considered themselves very fortunate! They were home on Tyneside for a long time. They had celebrated their

---

[4] Geordie for "hello" or "you ok?"

[5] The people of the Tyneside area, called Geordies, have a reputation for their distinctive dialect and accent. Tynesiders may have been given this name, a local diminutive of the name George, because their miners used George Stephenson's safety lamp (invented in 1815 and called a Geordie lamp) to prevent firedamp explosions, rather than the Davy lamp used elsewhere.

first wonderful Christmas since joining the war effort with their families, and life was returning to normal for them. Joe walked every night through his familiar neighbourhoods of Jarrow and Hebburn on the south bank of the River Tyne and often met his old companion. They were both enjoying the freedom and aloneness of walking out of their front doors and exploring their old haunts without being watched by guards.

"What you and I have been through together, my old marra!" said Joe. "We are now close to forty years old, most of that as marras."

"Why did we go, Joe?" asked Mike.

"Because we believed it was our duty to protect this country and our families from the Boche," said Joe, repeating his old refrain.

"Aye, that was it. But did we need to go?" asked Mike. "We had done our duty in South Africa and India. Why did we have to go to France for this bloody war?"

"I ask myself that every day, too, my marra," said Joe.

"I left Mary and our two bairns behind to go to a filthy trench war and German POW camps. They suffered; I suffered; we all suffered. Why? I don't know. So many men, young and old, joined the Army. We just got caught up in it and felt we had to join. I can't remember the details. I just remember we were at peace and enjoying our lives and work one day, and then we were signing up for war again the next."

"Aye. It makes little sense, does it?" mumbled Mike.

Back home, Joe slipped into bed with Mary, who was sleeping. She was warm through her nightclothes, so he fit his body into the contours of her form.

Then, after giving her a soft kiss on the neck, he fell asleep and soon dreamed he was on the Chemin des Dames above the River Aisne in France.

The night was black except for the constant flashes of guns and exploding shells.

"There's not much bloody protection in these trenches," said Mike. "How can we stay safe here?"

"Aye, I don't know where we should hide from the Boche aiming at us over there," Joe said. "They are so close we could reach out and touch them."

"Is this it?" asked their long-time marra Jack. "Two lines of soldiers facing and shooting at each other in the rain and mud? Is this our new war?"

"Looks like it," said Joe. "It's a bloody miserable state of affairs."

"Aye. There is no protection against those bloody Boche shells," said Mike. "Well, laddies, it was nice knowing ye. God knows how long we'll survive out here."

Then, from the trench, looking out across the scarred terrain to the German entrenchments, they saw movements. German soft uniform caps and spiked helmets appeared from time to time above their parapets as the German troops prepared for their attack. The morning was misty and dark, and the rain started pouring in sheets. Joe's fingers had stiffened, and they weren't sure they could fire their weapons should the enemy charge.

"Bloody hell," whispered Mike then. "I don't have a comfortable feeling, laddies. In these exposed, shallow ditches, enduring the downpour? It's bloody freezing and dangerous. We have the German Army staring at us from a few yards away, and those movements may mean they will soon attack us."

"Aye, Mike, this doesn't look good for us," said Joe. "We had better do our best if we want to survive. I reckon the Boche is just as wet and freezing as we are. Keep your heads low, and let's watch what's happening around us. Stay alive!"

"What about those darkies next to the West Yorkshires? Are they fighting men?" asked Jack.

"I bloody well hope so," said Mike.

Minutes later, the Germans launched a fierce attack along the Allied line. It began with the horrific storm of an artillery barrage. With the wind and beating rain, it became a storm of fire and water. Shells exploded before and behind the trenches and even overhead, raining shrapnel on us unsuspecting newcomers. German machine guns and rifles opened fire along the line. Bullets whizzed past them, embedded themselves in the earth mound behind them, or ricocheted off boulders and helmets. It was so loud they couldn't communicate with each other. The smoke, rain, and mist made it impossible to see the enemy. And it continued nonstop for over an hour.

"Keep your heads low, laddies, and return fire as best you can," yelled a corporal nearby.

"How?" cried Mike. "I can't see the bastards!"

"Just fire in their direction," yelled the corporal. "They'll get the message, and we might down a few."

After the first shocks, which had frozen them in their positions, they rallied their strength and nerve and fought back as hard as possible. The noise was deafening, the whizzing bullets frightening, and the sound waves and shrapnel from the exploding shells battered our line nonstop.

"We'll give you as much as you are giving us, you bloody Hun," yelled Mike while unloading his rifle over and over in rapid-fire towards the German line.

Mike's fellow Durhams, along the line, did the same, including Joe. After a few minutes of preparing their guns, the British artillery returned shells in rapid fire. Cannon blasts punctuated the Durhams' cries of pain.

The Moroccans on their right also came under a massive attack and were panicking and retreating. So, as the Moroccans pulled back, the Officer Commanding the 1st West Yorkshire Regiment moved one of his companies to cover the gap caused by their retreat. Then, the Moroccan officers rallied their men for a while, and they moved forward again. There was total confusion. Not knowing the British had moved into their position, the Moroccans opened fire on the 1st West Yorkshire

Battalion men, who suffered thirty casualties—friendly fire and complete chaos!

"I told you so," called Jack as loud as he could. "You can't trust those Wogs to get things right!"

"I think we are all in the same bucket here, Jack," I yelled, "no matter the colour of our skin."

"A bloody dangerous bucket!" screamed Jack.

"Look up there, laddies," called Joe. "It's a plane. I can see the pilot and a bombardier. They're coming our way. Watch them."

"They've dropped a bomb," screamed Mike. "It's coming straight for us!"

"Dive for cover," screamed Joe!

Joe awoke in a sweat. Mary had heard him groaning and calling out "bloody dangerous" and "dive for cover." So, she was awake too and comforting him.

"Relax, darling," said Mary. "You must have had a nightmare. I'll bring you some tea and a biscuit."

"I'm sorry I woke you up, my darling," said Joe. "A bomb was coming straight for us, and then I woke up, thank God."

"That's all right, Joe. You poor darling. We'll have some tea; you can tell me all about it. Then we'll go back to sleep, my love."

§

Empire and Tyranny

Joe walked every night, regardless of the weather, as soon as Mary and the children were asleep. He enjoyed breathing in the air of Tyneside despite, or because of, its familiar pall of industrial smoke. He had drawn breath in this smog-filled environment since his childhood. The breezes of the POW camps blowing off the Lüneburg Heath in rural North Germany had been so clean and healthy. But it was not the air of his homeland. He enjoyed walking wherever he pleased, unfettered in familiar surroundings. And he cherished the liberty of allowing his mind to overcome the turmoil of his last four years.

Joe and Mike often met, walking together while reminiscing about their exploits since they had first joined Queen Victoria's Army in 1900. As soldiers, they had shared many experiences in South Africa, India, France, Belgium, and Germany over two decades. The friends remembered many of the fun times and avoided reawakening their nasty episodes, the stuff of their inescapable nightmares. Yes, they lost many of their old marras, but they made many friends, too, along the way. And they treasured their medals and the King's letter to homecoming British POWs to honour their sacrifices. And both Joe and Mike still had their limbs and faculties intact!

"My God, Mike, how did we live through these last few years?" asked Joe.

"It's a miracle, Joe," said Mike. "We survived hell. I'm home, but I can't escape it. I dream about it every night. But what of those who didn't return?"

"Aye," said Joe as if from a distance, "I'm dreaming about it too, Mike. Billy, Jack, Fred, and the hundreds or thousands of others we left there in the blood and mud of the battlefields. Mary's three brothers died within a few miles of each other near Ypres. I'm miserable every time I remember them dying in those trenches. What has become of their remains?"

"Buried in the mud of France and Flanders," said Mike. "Far from their beloved Tyneside."

"Aye. Buried in the mud of France and Flanders. But their souls are now in heaven."

"Or maybe here with us, Joe."

Of the millions of Britons who went to fight in the Great War, 10% never came back. The official final and corrected casualty figures of the British Army for the Great War were 574,000 killed in action. Over 250,000 were missing and presumed dead. The war disabled or damaged another 1.7 million badly enough to qualify for a war pension. Surgeons amputated the limbs of over 40,000 men during the war; 272,000 suffered other debilitating injuries in the legs or arms; 60,000 were injured in the head or eyes, and 89,000 sustained further severe damage to their battered bodies. Many returning soldiers weren't as fortunate as Joe and Mike. Disabled soldiers needed continued care, many for the rest of their lives. Most of these men found it difficult, if not impossible, to regain employment on their return. It took over a year for the last soldier to leave St. Nicholas Hospital in Newcastle.

Empire and Tyranny

"Who do we blame for all that misery?" asked Mike. "The Boche Kaiser Wilhelm II and his generals, aye. But what of our generals, too? Did they give a damn about the thousands of men they sent over the top to their deaths? What did we mean to those arrogant bastards?"

"Aye, Mike. And they say the worst was Field Marshal Haig. They call him Butcher Haig. I've heard that his command endured two million British casualties. [6] [7] I reckon the generals had a job to do, Mike. They must win the wars, no matter how. They decided on the strategies and made their battle plans. We were just their cannon fodder!"

"Aye, that's true. But the generals had a job to do with us soldiers as cannon fodder! Are there not smarter ways to win wars without so many casualties?"

"Maybe. But we have seen that the generals don't know how!"

Joe and Mike surveyed the shipyards in silence for a long time, deep in their memories and thoughts. Then Joe concluded, "We must count our blessings and thank God that we and thousands of others are still alive and returning home to live and work again!"

They survived the horrific 1914-1918 Great War, which resulted in 17 million deaths and 20 million wounded. They lost

---

[6] *"Field Marshal Douglas Haig would have let Germany win, his biography says."* The Times. 10 November 2008

[7] *"World War I's Worst General."* Military History Magazine. 11 May 2007.

many more marras in the treacherous vermin, disease-ridden trenches, and the cramped German POW work camps. Towards the war's end, they were facing starvation through the chronic lack of food in Germany. They had survived the 1918 flu pandemic, which doctors described as one of the most significant natural disasters in human history. It may have killed more people than the Black Death of Medieval Europe. [8],[9]

"We must recover our strength as soon as possible and return to work, Joe. We are luckier than those poor bastards who have returned damaged."

Joe and Mike parted ways and returned to their sleeping wives. Once more, Joe slipped back into bed beside a sleeping Mary and soon fell asleep.

They crossed a bog, sinking to their waists in frigid water and mud, then reached a plowed field.

"Look after yourselves," said Joe. "They say we must cross this muddy field under fire while returning fire without protection!"

"Shite," said Jack. "Bloody madness!"

And then the attack began. Hundreds of British troops were shouting and running through the mud while firing through their comrades at the enemy. The Germans climbed out of their

---

[8] That pandemic went on to infect 500 million people worldwide and cause the deaths of 50 to 100 million people. Taubenberger, Jeffery K.; Morens, David M., *1918 Influenza: the mother of all pandemics*, 2006

[9] Potter, C. W., *A History of Influenza*, Journal of Applied Microbiology, October 2006

trenches and ran towards them, too. It was frightening! Bullets whizzed past them in every direction the whole time, while shells exploded randomly across the entire field. British guns were lobbing projectiles from behind their lines into the German defences on the other side of the Meteren Becque. The noise of battle was horrific, and smoke covered the entire battlefield, so it was difficult to see ahead of their bayonets! And men were dropping too often around them.

"Stick with me, lads," yelled Joe to his marras.

"Right next to you, Joe," called Mike.

"Right behind you, Joe," yelled Fred.

"I'm with you too," called Jack from just ahead of Joe.

So, on and on, they ran, weaving around their fallen, wounded, and dead fellows in the mud. Then Jack stumbled and fell face-first into the mire.

"Jack's hit," Joe shouted. "I'll check him out. Keep going."

Joe dropped to the mud and crawled back to check on his marra. But Jack had taken a bullet through his forehead.

"He's dead, a bullet to the forehead," Joe called to the others. "Jack's gone!"

"Keep going, my marra," said Mike, looking back. "Keep going as fast as you can. Catch up with me. They will collect and bury Jack after the battle."

So they ran through the hail of bullets and shrapnel from exploding shells. More men dropped to the mud when hit. Soon enough, they came upon the enemy.

They engaged in one-on-one combat, thrusting their bayonets into very young Germans as they went and dodging the German blades as best they could.

Joe saw a German soldier running straight for him, rifle and bayonet extended towards him, screaming. He tried as hard as he could to deflect the weapon as the soldier made his determined effort, jabbing his blade in Joe's direction. He yelled, "Halt," and then awakened, shaking and sweating as if from a fever.

His shouting awoke Mary. "Joe, Joe, you're all right, my darling. Wake up. It's all right. You're home with me." She was soothing him and stroking his brow as he emerged from his sleep. "Are you having another nightmare?"

"Jack," cried Joe. "We lost Jack! And a German soldier was about to stab me."

"I know, dear Joe," said Mary. "You told me about Jack. Stab you? My God, did that happen to you over there?"

Joe didn't reply. He looked into her eyes at first as the reality of being back in a warm bed beside his wife registered.

"I'm sorry, my darling," said Joe. "The memories keep pouring back. I can't get rid of them. But the soldier didn't stab me. I awoke."

"You will get rid of them, my love. You will once you have worked through them," said Mary, then kissed him on the forehead. "I'll make some tea, and we'll go back to sleep."

§

Empire and Tyranny

The sight of unemployed ex-servicemen on the streets became common and a scandal. The Gateshead Employment Exchange targeted local places of entertainment to see if they could use any more men. They considered the job of cinema projectionists ideal for those disfigured by war injuries since projectionists worked in darkness unseen by the public. They asked cinemas to project information about unemployed ex-servicemen on the screen each week to reach out to employers. [10]

However, many soldiers couldn't return to their original line of work because of injuries or the devastating effects of shell shock. [11] As early as 1916, schemes were being funded to offer workshops full of equipment for wounded returning soldiers to develop new skills, earn money, and gain independence and self-respect. This continued and grew after the war's end.

Luckier men had jobs kept open for them. But most others, able-bodied and wounded alike, competed for work in a changed and more complex environment. The war led Tyneside shipyards to an over-reliance on government contracts for a limited range of products, and they became vulnerable. So, engineering companies tried to diversify their post-war profile. For example, Armstrongs of Elswick,

---

[10] Jo Bath, *Great War Britain: Tyneside, Remembering 1914-18*, 2015
[11] We now know that these combat veterans were facing was likely what we now call post-traumatic stress disorder, or PTSD.

Newcastle, returned to making automobiles and vans to meet growing demand. They branched into locomotives, pneumatic tools, and combustion engines, too. However, many smaller companies lacked the capital to diversify. [12]

§

Back to Work

Once he had recovered enough, Joe found menial work, but it was not what he had done before the war and not what he had hoped for, either. But he was ready to contribute to the household and take the pressure off Mary without overexerting himself during his recovery.

It was a short-lived irony that the standard of living in England had improved during the war. Full employment, rationing, rent control, rising bacon imports, and increased milk and egg consumption meant that many working-class families were in a better position than before the war. Workers' incomes doubled on average between 1914 and 1920, and, in the war's aftermath, when price levels dropped, the war-boosted wage levels remained the same.

Mary spoke to his past manager, Gerald Robinson, at Hawthorn Leslie, whom she had kept abreast of his pending return to Jarrow and his recovery progress. When Joe left, she

---

[12] Jo Bath, *Great War Britain: Tyneside, Remembering 1914-18*, History Press, 2015

used his contacts at the shipyard to find employment for herself, ensuring income for their family. Now, the time was approaching to switch back from herself to Joe as the wage earner, and they agreed to do everything they could to make that happen.

The Government encouraged women to leave their jobs after the war to give them back to servicemen. The women received out-of-work compensation, but that didn't last long. In December 1919, Gateshead Council reminded the tram company they had only agreed to use female conductors during the war. Ex-soldiers' organizations condemned hiring women who were not widows or dependants, "thus depriving ex-servicemen, widows, and dependants of the means of making a livelihood." [13] These were still trying times for many on Tyneside and elsewhere. The *Newcastle Daily Journal* reported in December 1918 that in Newcastle alone, there were 15,000 unemployed women. The war claimed the lives of many former munitionettes, the name given to female munitions workers. [14] Unrest and dissatisfaction with post-war job conditions resulted in sporadic strike action. [15]

In many aspects of life, they continued hearing echoes of the Great War in the years after the Armistice. But conditions settled on Tyneside once more, and as with many others, Joe's strength returned. After three months, Joe was ready and keen to return to work. He met with his old boss at Hawthorn Leslie,

---

[13] Jo Bath, *Great War Britain: Tyneside, Remembering 1914-18*, History Press, 2015
[14] Ibid
[15] Ibid

Gerald Robinson, to discuss the possibility of returning, cap in hand.

"Welcome back, Joe," bellowed Gerald Robinson in his fashion as he thrust his hand to shake Joe's. "So canny good to see ye back home and healthy!"

"Terrific, Mr Robinson. Thank ye, thank ye so much," said Joe. "Ye don't know how canny good it is for me to be back here, believe me."

"Four years, Joe," said Robinson. "How did ye survive that?"

"I ask myself that every night, sir," he said. "If I had to survive, to look after my wife and children. I had to return, so I refused to die, even though the Boche tried their best to kill me."

"Well, it's an excellent thing, too," said the officer. "Now let's discuss the reason for this meeting, getting you back to work here. Joe, we don't have your old job anymore. Sam Mitchell has taken it, and I'm loath to remove him from it. But we can put you back in the yard, helping wherever they need you."

"That will be right with me, sir," said Joe, "I prefer to work out in the open."

"Good," bellowed the headman. "Well, that settles it then. You can start tomorrow."

"Terrific, Mr Robinson. Thank you so much!" said Joe as he backed out of his office, cap in hand out of respect, making his way home full of joy and pride.

"I have a paying job again, Mary," he proudly announced, "A good-paying job. Mr Robinson said I could start tomorrow."

"Oh, Joe," said Mary as she moved toward him, "I could see you needed that again. Now we can return to the old days as a family!"

"Aye. You can now return to raising our little ones," said Joe. "We'll have many more."

§

The Consequences of War

But for the people of Tyneside, as elsewhere, it was soon plain that they had lost the grand times of old. Gone were the gaiety and devil-may-care attitudes of pre-war Edwardian days. The war had punched a massive hole in the treasury of Great Britain. From being the world's largest overseas investor, it had become one of its biggest borrowers. Inflation doubled between 1914 and its peak in 1920; the value of the Pound Sterling and consumer expenditure fell by over 61%. [16] Reparations like free German coal depressed the British coal industry, one of the major employers on Tyneside. Germany could pay in kind or cash to offset its vast repayment commitments. Germany could settle reparations in kind with coal, timber, chemical dyes, pharmaceuticals, livestock, agricultural machines, construction materials, and factory machinery. The Allies deducted the gold

---

[16] *"Inflation value of the Pound"* (PDF). House of Commons.

value of these commodities from what they required Germany to pay.

Britain, with a population of 38 million in 1918, had changed! One significant change was the empowerment of women. During the war, women had filled in for men's jobs. After the Great War, women gained the right to vote directly, resulting in enormous political and social change for returning veterans to adapt to. Yet another significant development was Labour, emerging as a powerful social and political movement and a force for change.

Reminders of the war were everywhere in those early post-war days, and they couldn't forgive the Germans. In January 1919, the City of Newcastle Golf Club allowed no person of enemy origin to become a club member. They didn't even let "such persons" play on the course.

When Newcastle United played again, Joe and his marras attended one of the first matches at St. James' Park.

"Look, Joe," called Mike while pointing to an enormous poster at the entrance to the stadium, "Newcastle United players who fought in the Great War. I recognize a few of them who were in the Durham Light Infantry."

"Aye, Mike," said Joe. "I've heard that 100 ex-players and officials of Newcassel United served in the Great War. And a fine bunch of lads they were, too, both as football players and as soldiers! They awarded Thomas Rowlandson of Newcastle United a Military Cross and Donald Simpson Bell; remember him? They awarded him the Victoria Cross."

Empire and Tyranny

Within the stadium, they saw the disabled enclosure, full of injured men in hospital uniforms. Women were circulating through the aisles, passing the hat to solicit money for hospitals. Lines of blind veterans walked, each with a hand holding the shoulder of the one before, to the bleachers where volunteers commentated on the match for them. Mike and Joe thought they had seen everything, but the sight of blind veteran football fans entering the stadium in such a fashion was disturbing for them. During the match, the stadium rocked and echoed to "Tipperary" for the Irish and repeated strains of the trench favourite, "We're here because we're here because we're here." [17]

The Saturday evening after Joe's return to work, the marras met again at the Rolling Mill Pub, just as they had before the Great War and the Boer War. Joe had sworn off his Brown Ales while recovering and not working. But now that he and Mike are back at work and earning a living again, life can and should return to normal. A couple more ex-servicemen marras from the shipyard, and Joe's brothers William, George, and Thomas joined them.

"Well, here's to peacetime on Tyneside," toasted Mike once they received their ale. "May it be a long and prosperous peace!"

---

[17] Jo Bath, Great War Britain: Tyneside, Remembering 1914-18, History Press, 2015

The men clinked their thick beer glasses and called, "Cheers. We'll drink to that," in unison.

"Ye soldiers have been through so much," said William. "A fine lot you are, too, protecting our country and freedom as you did!"

"Coming from William, that was a genuine compliment," thought Joe.

"Aye," said Joe. "Two wars, my brothers. We have fought for the Empire in two wars."

None of Joe's brothers had ever enlisted in the army. Their father, the staunch Irishman he was to his end in 1910, wanted nothing to do with the British wars. Joe was the black sheep, and his father never forgave him for fighting in the Boer War.

"It was a right lark," boasted a reinvigorated Mike. "We had a grand time. Even with the bloody Boche in Germany, didn't we, Joe?"

"I wouldn't call it a lark, Mike," said Joe. "Still, we lived as best we could in the adversity's face!"

"Ooooh, where did you learn that haughty word?" asked Mike.

"From the Kommandant of Soltau Camp," Joe chuckled. "He used such haughty English military words often, ye remember?"

"Aye, stupid man," Mike growled, then quoting the Kommandant, said, "English Shweine! You have made me furious!" Mike and Joe both laughed. And laugh they could—now they were free of the Kommandant.

Then, the Rutherford brothers launched into a lively evening of questions on the Great War to copious pint glasses of Brown Ale.

"Were the trenches as terrible as they had heard?"; "Were there so many rats as they say?"; "Could they see the Bosch in their trenches?"; "What food did you get in the trenches and in the camps?" And many more such questions.

Joe, Mike, and their marras drank their ales and regaled their audience with tales of pain and starvation, cannons, guns, bayonets, blood, filth, vermin, weak soup, and black bread. They spoke of working full days when always hungry and of disease and injuries at the hands of the enemy. But as free men again, they could now relate their experiences with occasional doses of good-hearted joking and laughter. It had been a terrible time. But as life wore on and the darkest memories faded, better times and lighter moments arose. They could laugh again!

But Joe's nightmares weren't over yet. That night, he once again cuddled up to Mary in bed. He told Mary about his conversation at the pub and fell asleep beside her.

§

At 3:45 pm, they ordered the Durhams to advance at La Vallée and attack the village of Ennetières. Joe could see the advance guards walking on the grass verges to deaden their noise, passing groups of French cavalry. One of these groups was a detachment of cuirassiers, [18] their cuirasses, body armour, and helmets by then rusty. One shouted to Joe's company, "Hullo, Tommie, I was at Oxford."

La Vallée was at the edge of a rise on which the Lille fortresses stood. They began their demonstration under heavy shrapnel fire and sent Joe's company southeastward towards Fort d'Englos. The company advanced through a bog in extended order for 100 yards when a hail of bullets came from the right, left, and front. Shrapnel from exploding shells once more rained on them. Beyond the bog, they were into farm fields filled with turnips.

"Drop!" was the order at that point. "So Joe and his marras fell flat and attempted to conceal themselves behind the turnip greens while shrapnel from exploding shells rained down. They then rose and rushed forward through the turnip field with no cover.

"Drop," Joe shouted again. The bullets were so thick now that they could only lay their faces sideways on the mud and lie flat. "Are you injured, Fred?"

"Aye, sore but no open wound," said Fred.

They advanced again with caution, reinforced by the men before them, then dropped and remained there for two

---

[18] French cavalry regiments that still wore a covered cuirass, a piece of armour which covers the torso. and a plumed helmet, while on active service in the field

hours while the bullets were thick. Just before dusk, Fred risked a look over turnip tops and got a piece of shrapnel in the shoulder. With a pained cry, he raised himself above the turnip leaves. Then, a bullet struck Fred in the stomach. He collapsed into the mud between the vegetables, writhing in his death throes. Once again, assisted by Mike, Joe returned to help their marra, but to no avail.

"Fred is dead, Mike," shouted Joe. "They've killed yet another of our marras. What a bloody war." The Germans had reduced their small group of Jarrow shipyard marras to two.

They had no choice but to leave Fred where he was as they moved on. But despite intense rifle fire, the 2/DLI got as far as Ennetières before dusk. By 5 pm, they had taken Ennetières, and at 8 pm, the action over, they searched with caution for shelter. The roads were empty, or so it seemed. Joe and Mike entered a house on the principal street, encountering an appalling sight. They searched the entire house and found no one. Then they entered the cellar, where they found a horror scene.

"My God, Mike," whispered Joe. "Those are dead people down there."

In the dim light from the cellar door, they saw the outlines of many bodies — arms, legs, and heads scattered across the floor — a heap of bloodied, dead villagers. They concluded the Germans had herded and executed them into the cellar.

"Look, Joe," whispered Mike. "I think one of them is still alive over there."

In one corner, an older man and woman lay shattered by a grenade. They edged closer to help the old man, who was still alive and moving but died soon after they got to him.

It shook them deeply, so they left that house and moved through the village. There were no bodies of German soldiers anywhere. Their army had removed them. However, they came upon a small group of six French Dragoons they had seen patrolling the previous night. To their horror, Joe and Mike saw that someone had removed their eyes, ears, and noses.

"What the hell is this?" cried Mike. "These Boche are barbarians!"

Then, a little further along, they found a Frenchman standing erect but dead in the corner of a brick wall. They had removed his eyes, nose, and ears too.

"What are we dealing with here?" Joe murmured to Mike. "Savages? Let's get the hell out of here."

Joe awoke in a sweat but made no noise, so Mary didn't awaken. He then dressed silently, entered the street, and turned toward the river and shipyards.

When Joe and Mike met that night, he complained about his nightmares.

"I can't get rid of them, Mike," said Joe. "I have them every night."

"Aye, Joe, me too. I'm afraid that war will never leave us alone."

"Mary is so sweet. She takes it in her stride and makes me tea when I wake up, shouting sometimes."

"Aye, Ruth is an angel, too," said Mike. "Thank God we have them at our side now."

"Without me knowing, Mary spoke to our doctor about my nightmares. He said it was from what they call shell shock, caused by our time in the trenches. I remember having them in the camp, too. The doctor said they would stop in time."

"Well, I hope it's sooner rather than later," said Mike. "They are driving me crazy!"

§

Marking events at the war's end was essential for home-bound families. They had suffered long enough. It was time to remember and rejoice. The combatants signed the Treaty of Versailles on 28 June 1919 and declared 19 July as Peace Day. More celebrations occurred over the summer of 1919 on Tyneside, as in the other Allied Powers countries. The Treaty of Versailles was the most important of the many peace treaties that ended the Great War. This Treaty ended the state of war between Germany and the Allied Powers. They signed it precisely five years after the 19-year-old Gavrilo Princip assassinated Archduke Franz Ferdinand. It took six months of negotiations at the Paris Peace Conference to conclude the peace treaty. The Armistice, signed on 11 November 1918, ended the fighting. The Secretariat of the League of Nations registered the Treaty of Versailles on 21 October 1919. [19]

The most critical and controversial provision of the Treaty of Versailles required Germany and its Central Powers allies to accept responsibility for causing the damages of the war. A War Guilt clause forced Germany to disarm, make territorial concessions, and pay enormous reparation costs to countries of the Entente. Economists such as John Maynard Keynes predicted the Treaty was too harsh, declaring the reparations figure excessive and counterproductive. However, prominent persons on the Allied side, such as French Marshal Ferdinand Foch, criticized the Treaty as too lenient on Germany.

The newspapers covered the talks and the final Treaty at length. So Joe returned to his marras at the pub the following Saturday.

"So, what's all this talk about this treaty of whatever?" asked Mike.

"It's the final agreement between all sides in the Great War over what Germany should pay us for the damage they caused," said Joe.

"Well, I hope they are paying dearly," called another patron veteran who had overheard Joe.

---

[19] https://en.wikipedia.org/wiki/Treaty_of_Versailles

"Aye, they are," said Joe. "Not everybody's happy about it, even on our side."

"Well, they weren't there, like us," he said.

"A few are saying our demands are too high and could cripple Germany further," said Joe.

"What's wrong with that?" asked Mike.

"Well, a few wise men are saying it could cause another war down the track," said Joe. "Don't ask me how. That's just what they're saying." To which a few comments ran around the pub, calls like "idiots," "traitors," and "fools."

Joe understood and empathized fully with the reactions. "Well, as they say, don't shoot the messenger," said Joe with an enormous grin. "I'm only telling you what the newspapers have been saying. We should be thankful they have put it to bed. Even though the fighting stopped on 1 November last year, they had to work out a treaty. Now that's happened."

For the ordinary folk of Great Britain, the Treaty of Versailles marked the definitive end of a war that had affected them for so long. There were Victory Teas everywhere. They laid out feasts on decorated trestle tables. Music filled the air in streets and church halls, and revellers wore fancy clothes. They festooned the streets with bunting. Many parties moved into the fields and commons, adding sports events. In Gateshead, a £1,000 Council grant, supplemented by individual subscriptions, paid for a grand fete where army regiments paraded in uniform alongside bands and carousel roundabouts.

Empire and Tyranny

Displays included drills and gymnastics, circus performers, and a dog show. Thousands of visitors came in friendly spirits to Newcastle Town Moor on 24 June for the Newcastle Victory Festival. There was a musical festival, and the rides were favourites.

Most of these events were enjoyable and peaceful. But the men discussed a few unwanted incidents that evening in the pub.

"Did you hear about that 29-year-old woman, Gertrude Waller, whom a court of law found 'drunk and incapable' at a Victory Tea in Lambton Street, Gateshead?"

"The prosecuting constable said a few street parties had developed into drunken orgies! He also said that children were begging in the street to pay for admission to the events."

"Aye, and a few people were destroying trees for decorations," said Mike, unapproving. "What are we becoming, drunken vandals?"

"Aye, exactly, but then the constable refused permission for any new celebrations," said Joe. "That's not fair. That a few rowdies can spoil the fun for all the others?"

Word had circulated before the celebrations in Gateshead that the returned local veterans of Jarrow were planning a reunion. The Durham Light Infantry, the Royal Northumberland Fusiliers, the Tyneside Irish, and the Tyneside Scottish were to take part in a parade. They dressed in bright dress uniforms and put on a grand show. After the formal program, the regiments dispersed into informal groups intermingled with civilians. They swapped war stories, updated each other on the events since their return, and sang regimental and other favourite wartime songs over large mugs of ale.

Although most soldiers gathering at 28 June celebrations were born Geordies or living on Tyneside, a few had arrived from afar. Among these was Walter (Walt) Lane of 2/DLI C-Company, a close friend and fellow "Durham," even though he was born in Leeds.

He returned to Leeds to visit his family after being a 2/DLI prisoner with Joe and Mike in Germany, and he ended up staying.

But Geordie or not, he couldn't miss this reunion and went to Gateshead for the celebrations.

At first, the banter was alive and humorous.

"If ye have trouble understanding us, let me know, Walt, and we'll translate for ye," laughed Mike.

"I learned enough Geordie from ye chaps in Germany, so I'm sure I will cope," said Walt to the wild laughter of the assembled marras. And the Geordies had softened their dialect during the wars since, in the beginning, no non-Geordie had understood them.

"Where's your flintlock, Jimmie?" Walt called to a Fusilier he had met at Soltau. He was alluding to the 17th-century French word fusil, a flintlock musket that had given the Fusiliers their name.

"I left it with the Bosch," said the Fusilier. "They took it from me, so I told them they could keep it since they'll need it now more than me!"

"When they get up off the floor," called another over raucous laughter. After four years of fear and hatred of the Germans, they felt a soldier's empathy for the defeated enemy.

And then the conversation turned to more practical matters. Who had work, and who didn't? Were those unemployed being looked after by the military? Who had found their women waiting, and who had not? Whose families had expanded through their own loins or someone else's? And who had lost Tyneside friends and relatives? However, Joe and Mike decided not to discuss the war again after that day.

"That's it," said Joe, "the war is over, and we should stop going back over it."

"Agreed," concurred Mike and Walt. "We need to look forward to the rest of our lives!" And this vow held. They observed the Remembrance Days in silence and never discussed the wars again.

But for Joe, the war hadn't left his mind. As he joined Mary in bed that night, he worried her about his recurring nightmares.

"You know, Mary," said Joe, "when I go to bed every night, I worry about having another of those terrible dreams. I want to forget the war. My dreams mustn't remind me of it every night."

"You'll get over it, Joe," said Mary. "Your mind isn't ready to let it go. You've had a long and terrible time during the war, and your mind is still working through it. The doctor said you most likely suffered from mild shell shock and would take time to disappear. I'm sure you will get through it soon enough."

Joe accepted Mary's response, knowing she was often right about such matters. They discussed it for a few more minutes until Joe fell asleep.

Major Blake took two platoons of C-Company into a sugar factory near Ennetières. From there, they fired on the attackers from the upper story. Then, a massive German shell fell into the building, smashing the machinery and crushing and killing the men, including the Major. The other two platoons, under Lieutenant Norton, took part in bitter fighting after dark in the village's south.

Joe and Mike had always provided cover for each other, working as a compact fighting unit. They stood crouched with their backs against the wall of an abandoned house in Ennetières while looking over a low barrier in front. There was a fierce firefight. And it was so dark they couldn't recognize anything in the gloom except for the many flashes of rifle fire. Lieutenant Norton and the others weren't far from them, but they could hear the Germans approaching from every direction. Lieutenant Norton's company had retreated into the village. But it was only a temporary escape. It was now looking bleak for Joe and Mike. And they were alone and surrounded by Germans!

"Look out there, Mike," Joe whispered while looking into the darkness. "They aren't ours, that's for sure!"

"Aye, it looks like we're trapped here. Finished."

"Aye, I reckon you are right. The Germans have surrounded us. What happens now? I can't imagine, Mike. Could this be our end?"

"We can't run, or they'll shoot us for sure."

"Aye, let's stay put. I hope the Germans don't notice us.

"I don't think there's much chance of that, Joe. As far as I can see, we're finished!"

"Not yet, Mike. But if we raise our rifles, we will be."

Somebody cried out in the distance, "They shot Lieutenant Norton!"

Shots were still ringing out in that direction. Joe and Mike saw the distinct shapes of the many German soldiers approaching mere yards away. Their gleaming bayonetted rifles held from their hips at forty-five-degree angles, and their menacing pointed helmets identified them as German. Joe couldn't stop trembling. And he heard Mike's rapid breathing and gasping from time to time. Then, they listened to the tramping of boots on cobblestones.

"Where are they going?" whispered Joe.

"They are approaching us," whispered Mike.

"Hände hoch," snarled one of the approaching Germans. "Drop your weapons! No weapons! Hände hoch!"

Joe woke up and cried aloud, "Drop your weapons! No weapons! Hände hoch!"

"What, Joe?" called Mary in a state of shock. "Joe, are you all right? What's that you're saying?"

"I'm sorry, Mary. That's how the Boche got us. 'Drop your weapons! No weapons! Hände hoch!'"

"Well, they only had you for a while, my darling," said Mary. "Now you are back with me and recovering from your four years of hell."

"Aye, Mary," said Joe, calming. "That was it for sure. Four years of hell."

"You're not in hell any longer. Now you are back with your children and me in Jarrow," said Mary, embracing and kissing him.

"Aye, Mary. That I am," said Joe with a smile as he embraced her. "It's so good to be back, believe me. If only these nightmares reminding me of my time in the war would stop. I want to forget it all now."

Mary smiled back at him and said, "They will end, my dear; they will. Let me get us some tea and biscuits."

§

Another significant 1919 event was 18 July, unveiling the full-sized wood-and-plaster model of a Cenotaph to the "Glorious Dead" as designed by the Architect Edwin Lutyens.

Empire and Tyranny

The Government presented it to the public in its allocated position in London's historic Whitehall, within easy walking distance of the Prime Minister's residence at No. 10 Downing Street. To celebrate the end of the Great War, a committee chaired by the Foreign Secretary Lord Curzon declared a Bank Holiday in Britain on 19 July, Peace Day.

Victory parades across Britain celebrated the end of the Great War. That morning in London, many thousands of people who had arrived overnight gathered. It was a spectacle never seen before, with 15,000 troops taking part in the victory parade. Allied commanders, such as US Expeditionary Force Commander Pershing, Allied Supreme Commander Foch, and British Commander-in-Chief Haig, saluted the fallen comrades at the Cenotaph. Bands played, and the central parks of London hosted many performances entertaining the crowds.

Then, on 15 August, the "Restoration of Pre-War Practices Act" provided for returning servicemen to get their old jobs back. On the 30th day of August, they resumed the Football League four years after they had abandoned it because of the war. This was the most important announcement for working-class British workers who had missed their favourite sport for over four years.

On 26 September 1919, a Friday, Mary Rutherford gave birth to Margaret in Jarrow. The baby girl was their fourth child, third daughter, and the sixth member of Joe's growing family. But Margaret was too long for Molly, who was almost 5, so they called her Peggy. Women gave birth at home. Middle-class households often hire a live-in nurse for the two weeks before and a month after the birth. For working-class women, there was no such luxury apart from an overworked midwife on the day of the delivery. There was no paternity leave then for the husband to stay home and help! [20]

Mary's waters broke early that morning, and she sent Joe to alert her sisters that this was the day. Her younger sister Sarah sent Margaret to fetch the midwife while she went to Mary to prepare her for the birth. They dispatched Joe to work for the day while the women did their magic. Soon, the midwife Susan arrived with Margaret and Mary's other younger sister, Ellen. They had brought paraffin lamps to brighten the bedroom since electricity had not yet reached these terraces. They boiled the water and washed the bedroom furniture to ensure the most hygienic conditions for birth. The midwife cleaned her instruments and lined up her potions to prepare for her work. Then, they settled in to encourage Mary through her contractions. After several hours, they welcomed a baby girl at 227 High Street Jarrow.

"Another baby girl, Joe," said Mary when he entered their bedroom. "I hope that's all right with you?"

"Just what I wanted, Mary," said Joe. "Sure, I would like another son. But I love my girls."

---

[20] Ben Johnson, *The 1920s in Britain*, http://www.historic-uk.com/HistoryUK/HistoryofBritain/The-1920s-in-Britain/

Joe celebrated the recent Rutherford arrival that evening with two Brown Ales at the Rolling Mill Pub. The lads talked football, and Joe and Mike regaled their marras with entertaining stories of their team, the POWers, while in the German POW camps. Uplifting or fun war exploits were permissible memories. The following Sunday, Joe and his marras attended a local football match. The match was between the Jarrow football club, playing under the name of Palmers Jarrow, and Middlesbrough Res. They played at the Curlew Road ground, which had suffered through neglect during the war. /After a North Eastern League inspection of the field, they instructed the club to remove the pieces of broken glass and stones and try to keep the pitch playable. In March 1920, the club's name returned to Jarrow AFC, 'Palmers' being dropped from the title. [21] Other football news that year included Leeds City FC, of the Football League Second Division, being expelled from the Football League on 13 October amid financial irregularities. On 17 October, with the collapse of Leeds City, they formed a new football club in the city and named it Leeds United.

§

---

[21] Patrick Brennan,
http://www.donmouth.co.uk/local_history/jarrow_fc/jarrow_fc.html

Empire and Tyranny

Remembrance Day 1919

The British held the first Armistice Remembrance Day at Buckingham Palace on 11 November 1919. It started with King George V hosting a "Banquet in Honour of the President of the French Republic" during the evening hours of 10 November 1919. [22]

They held the first official Armistice Day events on the grounds of Buckingham Palace on the morning of 11 November 1919. Britain had decided early in the Great War to bring none of the fallen back to the islands. Those buried or left behind on the Western Front would stay there. Instead, they erected the Cenotaph in Whitehall to honour them on British soil. They also built memorials throughout the Empire with the names of the fallen engraved on them to remember their heroes on each Remembrance Day in perpetuity.

This set the trend for a Day of Remembrance for decades to come. In South Africa, Sir Percy Fitzpatrick, author of *Jock of the Bushveld*, proposed a two-minute silence to Lord Milner. This had been a daily practice in Cape Town from April 1918 onward. After a Reuters correspondent described this daily ritual to the office in London, it spread throughout the British Empire within weeks. [23] This two-minute silence at 11:00 am on 11 November local time shows respect for the 20 million

---

[22] Banquet in honour of The President of the French Republic, Monday 10 November 1919, Royal Collection.
[23] Royal Canadian Legion Branch # 138. *2-Minute Wave of Silence Revives a Time-honoured Tradition* The Royal Canadian Legion. Undated.

people who died in the war in the first minute. The second minute was for the living left behind. They understood the latter as wives, children, and families left behind but distressed by the Great War. They resolved to repeat this custom forever. The entire population, most of whom had lost family or friends, complied. Church bells and factory buzzers were announcing the hour before everyone downed tools. Everyone was to "give their thoughts, prayers, and thanks to those who gave their sacrifices with two minutes of impassive, deathly silence." Across Tyneside, trams stopped, and pedestrians stood in the streets, baring their heads to the falling snow.

Everything and everyone stopped. Buses, trains, and factories stopped; they cut electricity supplies off to prevent the trams; wherever possible, they brought even the men of Royal Navy ships to rest. Workers in offices, hospitals, shops and banks stopped working; schools became silent; court proceedings came to a standstill, and so did the stock exchange. Life paused altogether in what *The Times* described as "a great awful silence." There had been no instructions on where people should honour the silence. They assumed everyone should pause at their tasks, but most went outdoors to stand in silence in a public place. There were church services, and the forces' chaplain spoke at the Cenotaph.

Joe and Mike were at work in the shipyards along with many other veterans when the hour of remembrance arrived. They took off their caps, and the new Hard Hat by some workers bowed their heads in silence. Memories flashed through their minds, and a tear or two rolled down their cheeks. At home, Mary and the other women of Tyneside emerged from their houses into the streets, children in tow, and did the same. Those whose men had returned rejoiced, while those who had lost their menfolk mourned. This first day of remembrance was a solemn occasion filled with mixed emotions.

In France and Belgium, the battlefield recovery and the search for the fallen were in progress. They were restoring their decimated infrastructure, farmlands, and spirit. The Tour de France cycling race, not run since 1914, had restarted on ravaged French roads that summer. The 1919 Tour de France was the 13th, taking place from 29 June to 27 July over a total distance of 3,450 miles, longer than the earlier Tours. [24] Three former winners of the Tour, François Faber, Octave Lapize and Lucien Petit-Breton, had died fighting in the war. So, two other past winners, Philippe Thys and Odile Defraye, started the race. [25] The war had only ended seven months before, so most cyclists could not train enough for the Tour. [26] For that reason, there were few new younger cyclists, and the older cyclists dominated the race. [27]

---

[24] Augendre, Jacques (2016). Guide historique [Historical guide] (PDF). Tour de France (in French). Paris: Amaury Sport Organisation. Archived (PDF) from the original on 17 August 2016.
[25] Tom James (15 August 2003). "1919: Christophe in Yellow - but not in Paris"
[26] "1919: Wanhoopspoging levert Firmin Lambot Tourzege op" (in Dutch). Tourdefrance.nl. 19 March 2003.
[27] Sports Illustrated. Archived from the original on 5 August 2011

Worldwide, those pulled into the Great War looked forward to a more promising and peaceful future. The Rutherfords and Burgesses and their broader families and friends had overcome the turmoil, hardships, and lost men caused by the war. Joe and Mike had settled into peaceful lives with their ever-expanding families and were working at Hawthorn Leslie again. Mary had returned to her pre-war routine of looking after her husband and children. The football leagues had restarted, and their fans had reassembled behind them with passion as if nothing had happened, Joe and Mike included. Life was returning to normal, and memories of the Great War faded. Joe's nightmares were less frequent, and he had fewer interruptions to his sleep.

In the vanquished German Empire, the chaos of the German Revolution was over, and they had established a more stable Weimar Republic. But a hitherto unknown Great War German Corporal, Adolf Hitler, had already launched his journey to power.

§

The Rollercoaster Twenties

The year 1920 was uneventful in Britain. In February, the Council of the League of Nations met for the first time in London. War Secretary Winston Churchill announced Britain was to replace conscripts with a volunteer army of 220,000 men. In

Empire and Tyranny

March, Queen Alexandra unveiled a monument to Nurse Edith Cavell, the British heroine who had helped soldiers escape the Germans in Belgium during the Great War. The British Army promoted Sir William Robertson, who had enlisted in the British Army in 1877 as a private, to Field Marshal. He was the first soldier to rise from private to the highest rank in the British Army. Then, on 10 November 1920, the remains of an unknown soldier arrived from France aboard the Admiralty V-class destroyer HMS Verdun for burial in Westminster Abbey.

King George V unveiled the permanent version of the Cenotaph the next day. The permanent Cenotaph, designed by architect Sir Edwin Lutyens and constructed of limestone from the Isle of Portland, Dorset, replaced the temporary Cenotaph for "The Glorious Dead" in Whitehall. On the same day, they buried the "Unknown Warrior" in Westminster Abbey.

The following Saturday, the patrons of the Rolling Mill Pub discussed the Unknown Warrior.

"They've brought back and buried the bones of an unidentified fallen soldier in London," Joe told his marras. "They buried him beneath a black gravestone in Westminster Abbey. It's the only grave in the abbey where you cannot walk, a great honour."

"Why did they do that?" asked Mike.

"Because we lost so many of our fellow soldiers in the trenches and no man's land who never had a burial," said Joe.

"They buried others in the many cemeteries on the French and Belgian battlefields. But for their families, their dead are too far away to honour in those cemeteries. The British Army meant the Grave of the Unknown Warrior to honour them here in England. I think it's time they did that, don't you? Who knows? That unknown soldier buried in Westminster in soil brought from France could have been one of our marras."

"I'll second that," said Mike. Then, more veterans in the pub spontaneously stood up as one and, removing their caps, bowed their heads in remembrance before raising their glasses to the fallen.

"The French and Americans have done the same thing," said Joe.

The patrons of the pub grew solemn and silent at this news. Then someone at a nearby table asked: "Why are they calling it the Unknown Warrior?"

"It's the title they've given this grave to remember those without graves on the battlefields," said Joe.

"The Government is honouring those thousands of missing soldiers with this burial at Westminster Abbey among the many Kings and Queens of Great Britain. Westminster Abbey also contains the graves of Great Britain's greatest poets, authors, scientists, explorers, and politicians. But the Grave of the Unknown Warrior is the most honoured now."

"They should stop these bloody wars," said Mike. "Then we wouldn't need these graves and cenotaphs. I, for one, am finished with wars."

"Aye, Mike," said Joe. "I have to agree with you on that one."

That night, Joe had one of the last of his recurring dreams, brought on by the talk of the Unknown Warrior.

§

They stood in a dark and dismal Ennetières, cut off from their regiment and surrounded by German soldiers. Despite not knowing German, Joe and Mike understood the "hände hoch" order. Their captors' attitudes and hostile gestures reinforced their understanding. They had no choice but to yield; they dropped their arms, lifted their hands, and turned to confront their foe up close. It was the dreadful moment they had never reckoned on experiencing—eye-to-eye with the enemy.

"I'm ready to die," whispered Mike. "This is the worst thing that could have happened to us, Joe! But I'm ready to die for my King and country."

"Aye, that's true, Mike," murmured Joe while gathering his thoughts. "I have never even thought of this happening to us, but I'm not prepared to die. I can't die because I have a wife and bairns at home. And nor should you be my old friend, for your wife's sake. We will survive this war the way we did the last. I told Mary that, should I die, she was free to remarry. But this upset her; she cried, so we didn't discuss it further. We also discussed the possibility of injury. And she said she would nurse me back to full health as soon as I was home. But we never discussed the possibility of capture by the enemy. Our training didn't cover it, and it never occurred to me, although, based on our experience in the South African War, it should have."

"Aye, Ruth and I had more or less the same talk," whispered Mike. "She became upset, too. So, I guess that's a topic you should best leave unsaid with women."

"Nee, Mike," said Joe. "It's right to talk about it. You're tied together now, so you need to share such thoughts. It's how you speak of it that's important."

"Aye, Joe," said Mike. "I'm sure you're better at it than I am."

Their German guard rebuked them again, poking them with his rifle with a loud and stern warning, "Nicht sprechen!" A German officer nearby translated this command into English for the assembled British prisoners. "No talking. Take off your equipment and leave it here," he said, pointing to a pile of discarded rifles and other military equipment. "Keep quiet and do what the guards tell you." The men followed orders but held on to personal items such as letters, pay books or photos of their sweethearts and children. An interrogating German officer examined these later.

Empire and Tyranny

There was loud shouting and occasional gunshots as the Germans herded together more surviving Tommies of the 2/DLI and other battalions on the edge of the village. Joe and Mike couldn't see much at first, but soon enough, their companions appeared out of the acrid smoke-filled gloom, most of whom had glum looks on their faces. A few of these recent arrivals were resisting the guards. The Germans brought the few more challenging ones to heel through brutal blows to their bodies with rifle butts. They shot those who gave the enemy any reason to execute them, even if not permitted by the war conventions. Those Tommies, too, soon realized that any further resistance was futile. The marras recognized a sizeable group of Sherwood Foresters coming in their direction. The prisoners' numbers had swollen to a group of 100 or more. Then there were East and West Yorkshiremen, Moroccans and French soldiers too, many of whom Joe had fought alongside in his first battle. They appeared out of the mist and smoke, shuffling forward as a group. No one dared utter a word. They awaited their fate in stony silence while their captors barked incomprehensible blasts of commands and degrading insults in English or French.

Joe gave Mike a sideward glance and grimace, but he avoided provoking tension with the guards by talking. Their immediate future was very much on their minds. To the best of Joe's knowledge, they had received no information during training on the rules of war for prisoners. They couldn't know that Chapter II of the Geneva Convention, signed in October 1907 at The Hague, focussed on prisoners of war:

"Prisoners of war are in the hostile Government's power, but not of the individuals or corps who capture them. They must humanely treat all POWs. All prisoners' belongings, except arms, horses and military papers, remain the POW's property".

However, a Durham officer POW knew of this convention. He shared his knowledge with as many lower-ranking men as he could before being separated from them and officers going to separate camps.

"Remember, men; you are soldiers, not animals," he said. "You mustn't argue with them since you might provoke them. Just remember your rights and discuss any grievances you have at the right time with a German officer, not with lower ranks."

Now and then, they got another harsh nudge in their back or neck from a German rifle to move them on quicker, which they daren't protest.

But Mike couldn't hold back, muttering, "Bloody Huns!"

"Careful, Mike," Joe reminded him, but it was too late.

"Was? Was hast Du gesacht?" asked the guard, screaming. Mike looked surprised and shrugged his shoulders. But the guard wasn't happy with that gesture. He was sure he had heard "Hun" and knew it was an insult.

The guard grabbed Mike and spun him around to meet his rifle straight on. "Was has Du gesacht?" he yelled. Then, a

German officer, speaking to the guard, said, "Lass das sein, Korporal. Wir mussen weiter. Keine scheiße."

No one translated that for the British soldiers, but whatever the officer said defused a dangerous situation, sanity returned, and the column resumed its progress. The Germans herded the prisoners to a mustering point on the road out of Ennetières towards the new German lines. After a march of two hours, they arrived at a wire enclosure resembling a rough cage. There, the Germans had already assembled at least 200 to 300 or more British, French and Moroccan prisoners. There, they waited in groups as their captors rounded up more and more.

"Shite," cursed Mike in a whisper. "Are we animals or soldiers?"

"To these guards, we are animals," said Joe. "They could shoot us like animals, too."

Joe awoke then, shouting, "They could shoot us like animals."

And again, Mary awoke and calmed him through her tenderest embrace and gentle voice.

"It's all right, my darling," she said. "You're awake and home in Jarrow and fine. Just in time for tea and biscuits."

After the tea and biscuits, Joe and Mary slipped into a deep slumber.

But Joe was back in his dream, picking up where he had just left off. The march to the Dulag had not been without incident. The occasional stray friendly bullet or shell from the British side of the front lines had wounded or killed Allied soldiers and Germans alike. They had to circumnavigate the shell holes in the road, too. A fresh set of guards escorted them, including German lancers on horseback. But then, a few nasty incidents unfolded in front of them.

A few cantankerous Tommies defied the guards in one incident, and a scuffle ensued.

"Get back in line, you," shouted a German guard.

"Up yours, you bloody Hun," said one soldier. "I answer only to British officers, not you, Scum."

Then another such protest broke out a short distance away, and then another.

"You can't treat us like cattle," shouted another Tommy.

"Yeah," called another as the protests grew. "We're men, not animals."

The guards called in their Lancers, who charged into the ranks on horseback. Under direction from the German guards, they speared the protesting Tommies like wild pigs with their lances. To them, the objections voiced by the British prisoners were equivalent to resistance or trying to escape. It gave them an excuse to rid themselves of ill-tempered men and ensure the rest toed the line.

"Shite, Mike; did you see that?" murmured Joe to his marra. "They just did the same as the British officers' sport of

Pig-Sticking in India, with the same disgusting result. Do you remember that?"

"Aye, Joe," murmured Mike. "These are cruel bastards. We had better behave ourselves and stay out of trouble for now. Otherwise, we'll end up on the end of one of those lances."

A German soldier noticed them talking to each other and shouted, "Wovon sprechen Sie?" [28] while lowering his rifle in their direction. In this instant, so soon after their capture and the lancer incident, they froze in terror.

"I don't know what he is saying," whispered Joe. "Still, he looks like he could shoot us without a problem."

"Aye, Joe. Or bring one of those lancers back to stick us," said Mike, reaching his hands even higher and nodding to the guard. "Let's be careful."

Joe and Mike weren't sure what he was saying, but they understood his intent. So, they both held their hands higher in the air and called, "Nix, nix, nix." They had learned that this word meant "nothing" and hoped it would placate their antagonist. That satisfied the guard for the time being, who found their reaction with "nix, nix, nix" humorous, laughing with his buddies and humiliating the Tommies even further.

§

---

[28] "What are you talking about?"

Empire and Tyranny

And at that point, Joe awoke again. But this time, he didn't shout and wake Mary. Instead, Joe walked it off. He gathered his clothes, slipped out of the bedroom, and dressed downstairs. In the middle of the night, he left the house and went to the river. There, he worked through his dreams and memories by talking aloud about them as not being real.

§

By the start of the third decade of the 20th century, a great irony was about to play out in Britain and elsewhere. The principal players were those who inherited the wealth created by the Great War. The Nouveau riche, on the one hand, versus those suffering from the decline of the more traditional industries. They had helped make Britain wealthy and robust before the Great War.

Joe and his fellow workers of the North East were in this latter group. In the post-Great War world, a pivotal new decade began that became known worldwide as The Roaring Twenties. It proved to be a wild and joyous time for some but a more challenging time for the majority in parts of Great Britain.

Apart from ceremonies of remembrance and a period of grieving for many, the Roaring Twenties launched an exciting era of new and valuable changes and innovations. They were contributing to better social and cultural trends. These paradigm shifts, fuelled by a period of economic prosperity, were most visible in the principal cities such as Berlin, Chicago, London, Los Angeles, New York City and Paris. In the French Third Republic, they knew the decade as Les Années Folles (the Crazy Years), [29] emphasizing the era's chaotic social, artistic and cultural dynamism. For women, knee-length skirts and dresses, as well as taboo in Victorian and Edwardian times, became acceptable, as did bob-cut hair with a Marcell wave and listening to jazz. They often referred to women who pioneered these trends as flappers, [30] who became known for flaunting their disdain for what was before considered acceptable behaviour.

For the fortunate, the Great War had proved very profitable. Manufacturers and suppliers of goods needed for the war effort had prospered throughout the war years and became wealthy. Life had never been better for the "Bright Young Things" from the aristocracy and the more affluent classes. Nightclubs, jazz clubs and cocktail bars blossomed in the cities. Was the hedonistic lifestyle an escape from reality? This generation had missed the war, being too young to fight, and there may have been a sense of guilt they had escaped the horrors of war. Maybe, since Britain lost so many young lives on the battlefields of France and Flanders, the youth of the 1920s felt a need to enjoy life to the fullest.

---

[29] Andrew Lamb, *150 Years of Popular Musical Theatre*, Yale University Press, 2000
[30] Price, S (1999). *"What made the twenties roar?"* Scholastic Update, Vol. 131, Issue 10.

Empire and Tyranny

Women had gained confidence and become more integrated into the workplace. The 1920s was the decade in which fashion abandoned the customs of Victorian and Edwardian times and entered the modern era with gusto. They reflected this independence in the new styles. Hair and dresses were shorter, and women smoked, drank, and drove motorcars. Far more women entered the job market. Typewriters, filing cabinets, and telephones brought many unmarried women into clerical jobs.

But for the working people of Tyneside and the other traditional industrial areas of Great Britain, life had changed little. It was still the struggle it had always been. They were far from the nightclubs, jazz clubs and cocktail bars of the world's major cities in every respect. The daily grind for the workers of Tyneside was the norm, but it has improved a little of late through social reform laws and improved wages. They still shuffled their way to the collieries, shipyards and factories six 10-hour days a week. They performed the same work they had carried out for decades, interrupted only by wars. But even as the decade started and orders for warships declined, they knew that more challenging times were coming.

Life had returned to pre-war norms when Joe's second son and fifth child, Thomas Henry Rutherford, was born on 3 December 1920 at home in Jarrow. He would become known as Harry after his lost uncle, Mary's brother, who died in the war. This year saw the record highest annual number of births in Britain, as over a million love-starved soldiers had returned from the war. The Rutherford household was getting a "wee bit crowded" with five children and two adults.

"Well done, Mary," said Joe. "We now have two sons and three daughters!"

"Aye, Joe," said Mary. "I'm risking exhaustion!"

"I always wanted an enormous family, my love."

"Aye, that you did, Joe," said Mary, "I reckon we are there."

"Oh, I don't know," said Joe with a wink. "There's still room for a couple more."

Such conversations were typical. Families were often large since there were no contraception devices then. A homemade pension scheme was a tradition that produced extended families to look after their parents and grandparents in their old age.

"Well, I love every one of them," whispered Mary. "They are so precious!"

Satisfied that Mary agreed, Joe worked out where to put his many children. The babies slept in the parent's bedroom. They put the older ones, John Irwin, nine years old, Violet, seven years old and six-year-old Molly, in the back room.

Tyneside flats varied in size, having one or two bedrooms as the lower unit, made smaller by the staircase upstairs. Upper apartments could use the attic space for more bedrooms. It was possible to have three or four bedrooms spread over two to three floors, often with a dormer window to the front.

However, the Rutherford family's flat was a ground-floor unit with only two bedrooms for an expanding family. The kitchen and adjoining dining room contained a cast-iron coal range for cooking. They extended a small terrace to the rear by an outshot [31] serving as a scullery, a typical feature of Victorian terrace houses. They only provided water in this scullery, with a Belfast sink and often a separate stove heating a wash pan for laundry. They bathed there in a galvanized iron bath once a week. The kitchen and dining room were the house's most extensive and warmest rooms. It served as the social focal point, with two comfortable armchairs added for relaxing. As was typical, each flat had a small enclosed yard at the rear with an outside toilet or 'netty' as they called it in the local dialect. They built most of these terraces from the 1870s until the outbreak of the Great War in 1914.

§

'Normality' returned to politics after the Great War in the United States, Canada, Great Britain, France, and Germany. Conservatives defeated the leftist revolutions in Finland, Poland, Germany, Austria, Hungary and Spain. However, Russia became the base for expansionist Soviet Communism. [32] In Germany, the National Socialist German Workers' Party

---

[31] A pitched extension of a main roof similar to a lean-to but an extension of the upper roof serving as an additional room at the back of the house.
[32] Gordon Martel, ed. (2011). *A Companion to Europe 1900–1945*

(NSDAP), the Nazi Party, replaced the German Workers' Party (Deutsche Arbeiterpartei - DAP), founded in 1919. The Nazi Party emerged from the German nationalist, racist and populist Freikorps paramilitary culture, which fought against the communist uprisings in post-Great War Germany.

In January 1921, with unemployment standing at over one million people, the Government announced an increase in Unemployment Benefits. However, unemployment had reached over two million by June of that same year, with another two million workers involved in various pay disputes.

At supper one evening in August, the conversation centred on the pending school year. John Irwin had turned ten years old.

"You are a fortunate boy, John," said Joe. "When I was your age, they pulled me out of school and sent me to work in the pits."

"Why can't I do that, Da?" said John Irwin. "I wouldn't mind."

"Because I want you to turn out better than I have, young man," said Joe. "

"I want you to go to school for a few more years than I did, as required now by law, and you will become a better man. And believe me, you wouldn't enjoy working in the pits."

"You're a fine man, Da," said John Irwin. "You read and write, can do arithmetic, and know much about life. I think you are a much better man than the fathers of most of my friends."

Joe held firm despite his son's flattery.

"John Irwin Rutherford, I want you to be a better man than me, don't you understand? Better! I will never be more than a labourer. That is my lot in life, not that I mind since that is how I feed my family. My father was a labourer. My grandfather was a farmworker in Ireland. But I want to see my children achieve something more in life than just hard work in the pits or shipyards. Things are changing in these modern times. People will live better if they find better work. I will never be more than I am today—a hard worker, earning just enough to live in this house and feed my family. But I want my children to have more, don't you see? That's what I want for you, John. And the same for you, Violet, and for you too, Molly. That is why the Government now requires more years in school, so you can learn more and be smarter!"

In 1921, the 1918 Education Act came into effect, raising the school-leaving age from twelve to fourteen. State primary education was free for children from age five. They expected even the youngest children to attend for the entire day from 9 am to 4:30 pm. Classes were large, learning was by rote, and they shared books between groups of pupils, as books and paper were expensive. The teachers taught nature study, sewing, woodwork, country dancing and traditional folk songs. [33] This law was a milestone for developing the nation.

---

[33] Ben Johnson, *The 1920s in Britain*, http://www.historic-uk.com/HistoryUK/HistoryofBritain/The-1920s-in-Britain/

Empire and Tyranny

Life turned the corner from the Dickensian world of the Victorians when labourers worked until they dropped and were prisoners at the bottom of a class-obsessed society. From the 1920s onward, social classes were being shattered. In principle, anyone could rise above the squalor of the working classes if they were smart enough and worked hard. Joe was right. These recent laws opened up more rights and more chances in life for his children. England had one of the best educational systems in the world, including the most prominent and ancient universities of the time. However, up to that point, British education only catered to the middle and working classes of British society. Successive twentieth-century governments changed that by making primary school education available to the broader population and lifting them up through more prolonged exposure to learning. Dramatic social changes were underway, and these were to improve society!

The Great War had changed so much. That long and disastrous conflict had robbed so many young men of their lives. But the Great War had been a "Great Catalyst" for change. The men had gone to war; the women had gone to work in their places; society had been under enormous pressures from the war, which led to significant changes in the lives of male and female workers. The Great War was to prove a pivotal point in the history of the Western World.

§

Empire and Tyranny

One Saturday pub evening in October 1921, Joe arrived with a red cloth flower attached to his vest with pride. He noticed he was not alone at once, with most of the pub's veteran patrons wearing one, too. In the lead-up to Remembrance Day 1921, a new custom appeared in Jarrow and throughout the British Empire and America—the lapel Poppy.

"What a great idea," said Mike when seeing his marra wearing this symbol of remembrance.

"Aye, Mike, that is for sure," said Joe. "I hope it lasts. I, for one, will never be without one at this time of year for as long as I live."

"How did it happen, Joe?" asked Mike.

"As far as I know, the Americans started it, but General Haig announced Britain will follow the Doughboys this time."

"Well, it's good to know they will remember our time there."

"Aye, everyone's buying them, not just veterans."

In the autumn of 1918, Moina Michael was an American teacher working for the YMCA Overseas Secretariat in New York. On 9 November, Moina had a moment of inspiration when she happened upon a magazine illustration. It accompanied Canadian doctor, soldier and poet John McCrae's poem that began, "*In Flanders fields, the poppies blow*." Miss Michael vowed to wear a red poppy to remember those who had fallen in the war. From that moment, she devoted her energy to adopting the red poppy in the US as a national memorial symbol. At a conference in 1920, the National American Legion adopted it as their official symbol of remembrance. This inspired Anna E. Guérin to introduce the artificial poppies used today. Madame Guérin went in person to visit Field Marshal Earl Douglas Haig, founder and President of The British Legion. She persuaded him to adopt the Flanders Poppy as an emblem for The Legion. They launched the first British Poppy Day Appeal that year, in the run-up to 11 November 1921. It was the third anniversary of the Armistice ending the Great War. Proceeds from selling artificial French-made poppies went to ex-servicemen needing welfare and financial support.

§

Peace and remembrance were a part of the fabric of life throughout those countries the Great War had affected. But dissension was always present somewhere in the British Empire. Between 1919 and 1923, violence engulfed Ireland as the Irish Republican Army (IRA) fought a guerrilla campaign against the British state in pursuit of an Irish Republic. Britain itself was a theatre in the war, too. Cities such as London, Liverpool, Manchester, Newcastle-upon-Tyne, and Glasgow were fertile grounds for establishing IRA companies, Irish Republican Brotherhood circles, Cumann na mBan branches and Na Fianna Éireann troops.

"For too long, the British have ridden roughshod over the Irish," said Mike at one of their Saturday evening gatherings at the Rolling Mill Pub.

"It no longer concerns us, Mike. We are British now," said Joe.

"British my left foot," said Mike. "We are of Irish blood and will always be of Irish blood. You mustn't forget that!"

"Come on now, Mike," said Joe. "You and I married Geordie women, and we have Geordie children born here. We are working and making a living with Jarrow employers. Mike, we earn our living here in England, not in Ireland," said Joe. "What has Ireland done for us, apart from giving us our parents?"

"What about heritage?" said Mike, annoyed. "Once an Irishman, always an Irishman!"

Before long, the other pub patrons overheard these comments, raising a resounding agreement among the Irish and inciting the ire of the Geordie patrons. Joe tried to calm things. He leant across the table and spoke in muted words, "Don't start a fight on this, Mike. I'm not in the mood for a fight."

But it was too late. Before long, the shouting became physical, and the pushing and shoving started. Then, a full-on battle ensued, with fists and chairs and other objects flying in every direction until they broke a mirror. The publican rang the closing bell twice and chased the lot out of his pub. Under normal circumstances, when the publican rang the bell twice, the first time meant "last call" for more drinks and the second time announced that the bar was closed. On that night, he rang them both together. The door bolted behind them, and the brawl continued outside until the alcohol got the better of them in the chilled night air. They then collapsed in a heap on the road, gasping and laughing.

Mike had joined the Irish Self-Determination League (ISDL) of Great Britain, established in London, in 1919. He talked Joe into attending a few meetings, although Joe never became as drawn in as did Mike. For many years, the talk in the pubs of Jarrow had often swung towards Irish politics. Among the workers of Irish descent, there was a lot of sympathy towards the affairs of their homeland. And among the non-Irish, there was lots of apathy, but it turned to anger whenever Irish politics crept into a discussion. They made no impression on Joe, even after he had attended two meetings. But Mike had become politicized.

Mary heard of the battle at the pub and what had started it.

"I hope they didn't involve you in that fight at The Rolling Mill Pub the other night, Joseph," she asked sternly.

She only addressed him as Joseph whenever he was in trouble.

"Well, not quite, Mary. I mean, not on purpose."

Mary's look became sterner, her fists planted on her hips.

"Mary, it went like this. Mike and I were talking when he started his political shenanigans on the Irish and the British, just like Da.

"I didn't want to get involved in that, but Mike insisted. He had drunk a few too many ales and became too political. I tried to steer him away from the nonsense, but he insisted and became louder. And that's when the argument broke out with the English and Irish patrons ending in a fight."

"Joseph. How can you become involved in political talk? You know how hot-headed the Irishmen and hotter-headed Geordies around Jarra can be. It isn't worth getting involved. What will become of us if they hurt you or you end up jailed?"

Joe realized he had erred in his ways and vowed to Mary that he would never again become involved in such an argument. He would have a stern word with his best marras to ensure such an incident never happened again at the pub or anywhere else. During the early months of 1921, the Irish Republican Army carried out attacks throughout the region. Then, on 9 July, they agreed on a truce with the British Government.

§

On 16 June 1923, Mary Rutherford gave birth to Beatrice May, their sixth child at home in 227 High Street, Jarrow, who became known as Beattie.

That year, coal mining peaked in County Durham with 170,000 miners, up from 154,000 in 1919. However, many industries in North East England were experiencing more challenging times in the 1920s. Demand for traditional industrial products was fading, and the Great War had only provided a temporary boost. During the '20s, low demand and foreign competition beset coal mining in Britain. Between 1921 and 1925, the British Government subsidized the industry. However, the 1926 Mining Industry Act ended the subsidies and encouraged voluntary amalgamation of the marginal mines. So, coal mining in Great Britain faced tough times, consolidation, and closures.

"Our marras in the collieries are in trouble," said Joe one day. "Because of cheap, or even free, German coal, our mines struggle to stay alive."

"Aye, that is because of the money Germany has to pay back for the Great War," said Mike. "They are giving it away for free. How can our mines survive that?"

"You know, Laddies, Germany is getting stronger again while we are struggling," said Joe, "It's not right. The papers are talking about a troublemaker called Adolf Hitler. I know little about him, but from what I know, he gives these wild speeches and is getting a lot of support for his ideas."

The German term *Goldene Zwanziger*, or Golden Twenties, represented Germany's healthy economic recovery and growth after the Great War. However, the humiliating peace terms of the Treaty of Versailles provoked bitter indignation throughout Germany and weakened the new democratic Weimar Republic. That treaty stripped Germany of its overseas colonies, Alsace and Lorraine on the western border with France, and Polish and Czech districts in the East.

Germany had reluctantly agreed not to have an Army, Navy or Air Force to satisfy the demands of its Great War enemies.

The Allies' onerous reparation demands through shipments of raw materials and annual payments were biting. [34] They printed vast quantities of paper money to meet their needs, causing hyperinflation. The people of Germany needed wheelbarrows full of banknotes to pay for essential items. After a crippling war and the hardships that followed it, hyperinflation was a final blow. Germany's financial stability and prosperity returned only after the Weimar Republic started radical economic reform measures.

In the interim, the Nazis used a patriotic rally in a Munich beer hall on the night of 8 November 1923 to launch an attempted coup d'état. Nazi Party leader Adolf Hitler, Great War General Erich Ludendorff and other Kampfbund leaders tried to seize power in Munich, Bavaria. This putsch failed at once, but the following day the Nazis staged another march of 2,000 supporters through Munich to rally support. Troops opened fire and killed 16 Nazis. The police arrested Hitler, Ludendorff and others, and a court tried them for treason and imprisoned them in March 1924. While in prison, Hitler wrote the first volume of his autobiography and political manifesto, *Mein Kampf* (*My Struggle*). The Weimar Republic banned the Nazi Party but continued running under the "German Party" name. When they released Hitler from prison on

---

[34] Ian Kershaw, *Weimar: Why did German Democracy Fail?* St. Martin's Press, 1990

20 December 1924, he reorganized the Nazi Party, with himself appointed as its undisputed leader. He then gained widespread support by attacking the Treaty of Versailles and promoting Pan-Germanism, anti-Semitism, and anti-communism with charismatic oratory and Nazi propaganda.

"We must watch out for this Hitler," said Joe. "He is getting a lot of support in Germany. "

"Is he like the Kaiser?" asked Mike. "Could he start another war?"

"Ne, he comes from a low upbringing, but maybe because of that, the common people like him," said Joe. "That could become dangerous."

On 19 April 1925, Joe and Mary's seventh child, Dorothy, was born, and they called her Dolly. Joe and Mary decided they could not expand their little clan any further after that. Mary was 38 years old and felt she didn't have the strength to raise more children. Not only that, but their tiny flat couldn't accommodate over nine, not to mention the rising costs of such an extensive family. Joe was happy they had reached a family size of two sons and five daughters to care for him and Mary in their old age. Joe was a proud and caring father to them but became concerned about the economic conditions on Tyneside.

§

Empire and Tyranny

Closures Begin on Tyneside

By the mid-1920s in Britain, the postwar period of prosperity was over in areas of traditional industry, particularly coal. Poverty amongst the unemployed coal miners contrasted with the affluence of the higher classes.

Then, on 31 July 1925, the Government announced it would grant a subsidy to the coal industry for nine months to support existing wage levels. A Royal Commission conducted an inquiry into the emerging problems. The *Daily Herald* called this day Red Friday. Nine months later, the 1926 General Strike followed, with unemployment remaining over two million.

Shipbuilding was in decline, too. Whereas Great Britain had produced most of the world's ships during the 19th century, many emerging industrial nations had, by the 1920s, launched their own shipbuilding capabilities. Shipbuilding and engineering strikes occurred in North East England, including Tyneside, where they set up soup kitchens to feed starving families. The industrial growth of the 19th century went into a gradual decline, followed by closures and mergers of the smaller players throughout the industry.

"These developments worry me," said Joe after reading about the closures one day. "How long will it take to reach us here on Tyneside?"

"It's here now," said Mike. "Look at Armstrongs of Elswick across the river. They are closing a few of their works."

"Aye, they were a big supplier of weapons, ammunition and transport vehicles for the Great War. Peacetime is not good for those works," said Joe.

"What about colliery closures, Joe?" asked Mike. "That cheap German coal is closing our collieries too."

"Aye. That's why our miners are struggling. These are troublesome times for them. But so many strange things are happening in this world. Maybe coal and shipbuilding are no longer the place to be. Maybe our future is not here, but it is further south. I've heard that many new factories are opening down there."

While the traditional industries were declining, significant technological developments during the 1920s created enormous social and economic changes. A group of leading wireless manufacturers, including Marconi, formed the British Broadcasting Company on 18 October 1922. Daily broadcasting by the BBC began in Marconi's London studio, 2LO, in the Strand, London, on 14 November 1922. Karl Ferdinand Braun's cathode ray tube helped John Logie Baird, inventor of the first working television, in 1925. Record companies such as Victor, Brunswick and Columbia also introduced electrical recording on their phonograph records in 1925, resulting in a more lifelike sound. The Automated Musical Instrument Company launched the first jukeboxes in 1927. Warner Brothers produced the first movie with a soundtrack in 1926; silent films gave way to sound films. These pioneers and their innovations launched new entertainment industries that quickly became everyday phenomena. But they centred most of these new industries around London.

Then, the rise of automobiles led to new leisure activities and businesses. The car became the centre of middle and working-class life, supporting another vast industry with employment for thousands. This vehicle helped start the petroleum and petrochemical industries. But most of these industries were also in the South.

These brand-new industries in Britain and elsewhere would replace the traditional heavy industries of the Industrial Revolution that Britain had dominated for so long. Joe may have been right in his assessment—maybe the future was somewhere other than on Tyneside?

Faced with the poor employment prospects in Jarrow, the eldest Rutherford children moved south in 1926 to better pastures. John Irwin was only 15 but assumed responsibility for 13-year-old Violet and 12-year-old Molly when they migrated to Surrey. It had been a tricky move for the older Rutherford children, as with so many inexperienced people moving to the South. With their heavy Geordie dialect and accents, the Southerners had difficulty understanding them. For Violet, at 13, it was a major upheaval in her life. The daughters of Joe's older brother William, Betty and Jane, moved to Croydon, Surrey, too. Jarrow to Croydon was becoming a migratory path for the Rutherford family, but Joe, Mary, and the younger children remained in Jarrow for the time being.

§

Into the Tumultuous Thirties

"So, what the hell is going on now, Joe?" asked Mike one Saturday on a late October 1929 evening at the pub. "Everybody's talking about a financial crisis. What the hell is that all about?"

"I don't know either, Mike," said Joe. "It's all over the newspapers this morning. They say it's a serious crisis and will affect everybody. It has something to do with the stock markets, whatever they are, and banks and factories, too. I don't understand it, but they are saying it will kill a lot of businesses and cause more unemployment."

"Just what we needed, Joe," said Mike. "No sooner are we settled after that war than we may be out of a job? It's just one crisis after another!"

"Aye, Mike," said Joe. "We seem to be in a new war, or some other enormous problem, every ten years. But we will survive this as we did all the others."

The boom years of the Roaring Twenties resulted in reckless business practices and a frenzied buying of company shares. The market had a nine-year run that saw the Dow Jones Industrial Average increase in value tenfold, peaking on the 3rd of September 1929. Then, a significant slide in stock prices began on Wall Street on 4 September. On 24 October, known as "Black Thursday," Wall Street lost 11%. The Wall Street Crash had started. On the following Monday, 28 October, there was a sharp fall on the London Stock Exchange. The Wall Street Crash continued later that day, with the New York Stock Exchange falling by 13%. Then, 29 October 1929 became known as "Black Tuesday." Panicking sellers traded four times the average volume on the New York Stock Exchange. The Dow Jones Industrial Average fell by a further 12%. Many cite Black Tuesday as the start of the Great Depression. It became known as the Great Crash of 1929, and it was the most devastating stock market crash in the history of the United States.

The Great Crash signalled the start of the decade-long Great Depression that affected Western industrialized countries. The Crash forced many banks into insolvency. By 1933, 11,000 of the 25,000 banks in the US had failed. The failure of so many banks led to a nationwide loss of confidence in the economy. This led to much-reduced levels of spending and demand and hence of production, further aggravating the downward spiral. US manufacturing output fell to 54% of its 1929 level. The Great Depression was to have devastating effects on rich and poor countries. Personal income, tax revenue, profits and prices dropped, while international trade plunged by over 50%. Unemployment in the US rose to 25%, and in a few countries, it rose as high as 33%. [35]

When the 'Great Slump,' as they knew it in Great Britain, began, the British economy was still far from fully recovering from the effects of the Great War. Britain's world trade fell by half from 1929 to 1933. Traditional industry production dropped by a third, and profits plunged in most other industries. [36] The hardest hit by economic problems were the industrial and mining areas in the north of England, Scotland, Northern Ireland and Wales. These areas were hardest hit because of the structural decline in British industry. Staple industries such as coal, steel and shipbuilding were smaller, less modern, less efficient and over-staffed than their continental rivals. Unemployment reached 70% in a few regions at the start of the 1930s, with over three million out of work. Many families depended on payments from the local government, known as the dole, and for the poorest, soup kitchens became their only hope of survival. These soup kitchens, often offered by local churches or charitable groups such as the Salvation Army, became commonplace throughout the stricken old industrial regions of Great Britain.

§

---

[35] Frank, Robert H.; Bernanke, Ben S. *Principles of Macroeconomics (3rd ed.)*. Boston: McGraw-Hill/Irwin, 2007
[36] H. W. Richardson, "*The Economic Significance of the Depression in Britain*," Journal of Contemporary History (1970)

Empire and Tyranny

Tyneside, Wearside and Teesside were hard hit in the ensuing years. The workers of the shipbuilding industry endured times of continual apprehension as the companies they worked for approached closure. The Great Slump caused a collapse in demand for ships. Between 1929 and 1932, ship production declined by 90%, affecting the supply industries such as steel and coal. In towns and cities in the North East, unemployment reached as high as 70%.

"Palmers has shut their doors, Joe," said Mike one day in June 1932. "That closure has put so many outstanding men out of work—most of the men of this town. First, the mine closures, and now it's happening to us in shipbuilding."

"Aye, Mike," said Joe. "When Palmers shuts down after so many excellent years, Hawthorn Leslie must follow soon enough."

On 19 June 1932, the Palmer Shipyard, founded in 1852, launched its last ship, the HMS Duchess, at Jarrow and closed its doors in 1933. Palmers built the battlecruiser HMS Queen Mary, ten Royal Navy battleships, a dozen cruisers, over two dozen destroyers, monitors, gunboats, cargo ships, tankers, passenger ships, and tugs. It had a long and proud history of shipbuilding. That shipyard alone accounted for 80% of Jarrow's workforce, leaving 10,000 unemployed.

But it didn't end with Palmers. Although the smaller Hawthorn Leslie shipyard at Hebburn continued building ships, it had to reduce its workforce by 20% to 1,000 workers in 1933.

Empire and Tyranny

Joe Rutherford and Mike O'Brien were among the unfortunate workers dismissed by that reduction. They had retrenched Joe, 52, for the first time in his hard-working life. He entered his home on that fateful day and threw his arms around his waiting wife. Mary had already heard of the retrenchments from other women. The tension over the past few weeks had been too much for this hard-working, conscientious family man.

"They have let me go, Mary," he told her, tears welling up. "How could they do that after these many years I've worked for them?"

"Now, Joe," said Mary. "You know they must have had their reasons. We knew things were getting desperate. Look at how many men are out of work out here. These are tough times!"

"They are Mary," said Joe, pulling himself together, "I don't know what we will do. There isn't any work anywhere in the North East."

"We'll pull through, Joe," said Mary. "We will tighten our belts and live off the dole until you find more work. You've survived two wars; you can survive this, my dearest! I know you. We can do it."

"Aye, Mary," agreed Joe, somewhat relieved by Mary's response. "That we will. I'll apply for welfare right away."

In the 1920s and 1930s, Britain had an advanced welfare scheme compared to many industrialized countries. In 1911, the Liberal government of Herbert Henry Asquith put compulsory national unemployment and health insurance in place. However, with the mass unemployment of the 1930s, payments to insurance dried up, resulting in a funding crisis. So, in August 1931, a government-funded Unemployment Benefits scheme replaced that of 1911. For the first time, this scheme paid out according to need instead of the level of contributions. This unemployment help required a strict means test. A government official inspected the applicants for unemployment pay. They ensured the applicant had no hidden earnings or savings, undisclosed sources of income or any other means of support. For many poor people, this was a humbling experience and was much resented. But it provided much-needed relief.

Mary performed miracles in her little kitchen by changing her approach to cooking to accommodate the shortages of expensive ingredients such as meat. Soups, stews, and pies became the most important meals of the day.

She prepared these by stretching small portions of meat with gravies and ample vegetables. She used potatoes, carrots, cabbage, barley, or other inexpensive grains or beans when available to make tasty and nourishing meals. She created soups with stock derived from paltry amounts of lamb or cheap cuts of beef or marrow bones simmered with onions in an enormous pot. Then she added root vegetables, inexpensive brassicas, and stems to the meals as the week wore on and more ingredients became available. This she had learned from the time-honoured traditional French pot-au-feu. None of her family complained about the reduction in meat and praised her for such filling and delicious fare. But in those times, no one had the privilege of being fussy. In this way, Mary could support the strength and health of her family well within the constraints of their meagre dole.

One Saturday night at the Rolling Mill Pub, soon after the retrenchments, the conversation turned to the North East England crisis and the hardship of forgoing their favourite beverage.

"How long can we meet here over a few Broons?" asked Mike. "We won't be able to afford them anymore. So, enjoy these last ones, my marras."

"Aye," said Joe sadly. "These are tough times. So many men are unemployed in this town! I don't know who is working these days. I doubt I'll be able to afford a Broon much longer either."

"At least we have the Unemployment Benefits, thank God," piped in another. "Our government is in crisis! Will somebody ever fix this shite?"

"It's no wonder that those Fascists under Mosley are getting stronger," said Mike, "They are attracting many followers."

"Not only here, Mike," said Joe. "I have read that Adolf Hitler and his Nazi party are now heading the government in Germany. That is shite in the making!"

"Aye, that is for sure," said Mike, "I saw him on the News Reel in the cinema the other day. He's a madman, screaming and pounding his fists through his speeches. He will lead us into another war, mark my words!"

"Aye, you could be right, Mike," said Joe. "You could be right. God help us!"

The Nazi Party might never have seized power if not for the Reparations and the Great Depression of the 1930s and their effect on the people of Germany.

§

The year 1936 was notable in Britain for the death of George V, aged 70, on 20 January at Sandringham House, Norfolk, and the scandal surrounding his succession. His eldest son, Prince Edward of Wales, became King Edward VIII. On 21 January, King Edward VIII broke royal protocol by watching them proclaim his accession to the throne from a window of St. James's Palace. He was in the company of his still-married American lover, Mrs Wallis Simpson.

Frustration and disdain characterized the British people's unimpressed reaction.

"That is what's wrong with our Royals," said a bystander. "When they die, you never know how the next one will work out."

"Aye," said another, "George V saw us through the Great War. He was an excellent King. But that American woman has taken over his son."

"Maybe she pleases the poor bugger in bed," said another to laughter from all around him.

"Well, he won't have our problems wherever he ends up," answered another. "He won't starve like us or need to labour."

They had a point. Millions were starving in the traditional industrial regions of Great Britain while the shenanigans were playing out amongst their royalty, who had boundless wealth. It caused a lot of disdain.

The scandal surrounding the King's love affair continued. On 20 October, Prime Minister Stanley Baldwin confronted King Edward VIII about his relationship with Mrs Simpson, whom the king had fallen in love with and wanted to marry. After many meetings with the King, the Prime Minister informed him on 2 December that if he insisted on marrying Mrs Simpson, he must abdicate.

King Edward signed an instrument of abdication on 10 December at Fort Belvedere. His three brothers, The Duke of York, The Duke of Gloucester and The Duke of Kent, witnessed it. On 11 December, Parliament passed His Majesty's Declaration of Abdication Act 1936, providing the legislative authority for the King to abdicate. The King performed his last act as sovereign by giving royal assent to the Act. Prince Albert, Duke of York, or Bertie to his family and closest friends, became his successor as King George VI.

Empire and Tyranny

Another important event for North East England in 1936 was the Jarrow March, or Jarrow Crusade, from 5 to 31 October. The closing of Palmers' shipyard inspired 200 unemployed men to march the 274 miles from Jarrow to the House of Commons in London in protest against unemployment. Opposition from the British Iron and Steel Federation, an employers' organization with its own plans for the industry, had frustrated plans for Palmers' replacement. This led to the decision to leave on the hunger march. The "Crusaders" carried a petition to the British government requesting the re-establishment of an industry in the Jarrow. During their journey, local branches of the main political parties gave them sustenance and hospitality, and the public warmly welcomed them on their arrival in London.

The House of Commons received the petition but didn't debate it, and the march produced few immediate results. The Jarrovians went home, believing they had failed. However, despite a sense of failure among the marchers, the Jarrow March became recognized as a defining event. It helped foster a change in attitudes, leading to more social reform measures later.

§

Empire and Tyranny

South to Croydon for a New Start in Life

By 1936, 25-year-old John Irwin, 23-year-old Violet and 22-year-old Molly had jobs in the South. Violet was working in the house of a wealthy couple in Croydon and, at 21, had married Welshman Trevor Noel Hodge, born in Glamorgan, in 1934 in Surrey. They lived near Croydon with their first child and Joe's grandchild, Brian. Trevor Hodge's brother Reginald Hodge married Violet's cousin Elizabeth Mary (Betty) Rutherford in 1933 in Epsom, and he brought Violet and Trevor together. John Irwin found work in Croydon and met Mabel Mobley from West Ham, Essex, whom he married in September 1936 in Croydon. Molly also worked as a servant in a grand house in Croydon. They were encouraging their parents to follow them with the younger children. With every letter they wrote, they appealed to Joe and their mother to migrate to a new and more promising life. Those letters and Jarrow March convinced Joe to move at last.

"I'm moving south, Mike," said Joe one day in late October. "I will follow those Jarrow Crusaders and my eldest children with the rest of my family. All my children down there have paying jobs. That's where the jobs are. We spend our days in the employment queues getting no work. I can't stand it anymore. I'll be discussing it with the family tonight. Will you and Ruth come too?"

Empire and Tyranny

"I'd love to, Joe," said Mike. "Getting Ruth to move will take a lot of talking. She still has a paying job here, and her employers have put her in charge of the household. It's an excellent position she has always hoped for, so she will not want to leave. But I understand why you are going. There's nothing here for me, either. I'm unsure what will become of us, but I'll work on it."

"We've been through a lot together, my old marra," said Joe. "Please understand that I must go, and I hope you and Ruth can join us one day. I'm sure she'll find employment down there, and you too. It's boom time in the South. Please try to convince her. I've had enough of unemployment lines here, and I want to join my older children in Croydon."

"Is that where you are going, Croydon?" asked Mike. "I've heard talk of that place because of London airport being there."

"Aye, and that's where my older children are. And that's where there are many new factories and work, so we'll be going too," said Joe.

"Has life always been like this, Joe?" asked Mike.

"We have been through two wars, the trenches of France, the POW camps of Germany, the 1918 flu, and now the Great Slump. Why must we go through all these troubles?"

"I guess that's just how life is, Mike," said Joe. "It has nothing to do with us, and I reckon it has always been like that."

And so, on that note, the two close friends realized their paths were parting. "Aye, that's just the way life is," said Mike while giving Joe a forceful hug before turning and heading home.

§

Joe waited until the remaining children sat for supper one evening in 1936. Peggy, the eldest of the children still at home, was a young woman of 17 who was out searching for employment; Harry was 16 and looking for work, too. Beattie was 14 and had finished her education that summer, and Dolly, at 12, was the last Rutherford child still in school.

"Mary, children, I have been pondering our situation here, and I've decided it is time to follow John, Violet, Molly and the others to Croydon," he announced.

"We will follow whatever you decide, Da," said Mary. "If you think we should move, we will support your decision."

"Well, as you know, Da, there's no work here in Jarrow," said Peggy. "So, I'll support your decision for sure."

"What of our friends, Da?" asked Beattie.

"Aye, what of our friends, Da?" asked Dolly.

"Your friends will follow us, girls," said Joe, "I know of many families thinking along the same lines since the Jarrow March. We have no choice. No one, including the Government, knows what to do for work for us here, and we can't live here without work and money."

"Where will we live?" asked Dolly.

"John and Violet are working on that," said Joe. "They are looking for lodgings for us in Croydon.

"Where is Croydon?" asked Beattie.

"Just south of London, Beattie," said Peggy, "You know from Violet's letters."

"Just making sure," murmured Beattie.

"Well, Joe, we will pack our things right away," said Mary. "We will be ready when you are."

The entire family had agreed that Joe's decision was the right way to go, despite leaving their friends in Jarrow, and they followed his lead. So, once Joe had arranged transportation, he told his family that they should finish packing their things as soon as possible. There wasn't much to take with them in the working-class homes of the North East. Joe had found cheap transport shared with others going to Croydon to carry their belongings, including their beds and their few other pieces of furniture. John and Violet had reserved a "two up, two down" terrace house at 75 Cedar Road in East Croydon for them to occupy. It was within easy walking distance of East Croydon train station. They pledged to support the family as best they could until Joe found work. Joe scraped together enough to buy the one-way family train tickets to London, and they set out towards the unknown South, full of excitement and apprehension. They missed John's wedding in September but celebrated with them after the fact and settled into their new home in East Croydon.

Before they left, Joe and Mike met for one last time the night before at their meeting place above the yards.

"Aalreet, my old marra," called Joe.

"Aalreet, Joe," called Mike with a chuckle. "What are ye doing out here at this time of night?"

"I'm here to say goodbye to an old friend of mine," said Joe. "How about ye?"

"The same, Joe," said Mike, the tears rising.

The two men then threw their arms around each other and embraced for the longest time.

"Take care of yourself, Joe," said Mike. "Write to me from time to time. We mustn't lose touch with each other after all we've been through together."

"Aye, Mike, that's for sure," said Joe. "I'll let you know how it is down there. Can't be as bad as Germany, can it?"

But Mike couldn't respond. He just gave a parting gesture, turned and walked away. Joe understood his feelings and mirrored his gesture while departing, too.

It was a dramatic move for the Rutherfords. Joe, Mary, and their children were born and grew up in Jarrow. They had left the only home they had ever known and were insecure. But Joe found a temporary job at once washing dishes at the fashionable old Hotel Café Royale in Regent Street, next to Piccadilly Circus, London. This would tide him over until he could find a "proper job" closer to home.

"I did my first day of work in the South today, Mary," said Joe. "Getting there and back is no problem. The walk to East Croydon station takes 12 minutes. The train to Victoria Station, London, is quick, and then I have another short walk past Buckingham Palace and Green Park to Piccadilly and Regent Street. It takes a little longer than my walk to work in Jarra, but it's not bad."

But it wasn't long before Joe found work at a factory at Elmers End in Beckenham, a 14-minute ride there by train. He started on the assembly line at Muirhead and Co, a company involved in telecommunications since manufacturing the first electro-mechanic telegraphic equipment around the mid-19th century. This worldwide-known firm developed and produced many items used in wireless relays, multiplexers, recorders, and cables, and it was growing fast. Soon, Peggy found a job near home. A women's clothing shop in Croydon's town centre took Beattie on as a trainee seamstress. They enrolled Dolly in a school nearby, and the Rutherford family resettled and became comfortable in their new surroundings in no time.

§

Empire and Tyranny

Empires Reborn

By early 1937, the Rutherfords had settled into their new surroundings and soon found their life better than in Tyneside, even in another unfamiliar corner of England. At least there, they had work and wages to ease the stresses of everyday life.

Joe continued his practice of reading the daily newspapers to understand what was going on in the world. He bought a used radio from a fellow worker and listened to BBC News every evening after supper. The British newspapers blocked the government-run BBC from broadcasting news from its foundation in 1922. However, over time, it gained the right to edit the news copy and, in 1934, created its own newsroom. But it could not broadcast news before 6 pm. Joe was keeping up with the drama unfolding in Europe and around the planet, including places he had never heard of, where earth-shattering events were blistering. Of interest were the ongoing and worrying developments in Germany and Italy.

In Italy on 9 May 1936, Benito Mussolini, leader of the ruling National Fascist Party, announced that they had placed Ethiopia under the sovereignty of Italy. An assembled crowd of 400,000 before the Palazzo Venezia exploded into wild cheers. They continued rejoicing into the early hours of the following morning. Mussolini proclaimed the King of Italy to be the Emperor of Abyssinia. Mussolini declared to his masses, "Ethiopia's destiny is sealed." "Our shining sword has severed all knots. Italy, at last, has her Empire."

Mussolini coined the term "Axis Powers" in November 1936 when he spoke of the Rome-Berlin Axis as the treaty of friendship between Fascist Italy and Nazi Germany.

In August 1936, Hitler responded to a growing economic crisis in Germany with his vast rearmament program. He ordered Herman Göring to carry out a plan "to prepare Germany for war within the next four years." [37] The plan envisaged an all-out struggle between Judeo-Bolshevism and German National Socialism. Hitler believed his strategy needed a committed effort of rearmament regardless of the economic costs. [38]

One evening early in 1937, at the local pub, Joe often met up with his recent Croydon friends, other migrated Geordies, and his eldest son. The talk turned to the events unfolding in Europe.

"Can you believe what is going on out there?" asked Joe. "We watched this happening before the Great War. Is that where we are heading again?"

"Aye, the bloody Huns are at it again under this new maniac Hitler," said one of the other patrons.

"What about the Italians?" asked Joe.

"They fought with us against the Germans during the Great War, but now under that other nutter Mussolini, it looks like they are cozying up with the Germans."

---

[37] Overy, Richard, *Misjudging Hitler*. In Martel, Gordon. The Origins of the Second World War Reconsidered. Londn: Routledge, 1999

[38] Messerschmidt, Manfred, *Foreign Policy and Preparation for War*. In Deist, Wilhelm. Germany and the Second World War. 1. Oxford: Clarendon Press, 1990

"Aye, true," was the response, "We need not worry about the Italians. It's the Huns we need to be worried about once more!"

"What about the Russians?" asked Joe.

"They're too busy with their own internal shite," called another to peals of laughter.

"It's no joke," said Joe. "I've read that dictator Stalin has been busy with his Great Purge, as they call it, killing millions of his own people. I'm most worried about Hitler. He was only a corporal in the last war, but now he seems to fancy himself as a Kaiser. I've read somewhere that 'those who forget the past will repeat it.' We will have another Great War, mark my words."

George Santayana, the brilliant philosopher, essayist, poet, and novelist, once said: "Those who cannot remember the past are condemned to repeat it." [39] By the 1930s, it was the European Fascists who were forgetting the lessons of history so soon after the horrific Great War.

"Closer to home, what of our new King?" asked another patron.

"Aye, he's gone crazy for that married American woman," said Joe. Then, noting his companions' puzzled looks, he said, "Sorry, he's gone nutter for that married American woman; what's her name?"

---

[39] George Santayana, *Reason in Common Sense, volume 1 of The Life of Reason,* 1905.

Empire and Tyranny

"Simpson, Wallis Simpson," said someone, "She's a gold digger after our weak King. A bloody disgrace, that!"

"Aye," said another. "What do we need royals for, anyway?"

In the pubs and parlours of working-class Britons, the goings-on of their royalty during 1936 was a frequent topic of discussion. They had been following the drama surrounding King Edward VIII's love affair with "that American woman" and the King's abdication in December in favour of marrying her. The royal antics disgusted many and amused others. So, the most notable and happy event of 1937 in Britain was the coronation of King George VI.

Prince Albert, Duke of York, had ascended to the throne with Elizabeth Bowes-Lyon at the end of the previous year when his brother abdicated. They became King George VI and Queen Elizabeth of the United Kingdom, the Dominions of the British Empire, and the Emperor and Empress of India. This grand ceremony occurred on the 12th of May, 1937, at Westminster Abbey.

The BBC made its first outside broadcast covering the event. They broadcast the coronation procession on the BBC Television Service, which had only been operating since November. They laid several tonnes and eight miles of television cabling across central London to send the images from three Emitron television cameras to the transmission centre at Alexandra Palace. The BBC's Frederick Grisewood did the commentary from the cameras at Hyde Park Corner. In reviewing the transmission, The *Daily Telegraph* commented: "Horse and foot, the Coronation procession marched into English homes yesterday." The *Daily Mail* commented. "When the King and Queen appeared, the picture was so vivid that one felt that this magical television would be one of the greatest modern inventions." [40]

It riveted only the privileged elite who saw that event on their television sets while most subjects around the British Empire listened on their radios. The coronation service of George VI was the first filmed on TV, and it even required the forty camera crew members inside the Abbey to wear evening clothes. They then broadcast the service from these recordings, with the authorities censoring only one small section, a clip of Queen Mary wiping a tear from her eye. They later showed it in edited form as a newsreel in cinemas across the British Empire.

In the Rutherford home, there was both consternation and joy over the antics of their royalty.

"That coronation was wonderful," declared Molly, "I love these grand royal events." To which everyone agreed, the girls, in their excitement, exchanged comments on the uniforms, dresses, and horse carriages.

---

[40] *The story of BBC Television – Television out and about.* bbc.co.uk.

"Aye, but the antics of our last king were pukka disgraceful," said Joe. "I have lived through many of our great monarchs. I was a soldier for Queen Victoria, Edward VII, and George V.

"Victoria was a great queen I fought for when I joined the army and went to South Africa. Edward VII was a dandy and party animal, but I fought for him against the Boers when he became king in 1901. King George V was a fine monarch, and I fought for him during the Great War. I received a letter from him thanking me for my contribution as a POW in Germany, and I'm so proud of that. Edward VIII didn't act the way a monarch should. I hope King George VI will be a noble king for us again. However, he is coming into troubling times just as his father did in 1911 when your mother and I married!"

Joe's monologue had left his women speechless, so they shelved the topic for a while.

Preparations for war in 1936 and 1937 were everywhere, and progress on war readiness was being made in the UK. For example, on 6 November 1936, the Royal Air Force's Hawker Hurricane single-seat fighter plane performed its maiden flight at Brooklands, Surrey. In December 1937, the Royal Air Force at No. 111 Squadron entered service at Northolt with its first monoplane fighter.

On 25 November 1937, Nazi Germany signed a pact with the Empire of Japan. Hitler abandoned his plan of an Anglo-

German alliance, blaming "inadequate" British leadership. [41] At a meeting at the Reich Chancellery with his foreign ministers and military chiefs that November, Adolf Hitler restated his intention of gaining more "Lebensraum" [42] for Germans. He believed this territory was necessary for Germany's natural development and was ready to take it forcefully. Hitler ordered preparations for war in the East to begin as early as 1938 and no later than 1943. He felt he could correct the severe decline in living standards and the economic crisis in Germany by grabbing Austria and Czechoslovakia. [43] [44] Hitler had urged quick action before Britain and France gained a permanent lead in the arms race. [45]

"I heard the same from the Kaiser before the Great War," said Joe. "Here we go again. It's scary!"

On the 28th of May 1937, Neville Chamberlain became Prime Minister after Baldwin's retirement. Chamberlain signalled an intention to continue Baldwin's policies by changing the cabinet.

At the start of 1938, Hitler asserted control over the military-foreign policy apparatus. He dismissed Neurath as foreign minister and appointed himself as Oberster Befehlshaber

---

[41] Messerschmidt, Manfred, *Foreign Policy and Preparation for War*. In Deist, Wilhelm. Germany and the Second World War. 1. Oxford: Clarendon Press, 1990
[42] Living space
[43] Messerschmidt, Manfred, *Foreign Policy and Preparation for War*. In Deist, Wilhelm. Germany and the Second World War. 1. Oxford: Clarendon Press, 1990
[44] Carr, William, *Arms, Autarky and Aggression*. London: Edward Arnold, 1972.
[45] Messerschmidt, Manfred, *Foreign Policy and Preparation for War*. In Deist, Wilhelm. Germany and the Second World War. 1. Oxford: Clarendon Press, 1990

der Wehrmacht (Supreme Commander of the Armed Forces). [46] From then onwards, Hitler carried out a foreign policy aimed at war. [47]

Tensions were high across the entire globe but reaching worrying levels across Great Britain and Europe. The US government appointed Joseph P. Kennedy as United States Ambassador to the United Kingdom on 8 March 1938. Kennedy rejected the beliefs of Winston Churchill that any compromise with Nazi Germany was impossible. Instead, Kennedy supported Prime Minister Neville Chamberlain's policy of appeasement.

The Prime Minister met German Chancellor Adolf Hitler on 13 September 1938 to negotiate an end to German expansionist policies. On 30 September, Neville Chamberlain returned to the UK triumphant from Munich. He waved the resolution signed the day earlier with Germany at Heston Aerodrome, where he gave a brief speech to the gathered crowd. Later, in Downing Street, he gave his famous "Peace for Our Time" speech. George VI and Queen Elizabeth appeared with Chamberlain on the balcony of Buckingham Palace that day to celebrate the agreement.

By 1939, Hitler had disregarded the restrictions imposed on Germany by the Treaty of Versailles and annexed territories

---

[46] Overy, Richard, *Misjudging Hitler*. In Martel, Gordon. The Origins of the Second World War Reconsidered. London: Routledge, 1999

[47] Messerschmidt, Manfred, *Foreign Policy and Preparation for War*. In Deist, Wilhelm. Germany and the Second World War. 1. Oxford: Clarendon Press, 1990

populated by millions of ethnic Germans. He established the Dritte Reich (Third Empire) as the reborn German Empire. Hitler aspired to a much larger Empire than that which had collapsed a generation earlier under the German Kaiser. In Italy, the delusional Benito Mussolini saw himself as the saviour of the Roman Empire in the hopes and dreams of re-establishing Italy to its glorious Roman past. The Japanese Empire, which had existed since the Meiji Restoration in 1868, was reaching its zenith under the slogan Fukoku Kyōhei. Translated, it read, "Enrich the Country, Strengthen the Armed Forces."

On 31 March 1939, Britain pledged support to Poland in case of an invasion. Then, they formed the Royal Armoured Corps on 4 April and re-established the Women's Royal Naval Service on 11 April. On 27 April, the Military Training Act introduced the conscription of men aged 20 and 21 to undertake six months of military training. They created the Women's Auxiliary Air Force (WAAF) on 28 June. On 1 July, the Women's Land Army re-formed to work in agriculture, preparing for losing male agricultural workers for an eventual war. By mid-1939, they recalled Parliament, called up Army reservists and placed Civil Defence workers on alert. On 24 August, the 1939 Emergency Powers Act gave full authority to Defence Regulations and Emergency Regulations passed on the outbreak of war. During a conflict, these regulations became the fundamental principles of everyday life in the United Kingdom. Then, on 30 August, they ordered the Royal Navy to war stations.

Empire and Tyranny

And so it was that by mid-1939, mighty empires were on the rise again worldwide and gearing up for total war, just as they had a generation earlier.

"He is now calling Germany the Third Empire," said Joe one day. "The Second Empire was the Kaiser's Germany we fought. I thought we had ended the empires with the Great War, except for ours. But both Germany and Italy are talking about their empires. I don't like what's going on in Germany."

Anxiety was mounting in the Rutherford household, as in most other homes across the British Empire. Older adults could remember the horrors of the last war and had no interest in repeating that experience. One Sunday evening at the end of August, the talk digressed to this topic as the Rutherfords gathered for tea.

"I believe we are to become involved in yet another European conflict," said Harry. "What do you think, Da?"

"It feels just as it did in July 1914," said Joe. "I can't believe it, but it sure looks like we may fight the Huns again soon. But not me! I've been through enough wars, thank you."

"Aye, that you have, Da," said Mary. "I'll not have you going off again!"

"You're safe at your age, Da," said Peggy.

"Aye, but I don't know how safe we are," said Joe. "In the Great War, the Huns bombed England. I have read that the Germans raided London during most of the Great War, using airships, bomber planes and seaplanes. They have much better aeroplanes now and, I suppose, bigger bombs than they did then. It wouldn't surprise me if they tried it again."

"That goes for me, too," said Harry. "I've read how the Allies treated the Germans after that victory, demanding crippling financial penalties. That may have unknowingly paved the way for Hitler, the Nazis, and another Great War."

"Aye, you may be right, Harry," said Joe. "I've heard that often enough, too."

"Oh my God," cried an upset Peggy. "That is most worrying. They could bomb us again right here?"

That was a very sobering thought, and it left everyone quiet and reflective for the rest of the tea. There was the occasional "pass the" something or other and less consequential chit-chat.

"Well, if that could happen, we must be ready," blurted Peggy after contemplating the conversation. "Shouldn't we be talking to our neighbours about building a shelter we can go to if they bomb us? I've noticed that others in the neighbourhood have done that."

"Aye, now that's a superb idea," said Harry. "I'll talk to them."

Then they dispersed for the evening, knowing little of the changes soon to descend upon them.

§

2
Wartime Britain: September 1939 to July 1943

1939: Is this the Start of Another Great War?

It began on 1 September 1939, just as it had a quarter-century earlier with the Great War. Germany and its Axis allies marched into Poland. This first invasion of the war involved one and a half million German troops, 466,000 Soviets and 50,000 Slovaks. The campaign ended on 6 October, with Germany and the Soviet Union dividing and annexing Poland. In this lightning-fast occupation, there were 59,000 Axis casualties and 900,000 dead and wounded Poles. This start of WWII had as many losses in its first five weeks as in five months of the Battle of the Somme, our worst battle of WWI.

When Britain received news of the assault, it was obliged by its treaty with Poland to declare war on Germany. British Prime Minister Neville Chamberlain appeared before the House of Commons just after 6 pm on 1 September 1939 and stated:

> *"It now only remains to set our teeth and to enter upon this struggle, which we earnestly endeavoured to avoid, with determination to see it through to the end."*

Empire and Tyranny

"We shall enter it with a clear conscience, with the support of the Dominions and the British Empire, and the moral approval of the greater part of the world." [48]

At 9 pm, Sir Nevile Henderson, British Ambassador to Germany, handed an ultimatum to Nazi Foreign Minister Joachim von Ribbentrop. It declared that unless the British Government received satisfactory assurances, Germany would withdraw from Polish territory, "His Majesty's Government will without hesitation fulfil their obligation to Poland." One hour later, the French ambassador delivered a similar note. [49] That same day, Operation Pied Piper, a 4-day evacuation of children, began from London and other major British cities. The Government imposed a blackout across Britain and mobilized the Army.

At 7:44 pm on 2 September, Neville Chamberlain informed the House of Commons that they had not yet received a reply from Germany to the previous night's ultimatum. [50] So, on 3 September, Britain declared war on Nazi Germany. Just after 11:00 am, Chamberlain announced this news on BBC Radio from No. 10 Downing Street. Chamberlain created a small Imperial War Cabinet, including Foreign Secretary Viscount Halifax and First Lord of the Admiralty Winston Churchill. Churchill had been in the same role at the start of the

---

[48] *Hansard – Parliamentary Debates*, British Note to Germany. 1 September 1939

[49] Shirer, William L. (2011). *The Rise and Fall of the Third Reich: A History of Nazi Germany*. New York: Simon & Schuster.

[50] *Hansard – Parliamentary Debates*, Germany and Poland, Italian Proposals, 2 September 1939

Great War. The Prime Minister also invited the old Boer General Jan Smuts to the Imperial War Cabinet. Smuts had served as a Boer general during the 2nd Anglo-Boer War and a British general in Africa during the Great War. General mobilization of the armed services began. The Admiralty sent the signal "Total Germany" to the ships of the Royal Navy, marking the start of the war. Parliament passed the National Service (Armed Forces) Act, introducing National Service for men aged 18 to 41.

Prime Minister Neville Chamberlain appointed Lord Gort as the Commander-in-Chief of the much-reduced British Expeditionary Force (BEF) on 3 September 1939. The BEF started moving to France the next day and assembled along the Belgian–French border. They posted the BEF to the left of the French 1st Army Group (1er Groupe d'armées) on the North-Eastern Front in France.

Joe had followed these events through the newspapers and listened to BBC Radio broadcasts every evening. He kept his fears from his women but had the attentive ear of his youngest son.

"I don't believe this, Harry," said Joe. "I've been through all this at the start of the last war. It's the same as in August 1914, 25 years ago! This time, the Boche invaded Poland, but I'm sure they will move towards Belgium and France again, and maybe us, too. And they even call our British Expeditionary Force insignificant, just as the Kaiser did then."

Empire and Tyranny

"Aye, Da," said Harry. "We are at war with Germany again. And I can't even enlist because of my heart issues. I'm so annoyed about that! I want to make my contribution just as you did."

"Well, I'm not, son," said Joe. "I am most anxious about it. I've seen enough wars to know it's even worse for your health. Look to see how else you can help here on the home front. Meanwhile, I can't help myself. I'll be following events every day as they unfold."

And unfold they did, with astonishing speed. The first naval disasters occurred early in this war. British liner SS Athenia became the first civilian casualty of the war on 3 September. The German submarine U-30 torpedoed and sank her off the northwest coast of County Donegal, Ulster, Ireland. The Royal Air Force bombed Wilhelmshaven and Brunsbüttel in Germany on the North Sea on the 4th of September, the first such bombing by the Allies during this war.

From the beginning, the war had a tremendous impact on life in Britain. On 5 September, Parliament passed the National Registration Act, introducing identity cards. It stipulated that citizens must produce them on demand or present them to a police station within 48 hours. By 9 September, the British Expeditionary Force (BEF) had crossed the channel to France. On 11 September, *Time* magazine first named this conflict World War II. This magazine first referred to the Great War as World War I on 12 June that year.

Empire and Tyranny

The first trans-Atlantic convoy of the war sailed from Halifax, Nova Scotia, to the United Kingdom on 16 September, escorted by British cruisers and two Canadian destroyers. But they kept this a secret. Britain depended on vital supplies from North America as a small island, but the Germans launched a submarine 'tonnage war,' known as the Battle of the Atlantic. From then on, they assembled all trans-Atlantic ships into convoys, escorted by vigilant warships.

The Aircraft carrier HMS Courageous sank when torpedoed by German submarine U-29 on the 17th of September in the Western Approaches. It lost 519 crew, the first British surface warship loss of the war.

On 18 September, the American-born Irish Fascist politician William Joyce began broadcasting Nazi propaganda on the German radio's English service. The British listeners were to name him Lord Haw-Haw.

The Cabinet introduced petrol rationing on 24 September and announced the first war tax on 27 September, including a significant increase in income taxes. They published a "Call-Up Proclamation" on 1 October, requiring men aged 20 to 21 to register with the military authorities. The Government increased the Call-Up Proclamation age from 21 to 23 on 21 October.

On 14 October, a German U-boat torpedoed the Revenge-class battleship HMS Royal Oak, built for the Great War and known as The Mighty Oak. They sank it in Scapa Flow, Orkney Islands, with the loss of 833 crew.

Then, on 30 October, U-56, under the command of Kapitän Wilhelm Zahn, attacked the British battleship, HMS Nelson, off Orkney. Although hit by three torpedoes, none exploded, so HMS Nelson avoided severe damage. Onboard that ship was First Lord of the Admiralty Winston Churchill, First Sea Lord Admiral of the Fleet Dudley Pound and Commander-in-Chief Home Fleet Admiral Charles Morton Forbes. Kapitän Zahn came close to an earth-shattering hit that day! [51]

"Bloody hell, Harry. They are already battling it out at sea," said Joe. "Looks as if the Boche have upgraded their navy for this war. We beat them on the sea at the Battle of Jutland in the last one."

"Aye, Da. It's moving fast," said Harry.

"They are doing the same thing on land as in 1914," said Joe.

"They raced into Belgium and would have continued racing to Paris if we hadn't stopped them. But stop them we did, at the River Marne. I got there soon after, at the River Aisne. Then we raced them to the North Sea to stop them from getting around us to Paris. But again, we stopped them. The question is, can we stop them again in this war?"

"I don't know, Da," said Harry. "This time, they have a modern Air Force and a huge, fast-moving army with modern

---

[51] Doyle, Peter (2010), *ARP and Civil Defence in the Second World War*. Oxford: Shire Publications

tanks. We might still hold our own at sea, but I've heard our army is too small again compared to theirs on land. And what kind of Air Force do we have?"

The German army of September 1939 totalled 3.7 million men and 105,000 officers in 103 divisions, including 86 infantry units. The British Army had a full-time regular army of 900,000 officers and men and a part-time Territorial Army (TA). But the regular army could only muster 224,000 men for the BEF, supported by a reserve of 174,000 men.

Germany had an operational Air Force of 1,000 fighter aircraft and 1,050 bombers in September 1939. Britain's Royal Air Force had the same number of planes.

The Kriegsmarine was the War Navy of Nazi Germany from 1935 to 1945. It replaced the Imperial German Navy of the German Empire (1871–1918) and the inter-war Reichsmarine (1919–1935) of the Weimar Republic. In 1938, Germany drew up the major naval rearmament program, the 'Z' plan, to bring their War Navy closer to equality with Britain by the mid-1940s. That year, they launched their uncompleted carrier, Graf Zeppelin. At the outbreak of WWII, the Kriegsmarine only had two battleships, two battle cruisers, three armoured cruisers, three heavy cruisers, six light cruisers, 22 destroyers, and 59 submarines. In September 1939, they completed the Battlecruiser Scharnhorst. They had launched their battleships, Bismarck and Tirpitz, before September 1939 for commissioning in 1940 and 1941. At 41,700 tons, they considered Bismarck the most powerful warship in the world. German U-boats and two pocket battleships sailed for their war stations in the Atlantic in late August 1939.

However, the Royal Navy was still the most powerful globally, with the most warships and naval bases. The Fleet, including the Canadian, Australian, Indian and New Zealand fleets, comprised 15 battleships and battlecruisers, and five modern King George V class battleships were under construction. Britain had one new carrier, and five planned fleet carriers were still under construction. There were 66 battle-ready cruisers, and they had laid the keels of another 23. There were 184 destroyers of various types, with over half modern and another 52 under construction or on order. There were 66 submarines, too, and another nine submarines under construction. [52] [53]

"I'm sure England won't win alone," said Joe.

"Just as in the Great War, we will need the help of the whole Empire and more, including our ally, the Americans. They helped us win the Great War."

"Aye, but didn't the Americans arrive late?" asked Harry.

"Aye. That's why we called the Yanks doughboys," [54] said Joe. "Let us hope they won't take as long this time."

§

---

[52] https://WWII-weapons.com/fleets-1939/
[53] http://www.naval-history.net/index.htm
[54] Indelibly tied to Americans, "Doughboys" became the most enduring nickname for the troops of General John Pershing's American Expeditionary Forces, who traversed the Atlantic to join war weary Allied armies fighting on the Western Front in World War I - The National WWI War Museum and Memorial

Empire and Tyranny

The Canadian Army Mobilizes for a New World War

Britain's declaration of war against Nazi Germany included the Crown Colonies and India but did not commit the Dominions of Australia, Canada, New Zealand, South Africa, and Newfoundland. But every country of the British Empire soon pledged support for their King and declared war on Germany. Ireland stayed neutral throughout the conflict.

For the Canadians, including politicians, memories of WWI and its horrific loss of life and the resulting heavy burden of debt made them reluctant to enter another such conflict. In addition, there was strain imposed by conscription threatened the country's unity. At first, Prime Minister William Lyon Mackenzie King supported British Prime Minister Neville Chamberlain's policy of appeasing German leader Adolf Hitler to avoid war. When Chamberlain postponed war by sacrificing the Sudetenland in the Munich crisis of September 1938, King thanked him, and the Canadians agreed. But when the German invasion of Poland forced Britain and France to declare war on Germany, Prime Minister King summoned Parliament to decide, as he had pledged. They postponed proclaiming war for a week, during which Canada was neutral.

When the Germans torpedoed the transatlantic passenger liner Athenia on the 3rd of September 1939, it resulted in the first Canadian deaths of the war. She was the first British ship sent to the bottom by Germany during World

War II. The incident was the Donaldson Line's single most significant loss of life at sea.

Of the over 1,400 onboard, they killed 98 passengers and 19 crew. The dead included 54 Canadians and 28 US citizens, leading Germany to fear that the US might react by joining the war on the side of Britain and France. The people of Canada condemned the sinking as a war crime. German authorities denied that one of their vessels had sunk the ship. Hitler ordered that they keep their involvement in the incident a secret, and the Kriegsmarine did not admit responsibility until much later.

Among the first Canadians killed by enemy action against Athenia was the 10-year-old Margaret Hayworth. Newspapers publicized and hyped the story, proclaiming "Ten-year-old Victim of Torpedo" as "Canadians' Rallying Point," and set the tone for their coverage of the rest of the war. 1,000 people met the train that brought her body back to Hamilton, Ontario. The mayor of Hamilton, the city council, Lieutenant Governor Albert Edward Matthews, Ontario Premier Mitchell Hepburn attended a public funeral, and the entire Ontario cabinet. [55] The Athenia's sinking contributed to Canadian determination to support the British Empire in the war effort.

On the 10th of September, the Canadian Parliament declared war on Germany. The Cabinet agreed to dispatch the

---

[55] Houghton, Margaret, *The Hamiltonians: 100 Fascinating Lives*. Toronto: James Lorimer & Company, 2003.

Empire and Tyranny

First Canadian Division to Europe. The Canadian Army had mobilized the 1st Canadian Division before Canada's formal entrance into World War II, alongside the 2nd and 3rd Canadian Infantry Divisions. Elements of the 1st Canadian Division lacked equipment for mobilization. Most available artillery and machine guns were obsolete, and the troops lacked steel helmets. More modern weapons, equipment, and transport supplies only reached the division overseas in 1940.

With the outbreak of World War II, Canada's tiny armed forces increased dramatically. In September 1939 alone, over 58,000 Canadians enlisted, including twenty-one-year-old truck driver George of Montreal, Quebec. As usual, in times of the outbreak of war, young men fell over each other to join up for a new and adventurous job as a soldier. Young women also enlisted in large numbers for this war to work as nurses, administrative staff, or radio operators. The whole of Canada was rallying to the call to support the pleas of the mother country.

George was having a few beers with his buddies Jock McTavish and Paddy McCaffrey when the news came through on the radio in the tavern.

"Shit," said George. "We're joining Britain in the war against the Germans."

"That's it," said Jock. "I'm signing up for that."

"Me too," said Paddy. "Are you in, George?"

"Just try to stop me," said George. "Drink up, laddies. I know where I'm going now. I expected this would happen and investigated it, and I'm joining the Artillery."

They all rushed off to join the war effort at once. On the 19th of September 1939, George joined the 7th Battery, 2nd Field Brigade Royal Canadian Artillery as a Gunner Driver Mechanic with the ID D6618. He entered this unit because of his passion and experience with vehicles and driving. His buddies Jock and Paddy enlisted with him as gunners. At the time of their enlistment, the army had headquartered the 2nd Field Brigade at the Craig Street Drill Hall under Lieutenant-Colonel A.E.D. Tremain. Its motto was "Quo Fas et Gloria Ducunt," or "Whither right and glory lead."

The regiment originated in the 3rd Montreal Battery, formed in 1855 after the departure of British regular troops for the Crimean War and the Militia Act of 1855. For the first time, the Canadian public funded the maintenance of militia forces, including the five field batteries. They created the Battalion of Montreal Artillery in 1856 and renamed it the 2nd Montreal Regiment in 1895. [56] In WWI, they raised several artillery batteries in Montreal, and the 2nd Brigade included the 3rd Montreal Battery among its four batteries. During the war, the unit took part in every action of the 1st Canadian Division and later with the Canadian Corps. In a series of reorganizations,

---

[56] Volume 3, Part 1: *Armour, Artillery and Field Engineer Regiments - Artillery Regiments and Batteries*. www.cmp-cpm.forces.gc.ca.

they renamed it the 7th Field Battery. Major Andrew McNaughton, wounded at the 2nd Battle of Ypres in World War I, commanded the battery at the outbreak of WWII.

George lived at 3884 Evelyn Street, Verdun, an inner suburb of Montreal, Quebec. It was the home of his grandmother, Sarah Downes and his step-grandfather, William Frederick. Born on the 8th of June 1865 in Tenbury Wells, Worcestershire, England, Sarah Downes emigrated to Canada from England around 1880. She married a much older George 'senior' on the 25th of September 1889 at the historic red-roofed St John the Evangelist Church at 137 Ontario Street in Montreal. George Senior was born on 13 November 1848 but didn't give his place of birth. He emigrated from England to Montreal around 1860, becoming a bookkeeper after a few years of labour. He was working as an established and comfortable accountant when he married Sarah. They had two surviving children: Ernest Alexander, born on 7 July 1889, and Beatrice, born on 2 July 1911. George Senior died on 29 February 1912, after which Sarah married William Frederick Jenkins, 24 years her junior. Jenkins was born on 2 January 1888 in London, England.

At the time of William Jenkins' enlistment for WWI, he was working as a clerk, and he and Sarah were living at 22 Ontario St. West in Montreal, moving to 3884 Evelyn Street in Verdun following WWI.

Empire and Tyranny

George Alexander was born on 30 January 1918 at the Royal Victoria Hospital, Montreal, to Janet McRae of Hope Town, Quebec, Niagara, Ontario and Ernest of Montreal. George was working for the Drummond Transit Company when he enlisted in the army. He had worked there as a truck driver since 1935. George was earning a weekly wage of $20 at Drummond Transit. In the army, he could only make $15 a week, but the military would pay for his accommodation, living expenses and clothing, not to mention world travel costs. So, most recruits considered it a good move from a financial perspective, with the bonus of travel and adventure. George's highest level of education was the 7th Grade, which is typical of most working men since that was the level required by law. When joining the army, he was 21, five feet six inches tall, slim but muscular, blond, blue-eyed, handsome, full of life and raring to go.

"I can't wait to get going," said George as he and his buddies enjoyed a few beers to celebrate their new status. "I've always wanted to leave this town for a while. But I never dreamed I'd see the world."

"Yeah. Me too," said Paddy. "I'm very excited."

"Me too," said Jock. "Maybe we'll get to Scotland, where my ancestors were from."

"That's an excellent point," said George. "I'm half McRae, with Scottish ancestors too. This is so exciting, Guys!"

On 13 November, an advance party of Canadian officers landed in Britain. The 1st Canadian Division was under the command of the promoted Major-General McNaughton. It comprised a Headquarters (HQ), the Royal Canadian Infantry Corps, the Royal Canadian Armoured Corps, the Royal Canadian Artillery and the 1st Canadian Armoured Brigade. Signals, Engineers, Army Service Corps, Medical Corps, Ordnance, Army Pay, Postal, Dental, and Provost Corps supported these fighting units. The 1st Canadian Division left Halifax from Pier 21 in two escorted convoys; the first left on 10 December, three months after declaring war, and the second left on 22 December 1939, with added troops reaching England in February 1940. [57]

§

Crossing the Atlantic to defend the Mother Country

After kitting up and drill training for two months, George's regiment arrived in Halifax by train from Montreal. It then boarded the Empress of Britain for England on 9 December 1939. The 1st Canadian Division aboard the Empress left Halifax with Convoy T.C.1 on 10 December with 7,449 officers and men.

The RMS Empress of Britain was a three-funnel ocean liner built between 1928 and 1931 by John Brown shipyard of Clydebank, Scotland, owned by the Canadian Pacific (CP)

---

[57] C.P. Stacey, The Canadian Army 1939-1945: An Official Historical Summary (1948)

Steamship Company. This ship was the second CP vessel named Empress of Britain. HRH Prince of Wales, the future King Edward VIII, launched her on 11 June 1930. This was the first time they broadcast the launching ceremonies on the radio in Britain, Canada, and the United States. [58] Her maiden voyage to Quebec started on the 27th of May, 1931. [59] The Empress of Britain provided scheduled trans-Atlantic passenger services between Canada and Europe from spring to autumn from 1931 until 1939. At 42,348 gross tonnes, she was the largest, fastest, and most luxurious ship between England and Canada. Her proudest moment came when King George VI and Queen Elizabeth completed their goodwill tour of North America in June 1939 and chartered the Empress to return to England. The royal couple and their entourage occupied many of the ship's luxury suites for the voyage.

On 2 September 1939, one day before Great Britain declared war and seven days before Canada entered the war, the Empress of Britain sailed from Southampton. That voyage marked her last as a Canadian Pacific Line passenger liner, as the British government requisitioned her as a troop ship. Filled beyond capacity with Canadians returning home and with temporary berths in the squash court and other spaces, the Empress of Britain zig-zagged across the Atlantic to avoid U-

---

[58] Miller, William H. (1985). *The Fabulous Interiors of the Great Ocean Liners in Historic Photographs*, New York, Dover Publications.
[59] Musk, George, *Canadian Pacific: The Story of the Famous Shipping Line*. Newton Abbot, Devon: David & Charles, 1981

boats, arriving in Quebec on 8 September. [60] Upon arrival, they refitted the ship, painting it grey. They then laid her up, awaiting orders. On 25 November 1939, the Government requisitioned the Empress of Britain as a troop transport.

The buddies couldn't believe the luxury accommodation and cruise liner service that "spoilt the soldiers rotten." The gunners slept in comfortable staterooms, where stewards made their beds. They enjoyed superb meals at tables dressed in clean linen and set with gleaming silverware and glassware. Attentive waiters hovered around them to fulfil their slightest wish. There was no rationing at the many bars onboard, but the Military Police (MP) watched them to ensure the soldiers behaved. They filled the days at sea with physical training (PT), medical inspections, pay parades, boat drills, guard duty, and manning the ship's makeshift guns. [61] For the 1st Canadian Division, it was an effortless and impressive start to the war.

On the first morning out, a Sunday, the soldiers had time out on deck to enjoy the departure through the Halifax narrows and on out to sea. The sea was calm, so no one was seasick despite feeling uncomfortable.

"Hey George, I bet you've never had it so good, eh?" called Jock.

---

[60] Musk, George, *Canadian Pacific: The Story of the Famous Shipping Line*. Newton Abbot, Devon: David & Charles, 1981
[61] G.W.L Nicholson, *The Gunners of Canada, The History of the RCA, 1919-1967*, McClelland & Stewart, 1972

Empire and Tyranny

"You can say that again, McTavish," said George. "I've never lived so high in my life!" Jock McTavish and George had grown up together in Montreal. He was a good-natured, stocky, ginger-haired fellow.

"I think it's a screwup," said another soldier. "The army didn't have enough time to organize something less fancy for us soldiers."

And he was correct to an extent on that point. Despite the warnings, the speed of events leading to declaring war against Germany surprised the world and Canada. They had no troopships ready and waiting, so they had to requisition one quickly. The Empress of Britain had become available just when they needed her.

"I think you're right, Smith, but it's fun living like this for now, eh?" And they all agreed with that sentiment. Dave Smith enlisted on the same day as George, and they had since connected. He was a Canadian of English descent, tall, blonde and intense. Smith's father, a soldier, had died near the end of World War I before meeting his son, and Dave had grown up without a role model. So, he had developed a lifelong hatred of the Germans.

"Can you imagine how the officers are living," said George? "Have you seen the First Class dining room? They sent two of us up there yesterday to help with heavy lifting. It was like being in a palace. Not that I've been in one of those, mind you, but I have seen pictures of a few. Gold, silver, fine paintings, statues and mirrors everywhere."

Unbeknown to George at that stage, the Major he would chauffeur throughout the war was among them.

"We're living like kings," said another gunner nearby, a French Canadian 'Québécois' named Jean LaFleur. Jean was a short man with curly black hair and a protruding jaw. He said he had sported a full beard before joining, but the army barber got rid of that pronto. George had noticed that he had a nervous disposition and kept to himself.

"First Class," called out George's old friend Paddy McTavish. He was a Canadian of Irish ancestry with a medium build and dark curly hair, and he was always looking for action and fun.

"Just look at that ocean," said George. "Has anybody ever seen so much water?"

"Fantastic," said Jock. "No, I've never seen so much water!"

"I saw Lake Ontario once when visiting my mother at Niagara as a kid, and it was so big you couldn't see the other side," said George.

"This seems to go on forever."

"Did you see those jumping fish back there?" asked Smith.

"Yeah, but I was told by a sailor they are porpoises, not fish," said Jock, "Amazing!"

"What a great day," said George. "This is my first time at sea, and I love it."

"It would be better if this ship stopped rolling around," said Jock.

"Ah, come on, Jock. It ain't that bad yet," said Paddy.

"Just think," said Jean, "Our ancestors crossed this ocean so long ago in tiny sailing ships from Europe before they settled in Quebec. I think mine came 200 years ago. They were poor farmers from southern France when the French king sent them to populate the colony."

"We all came from France, England, Scotland, Ireland or wherever," said George. "Sent by those countries to conquer the American Continent and displace the natives… and other conquering countries. My McRae ancestor was a Scottish soldier at the Battle of the Plains of Abraham to boot out the French King."

It was a frigid North Atlantic day, but the sun was bright. The sky was a vivid blue as the fluffy white clouds floated by in a steady prevailing west wind. It wasn't a storm wind, so the sea's surface was tranquil but undulating with a considerable swell. As a new cruise liner with the latest stabilization technology, the Empress wasn't pitching or rolling much and easily cut through the waves. The soldiers hanging out on the main deck bundled up in their new greatcoats, with regulation army scarves wrapped around their ears and noses beneath army hats; only their eyes were visible. In time, the conversation shifted towards more pressing matters.

"To think we are heading towards another war in Europe. They are calling it the Second World War or World War Two, you know," said George.

"Yeah, and they are now calling the Great War the First World War or World War I. My grandfather died in that one. My father just missed it," said Jock.

"Was your grandfather in the Canadian army?"

"No, he was in the British Infantry and died at the Somme," said Jock.

"My grandfather was in that one, too," said George. "He was with the Canadian Black Watch from the start of 1917 to the end of the war. Imagine a Welshman in the Black Watch! That's our Canadian Black Watch, mind you. His name is Jenkins."

He didn't mention that his father had signed up for service in March 1915, but they discharged him three weeks later. "Why? No point raising that sticky little topic here," he thought. He also didn't explain that his grandfather was his step-grandfather since he didn't consider that necessary either.

"Ah, the Royal Highland Regiment," said Jock. "An elite regiment going back to its beginning in Montreal in 1862 as the 5th Battalion, Volunteer Militia Rifles of Canada. The Canadian Black Watch was at Ypres, Vimy, Passchendaele, the Somme, and more. An excellent reputation, eh?"

"How do you know?" asked Dave.

"I wanted to join them before George talked me into joining the artillery," said Jock, "I did my homework on them."

Empire and Tyranny

"Yup," said George. "My grandfather was mighty proud of being in the Black Watch. I never understood how he survived that war. Grandpa must have had a guardian angel, eh? He didn't talk about it much, though. But ever since I've known him, he has said it was a terrible war and that he never again wanted to fight in another."

"My father died in that war," said Dave. "I never got to know him. The Germans killed him at the Battle of Passchendaele. Ever heard of it? What a disgusting war that was! They told my mother he had drowned in the mud! Can you believe it? Drowned in mud! Shit! The Germans were at fault for that war. And now they've started another! They are not fit to live on this Earth. I have killed as many of them as possible. That's why I joined the artillery. You can kill many more Germans with 25-pounders than with rifles."

"Just to change the topic somewhat, where do you believe we'll end up?" asked Jock.

"I've heard they'll first post us to England," said George. "Then they will determine our assignment location. Who knows, I suppose we could end up anywhere on the Continent after that? France isn't that far away from England, eh? Just across the English Channel. I've heard that the British Expeditionary Force is already there."

"We only have a few guns in the RCA, so I don't know what we will fight with," said Dave.

"Rifles, Dave," laughed Jock.

"Hilarious," mumbled Dave.

"Yeah, but I was told they'll find us more by the time we fight," said George. "I'm sure we'll have everything we need when needed."

"Well, I've heard the English maidens are open and friendly," said Jock. "I intend to find out just how friendly they are."

That statement received total and enthusiastic agreement from everyone within earshot. These men were robust young bachelors and keen to meet the English lassies or any lassies except Germans at this stage.

While underway to England, the ship's captain kept the soldiers updated on the latest developments in the war.

News circulated on 12 December of the disaster of the escorting D-class destroyer HMS Duchess (H64). She sank after a collision with the British battleship HMS Barham off the Mull of Kintyre in thick fog, with the loss of 124 men.

"How the hell are we going to win this war if we bump into each other?" asked Dave, getting a few laughs and groans.

Later in the voyage, news arrived on the Battle of the River Plate in Argentina and Uruguay. It occurred between HMS Exeter, HMS Ajax, HMNZS Achilles and the German Pocket Battleship Admiral Graf Spee on 13 December. The Battle of the River Plate was the first naval battle of the Second World War and the first of the Battle of the Atlantic in South American waters. But most of the actions in Europe they heard of were on the Western Front, again! This news was extraordinary for the young Canadian soldiers, even though it was familiar to the older men who had experienced World War I a generation before.

"This war is real," said George. "We're on our way to a proper fight!"

"Sure looks like it," said another. "The Huns are up to their old tricks, eh?"

"I hope we're safe on this ship," called yet another, looking out to sea.

"I've heard the U-boats are out on the hunt already, eh?" This caused immediate consternation among the troops within earshot! They hadn't thought of that peril at this stage of their journey.

"Yeah, they did enough damage in World War I," said Jock. "The Germans got the US into that war by sinking the Lusitania and many American merchant ships."

When World War II started, Germany had 65 U-boats, 21 at sea, ready for war. During World War II, U-boat warfare was the core of the Battle of the Atlantic, which lasted the duration of the war. Germany had the most extensive submarine fleet at that stage. This had happened since the Treaty of Versailles had limited Germany's surface navy to six battleships of less than 10,000 tons each, six cruisers, and 12 destroyers. [62] Winston Churchill wrote, "The only thing that frightened me during the [Great] War was the U-boat peril." [63]

---

[62] Hakim, Joy, A History of Us: War, Peace and all that Jazz. New York: Oxford University Press, 1995.
[63] Winston Churchill, The Second World War, Volume 2, Published by Cassell, London,1949.

With a sweeping motion of his right arm, George echoed this sentiment. "If they are out there, I sure as hell hope our navy escorts will get to them before they get to us."

For the rest of the trip to England, the buddies spent most of their time outside on the main deck despite the North Atlantic winter conditions.

The Canadian convoy arrived unscathed in the British Isles on the morning of 17 December. They first saw the impressive rocky islet of Ailsa Craig, rising 1,109 feet out of the Firth of Clyde south of the Isle of Arran.

"Just look at that rock; amazing!" said a soldier.

"Yeah, Scotland, the land of my forefathers," said Jock McTavish.

"My ancestors, too," said George to a broader audience, "My mother was a McRae. In fact, her ancestor Duncan McRae arrived in Canada with the British Army during the Siege and Battle of the Plains of Abraham in Quebec City. She'd be so excited and proud to know I have come here. I must buy postcards for her when we get ashore."

As they sailed past the impressive island of Ailsa Craig, the captain announced the German Pocket Battleship Admiral Graf Spee had sunk off Montevideo harbour, Uruguay. A wild cheer arose on deck. But the captain didn't mention that the Germans had scuttled their ship rather than let the enemy capture it. The Uruguayans questioned its captain, Hans Langsdorff, then let him go. On 20 December, Langsdorff shot himself in full dress uniform while lying on the ship's battle ensign in his room in a Buenos Aires, Argentina, hotel.

§

Arrival in the United Kingdom

Moving up the Firth of Clyde, the convoy dropped anchor in the afternoon off Gourock near Greenock, twenty-seven miles downstream from Glasgow. The troops disembarked on 18 December. After saying goodbye to the Empress of Britain, they began an arduous journey via Glasgow to Aldershot, Hampshire, calling the trains "tiny" compared to those in Canada. Aldershot was and still is the home of the British Army on heathland 37 miles southwest of London. A four-mile march took the 1st and 2nd Field Brigades from Fleet Station to Leipzig Barracks, Church Crookham, Hampshire.

They treated the Canadian gunners who arrived in the United Kingdom in December 1939 to a welcome seldom experienced by troops anywhere. That first Christmas, so soon after their arrival, was the merriest of the wartime Christmas seasons they would experience during their stay in England. The 1st Canadian Division arrived just before Christmas. It provided a massive boost to the morale of the British people after the constant unpleasant news from Europe and the icy dampness of that brutal winter of 1939-1940. [64]

---

[64] G.W.L Nicholson, *The Gunners of Canada, The History of the RCA, 1919-1967*, McClelland & Stewart, 1972

They sent half the personnel of each artillery regiment on five-day Christmas leaves, with the other half going for a New Year's break. The Canadians encountered the warmest hospitality everywhere they went. During that early period of the war, the better things in life were still available, and the people of England were so generous. They found the Canadian "boys" to be so different, open, friendly, and refreshing. It was a cheerful atmosphere in which the gunners mingled with the inhabitants of this country, which was to become their new home. They found little sign of the aloofness reputed to be a characteristic of the British. Hitherto, complete strangers heartily welcomed Canadian soldiers and made them comfortable wherever they travelled. They bought their first drink in the pubs, and the patrons treated them for the rest of the evening. In those momentous times, they established lasting friendships between the British people and their guests from across the ocean. [65]

George contacted his step-grandfather's brother, Ernie Jenkins, who lived with his wife Nellie in London. They invited George to join them for Christmas. Uncle Ernie and Auntie Nellie, as they insisted on being called, were living in a tiny upstairs flat in the Kensington Mews. The Jenkins welcomed George into their home with open arms and led him to a bunk they had prepared on the sofa in the little living room.

---

[65] G.W.L Nicholson, *The Gunners of Canada, The History of the RCA, 1919-1967*, McClelland & Stewart, 1972

Empire and Tyranny

Uncle Ernie and Auntie Nellie, both small people in stature, poured generous love and hospitality on their young Canadian godson visitor. They looked after him in their modest home and gave George the classic introductory tour of the highlights of London. On his first day with them, they walked the short distance to Kensington Palace. From there, they walked through Hyde Park and beyond to Buckingham Palace, Green Park, St James's Park, Westminster, the Houses of Parliament, and the Horse Guards Parade.

They jumped on a double-decker bus at Piccadilly Circus and travelled through The Strand and Fleet Street to the City of London. They visited St Paul's Cathedral and the Tower of London. For their return, Uncle Ernie decided they should take the tube to introduce George to another convenient means of transportation in this magnificent city. From Montreal, his experience on the underground railway was enlightening, as he had never seen one before.

Over the next couple of days, George walked around London despite the freezing rain of winter. He visited the Natural History Museum in Kensington and spent hours of fascination while exploring its vast collections. George also visited the Imperial War Museum, founded in 1917. There, he studied the dozens of WWI exhibits. It was a real eye-opener for him. Montreal had museums but none on the scale of these elite London institutions.

Empire and Tyranny

He found his way to the Oxford Street shopping district. Holiday decorations adorned every shop and building. However, there were no coloured lights that might have adorned the shopping streets of London in the evening because of the blackout. And everywhere, he met other Canadian soldiers and sailors. They had wasted no time, and many had young ladies in tow arm in arm, whether promenading on the streets or languishing over drinks in the pubs. Before returning to their barracks, they wanted to see and live as much of this historic city as possible.

George relished the joys of the pub lunch. These meals were different from the taverns of Montreal. They were just as down-to-earth but far more comfortable. They provided the convenience of a well-priced menu—fish & chips, bangers and mash, gammon and fried egg with bubble and squeak, etc. He found this to be fantastic food, distinguishing them from Montreal taverns, which didn't serve meals. George swore to frequent the English pubs for as long as he was in England. One day, he met up with a few of his newfound buddies on a minor road off Oxford Street. Bored with the shops, it didn't take long for them to propose a visit to a pub that had only just opened at 11 am. As they entered, they saw they weren't alone. The pub was already half filled with patrons, including more Canadian soldiers and a few young ladies in the ladies bar. England kept vulgar men and sensitive ladies apart in those days. Two old fireplaces were hot with coppery red anthracite coals.

"Yes, my friends, just what we need on such a dismal day in Jolly Old England," called George over the rising din of the pub as they entered. Since it was an overcast day, the interior was gloomy, and it took a few seconds for their eyes to adjust. Then, finding an empty table surrounded by a padded bench, they settled in for what became a most enjoyable afternoon of drinking and socializing.

"This is the life," said Private Johnny Anderson of the Royal Canadian Regiment from Petawawa, Ontario.

"Yeah, that's for sure," said a Private Jack Black of Princess Patricia's Canadian Light Infantry (PPCLI) from Edmonton, Alberta.

"I love it," said George. "Who'd have thought we'd get to London so fast? This sure beats Canada in the middle of winter, eh?"

"Have you seen much of London, George?" asked Jack.

"I think I've seen the most famous parks and buildings," said George. "I swear my brand new army boots are wearing thin."

Just then, a sergeant from the RCA joined them.

"You're most welcome, Sergeant," Johnny blurted out. "Just as long as you don't expect us to do drilling."

"No chance of that, Laddie," said the older sergeant, a veteran of the Great War. "I mellow after two of these good old English Brown Ales. I got a taste for them in the last war over here."

"Ha, I bet, but I still haven't been able to stomach the stuff. Did you ever think you'd be back, eh?" asked Johnny.

"Nope. I sure didn't. That was one hell of a war. I never wanted to get back into another European war, and I sure hope this one won't be as wicked!"

"Where were you during that war, Sergeant?" asked George. He remembered his step-grandfather William, Ernie's brother, who had told a few stories of his time in France and Belgium during WWI.

"I fought for a while in the trenches of France, around Ypres, but then they captured me at Passchendaele in October 1917. I then spent a year in two POW camps in Germany. I ended up at Soltau, happy to be alive but lost much weight."

After mentioning Ypres, Passchendaele and POW camps, words familiar to his audience, his admiring drinking partners elevated the sergeant to hero status. They paid for his ales and listened for hours to his experiences in the First World War.

After an afternoon of English beer, a nutritious pub supper, and many war stories, George returned to the Kensington Mews relaxed and invigorated. Then, having said goodnight to his anxious hosts after tea, he crashed on the beckoning sofa for a good night's beer-induced sleep.

On his return to the Mews every other evening, Auntie Nellie had prepared a hearty meal despite their limited means. They wanted to give their Canadian "nephew" the best stay. The conversations ended up with family matters. His English hosts wanted to know everything about George's Canadian family, Grandpa Jenkins and Grandma Sarah. They learned of Sarah's history from Ernie's brother William, her second husband.

"Tell us about your family, George," Uncle Ernie said one evening.

"Well, what can I tell you that you don't already know?" said George?

"My mother was from Hope Town on the Gaspé Peninsula, where her parents had farmed before retiring to Niagara Falls. My father was a drunk and a womanizer. He left my mother and us kids when I was young, and I never saw him again. We then moved from Montreal with my mom to Niagara for a while. Those were marvellous years! I played around the falls on the Canadian side with my friends. We even walked behind the falls."

"Wasn't it dangerous?" asked Auntie Nellie.

"Yeah, I guess so. But we never worried about that. I remember two kids falling from the cliffs or drowning in the whirlpool—not my friends, though."

"How long were you there, George?" asked Uncle Ernie.

"A few years, Uncle Ernie. Most of my earliest school years were carefree times for me. I loved my great-grandparents, Peter and Isabella McRae. They were wonderful people who moved up to Niagara from the Gaspe Peninsula of Quebec with my grandmother. The McRae family had been around Hope Town since our ancestor from Scotland, Duncan

McRae, received land there from the Crown. He joined the army in Scotland and served during the Battle of Plains of Abraham in Quebec City. My grandfather told me many residents of Hope Town were McRaes or married to one; everyone descended from Duncan. Grandpa McRae made money from selling his farm because we always had enough food. I have fond memories of those times, but I ended up with another grandmother back in Montreal."

"That is a wonderful story," said Auntie Nellie. "When did you meet Ernie's brother William?"

"Well, I finished grade four in school there and then moved back to Montreal and lived with Grandma Sarah and Grandpa Jenkins on Evelyn Street in Verdun. Grandma Sarah is also a wonderful woman, and I am very fond of Grandpa Jenkins, as we call him. I finished my schooling in Montreal and worked odd jobs here and there in Verdun and Montreal. Then I joined Drummond Transit as a driver when I was seventeen in 1935, working there until I joined the army."

"What about your sisters, George? Tell us about them," asked Auntie Nellie.

"Ah, my sisters," began George. "My older sister is Sadie Isobel. She was born in 1915 and is three years older than me. She has had a cleft pallet and a crippled arm from birth. My younger sisters were Mary, born in 1920, and Millie, born in 1925. It was just after Millie was born that we moved to Niagara, so I guess I was about seven or eight when we moved there.

Mary and Millie have joined the Royal Canadian Air Force at home. They are wonderful sisters, but Sadie gave me a rough time because she was older and said I was a brat. The younger ones were sweet but naughty sometimes when they were little. Mary is a character with a sense of humour. I love them, every one of them. They are still in Niagara. They made me promise to write to them from time to time."

"So you grew up without your mother and sisters?" asked Auntie Nellie.

"Yup. It was just me with Grandma Sarah and Grandpa Jenkins," said George. "Still, they were always good to me, and I call my grandma my sweetheart."

"Ah, that's so good to hear, George," said Nellie while Ernie nodded in agreement with an enormous smile.

However, this British family visit was soon over. George returned to Aldershot by train from Waterloo Station, memories of his first ocean voyage and his first English Christmas in London swirling around in his head. "What a month," he thought. "What a fantastic month and start to my stay in England!"

§

The friendly influx of thousands of Canadian soldiers would positively impact Joe Rutherford and hundreds of other families throughout Britain. The Germans invading Poland caused severe consternation among the British since they feared the Nazis could try the same on their shores. The press jumped on the German term 'Blitzkrieg,' or lightning war. The implications for Britain caused apprehension among its citizens so soon after WWI. The memories of that conflict were still fresh in the minds of the older generation. They recalled the German bombings of London and other towns, and the horrors of the trenches returned to their nightmares. Thus, everyone welcomed the first arrival of the Canadian forces. Little did they know at that stage how well they could get to know the young Canadian soldiers or how close they might become to those with marriageable daughters.

At 57 years of age at the outbreak of war in 1939, Joe was a hard-working labourer and veteran of two wars with two sons and five daughters. His eldest daughter Violet had married Trevor Hodge, a Welshman from Glamorgan, in 1934 in Surrey. His eldest son, John Irwin, was 28 and had married Mabel Mobley of West Ham in September 1936 in Croydon, Surrey. His younger son Harry was 19 years old and still unmarried. His youngest daughters, living under crowded conditions at home, were Molly, Peggy, Beattie and Dolly, who, at 14, was still in her last year of school. The entire family was now living in or around Croydon. As mentioned, when BBC News announced the war, Joe said he had fought in enough conflicts and wasn't going anywhere!

§

1940: Training in Britain

Intensive training began for the Canadian gunners right after the Christmas and New Year leave. But it soon became clear the regiment was not ready for this war. There was a severe shortage of equipment, and this made training difficult. On 27 December 1939, the field regiments drew their first 18/25-pounder guns, four per regiment only, far from enough for proper training. The new 25-pounder Howitzer guns had gone into production but were unavailable. The old 18-pounder Mark IV guns were re-bored to take a 25-pounder shell as a temporary solution. But they still mounted them on the old 18-pounder carriages. [66]

The lack of proper equipment required improvisation, ingenuity, and a vivid imagination during artillery training. The learning process began with an introduction to the drill instructors who would train each crew, followed by an instructional film. The film showed how an efficient gunnery team functioned, illustrating the movements and actions of each team member as they loaded and fired their gun. This gave the recruits an idea of what their future roles would be. Then, on the training grounds, Driver/mechanic George observed groups of six men, each without guns, in odd postures. Some were standing, and others were kneeling,

---

[66] Duncan, George. *Lesser-Known Facts of World War II*, http://members.iinet.net.au/~gduncan/index.html

making strange movements in response to orders barked out by the drill instructors. They ended these antics by breaking up and playing a game of follow-the-leader around the parade ground. [67]

"It was a madhouse. I watched on the sidelines from my truck," said George.

"Yup. It was bedlam," said McTavish. "Crazy!"

"The stupidest thing I've ever taken part in," called Dave with more expletives.

"When the hell are we going to get our goddamned guns so we can practise with the genuine thing?"

The rest of the buddies howled with laughter that evening as they enthusiastically reviewed the day's antics in the mess tent over bangers, beans and mash. They still felt pride in their ingenuity in practising with imagined guns.

Military vehicles lacked guns to train, too, until well into the summer of 1940, civilian vans were the principal means of towing guns and transporting men and supplies. These were each driven by a civilian driver with a gunner driver beside him. The 2nd Field Regiment was fortunate to add to its mobility and the experience of its drivers by finding a few "dragons." These vehicles with tracks towed a gun and carried the gun teams. The army introduced the dragons during the early stages of mechanization to replace horses, a few showing up at Camp

---

[67] G.W.L Nicholson, *The Gunners of Canada, The History of the RCA, 1919-1967*, McClelland & Stewart, 1972

Petawawa, Ontario, in the 1930s. They created the name by contracting their original name of drag guns. [68]

VIP inspections interrupted training from time to time. On 24 January 1940, His Majesty King George VI, accompanied by Maj.-Gen. McNaughton, the Canadian High Commissioner, and the future Governor-General of Canada, the Honourable Vincent Massey, reviewed the four regiments of the 1st Divisional Artillery. King George VI was the Colonel-in-Chief of the Royal Canadian Artillery. But on that day, the temperature was well below freezing. The troops looked much 'smarter' in their dress uniforms than if they had been wearing their ill-fitting greatcoats. But for a long time afterwards, they recalled how chilled they became despite the quick march time prescribed by a considerate Commander Royal Artillery (CRA). They made King George aware of the deficiencies in the Canadian equipment. When presenting the COs to him, General McNaughton introduced Lt.-Col. Johnston of the 1st Anti-Tank Regiment was "the man who has not yet seen his guns." His Majesty confided in Johnston: "You know, I find these organizational changes very bewildering, don't you?" ·

"It was bloody freezing out there today, eh?" blurted McTavish that evening.

"Bloody right it was, even by Canadian standards," agreed George, "We came close to freezing our balls off, eh?"

---

[68] G.W.L Nicholson, *The Gunners of Canada, The History of the RCA, 1919-1967,* McClelland & Stewart, 1972

"Yeah. But what an honour for the King to review us!" said Dave.

"That it was," said George, "a damn fine-looking man."

News arrived on 9 April 1940 that Canada had created a Department of Munitions and Supply to manage war material production. They established the Wartime Industries Control Board.

"Oooh, now we are getting serious, Guys," said McTavish on that announcement. "Maybe now we'll get everything we need?"

"Don't hold your breath," snarled a frustrated gunner, Dave, "When the hell are we going to have time to shoot our 25-pounders at a few Jerries? I want to see more of those buggers dead!"

When spring came to southern England, it was a refreshing change for the gunners who had endured the wet English winter. The harsh Canadian winters had hardened the gunners, but most only knew the dry, icy-cold, snowy, and sunny high-pressure days of the continental Canadian winters. However, while these boys were still training in the peaceful English countryside, the war raged with the British and French forces on the Belgian border across the English Channel. And Germany had just invaded Denmark and Norway.

By then, the gunners were in top physical condition. As they strode along in their periodic route marches through the English countryside, a safe distance from the battles in Europe, it felt good to be alive.

At the end of April, the 1st and 2nd Field Regiments moved by road and rail to Larkhill, the vast gunner stronghold north of Salisbury. They carried out firing practice there while living in a tent city at Fargo Camp at the northern tip of Fargo Plantation, within a mile of prehistoric Stonehenge. [69]

George and his buddies visited the famous ancient Stonehenge monument to see first-hand what it was. Dave found a booklet explaining the region's history, including Stonehenge. They entered the site at dusk when Stonehenge took on an eerie atmosphere.

"Was this a graveyard?" asked Paddy.

"Or a temple where they worshipped?" asked George.

"It says here they worshipped the sun and the stars," said Dave.

"They met every year here on the first day of summer when the sun fell on that stone over there."

"Oh, now I can sense them," whispered Jean. "They are haunting this place!"

"Get out," said Dave. "How can you sense them?"

"I don't know," said Jean. "I just do."

And with that eerie thought, the men decided it was time to retreat to base for a few pints of warm English beer.

§

---

[69] Ibid

Empire and Tyranny

On 10 May 1940, hours before the German invasion of France by a lightning-fast advance through the Low Countries, Prime Minister Chamberlain resigned. Lord Halifax refused the post of Prime Minister. He wanted someone who could command the support of the three major parties in the House of Commons. So, a meeting between Chamberlain, Lord Halifax, Churchill and the government Chief Whip David Margesson led them to recommend Winston Churchill. Then, as the constitutional monarch, George VI asked Churchill to be Prime Minister. Churchill's first act was to write to Chamberlain to thank him for his support. [70]

Churchill's speech on the 13th of May 1940 was the first of three addresses he gave during the Battle of France, which had begun on the 10th of May.

> *"We are in the preliminary stage of one of the greatest battles in history; the air battle is continuous, and many preparations have to be made here at home.*

> *"I have nothing to offer but blood, toil, tears and sweat. We have before us an ordeal of the most grievous kind. We have before us many, many long months of struggle and suffering.*

> *"You ask, what is our policy? I will say: It is to wage war, by sea, land and air, with all our might and*

---

[70] Self, Robert, *Neville Chamberlain: A Biography*, Vermont, Ashgate, 2006

with all the strength that God can give us; to wage war against a monstrous tyranny, never surpassed in the dark and lamentable catalogue of human crime. That is our policy. You ask, what is our aim? I can answer in one word: Victory. Victory at all costs—Victory despite all terror—Victory, however long and hard the road may be, for, without victory, there is no survival."

Then Churchill made a short wireless broadcast on the afternoon of the 17th of May:

> *"We have become the sole champions now in arms to defend the world cause. We shall defend our Island home, and with the British Empire, we shall fight on unconquerable until the curse of Hitler is lifted from the brows of mankind. We are sure that in the end, all will come right."*

§

Back in Larkhill, towards the end of May with the 2nd Field Regiment RCA, they focused the talk on events developing across the channel in France.

"Our British brothers are in deep trouble over there," said George to the rest of his group.

"Shit, that's for sure, the German bastards," said Dave. "The BEF has the Jerries strafing them and closing in on land for the kill!"

"What the hell are we doing for them?" called Jock. "We can't just let those bloody Jerries slaughter them!"

"We need to get over there," called another.

"Yeah, I agree," said George, "we can't just sit here shooting at false targets. The division needs to go to their aid right now! What are our generals doing about this situation?"

§

Participation in the Dunkirk BEF Rescue May-June 1940

As already mentioned, when the BEF moved to France in September 1939 under the command of General Lord Gort, they assembled along the Belgian–French border. They were on the left of the French First Army as part of the French 1er Groupe d'armées[71] of the Front du Nord-Est[72]. Most of the BEF troops spent the Phoney War[73], as it became known, digging field defences on the French–Belgian border.

The Battle of France began on the 10th of May 1940. However, the BEF was tiny, making up a mere 10% of the Allied forces in Europe. They took part in a rapid advance into Belgium to the line of the river Dyle. However, the German breakthrough forced them and the rest of the French troops to retreat through Belgium and north-western France.

---

[71] 1st Army Group
[72] North-Eastern Front
[73] The Phoney War was the eight-month period at the start of World War II (3 September 1939 – 10 May 1940), during which there were no major military land operations on the Western Front.

By the 26th of May, the Germans had caught the BEF and French 1st Army in a narrow corridor to the sea 60 miles deep and 25 miles wide. Most of the BEF was still around Lille, over 40 miles from Dunkirk, with the French farther south. Then, two massive German armies flanked them. General Fedor von Bock's Army Group B was to the east, and General Gerd von Rundstedt's Army Group A to the west.

What happened then became one of the war's most baffling and debated decisions. The Germans halted their advance on Dunkirk. Contrary to popular belief, the Halt Order did not originate with Adolf Hitler. Field Marshal Gerd von Rundstedt and Günther von Kluge proposed the German forces around the Dunkirk pocket should halt their advance on the port to avoid an Allied breakout. Hitler sanctioned the order on 24 May with the support of the Oberkommando der Wehrmacht[74] (OKW - the German armed forces high command). [75] The German army was to stop their advance for three days, which they did.

Despite the Allies' gloomy situation, Britain even considered a conditional surrender to Germany. The German halt unknowingly gave the Allies enough time to evacuate the trapped BEF from Dunkirk. The War Office recalled the British forces on 25 May, and the removal began at once. Winston Churchill motivated the help of anyone who owned a boat, no

---

[74] High Command of the Armed Forces
[75] David Stahel, *Operation Barbarossa and Germany's Defeat in the East,* Cambridge University Press, 2009.

matter its size. The alarm went out along the southern coast of England, rallying hundreds of vessels and rescuers to rush into the fray. The Germans had damaged the docks at Dunkirk beyond use, but the sea walls protecting the harbour, known as the East and West Moles, were intact. Captain William Tennant, the officer in charge of the evacuation, used the beaches and the East Mole to land the ships. This favourable decision increased the number of troops embarked on each day. At the rescue's peak, on 31 May, they evacuated over 68,000 men. [76] The last of the British Army left on 3 June, and at 10:50, Tennant signalled Ramsay to say, "Operation completed, back to Dover.

But Churchill insisted on returning for the French and other troops at Dunkirk. So, the Royal Navy returned on 4 June to rescue as many French rear guards as possible. They evacuated over 26,000 French soldiers on that last day. But rescuers had to leave behind 30,000 to 40,000 to surrender to the Germans. [77]

The 1st Canadian Division answered the call to help. They assigned scores of RCA soldiers to help the battle-weary BEF soldiers returning to England. George and his fellow gunners were among them. They dashed off to Dover to help receive the exhausted BEF troops back into their home country. There, they

---

[76] MacDonald, John. *Great Battles of World War II*. Toronto, Canada: Strathearn Books Limited, 1986
[77] Lord, Walter. *The Miracle of Dunkirk*. New York: The Viking Press, 1982 / London: Allen Lane, 1983.

saw the survivors' harried, dirty and bloodied faces as they helped them off the various rescue craft. They heard them laugh and cry, thanking everyone for supporting them with their rescue. These were the first distressed faces of World War II that the gunners saw that day, which profoundly affected them.

"Careful, soldier, watch your next step," said George to the first of his evacuees.

"Cor blimey, a Yankee," the relieved soldier said with a gigantic smile. "It's about time you got over here. How good to place my feet on this home soil!"

"I'm not a Yankee, soldier," said George, "I'm a Canadian. The Yanks are not here yet. I don't even know whether they are coming. But we're here as part of the British Empire. Mind your step."

George passed the soldier to the next helper, then turned to help another. "Welcome back, soldier. Watch your step." The boat was bobbing and lurching in the choppy conditions within the busy harbour.

"Watch your hands on that gunwale," warned George, an expert angler and boatman.

"Blimey! Great to be home again, Canuck. Enough said, eh?" said the next soldier. "Thank you. You do not know how good it feels to be here with you, blokes!"

Next to him, George could hear McTavish welcoming a Scottish soldier back on UK soil. "Hey, Jock, we are now in the thick of it, buddy?"

"Yup, we sure are," said Jock. "Meet my recent friend Highlander Private Anderson, and take care of him!"

But that was just the beginning. By the time the gunners had finished this first war assignment, many hours had flown by with occasional sandwiches and quick power naps in shelters in the harbour. By the time it passed, they had helped hundreds of returning soldiers off the English and French boats, directing or leading them to the temporary medical stations. They sent the less distressed soldiers to feeding and resting stations in the docks.

Throughout the Dunkirk evacuation, the people of Dover could hear the battle at Dunkirk, 28 nautical miles away. They could even see the dogfights above the evacuating Armada, their smoke streams filling the sky. Bombs were exploding nonstop on or near the rescuing Navy ships and on men and vehicles ashore. Naval guns were firing at the German troops and transporters behind the beaches, and anti-aircraft weapons were shooting nonstop at enemy planes swooping on the fleeing soldiers and boats. It was total pandemonium!

Exhausted, the gunners of the 2nd Field Regiment made their way back to Aldershot, proud of their modest contribution to the historic evacuation and rescue mission of Dunkirk. The tortured faces of their rescued colleagues imprinted on their memories, whether grimacing or smiling. And these memories endured for the rest of the war and for many the rest of their lives. For George, Jock, Paddy, Dave and the others of the rescue squad had crossed the line from training into the actual war arena. Even if they were still a few miles away from the actual fighting, it galvanized them to support the war effort in any way they could.

"Helping rescue those guys sure felt good, didn't it?" said McTavish.

"It sure did," said George. "They had gone through hell and back. Welcoming them back was such an honour."

"What happens now," asked Dave. "So the BEF is back, and the French have surrendered. What now?"

"As the Jerries finish their invasion of France, we must wait here for them to attack us?" said an angry McTavish.

"Well, I hope our leaders have a plan to stop that," said George.

And Commander-in-Chief of the 1st Canadian Division General McNaughton, among others, had a plan. In a personal letter to General Sir John Dill, the new Chief of the Imperial General Staff (CIGS), he wrote:

"We are now squarely set for what I have long thought was the important task, the defence of these islands."[78]

§

---

[78] G.W.L Nicholson, *The Gunners of Canada, The History of the RCA, 1919-1967*, McClelland & Stewart, 1972

On the Move for More Training

The day after France fell, the Canadians moved to Oxfordshire. General McNaughton had convinced General Headquarters (GHQ) Home Forces that having his brigade groups shifted from the restrictive setting of Aldershot was important. He worried they couldn't hide their vehicles from above in the confined spaces available in barrack areas, nor could a rapid escape be possible. And the vast military camp was an obvious priority target for enemy bombers during an invasion.

"The thing to do is to exploit what the English have— those lovely parks." He was referring to the grand English estates surrounding the noble houses of Britain.

The Canadian units camped in great tree-studded country estates, ready at an hour's notice to move from their bivouacs in any direction to help oppose seaborne or airborne attacks. The 3rd Field Regiment's temporary home was in the magnificent grounds of Blenheim Palace, where Prime Minister Winston Churchill had been born. Headquarters 1st Anti-Tank Regiment was in Holton Park. They encamped the gunners of the 2nd Field Regiment near Brill in the adjacent Aylesbury Vale, a region of rolling farmland. There, the 2nd Field experienced their first bomb of the war, which fell with a tremendous explosion five miles away. [79]

---

[79] Ibid

But the Canadian stay in Oxfordshire was brief. When they revised anti-invasion plans, this led to a mobile corps stationed north of the Thames, comprising the British 2nd Armoured and 43rd Divisions. They moved another unit south of the river, including the 1st Armoured and 1st Canadian divisions. Because of the many moves they were making, a sarcastic Canadian soldier came up with the nickname "McNaughton's Travelling Circus."

The resulting joint Corps came into existence on 21 July 1940. Its headquarters was at Headley Court, near Leatherhead, Surrey, a town southeast of Croydon and 20 miles from London, to which the Canadian Forces now moved. In this region, it placed General McNaughton's formations well to work with speed against enemy landings between Beachy Head and North Foreland on the South Coast. That was the region most likely prone to German seaborne attacks. And from their position, they could better counter any airborne assaults on the North and South Downs. The Canadians were in a convenient spot for carrying on training. For the gunners, the distance from Leatherhead to the training grounds of Larkhill was 70 miles and less to the artillery ranges at Lydd on the Kentish coast. [80]

The 2nd and 3rd field regiments and the Anti-Tank Regiment took up a new position of readiness and began a busy twelve more weeks of training. They took part in manoeuvres over broad areas of the Southern Counties, an opportunity to test

---

[80] Ibid

new deployments and record the times needed to move from place to place. The regiments were developing anti-tank tactics and comprehensive defence systems, and they rehearsed procedures in line and radio communications. And, they found time for another firing practice at Larkhill. [81]

Towards the end of George's driver mechanic training, he became acquainted with the Universal Carrier, an army vehicle that became popular and widespread during the war. The Universal Carriers were small, incomplete tanks without a gun, used for transporting personnel and equipment, support weapons, or as machine gun platforms. Known as the Bren Gun Carrier from the light machine gun armament they often carried. On 24 July 1940, George passed his skill test as a Driver Mechanic. Throughout the rest of that summer, they attached him to the Royal Canadian Army Service Corps (RCASC) as a driver.

September came, and it was time to find more weatherproof accommodation than the tents and bivouacs served during the summer. Yet another move was in the offing. The gunners of the 1st Canadian Division fondly remembered the 18th of September. Winter quarters into which each field regiment moved on that Wednesday turned out to be home for the next fourteen months. They quartered 2nd Field in Addington, Surrey, less than five miles from Beckenham and Croydon. [82]

---

[81] Ibid
[82] Ibid

As in other parts of England, the Canadian gunners received a warm welcome from their civilian neighbours, who were most friendly in this challenging period. Local homes opened their doors to the newcomers, and it was not long before they had adopted a Canadian soldier into their family circle. Not a few of these adoptions led in time to the one or other daughter of the house becoming the bride of a Canadian soldier. [83]

Towards the end of October 1940, the Canadian brigade groups began a series of three-week tours on the south coast, as each became responsible for guarding a 15-mile zone around Brighton. [84]

§

"Those bloody Nazis got our ship!" cursed Dave. "Why can't we get over there and put them out of action?"

On 28 October 1940, the Empress of Britain was on a troop transport mission between England and Suez via the Cape of Good Hope, South Africa. On her way back, she called at Cape Town. With 643 people aboard, no one knew this would be her last journey. On 26 October, when this magnificent Canadian ship was off the West Coast of Ireland, a German long-range Focke-Wulf Condor plane attacked her. They set the vessel on fire in the

---

[83] Ibid
[84] Ibid

assault, and it did not take long before the crew lost control of the raging blaze. Captain Sapworth ordered them to abandon the ship, but a skeleton crew remained to save it.

The Polish destroyer Burza and the tugs Marauder and Thames took the burning vessel in tow and headed for safe waters. But the German plane had reported the ship's position via radio, and soon, the German U-boat U-32 was on the Empress' tail. The U-boat stalked its prey for 24 hours before, on 28 October, it fired three torpedoes towards the Empress of Britain. One detonated too soon, but the other two found their target and wounded her beyond hope. The Empress sank northwest of Bloody Foreland, County Donegal, Ireland. There were 49 casualties, most killed in the earlier air attack. Two days later, the U-32 paid for this heinous act when the HMS Harvester sank it. [85]

When the buddies heard of this tragedy, it upset them. The Empress had been their first ship, and they had become attached to her during their Atlantic crossing.

"She was a fine ship," said Jock with sadness. "I can't believe she's gone. Hell, I was hoping to travel back to Canada on her with my bride."

"Yes, a damn shame that! But they got most of the passengers off," said George.

---

[85] http://www.thegreatoceanliners.com/empressofbritain2.html

"Bride, Jock?" asked Paddy. "Have you been keeping something from us?"

"No, Paddy," Jock said, "I ain't found her yet. But I have been trying. Splendid fun that!" he said with a chuckle.

"I'm in no rush, and I want to make sure I get the right one, seeing as she will be with me for the rest of my life."

"Well, let us know your secret," said Dave. "So we can gain from your experience."

"Ha, fat chance of that," said Jock. "I'm not giving away any secrets!"

To which they had a friendly chuckle.

§

The Blitz and Battle of Britain

The first German bombing raid of the war on Britain happened on 16 October 1939 when the Luftwaffe targeted ships in the Firth of Forth in Scotland. Daylight raids on civilian targets began in Britain in early July 1940. On the 1st of that month, a bombing killed 15 people in Wick, Caithness, at the northernmost tip of Scotland, when German bombers attacked the town's aerodrome. On 9 July, 27 people died in Norwich during attacks on factories and ironworks. There were more attacks throughout July, including raids on Newport, Wales. However, as the month wore on, they hit many towns on the south coast as the Luftwaffe targeted the Channel ports and their defences as part of Operation Sealion. The Luftwaffe bombed Southampton from June onwards, and the International Cold Storage Depot in that city burned for over a week. They hit Coventry in July and August, losing several dozen lives. The bombing continued at Liverpool, Wrexham, Bradford and Birmingham, and they carried out occasional raids on London. [86]

The run-up to WWII saw a rapid increase in passenger numbers as British holidaymakers rushed to return from Europe. In the last days of August 1939, before the outbreak of war, Croydon Aerodrome, London's and Britain's first international airport, saw passenger numbers increase threefold to 1,500 a day. However, on 30 August 1939, Croydon reverted to its original role of defending Britain from aerial attack. Commercial airlines moved out, and the authorities renamed London Airport RAF Croydon, an operational frontline fighter airfield within 11 Group, Fighter Command. Purley Way in Croydon was busy with factories and warehouses clustered around the Aerodrome. In June and July 1940, the No. 1 Royal Canadian Air Force Squadron arrived, and they gave them a hangar for their Hurricanes. In the same month, No. 111 Squadron from North Weald came to recover its strength after being engaged in extensive patrols over France.

On Thursday, 15 August 1940, around 7 pm, they spotted twin-engine planes approaching. These were a

---

[86] http://www.bbc.co.uk/history/events/germany_bombs_british_towns_and_cities

German 'testing or exploration group' unit, Erprobungsgruppe 210, formed to conduct preliminary attacks on the British Isles. They bombed the airfield for five to ten minutes. The Air Force scrambled nine Hurricanes from No. 111 Squadron thirty minutes before the attack, and they intercepted the bombers before they could line up their targets. This interruption meant that the planes dropped most of their loads outside the aerodrome, causing casualties among the civilian population. Six Bf 110s and one Bf 109 were downed that day. It was a costly exercise for the Luftwaffe since the bombers never reached their target of RAF Kenley, South Croydon, a strategic airfield in the Battle of Britain.

The Rutherfords could hear the attack from their home on Cedar Road, which was not two miles from the aerodrome.

"What's that, Da?" asked Dolly. "Do you hear those explosions?"

"Aye, I hear them, Lassie," said Joe. "I hear the planes too."

"What does this mean?" asked Beattie.

"Sounds as if we are in the war," said Harry. "The bloody Jerries have brought the war to Croydon."

Dolly sobbed at the thought of bombs falling so near their home.

"Let's not jump to conclusions, children," said Joe. "We need to wait to hear what the papers say."

The next day, Joe learned of the attack on the aerodrome.

Empire and Tyranny

"I'm afraid Croydon Aerodrome suffered serious damage," he told his family. "They say the bombs made large potholes in the airfield. There was a direct hit on the armoury, and they hit the C hangar used by Rollason Aircraft Services with incendiary weapons, destroying the training planes. The Germans also bombed the Rollason factory and workshop, which caused many civilian casualties. They fired on D hangar, causing blast damage. A hangar only received minor damage, but they reduced the officers' quarters to rubble when hit by a bomb blast."

The rest of the Rutherfords sat speechless as they listened to him. Mary continued preparing the supper in the kitchen without comment. However, before Joe explained the grim details of the loss of life in that raid, Mary summoned everyone to the table for supper. So, they added a few more thoughts in their prayers for the people killed at the aerodrome.

"The Jerries have bombed London," called Jock one day in September. "There was a massive attack yesterday, and I heard hundreds of innocent civvies died."

"Goddamnit, I have family there," called George. "I hope they are all right."

"Me too, damn it," called Dave. "I must try to contact them to see whether they are OK."

Then, on the 5th of September 1940, Hitler ordered the Blitz as he prepared to invade the British Isles. The Blitz, shortened by the British Press from the German word Blitzkrieg or lightning war, brought WWII to Britain's doorstep. The Luftwaffe used aerial bombing to speed up their advance through Europe. And they had no aversion to bombing civilian targets. When they invaded Poland in 1939, they destroyed houses to force refugees onto the roads and create chaos. Warsaw surrendered after two-and-a-half weeks of continuous bombing. [87] In May 1940, the Germans subjected Rotterdam to carpet bombing to hasten a surrender. This latest use of air warfare had a terrifying psychological effect, one not seen in WWI. For civilians, it was akin to being hunted by mechanical birds of prey. The Nazis fitted Stuka dive bombers with wailing 'Jericho trumpets' that screeched as the planes entered their terrifying low-lying dives, strafing fleeing civilians with machine gun fire.

The Germans designed the enormous aerial assault to destroy the morale of the British people and force the country to seek peace and surrender. Luftwaffe chief Hermann Göring oversaw the first mass attack on the warm evening of the 7th of September, known as "Black Saturday"; 350 bombers supported by 650 fighters attacked the city.

The first squadron to meet the German bombers was the 602 Squadron, which scrambled together with the 43 Squadron from RAF Tangmere, Sussex. They climbed through the haze to 16,000 feet and spotted them as they broke through the top.

---

[87] http://www.bbc.co.uk/history/events/germany_bombs_british_towns_and_cities

Their squadron leader, Sandy Johnstone, recalled, "I almost jumped clean out of my cockpit. Ahead and above a veritable armada of German planes, Staffel after Staffel as far as the eye could see. I have never seen so many planes in the air at one time. It was awe-inspiring." [88] The bombing lasted until the morning, and 400 civilians died in that raid.

The Blitz onslaught began in London just before the 2nd Field Regiment moved to a new location.

"They are calling these fresh bombing attacks on Britain the Blitz," said George. "The raid on Saturday involved almost 1,000 German planes in broad daylight. It was horrific!"

"Yes, and they killed 448 civilians that afternoon and evening," said Dave. "Mostly in East London, I've heard. The bastards!"

In that first raid, German planes dropped 337 tons of bombs on London. Even though civilian populations were not the primary target that day, the poorest of London slum areas in the East End got the brunt of it. They received direct hits from wayward bombs and the fires that broke out and spread throughout the district.

But that was still only the beginning. Between 7 September 1940 and 21 May 1941, the Germans conducted a mass air offensive against industrial targets, towns and cities. The Luftwaffe attacked and bombed London 71 times over 57

[88] Stephen Bungay, *The Most Dangerous Enemy: A History of the Battle of Britain*, Aurum Press, 2001

consecutive nights. Meanwhile, the Battle of Britain raged overhead as Britain's RAF pilots met the attackers head-on, downing many German aircraft.

The massive loss of German planes during the early raids was partly because of the flawed strategy of targeting cities and not British airfields during the daytime. This caused the Nazis to switch to night-time bombing raids instead. One of the most brutal attacks on London occurred on the night of 29 December 1940. 136 bombers dropped 127 tonnes of high explosives along with 22,000 incendiaries, causing a massive firestorm. The last major attack of the London Blitz was on 10 May 1941, creating 2,000 fires and killing 1,436 Londoners. [89] They carried out another raid on 11 and 12 May 1941. [90] It damaged Westminster Abbey and the Law Courts, and it destroyed the Chamber of the House of Commons. One-third of London's streets were impassable. Only one railway station line was open for several weeks. [91] This raid was dramatic since they sent 63 German fighters with the bombers to counter the effectiveness of RAF night fighter defences. [92]

The Nazis also carried out bombing raids on the cities of Belfast, Birmingham, Bristol, Cardiff, Coventry, Glasgow, Hull,

---

[89] Calder, Angus. The Myth of the Blitz. Pimlico, London, 2003.
[90] Hooton, E. R., Eagle in Flames: The Fall of the Luftwaffe. Arms & Armour Press, 1997.
[91] Calder, Angus. *The Myth of the Blitz*. Pimlico, London, 2003.
[92] Hooton, E. R., Eagle in Flames: The Fall of the Luftwaffe. Arms & Armour Press, 1997.

Liverpool, Manchester, Plymouth, Portsmouth, Sheffield, Southampton, and Swansea. They destroyed or damaged over one million London houses and killed over 40,000 civilians, half of whom were in London.

The British government issued over 40 million gas masks and enforced a blackout to hinder enemy planes' navigation. They evacuated over three million people from towns and cities, including over a million children. Preparations included piling up 400 million sandbags around buildings. Fears of bombing led to 750,000 domestic pets being euthanized. London Zoo destroyed its poisonous snakes and spiders out of fear of them escaping. [93]

"A few of my buddies and I went to London the other day," said George to Major Walker, the regimental second in command. "I wanted to check on my aunt and uncle, and we wanted to see the damage for ourselves. It was unbelievable."

"That was risky, George," said the major. "Sure, the raids are now happening at night. But you never know with Hitler. He could change his mind at the drop of a hat."

"I know, Sir," said George. "I had to check in on my elderly relatives. Thankfully, they were okay. They told me they go to an air-raid shelter every night now. Imagine that, Sir. Their lives have changed so much, poor old folk."

---

[93] James Moore, *The Blitz Spirit - 75 years on!*, Express, Sun, Sep 6, 2015.

Shelters helped to save lives, although only one in seven people ever used them. They produced over 2.5 million corrugated iron Anderson shelters for private gardens. Six feet tall, 6.5 feet long, and 4.5 feet wide, the corrugated metal shelters were a tight fit for a family of six. Wealthier residents could buy one for a small fee. They often buried them four feet under the owners' gardens, their arched roofs covered with a layer of soil, and many planted vegetables and flowers on top. They distributed the shelters for free to more impoverished residents. By the time the Blitz began, they had erected over two million Anderson shelters. [94]

There were public bomb shelters, too, including 79 London Tube stations. Underground bomb shelters provided the most protection against a direct hit. However, the government in 1939 refused to allow Tube stations as shelters so as not to interfere with the travelling of daily travellers and troops. But by the second week of intensive bombing, the government relented and ordered the stations to open as shelters. Each day, well-ordered lines of people queued until 4 pm when they entered the stations, and by mid-September 1940, 150,000 slept in the Tube overnight.

The Germans dropped 50,000 tonnes of high-explosive bombs and 110,000 tonnes of incendiary weapons filled with chemicals designed to cause fires during the Blitz. They used

---

[94] https://en.wikipedia.org/wiki/Air_raid_shelter#Anderson_shelter

massive parachute mines, too. These caused much more destruction by exploding at the level of roofs. However, despite the damage to factories, industrial production increased.

"You know, Sir," said George to the Major. "They don't complain. Everywhere we went, the people were just as friendly as ever, smiling and laughing as they did their daily business. It was amazing."

"I know, George," said the Major. "The resilience of the London inhabitants is phenomenal. They are an amazing bunch of people—the best!"

Officials expected panic, but that never happened. In fact, psychiatric clinics they had opened to treat bomb shock victims were closed because of a lack of demand. The level of suicides and drunkenness decreased. Prime Minister Winston Churchill and King George VI toured bomb sites, and when the Nazis hit Buckingham Palace, the Queen said: "I'm glad that Buckingham Palace has been bombed. Now I feel we can look the East End in the face." Other famous buildings the Germans hit included Westminster Abbey, the British Parliament as mentioned and Lambeth Palace, the official London residence of the Archbishop of Canterbury in England .

During the Blitz, PM Winston Churchill and his government oversaw operations from the Cabinet War Rooms, a secret underground complex in Westminster protected by a 5-foot layer of concrete. As the bombs dropped, Churchill commented on Hitler. "He hopes by killing large numbers of civilians and women and children, he will terrorize and cow the people of this mighty imperial city. He thinks it will make them a burden and anxiety to the government. Little does he know the spirit of the British nation."

In the Rutherford household, the bombing didn't upset their routine much, but it had a profound psychological effect. Together with neighbours, they had built a shared bomb shelter in the lane at the back of the house. The men made it with bricks and a rounded corrugated iron roof. It was more substantial and durable than the Anderson shelters that had become so common around London and Croydon.

Every night, as the bombing started, the families rushed to their bomb shelters. In the suburbs and outlying areas, people and pets scrambled into their cramped garden shelters and slept as best they could until the bombing subsided. In London, they rushed to their nearest converted Tube station for protection.

In his third major war, Joe developed a slight tremor in his hands and, to an extent, his head and body. At first, Mary worried it might be the 'tremor disease' onset.

"Are you OK, Da?" asked Mary in private.

"Aye, Ma, I am," said Joe. "This bombing reminds me too much of my time in the trenches and during the Boer War. I can't stop myself. But I'm all right, Mary, believe me," he insisted. Joe's harsh life had taken its toll but remained steady under most circumstances. And he wasn't alone. Many victims of those bombings experienced similar symptoms.

But as the Blitz continued, so too did Joe's suffering. His shaking became more pronounced. He did what he could to hide it, but the Blitz awakened long-suppressed deep memories, causing Joe psychological pain. Joe and a few of his children had various factory jobs at that time, supporting the war effort. The bombing nights, with deprived sleep, influenced even the youngest, Dolly. This sleep deprivation had become widespread during the Blitz, but employers became tolerant and understanding.

Everyone had to adapt. Bomb sites were often cleared and used to grow extra food in so-called Victory Gardens. [95] They used over 750,000 tons of bomb site rubble to build airport runways for the RAF, too. [96] They drafted 78,000 women to crew the 2,000 anti-aircraft guns used during the Blitz. Defences included 1,400 barrage balloons and 4,500 searchlights. One million Women's Voluntary Services for Civil Defence members organized evacuations, salvages and canteens. The Government recruited one and a half million air raid precaution wardens for sounding air raid sirens, dubbed "moaning Minnies." They armed the wardens with wooden rattles to warn of gas attacks. They drafted 95,000 Britons into the Auxiliary Fire Service. Brave bomb disposal units dealt with 40,000 unexploded bombs, one in every

---

[95] Way, T. *The Wartime Garden: Digging for Victory*. Oxford: Shire, 2015.
[96] Nicol, Patricia. *Sucking Eggs*. London: Vintage Books, 2010.

ten dropped. 750 bomb defusers perished while trying to make the devices harmless. [97]

While the aerial blitz on London was at its height, many high-explosive bombs and incendiaries fell in the areas where they stationed the Canadian artillery units. This included the surroundings of Croydon. Soldiers soon became skilled in putting out firebombs, and volunteer rescue parties were often at work with the local Auxiliary Fire Services. Unit commanders received many expressions of appreciation from municipal authorities and individual householders whom the regiment's men had helped.

One testimonial on the bombings came from an Air Raid Precautions warden following his experience with an oil bomb that fell near him while cycling along the road. He took cover when he heard the weapons dropping, and when the incendiary exploded 250 yards away, he rushed to the spot. He reported arriving only seconds after the explosion to find six members of the 3rd Field Regiment at work with shovels. They could detect a note of frustration in his following comment: "The damn Canadians are dropping with the bombs!"

Then, there was the night of a vicious incendiary bomb attack on Croydon. The Canadians reported over 100 men of the 2nd Field Regiment absent without leave (AWOL) at the 11:00 pm tattoo roll call.

---

[97] James Moore, *The Blitz Spirit - 75 years on!*, Express, Sun, Sep 6, 2015.

Empire and Tyranny

But these missing men were still amid the air raids. George and his buddies were among the group enjoying a dance party with gorgeous young Croydon ladies in a church hall when the bomb struck nearby. The building shuddered, sending dust and plaster to the floor.

"My God, lads, that was a big one," yelled Paddy McCaffrey, "It sounded as if it was across the street!"

"Hey, Paddy, where did you come from?" asked George.

"Uh, just getting to know a lovely young lady better," said Paddy. "It's a pity, but it's time to see what is going on out there!"

The men ran out of the hall to see several buildings close to where they stood ablaze. They sprang into action at once.

"We have to help, Guys; let's go," called George.

"Damn," called Jock. "I was also making progress with a lovely young English girl!"

At the site, they immediately searched for survivors to assist, a few emerging dazed and blackened from the burning rubble. They escorted these to the arriving ambulances. The soldiers pitched in to help the firemen extinguish the blaze, too. The bombing continued through the night, and the gunners moved from one blast site to another, repeating the same rescue activities as often as possible.

Dave's anger with the enemy grew with every corpse he discovered. "Those goddamned Nazis will pay," he swore. "How the hell can they bomb innocent civvies?"

"They are trying to make Britain surrender, the bastards," said Jock. "Don't worry, we're getting ours back with bombings in Germany. And we will beat them into the earth!"

"Yeah, but they are not defeating the British spirit or forcing them to surrender," said George. "You heard what Mr Churchill said—we will never surrender!"

They dragged themselves into camp the following day, exhausted, tattered and blackened, some even with burns.

"They charged the gunners," records the unit historian. "However, the cases never came up for punishment. The work these lads, who had gone out for an evening's amusement, had done to save Croydon and help her blitzed citizens. These acts brought forth such demonstrations of praise and thanks that Colonel Tremain must have swelled with pride to have such men under his command." [98]

§

1941: In Defence of These Islands

By 1941, in London and Croydon, and the other areas under attack, people carried on as best as they could. A wartime routine had become ingrained in them. The city authorities considered the days safe enough to move around and filled them with rescue or rubble-clearing operations. People went about their daily chores and employment as usual.

---

[98] Ibid

Empire and Tyranny

The youth, including the Canadian soldiers, airmen and airwomen, sought solace from the war and joined the residents of the opposite sex as often as the war allowed them.

George, his friends, and many others from camps in the Croydon region visited the town every free weekend, attending dances and inviting young ladies out to the cinema or dinners. The Canadians had a reputation for being well off compared to British men, so they became popular among British girls. One Saturday, early March 1941, a friend asked George to stand in for him since he was still under the weather from partying through the night. The friend had a date with a young lady named Dolly Rutherford, and he asked George to go to her house at 75 Cedar Road, East Croydon, to deliver his buddy's apologies. George agreed and went via East Croydon station to Cedar Road nearby. Joe Rutherford opened the door of his home that evening to welcome a fresh-faced and handsome blond Canadian soldier dressed in his best uniform. By this stage, George was sporting a trendy moustache. Joe's daughters had sworn their father to secrecy so as not to let on to the fact that Dolly was still a few weeks from her sixteenth birthday.

"Hello, Sir. My name is George. I'm a Canadian soldier from Montreal, and I am here with a message for your daughter, Dolly."

Joe greeted George and escorted him to the dining room, where his wife and four unmarried daughters were waiting.

Empire and Tyranny

"This is George, a Canadian soldier from Montreal. George, my wife Mary, my son Harry, my daughters Molly, Peggy, Beattie, and Dolly are on the right." Beattie, 19, wore her WAAF uniform. She had joined the Women's Auxiliary Air Force (WAAF), the female auxiliary of the Royal Air Force during World War II, established in 1939. Beattie was in a barrage balloon crew.

"Good evening, ladies," began George in his best-mustered Canadian demeanour, "I'm pleased and honoured to meet you; I have a message from Jack for Dolly. He couldn't make it tonight because he was not well. So he asked me to drop by and give you that message."

The girls greeted George, and Molly, the eldest, asked, "Won't you stay and have tea with us?"

"I'd love that," said George, "I've had a hectic day, and that's just what I need."

They invited George to sit while the girls rushed to the kitchen to prepare the tea and sandwiches. On their return, George told Joe and Mary about his life in Canada.

"How do you take your tea, George?" asked Dolly.

"Milk and two sugars if you have them, please," said George, knowing how difficult it was to get sugar then. "If you don't have sugar, milk will be fine. We can't be choosy these days."

He looked closely at her and noted how lovely and bubbly she was.

Empire and Tyranny

"Oh yes, we have sugar," said Dolly. She emptied two teaspoons of the precious rationed commodity into his cup while her sisters poured tea for their parents and themselves. Official rationing began on 8 January 1940 with bacon, butter, sugar and other commodities according to weight, monetary value or points. A person's standard weekly allowance was one fresh egg, 4oz margarine, four rashers of bacon, 2oz butter, 2oz tea, 1oz cheese and 8oz sugar. Meat prices varied, and cheaper cuts became popular. Citizens could pool or save points to buy pulses such as dried peas, beans, lentils, chickpeas, cereals, tinned goods, dried fruit, biscuits, and jam. [99] But the Rutherfords always ensured they had sugar available for guests, even if they went without. They had become talented at ensuring they still had sweet biscuits and fruitcakes in the pantry for such occasions. They then sat and began a lively conversation, questioning George on his life in Canada and the army.

"Well, I left an excellent job as a truck driver for Drummond Transit in Montreal to join the military and help you Brits beat the Nazis," said George.

"I was born in Montreal in the Province of Quebec and grew up in Montreal and Niagara Falls in Ontario, where my mother and sisters still live. I have three sisters—Sadie, Mary and Minnie, but I'm closest to Mary. Before retiring to Niagara, my mother's parents were farmers in Quebec, but I don't think

---

[99] http://www.bbc.co.uk/history/topics/rationing_in_WWII

I could be a farmer. Instead, when I get back to Montreal, I want to start a transport company."

It had flowed without effort and nonstop from his lips. His life and future dreams poured out as if lubricated by the tea. He wanted to make an impression on these young women.

"A sandwich, George?" asked Beattie. "Dolly, offer George a sandwich or two."

"Oh, thank you. I have eaten little today, so I'd love that," George said, selecting an egg and cucumber sandwich while assessing Dolly further. "Ummm, a most delicious sandwich, thank you," he told her. Dolly was a petite, brunette woman wearing a fashionable dress and her hair in a net. George looked at her for a long time as she served him the sandwiches, and he was most impressed. She seemed so mature and gorgeous, he thought.

"How long have you been in the army, George?" asked Harry.

George then turned his attention to Harry and engaged in small talk with the only other male of his age in the room.

"I joined as soon as Canada got into the war," said George. "We arrived here in December 1939."

"That's grand," said Harry. "I see you are in the artillery."

"Yup, that's right. Are you in the service, Harry?" asked George.

"No, George," said Harry. "My older brother John and I are both working at Creeds Munitions Factory, a short distance from here on Cherry Orchard Road. We have a heart condition and couldn't enlist. But I would have."

"Well, I guess working in a munitions factory is dangerous enough in these times," said George. "You wouldn't find me doing that. I prefer to be out and about as a driver." The girls giggled at George's Canadian pronunciation of "out and about." He learned too that Molly was working in the office at the munitions factory and that Peggy was working at De Witt's Pharmaceuticals factory across the road from Creeds. Beattie was working as a seamstress in Croydon High Street.

"What about you, Dolly," George asked, "Are you working there too?"

"No, George," she said with a giggle, "I'm working as a seamstress at a uniform factory near here."

In this first contact with the Rutherfords, he didn't overstay his welcome even though they assured him he wasn't and that he was welcome to visit whenever he wished. He thanked his hosts and the girls, and Joe escorted him to the front door.

"I see you've had your share of bombs in this neighbourhood," said George.

"Aye, that we have, Laddie, that we have," said Joe. "We haven't had a hit on Cedar Road yet, touch wood."

"I saw the damage on my way from the East Croydon Station," said George, pointing in the general direction. "It looked as if the bomb had taken out part of the station and a few houses over there."

"Aye, you're right. At the bottom of Colson Road," said Joe. "Not 250 yards from us and even closer to the factories! The blast was next to the train station, across from the factories. But we were lucky that there wasn't more damage done or that the munitions ignited. They've cleaned up most of the mess made by the bombs, but there's still some around. There was another blast on Tunstall Road, which was 300 yards from us that way. The bombs inflicted a lot of damage on Tunstall and Canning Roads. Eight or ten bombs fell together one night—a terrible night for us!".

"That's the tragedy of war, Mr Rutherford," said George,

"I witnessed a terrible blast in the centre of Croydon, where my buddies and I helped the fire department rescue survivors and put out the blaze. Please stay safe with your family. So long."

He had adopted the custom of the times never to say goodbye. And with a wave, he scurried off, vowing to return as soon as possible. To use an angler's expression, he admitted young Dolly had hooked him!

George impressed the Rutherfords, too. It impressed Joe that George had been among the Canadian soldiers who had helped at the bomb blast in town. He had heard the whole story. They agreed George was an upstanding man they hoped to see again. That didn't take long since George was starting a 7-day leave on 7 March, and he tried to see Dolly again.

Two months of raids after that visit saw another one of the most brutal bombing campaigns unleashed on Croydon by the Nazis during the Blitz. It resulted in a destroyed bus depot. Between 10.50 pm on 10 May 1941 and 5:50 AM the following day, the Nazis unleashed a relentless bombing attack on Croydon. It claimed 14 lives across the borough, including seven at the bus depot. But a horrific hit on the bus garage in Brighton Road earned a prominent place in Croydon's own war records. The London Transport Museum has described the bombing campaign of 10 May 1941 as its worst night during the Blitz. Not only were 65 buses destroyed at the South Croydon depot, but there were 20 direct hits on London Transport railways elsewhere in London. In four separate locations, tunnels of the Underground network collapsed.

The last major Blitz attack on London was from 10 to 11 May 1941, when the Luftwaffe flew 571 sorties and dropped 800 tonnes of bombs on the city. This caused over 2,000 fires, killed 1,436 people and injured 1,792.

Over 1300 German bombs, including five parachute mines, fell on Croydon from 7 October 1940 to 6 June 1941. The blasts from the parachute mines exploding above ground caused extensive damage, demolishing many houses in the vicinity, sometimes an entire city block. It shattered windows as far as a mile away. The air raids destroyed or damaged 60,000 homes and killed or injured 5,000 people. [100] But aside from two bombs in July 1941, the Germans didn't target Croydon again until January 1943. [101]

By May 1941, it had become clear to the Nazis that their strategy of wearing down the Britons had failed. The bombing did not demoralize the British into surrendering or doing much damage to the war economy; eight months of attacks didn't hamper British war production much, which continued to increase. [102] The most significant effect was forcing the British to disperse planes and manufacture spare parts. British wartime studies concluded cities took ten to fifteen days to recover when hit, but exceptions such as Birmingham took three months. [103] So, the Nazis turned their attention to "Operation Barbarossa" to attack the Soviet Union in the East. Thus, the threat of invasion to the West receded for a while.

§

---

[100] Moss, Richard, *Croydon Museum and Clocktower remembers the Blitz and the Battle of Britain*, 22 September 2010

[101] Croydon's struggle during the Second World War is well-documented at the Croydon Local Studies Library and Archive Service at the Clocktower in Katharine Street.

[102] Cooper, Matthew. *The German Air Force 1933–1945: An Anatomy of Failure.* New York: Jane's. 1981.

[103] Hooton, E. R. (1997). *Eagle in Flames: The Fall of the Luftwaffe.* Arms & Armour Press.

Exercise "Bumper"

On 30 June 1941, the Army posted George as Driver Mechanic to 2nd Field Regimental Headquarters (RHQ) Addington. There, he became the driver for Major G.M. Walker, 2nd in command of the 2nd Field Regiment. Impressed by George's CV and his story of helping during the Croydon Blitz bombings, the Major selected him.

The summer and autumn of 1941 saw the start of the grand-scale manoeuvres. They exercised large formations in carrying out their role in defence of Great Britain and later rehearsed for offensive operations beyond Britain's shores.

The most significant anti-invasion rehearsal attempted during the war, and one of the most extensive military manoeuvres ever staged in Britain took place as "Exercise Bumper." It began on the 25th of September 1941 and continued for two weeks. It involved a quarter of a million troops, including the Canadian Corps. In this exercise, a "German" invasion force that had overrun part of East Anglia was successfully engaged by "British" troops in the Chilterns, northwest of London. They designed the exercise to give senior commanders and their staffs of the two headquarters, four corps, and twelve divisions involved an opportunity to handle sizeable mobile forces. Those concerned with the movement, administration, and supply of enormous bodies of men in the field learned many valuable lessons. Moving from one concentration zone to another without firing, a few Canadian artillery units found the proceedings monotonous. Yet most Canadian artillery engaged in the simulated fighting reported an enjoyable two weeks since the weather held fair throughout the exercise·

The primary goal of "Exercise Bumper" was to practise an entire Command in an anti-invasion role. At the same time, they intended the scheme to "test the organization for an assault action across the Channel." After "Bumper," they emphasized to prepare for an invasion.

George had become a very conscientious driver for Major G.M. Walker. He was the Major's personal chauffeur, and he drove him anywhere he needed to be while on duty or desired to go during his free time. They had mutual respect for one another. The Major had developed a liking for George's driving abilities and his discretion on the Major's movements. George respected the major's rank and position within the regiment. But he had grown to admire him, too, as a person and soldier. Then, on 19 November 1941 at 1600, George and the major had an unfortunate car accident at Titsey, a tiny village in the North Downs of Surrey. The North Downs is a ridge of chalk hills south of Croydon that stretches from Farnham in Surrey to the White Cliffs of Dover in Kent. It's a region known for its "outstanding natural beauty."

They were on their way in an Army Ford Sedan from Addington to Tandridge in Surrey for a conference at the 2nd

Canadian Infantry Brigade. But as they drove down Titsey Hill, the brakes failed, and the axle broke.

"What the hell was that, George?" asked the Major.

"The axle has broken, Sir. And we don't have any brakes," said George. "Hold on, Sir. I'll get us down safely."

But the vehicle's left rear was on fire since the gasoline tank had caught fire, caused by sparks generated by the axle and wheel dragging on the road.

"We're on fire, George," said the Major calmly.

"That we are, Sir," said George over his shoulder. "Don't worry, Sir. I've got it under control."

"Well, I'm glad to hear that, gunner," said the Major.

George kept the car on a straight run 300 yards down the hill until they stopped. Soldiers nearby and two civilians rushed to their aid and helped George extinguish the fire. George removed tools and Tommy gun parts from the boot, then recovered the left rear wheel and tyre on the road 40 yards back.

After the accident, the shaken driver gave his statement in his own words to the Military Police. A calm and collected Major Walker also declared in his own words. A local resident, E.J. Barrows of No. 3 Evelyn Ave, Titsey, Oxted, saw the accident's aftermath and gave a short testimony. His home was across a field opposite Titsey Hill.

The police deemed George to be free of fault and dropped the matter. George even received a commendation from Major Walker for handling what could have been a far worse accident with a less skilled driver.

When George returned to camp that evening, he found his companions had gone to a local pub, so he joined them.

"I had an accident today, Guys," said George to the assembled buddies, "with the major as a passenger!"

"An accident, George? No. How serious?" asked Paddy.

"Serious enough, but it hurt no one, thank God," George said. "The axle broke while descending Titsey Hill and the car caught fire!"

"Thank God it hurt no one," said Jock. "Was the major angry?"

"No. Not at all. The major was calm about the whole incident. He realized that the accident happened because of mechanical failure," said George, "It shook me somewhat. I have never had an accident. So that was my day ruined. I need a good slug of whisky. How was yours?"

This prompted mirth within the small group. So, they fetched another round of beer and a double measure of Scotch to celebrate George's survival of his first "battle" of the war. They gave a toast: "Here's to George and the major!" The talk then turned to more exciting topics, such as English beer and women.

§

Empire and Tyranny

America Enters the War

On Sunday, 7 December, the first news of the Imperial Japanese Navy's morning surprise attack on the American naval base at Pearl Harbour in Honolulu, Hawaii, arrived in England.

A fleet of 353 Imperial Japanese planes, including fighters, dive bombers and torpedo bombers, attacked the in two waves from six aircraft carriers. [104]

The attack ended ninety minutes later, with 2,403 Americans dead and 1,143 injured. [105] They sank eighteen ships, including five battleships. [106] Most Americans killed or wounded during the attack were non-combatants, given there was no state of war when the assault occurred. It led to the US entry into World War II the next day, and these famous words from President Franklin D. Roosevelt relayed the news over the radio, including to the BBC.

"Yesterday, 7 December 1941, a date which will live in infamy, the United States of America was suddenly and deliberately attacked by naval and air forces of the Empire of Japan."

The Japanese torpedoed American ships between San Francisco and Honolulu on the high seas. They also attacked

---

[104] Parillo, Mark (2006), *"The United States in the Pacific,"* in Higham, Robin; Harris, Stephen (eds.), *Why Air Forces Fail: The Anatomy of Defeat*, The University Press of Kentucky

[105] https://www.thoughtco.com/pearl-harbor-facts-1779469

[106] Conn, Stetson; Fairchild, Byron; Engelman, Rose C. (2000), "7 – *The Attack on Pearl Harbor,"* *Guarding the United States and Its Outposts*, Washington D.C.: Center of Military History United States Army & GPO 1946

Empire and Tyranny

Hong Kong, Guam, the Philippine Islands, Wake Island and Midway Island.

On 8 December 1941, the United States Congress declared war on the Empire of Japan in response to that country's surprise attack on Pearl Harbour the previous day. They planned it an hour after the 'Infamy Speech' of US President Franklin D. Roosevelt.

"The Yanks are finally in the war," called Dave.

"It's about bloody time," said Jock. "What happened?"

"The Japanese bombed their naval base in Hawaii," said Dave. "This means that Japan has joined the Axis in the Pacific."

"That means the British Empire will fight the Japanese, too," said George. "This war keeps getting worse and worse by the day! It's now truly a World War."

§

The United States of America was not an empire in the word's traditional meaning, but it had foreign possessions and much influence in the Pacific and the Atlantic. Despite its limited geographical extent, it was a nation with a massive and educated population for its time, immense wealth, vast military strength and unlimited industrial power. From this day on, the world would experience a global war clash of armed forces and weaponry of epic proportions never imagined.

§

1942: A Year of United Nations, Romance and Disaster

US President Franklin D. Roosevelt coined the term 'United Nations.' It was first used on 1 January 1942. Representatives of 26 nations at war with the Axis Powers met in Washington to sign the "Declaration of the United Nations." They endorsed the Atlantic Charter, pledging to use their resources against the Axis and agreeing not to make a separate peace. President Roosevelt, Prime Minister Churchill, Maxim Litvinov of the USSR, and TV Soong of China drafted a brief document later known as the "Declaration by United Nations." [107]

On 14 January 1942, the US and Britain concluded the "Arcadia Conference" in Washington, DC.

US President Roosevelt and Prime Minister Churchill agreed to set up a combined chief of staff and make defeating Germany their priority. WWII was a global conflict involving two great theatres of war. Twenty-six Allies were at war with the Germans in Europe and the Atlantic and the Japanese in the Pacific. The Arcadia Conference decided that winning the war in Europe took precedence over winning the war in the Pacific.

---

[107] The original twenty-six signatories were: The United States of America, the United Kingdom of Great Britain and Northern Ireland, the Union of Soviet Socialist Republics, China, Australia, Belgium, Canada, Costa Rica, Cuba, Czechoslovakiam, Dominican Republic, El Salvador, Greece, Guatemala, Haiti, Honduras, India, Luxembourg, Netherlands, New Zealand, Nicaragua, Norway, Panama, Poland, Union of South Africa, Yugoslavia

On 26 January, the first United States troops arrived in Belfast for the European Theatre. The US sent American bombers to bases in England, and the British strengthened their forces in the Pacific. [108]

The New Year of 1942 opened with a world struggling with the second world conflict in a quarter-century, with its unprecedented violence. In England, on 10 January, a Blitz on Liverpool ended with German bombs dropping on Stanhope Street, killing nine people and injuring far more. Among the houses destroyed in the bombing was the former home of Adolf Hitler's half-brother Alois. Alois Hitler lived at 102 Upper Stanhope Street with his Irish wife, Bridget Dowling and their son, Patrick William Hitler, born in 1911. The Hitlers were long gone, but four more died because of their injuries from that blast the following day.

On 30 May, over 1,000 RAF bombers attacked the German city of Cologne. Cologne Cathedral endured fourteen hits by bombs during the war but survived without too much damage. So, as with St Paul's Cathedral in London, Northern Europe's largest Gothic cathedral stood as a sign of courage above an otherwise destroyed city.

Soon after the Cologne bombing on 1 June 1942, the Germans retaliated with a bombing raid on Canterbury. In the early hours of this day, German planes dropped 130 high

---

[108] William Hardy McNeill, *America, Britain and Russia: Their Cooperation and Conflict 1941-1946* (1953).

explosives and 3,600 firebombs on the city, killing 43 and injuring 40 others. Canterbury Cathedral, one of England's oldest and most famous Christian structures, escaped with minor damage, but they reduced much of the St George's area to rubble. A further raid, this time in daylight on 31 October 1942, claimed 33 lives and 54 injured.

§

Romance in Croydon

But despite these terrible events, life continued as usual in England. The Germans had stopped bombing Croydon for the time being, and the Rutherford family was busy with their everyday lives and romances.

Peggy had formed a close relationship with a Canadian soldier named John (Jack) Bass. Beattie was in a relationship with a real estate businessman named William Henry (Bill) Simpson. Both he and Beattie met in Croydon's central shopping district of George Street. He worked for Hooker and Rogers Real Estate, and she worked in a dress shop nearby as a seamstress. Bill also ran the local stretcher service as a volunteer. Then, on 14 March 1942, Beattie Rutherford, at 19, married Bill Simpson, 31, in Addiscombe Congregational Church, Croydon. Dolly and Bill's sister Queenie were bridesmaids. Beattie and Bill had an honour guard of WAAFs and Bill's stretcher-bearers at their wedding.

Empire and Tyranny

George had been pursuing a courtship with Dolly. He took a few leaves of absence that year and visited Croydon as often as possible. He and Dolly went to the Shirley Hills nearby, spending many pleasant hours walking, talking, and relaxing together. The heather-sprinkled meadows and forests of Shirley Hills were a welcome rural escape from the horrors of war on the outermost reaches of London and Croydon.

Dolly and Beattie were the two youngest sisters and were close. So, when Beattie married and moved out of 75 Cedar Road, Dolly, short of 17 and working as a seamstress, lost her closest friend and confidante. But it wasn't long before George asked Dolly to marry him. George had army leave again from 14 to 21 July, when he spent most evenings with the Rutherfords. His time off included a weekend, so he and Dolly were inseparable. George collected her early Sunday morning, and they grabbed a bus again to the Shirley Hills.

Dolly had prepared a picnic basket. It was a lovely summer's day and not too hot. So, they found an ideal spot out of sight of the other visitors and spent the day talking. George told her of Montreal, the city he knew so well and loved. He described Verdun, the inner suburb of Montreal, and Lac Saint Louis, where he spent time in the summers.

"We have pleasant summers and colourful autumns, which we call 'falls' in Canada," he explained. "Our winters are much colder than here, but we have a lot of snow, making both more work and fun. Then we have short explosive springs that are as pleasant as here."

"Is it freezing in winter?" asked Dolly.

"Yes, Dolly, it can be icy cold," he said. "Then, after the snow falls, the sun comes out, and we have several days of clear blue skies. We see the sun much more in Canadian winters than in England. Yes, it's cold, but you dress for that, and the days are lovely. We go skating or tobogganing in winter on Mount Royal or on toboggan slides Verdun builds along the Boardwalk on the riverbank. There are ice-skating rinks everywhere. It's a lot of fun, for children in particular," he ended with a wink.

"I remember the snow in the North," said Dolly. "We get little of that here."

"In summer, I go to a place upriver from Montreal called Beauharnois on the shores of Lake St Louis where the St. Lawrence River widens," said George.

"I keep a fishing boat and outboard motor there at an old clubhouse. Close by, I have close friends from when I lived there as a boy. There are lovely beaches on islands near Beauharnois, where I swim and fish. The water is crystal clear and full of fish you can watch swimming in and out of the reeds. It's a paradise."

"Oh, that sounds like fun, George," said Dolly. "I don't think I'd be good at fishing."

"Maybe not, Dolly," he said. "I guess it's not a woman's thing. But children love it."

"Tell me about your family over there, George," said Dolly.

George told her of his family, his grandmother Sarah and her husband Bill, his aunt Bea and her husband John, and their children, who lived in Verdun. He told Dolly of his long-term plans to build a transport business with a fleet of delivery trucks. His words impressed Dolly. And George had his mission in mind as he explained these home truths of life in Canada.

"It's a wonderful life there, Dolly, but just a little different to here," said George, downplaying the Montreal winter. "I'm sure you would adapt well to it."

"Yes, George, I might enjoy it there," said Dolly, even though she wasn't sure of the Canadian outdoor life activities he had described. But she contemplated its advantages for raising children. George appealed to Dolly. He appeared to be a reliable, upstanding, good-looking man and one she could love. A man, she believed, who could be a proper provider and father to her children too. Despite her young age, she had learned from her sisters and the other women in her family that it was necessary.

"Well, if you were to come with me after the war, you wouldn't be alone there," he said. "Apart from me, the Martins are decent people, and I love my aunt Bea. She has an enormous heart and could become a mother to you. And my grandmother is a wonderful person. She immigrated from England too, so she could offer advice."

"Okay," said Dolly. "Sounds good, George."

Dolly was mulling it over. She understood well where this conversation with George might be heading. Could she become one of the thousands of young women who had married Canadian, Anzac or American military men? The armies listed them as "war brides" who were to emigrate with their military husbands when the war ended. The unstoppable tide of positive sentiment towards such an idea enveloped her.

"You know George, I might enjoy that," said Dolly, "I might like that very much." She wasn't too enthusiastic, but it was enough for George. She was young, he thought, and it was a big decision for her. But she had shown a 'maybe,' so as evening approached and George had worked up his courage, he asked her whether she might marry him. She had given it careful consideration in the interim and agreed.

"I'd love to go to Canada and build a home for our children with you, George," she said. "I know I wouldn't be alone. Some of my friends have already married soldiers and will end up in Canada, too. I like you too, George. I've gotten to know you over this past year, and you are a decent man and will make a wonderful husband and father. So, yes, I'd love to marry you."

When George returned to camp that night, it felt like he was floating in the clouds. Mission accomplished! Now, he just had to buy a ring or two and get permission from the army to marry, then get married. Oh yes, and survive this bloody war!

§

The Canadian Dieppe Disaster

In August 1942, rumours circulated that a significant invasion of the European mainland was again in the offing. Excitement among the gunners of the 1st Canadian Division was growing, and the talk was everywhere the same.

"Do you think we might invade the Nazis in France at long last?" asked Jock.

"I've heard rumours, but nothing more than that," said George. "I cannot go now because of my love life."

"Well, my friend, if they call upon us to go, you will go too," said Jock.

"Oh, I know," said George, "I'm getting married just as soon as the army grants me permission. Don't let me spoil your fun, though," he said to lighten the conversation. "You can go on my behalf."

They proved the rumours correct. On 19 August 1942, British and Canadian troops attempted the disastrous Dieppe Raid on the northern coast of France. They selected 5,000 Canadian troops, 1,000 British troops, and 50 top United States Army Rangers for the raid. None of the 2nd Field Regiment RCA soldiers took part in this assault, much to their disappointment.

Empire and Tyranny

The Dieppe raid was a significant action planned by Vice Admiral Lord Mountbatten of 'Combined Operations Headquarters'. Its objectives included briefly seizing and holding a port to prove it was possible and gathering intelligence. Upon retreat, the Allies wanted to destroy coastal defences, port structures and strategic buildings. The raid had the added objectives of boosting morale and showing the firm commitment of the British Empire to open a Western Front in Europe. Bernard Montgomery had taken part in the early planning for the assault but had suggested that they should abandon the action.

The attack began at 5:00 am on 19 August, but by 10:50 am, the Allied commanders called a retreat. Of the 6,086 men who made it ashore, 3,623 or 60%, including 48 Canadian artillerymen, were dead, wounded or captured. The Royal Air Force lost 106 planes compared to the 48 Luftwaffe planes downed. The Royal Navy lost 33 landing craft and one destroyer. And they met none of their objectives, which severely affected their confidence. Allied fire support was inadequate, and the Germans trapped the raiding force on the beach by obstacles and heavy fire. Less than ten hours after the first landings, the last Allied troops were dead, evacuated, or left behind and captured by the Germans. Instead of a positive outcome, the bloody fiasco of Dieppe showed the world that the Allies could not hope to invade France for the foreseeable future. [109] But despite the failure and embarrassment, the amphibious assault at Dieppe taught the Allies many lessons, including the need for overwhelming fire support for later beach landings[110].

§

George Gets Married

George requested permission from the army to marry Dolly, and they granted it on 24 September 1942. Then, on 17 October, George, 24, married Dorothy Rutherford, 17, in St. Mary Magdalene Church in Addiscombe, officiated by the Curate Frank Leslie Taylor. Dolly's older sister Peggy, her bridesmaid, and her brother Harry, who acts as the best man to George, witnessed the marriage certificate. Dolly's father, Joe Rutherford, gave her away, and her proud mother, Mary, was in attendance, too. Uncle Ernie and Auntie Nellie Jenkins represented George's parents and grandparents. The rest of Dolly's sisters, brothers, and a few friends attended, too. They held a modest wartime reception at the church hall, and it was a happy but sober occasion—no heavy drinkers were in attendance.

---

[109] https://en.wikipedia.org/wiki/Raid_on_Dieppe
[110] Colonel C.P. Stacey, *Six Years of War : The Army in Canada, Britain and the Pacific* (The Official History of the Canadian Army in the Second World War) Volume I Hardcover – 1966

Empire and Tyranny

Addiscombe was a lovely setting for the wedding. It's in an old part of Surrey, near East Croydon, a rural suburb of Croydon and London. But when Elizabeth I reigned in England, Addiscombe was a country estate owned by the Heron family, just a mile from Croydon on Shirley Road.

During the reception, George pulled Dolly aside.

"Well, Dolly, how do you feel being a married woman and to a Canuck?" he asked.

"Oh, I don't know George. It's wonderful, and I am thrilled, but it has happened so fast!"

"Fast, my darling? We have been seeing each other for eighteen months!"

"Yes, but it's only been a while since you asked me to marry you. But I'm thrilled, my darling. I am."

At seventeen and the spoiled baby of the family, Dolly was apprehensive of what lay ahead for her in Canada once the war had ended, thought George. He considered girls matured into womanhood quickly and married younger. But she wouldn't be leaving the womb of her family just yet. Even though officers often took up marriage quarters away from the base, they expected other rank soldiers to be at their regimental billets for instant availability if needed. But lower-ranking soldiers couldn't afford much in terms of housing. So George and Dolly were to live apart for the foreseeable future.

"Well, let's get out of here, my Love," said George. "I've found us a lovely little spot in the Shirley Hills to spend two lovely autumn days. The Major has allowed me to fill the car with gasoline at the army's expense and use it until Tuesday. We can explore the North Downs if you'd like?" Despite being in England for three years, George still used his Canadian automotive jargon, such as gasoline instead of petrol or hood instead of a bonnet. But he spent most of his time with other Canadians.

With the wedding and reception over, George and Dolly vanished for their short 2-day honeymoon in the Shirley Hills. They wasted no time, having conceived on that honeymoon, as they soon discovered. The Rutherfords were busy expanding their family with two more daughters married and at least one child on the way. But it was too early for George; the romantic side of October 1942 was over, and he had to return to his camp to continue his military duties. Married or not, England and Canada were still at war with the Axis!

§

Meanwhile, in North Africa, the German Afrika Korps had recaptured Tobruk, Libya, from the British on 21 June. However, the British won a considerable victory. From 30 August to 2 September, General Bernard (Monty) Montgomery led the British Eighth Army to victory over Field Marshal (Desert Fox) Rommel's Afrika Korps at the Battle of Alam el Halfa in Egypt. Then, on 23 October, British and Commonwealth forces launched a major attack against German and Italian troops in the Second Battle of El Alamein in Egypt. By 4 November, the Second Battle of El Alamein ended with Erwin Rommel compelled to order his forces to retreat. Then, on 13 November 1942, the Allied troops recaptured Tobruk. Both generals continued their illustrious careers following the battles in North Africa but with very different endings.

Also in Northern Africa, Operation Torch from 8 to 16 November 1942 was an Allied invasion of French North Africa - Morocco and Algeria. Torch met the British aim of securing victory in North Africa while American armed forces also engaged in the fight against Nazi Germany. It was the first mass involvement of US troops in the European–North African Theatre, and it saw the first major airborne assault carried out by the United States. American General Dwight D. Eisenhower, supreme commander of the Allied forces in the Mediterranean Theatre of Operations, planned the operations from his headquarters deep inside the Rock of Gibraltar.

He devised a three-pronged attack on Casablanca (Western), Oran (Center) and Algiers (Eastern). He planned a rapid move on Tunis to catch Axis forces under Erwin Rommel and Ernst Kals in North Africa from the west with the Allied advance from Egypt.

The other Allied commanders included the American Generals George S. Patton, Henry Kent Hewitt, Lloyd

Fredendall, and British Generals Andrew Cunningham and Kenneth Anderson.

The successful Operation Torch saw the American armies gain their first significant victory in World War II. The US Army also successfully deployed paratroopers and Rangers for the first time in the Oran, Algeria landings.

§

1943: New orders for the 1st Canadian Division

During their meeting in Casablanca, Morocco, in January 1943, the Allied leaders used their joint military resources in the Mediterranean to invade Italy.

British Prime Minister Winston Churchill called Italy the "soft underbelly of Europe."

The war had continued unabated, but by this stage, the Allies were well into planning and preparing for their invasions of Europe. Their objectives were to remove Italy from World War II and secure the Mediterranean Sea. That was to force Germany to divert its divisions from the Russian front and northern France, where the Allies were planning to launch their cross-Channel landing at Normandy.

On 14 January, the Royal Air Force switched its bombing campaign from industrial targets to U-boat bases in France. They planned to counter a significant increase in U-boat operations, starting with attacking the Keroman Submarine Base. That base was at Lorient, Brittany, on the Atlantic and the deepwater port of Cherbourg-Octeville, Normandy, on the English Channel. The US started its raids on Germany by bombing the port city of Wilhelmshaven on the North Sea. Of the 64 planes taking part in the attack, 55 bombers dropped 137 tons of bombs on warehouses and industrial plants, losing only three planes.

In Africa, on 23 January 1943, British forces under the command of Field Marshal Montgomery grabbed Tripoli from the Nazis. They staged Exercise Spartan, from 4 to 12 March, as a rehearsal for the Allied Invasion of northern France. In April, the Germans began withdrawing from Tunisia in North Africa, and US and British forces met in North Africa. From Tunisia, they readied the Allied troops to invade Europe.

§

Joy and Sadness in a Growing Rutherford Family

In England in March 1943, the younger son of another Rutherford, Harry, at 22, married Grace Helen Blandford, 20, in Croydon. It was another joyous occasion in the Rutherford house. In May, following Harry's wedding, the Rutherfords had more joy when John Irwin and his wife Mabel welcomed their third daughter, Patricia Anne, into a troubled world on the 24th.

But the joy was short-lived as tragedy struck the Rutherford family. Harry died from massive aortic trauma three months after his marriage in June. A family who had just experienced the happiness of his wedding and welcomed another niece and granddaughter into the family descended into deep mourning. At the funeral, the entire family came together. The vicar of their church performed the ceremony and delivered a eulogy. He had officiated at Harry and Grace's wedding three months earlier. So Harry's death had shaken him to the core.

"I didn't christen Harry because he came to us here from Jarrow, where he was born," said the vicar in closing. "Still, I got to know him well over the years since his arrival in Croydon. He was a fine, energetic, and hard-working young man, and we will all miss him so much. But God must have had His reasons for taking Harry from us. He sent Harry to give us joy for the 22 years of his life. We find it so hard to lose him. But we must remember him from the beautiful years of his brief life. These memories will continue to give us joy and strength as we endure these desperate times."

"How can God be so cruel?" Dolly asked as they emerged from the church. "Harry was such a life- and fun-filled soul. Why take him now in the crowning moment of his youth?" Then she broke down and cried.

"It is a terrible tragedy," said George, putting his arms around her. "I liked Harry a lot. He was such a smart and fine man. I will miss him for as long as I live."

"I cannot believe it," said Joe, who had been close to Harry. "Harry was so young and vibrant. He looked so healthy! He was a good, hard-working man and had just married his lovely bride, Grace. Why did God have to take him now? The vicar didn't answer that question; he couldn't."

Joe had become acquainted with death. He had lost close friends during his war in South Africa, France and Germany. But losing his son in this way struck him very hard.

"It was God's will, Joe," cried Mary. "He wants us to remember Harry as a young man. He gave us Harry for 22 years. And we must be thankful for that, Joe." She then collapsed in tears, comforted by her husband and girls, who surrounded her.

It had devastated Mary, too, but she was better equipped to handle the tragedy than Joe and the others. She had lost her mother when she was 13. And Mary had lost her three closest brothers, including Harry's namesake, during World War I. And as a mother, she had an uncanny sense that Harry might die young. The Army had rejected Harry and John Irwin from military service because of the weaknesses of their hearts. She had known of these weaknesses since they were boys. She cared for and nurtured them, and a mother knows, somehow. But the first loss of a child, his pride and joy, devastated Joe.

§

Exercises and New Orders in Scotland

During April 1943, George and his friends were involved in "Exercise Stymie" when the 1st Canadian Division took part in an invasion landing training exercise at Troon, Ayrshire. On arrival in Scotland by train, they concentrated the units of the 1st Division within easy reach of Troon. That town lies on the Firth of Clyde opposite the Isle of Arran. The army billeted the 2nd Field Regiment under Lt. Col. H.M. Hague at Kilmarnock, less than ten miles inland from Troon.

Kilmarnock is the original home of the Scotch whisky brand Johnnie Walker, known as Walker's Kilmarnock Whisky when it was first traded from the town in the mid-1800s. The Johnnie Walker brand, now one of the best known and consumed worldwide, is a legacy left to us by the grocer John Walker. He distilled the whisky in the Johnnie Walker Bond room in the town centre of Kilmarnock, Ayrshire, Scotland and sold it in 1850 in his grocery store.

This training program for the artillery comprised hardening exercises through long route marches with heavy equipment and gritty sessions manhandling guns over challenging country courses. Later, most of the artillery units spent a strict eight days at the Combined Training Centre known as Duke's Camp at Inveraray. That was a former royal burgh and ancestral home to the Duke of Argyll on the western shore of Loch Fyne, on the rugged coast of Argyll. Duke's Camp was the leading centre for amphibious training in the British Isles for much of the war. The 2nd and 3rd Fields also took their 25-pounders to Kirkbride, in Dumfrieshire, for calibration. In this way, the 2nd Field Regiment covered lots of Scottish territory in the name of training.

Empire and Tyranny

"What a lovely country, eh?" said George one day.

"Yup, I can say with confidence God's country," said McTavish.

"So much wonderful Scotch whisky, too," said another.

"I could spend much more time looking around this country, and maybe I will revisit with my family one day," said George.

"It has such different scenery within such a small country," said Jock. "Flat at Troon, then hillier up the firth, then mountainous in the Highlands. Amazing!"

"Such good fishing," said George.

"Such bonnie lassies, too," said another.

"Such ugly legs under those kilts," joked Jock. "We've lost that custom in Canada, except during Highland Games in Nova Scotia."

George got in a "wee bit of fishing," as he learned to say there. He had made the acquaintance of a Kilmarnock shop owner by the name of Hamish McClintock, who invited him out onto nearby trout waters very early one Sunday morning. When George arrived at his shop, where he lived in the back, Hamish handed him a fly rod. Now, George has done lots of fishing in his life in Canada, but never with such a strange rod, reel, line, and lure. History has it that the Romans invented the fishing fly, but the English, Scottish and Irish gentry perfected the art of fly-fishing. However, only the upper classes and professional anglers in Canada knew how to fly fish. Most anglers did game fishing with metal or plastic fishing lures or live bait.

"Uh, Hamish, I've done lots of fishing in my time but never with something like this," he confessed to his host while holding the fly.

"Don't worry yourself about it, George. You'll soon get the hang of it," said Hamish in a thick Scottish accent. Hamish gave him a few lessons in fly casting basics and left him alone on his own stretch of the river. "For a start, George, you use the weight of the line to cast, not the light fly. Cast the line; the fly will follow. Do the best you can. The fish are close to the bank, so ye needn't cast too far."

George didn't understand all of what Hamish said with his thick accent, but he got the gist of fly fishing. He just tried and tried and did the best he could. After an hour or two, Hamish returned.

"How did ye do, George," he asked?

George held up two gorgeous, two-pound Rainbows and smiled from ear to ear.

"Well then, Laddie. I see you've mastered the art!"

"Thank you, Hamish," said George while handing back the rod, "I wouldn't say mastered, but I got the hang of it. And I enjoyed that. I'll return the favour if you ever make it to Montreal. Then, I'll teach you a thing or two about how to catch our big Pikes, Muskies and Sturgeons. That you must try too."

During the 1940s, Scotland was a peaceful country that took one far back. Apart from Glasgow and Edinburgh, there was none of the hurly-burly of a world obsessed with business and making money. The countryside was quiet and clean and wet and fresh. The people were level-headed and genuine. They were a pleasant change from the greed and hypocrisy in many other parts of the developed world. The army first introduced the Canadians to the lowlands along the West Coast. Then, as they moved north, the land rose from the sea and became less arable until they moved into the rugged Highlands of West-Central Scotland. There, humans were scarce, and sheep were many. It introduced the soldiers to the long-haired Highland cattle grazing unattended in the Glens, something they had never seen. They saw the occasional stag and a small herd of does just visible in the bracken and heather lining the hills and mountains. They heard the eagles calling from high above them. It was magnificent and peaceful, like their native Canadian bush, but very different and steeped in history.

"There's water everywhere," said George, the avid fisherman. "Everywhere you look, the brooks are bursting from the hills. You see dozens of waterfalls as you look up. You're never far from calm lochs; water is everywhere. It is very much like Canada in that way."

"Very much like my home," said a Cape Breton Islander named Iain MacDonald, who had lost his way into the Montreal-based 2nd Field Regiment. "The hills and the sea. Just like Nova Scotia—New Scotland. I love it here, too! Maybe when we're done with this war, I'll return to my ancestral roots on the Isle of Skye and marry a sweet Scottish lassie."

Then, into this paradise, the roar of army vehicles and the booming of the practising gunners shattered the peace in the name of defence of the British Isles. How could people or fauna understand such intrusions in this peaceful place?

"Hey, Guys," called out Dave. "These Brits have a few interesting ideas. I've just heard that a group called the Dam Busters has invented a bomb for blowing up German dams. They drop the bombs at low levels that bounce across the water's surface to the dam wall, where they sink and explode. They have just blown up dams in Germany, causing enormous damage and loss of life."

"Special bombs for dams. How about that?" said George. "Good thinking!"

On 16 and 17 May 1943, "Operation Chastise," known as the Dambusters Raid, took place. RAF 617 Squadron, using a bouncing bomb invented and developed by Barnes Wallis, attacked dams in the industrial heart of Germany, the Ruhr. They breached the Möhne and Edersee Dams, causing catastrophic flooding of the Ruhr Valley and villages in the Eder Valley; a third target, the Sorpe Dam, sustained only minor damage. The flood destroyed two hydroelectric power stations and damaged several more. It crippled or destroyed factories and mines. 1,600 civilians drowned, of whom 600 were Germans, and 1,000 were Soviet forced labourers.

"I have heard rumours of us getting ready for an invasion," said Dave. "We will blow those bloody Jerries to pieces!"

"What, the 1ˢᵗ Canadian Division?" asked George. "I thought we were supposed to be guarding these islands."

"Well, that's what we've been doing: protecting these islands, training and preparing to invade France," said Dave. "It's about bloody time. We've got our guns, and we know how to use them. So, let's go!"

Two other guys within earshot concurred with Dave. "We've heard those rumours too. Maybe our time has arrived!"

§

Departure for Churchill's "Soft Underbelly of Europe"

Between 13 and 16 June 1943, after a quick visit by Major-General Simonds, the assault troops of the 1st Canadian Division embarked at Gourock. That was where they first landed when arriving from Canada in December 1939. The Divisional Artillery left behind only the 1ˢᵗ Field Regiment for the next sailing. But if the men on board the ship thought they were on their way into action, the planners disappointed them. First came "Exercise Stymie," which the armed forces designed as a complete rehearsal of the assault landings in Europe. On 17 June, a dozen loaded ships sailed out of the Clyde along the western Ayrshire coast to within five miles from Troon. Under grey dawn skies, troops clambered down the sides of their ships into assault landing craft and began the approach run into shore in driving rain. Spitfires roared low overhead, adding a note of frightening realism by churning up the water around the craft with machine-gun bullets. Worsening weather halted and then cancelled the exercise. Late the following evening, the men boarded their ships again after rough passages and a hazardous climb up scramble nets and rope ladders. Despite a few discomforts, they learned lessons which would prove helpful if they encountered rough seas during the actual landing operations in Europe.

After Stymie, the troops waited impatiently on board their ships in the Clyde. The first of the slower convoys carrying vehicles, guns, and stores left on 19 June. There were nine more days of lectures, physical training, weapon-cleaning and other routine tasks assigned to dispel monotony before the troopships hoisted anchor at last. On the evening of 28 June, the vessels of the Fast Assault Convoy steamed down the Clyde with naval escorts and headed out to the open sea. The divisional headquarters, including Headquarters RCA, travelled in HMS Hilary, a former passenger liner launched in 1931 and requisitioned by the Royal Navy in 1940. This ship carried Vice Admiral Sir Philip L. Vian, Commander of Force V, transporting the 1st Canadian Division to the Mediterranean Sea.

Their course took the troopships around the rocky islet of Ailsa Craig, which they had first seen on their arrival from Canada. Then, they sailed west around the northern coast of Ireland and turned south, giving the choppy waters of the Bay of Biscay a wide berth. The weather was bright and warm, so officers and men donned their tropical kit. There was a lot of excitement at the prospect of the impending action after such a long wait.

They kept the convoy's destination secret, which caused much speculation among the Canadian gunners, conjectures varying from Norway to the Solomon Islands in the Pacific. The suspense ended on Dominion Day, 1 July. The loudspeaker systems in the troopships broadcasted the announcement that the 1st Division was on its way to assault Axis-held Sicily. The foreseen day of the landings was 10 July. All ranks cheered at the news they were entering the Mediterranean theatre of war and were to become part of the famous Eighth Army. A greeting from General Montgomery, which they read on all ships, carried a warm welcome to the Canadians:

"I know the fighting men from Canada well. They are magnificent soldiers, and the long and careful training they have received will now be put to good use to the great benefit of the Eighth Army."

There were also messages from the Commanders of the First Canadian Army and the 1st Canadian Corps, wishing the troops the best of luck. In an Order of the Day, Major-General Simonds called on all ranks of the 1st Canadian Division to live up to the fighting tradition that they had inherited from WWI. He reminded them that with the co-operating naval and air forces, the division was a part of the best-formed expedition ever to set sail to invade a hostile country.

"It remains only to apply our training lessons under the stress of actual operations. I am not trying to tell you the task will be easy. War is brutal. It's a complex and bitter struggle— the ultimate test of moral and physical courage and skill at arms.

"We will launch you into battle on a well-rehearsed plan, and if you apply what we have taught you during three years of preparation, success will be ours."

The news and the words of praise from their Commanders raised the gunners' morale and made the shipboard routine less tedious. There was something now to occupy every officer and man. It was part of General Montgomery's policy that they should brief all troops at length on the proposed operations. They opened the sealed bag of instructions on every ship, and each unit received its quota of maps, air photographs, operations orders and intelligence pamphlets. Every vessel carried a large-scale relief model, and saloons became briefing rooms in which officers and men studied the details of the operational plan. They memorized the terrain of the beaches and the interior of Sicily where the Canadian assault was going.

They tried to keep officers and men in the best physical condition. Divisional headquarters issued a directive for training during the voyage, which insisted on "maintaining regular hours for physical training, washing, eating, fatigues, games and lectures." These lectures emphasized first aid, sanitation and the proper treatment of prisoners of war and civilians. They warned the men that they would deal with looters in the "severest manner." Preventing tropical disease infection beforehand was so vital to General Montgomery that he asked commanders and medical officers to ensure everyone was aware of malaria risks. To raise malaria awareness, medical officers lectured the men on the dangers of tropical diseases, stressing the use of mosquito repellent and mepacrine tablets. Malaria was still present in Italy during WWII.

By such activities, as the convoys pursued their course toward Sicily, the members of the 1st Division groomed themselves to fulfil their Commander's orders. They would "go ashore fit, with everyone knowing his job and what they require of him."

§

George Granted Leave to Stay Behind for Personal Reasons

But George was not travelling with this convoy. The major had given him special permission to stay behind in England to attend the birth of his first child in Croydon. He should then catch the next available ship to Sicily.

His buddies, Dave Smith, Paddy McCaffrey, Jock McTavish and Jean LaFleur, were on board and filled with anticipation.

"It's bloody time we are being sent to give the Nazis a bloody nose in Italy," said Dave.

"Yup, we're on our way. This is amazing. Look at all those ships," said Paddy. "Unbelievable!"

Empire and Tyranny

On 1 July, the last group of transport ships weighed anchor in the Clyde. They followed the other convoys out into the North Atlantic en route to the Mediterranean. 125 vessels, including the escorting naval craft, were now forging forward with their Canadian troops and equipment. They grouped the ships at various intervals off the treacherous coast of Western Europe, watching for German U-boats.

"Goodbye, the homeland of my ancestors," lamented Jock. "Who knows whether I'll ever see ye again."

"You'll be back there in no time," said Dave. "It won't take us long to finish this war."

"Just look at this flat sea, thank God," said Paddy. "I love this voyaging at sea."

"Yeah, well, you can keep this sea stuff," said Jock. "I feel ill, even on this flat sea."

They voyaged southward through calm seas and under cloudless skies, and as the weather grew warmer, the men exchanged their serge battledress for khaki. Opposite the south coast of Spain, the Fast Assault Convoy turned eastward. In the early hours of 5 July, they passed through the Strait of Gibraltar into the Mediterranean.

It continued along the North African coast, rounding Cape Bon, Tunisia, and sailed southeast toward Tripoli. On the morning of D minus 1, 9 July, it turned northward towards the appointed rendezvous south of Malta. When each convoy was well inside the Mediterranean, a flotilla of destroyers replaced the group of smaller escort craft which had led the transports through Atlantic waters. The weather remained fair. After their weeks of hard training amid the cold Scottish mists, the troops found the cloudless skies and the deep blue waters of the Mediterranean a welcome change.

The Fast Assault Convoy successfully completed its entire voyage. However, there were alarms which set the ships weaving in complicated emergency turns. The troops on board saw at least one enemy submarine blown out of the water by the depth charges of the escorting destroyers.

They based the schedule on the speed of the various convoy ships so that the whole convoy simultaneously arrived at the rendezvous point off Sicily.

The first tragedy of the Sicilian campaign struck the 1st Canadian Division at sea. German U-boats sank three ships, the St. Essylt, the City of Venice and the Devis, in the Mediterranean on 4 and 6 July. It sent forty guns to the bottom of the Mediterranean along with over 500 vehicles, including those for the Headquarters, 1st Canadian Divisional Artillery. Of the 900 troops aboard these three ships, 593 were Canadians. In the first two sinkings, there was a minor loss of life; among the Canadians, they listed one officer and five other ranks as missing. Casualties were more severe on the Devis, which carried 261 Canadian and 35 British officers and men. The first explosion killed or injured several soldiers, trapping men in the hold when the companionway burnt out. Despite prompt rescue operations, they reported 52 Canadians as missing and presumed killed. The 2nd Field Regiment lost an entire troop of personnel. A rescue ship took the survivors to Algiers, not to rejoin the regiment for another seven weeks. The cargo's loss across the three vessels had a significant impact on many units.

§

George heard nothing of these sinkings until much later. He was with his wife, who was preparing for their first child. Dolly had only just turned eighteen and was apprehensive about giving birth. Hers would be the first child of the younger Rutherford sisters. John Irwin's wife, Mabel, had given birth to four children, including baby Patricia Anne. Violet's Brian and Sally were born before the war. But Dolly was the first of the remaining four Rutherford daughters to give birth, even though she was the youngest.

They admitted Dolly to the hospital on the evening of 22 July. George and her sister Beattie had escorted her there and waited with her. Dolly gave birth to their first child at 12:45 pm on 23 July at St. Mary's Maternity Hospital in St James Road, Croydon. George sweated and paced through the entire labour in the waiting room, with only occasional conversations with the other expectant fathers waiting with him. But following the birth, they admitted him to the maternity ward to see his wife and baby.

Empire and Tyranny

"A son, Dolly," he said while taking the baby's tiny hand. "He's our handsome son, Dolly. And he has all his fingers and toes!"

"Oh, George, it was a hard night. Terrible! If I had known. But I'm so pleased that it went well. I'm exhausted!"

"I bet you are after that hard work and pain, but you look wonderful, my dear, and you've done a marvellous job. What a fine little boy we've got!"

She could only muster a weak smile before she and the baby fell asleep. George had another hour with his sleeping wife and baby son, then had to run off to return to his unit at Seaford, East Sussex. This was where the 2nd Field Regiment had nestled among the white chalk cliffs on the coast of the English Channel between Brighton and Eastbourne opposite Le Havre, France. He kissed them both and then crept out of the ward. The proud new father with a cheerful demeanour then travelled on a Third-Class ticket from Seaford to Glasgow on 24 July.

While on the train, he caught up with events transpiring in Sicily. The English papers reported daily on the Allies' progress during what they now knew as the Italian Campaign. In fact, he had little else to do while waiting for his convoy to leave. News circulated among the waiting troops. For the first time, the realities of this war felt personal—soon, he would be in the thick of it. While alone, he felt that strange apprehension in his stomach. As a new father, this war posed a higher risk.

But as he and his companions gathered in the temporary tented accommodation near Glasgow, they talked up their courage over beer and sandwiches. Nothing was worse than waiting to go into battle. They embarked in Glasgow on the 16th of August on the sea journey to Italy, and the waiting and apprehension of the unknown continued at sea. During the voyage, George heard of the ships sunk in the Mediterranean on 4 and 6 July.

"We've had our first disaster of this war," said George to another 2nd Field gunner he was travelling with. "One officer and 57 gunners lost at sea. Three ships, forty guns and 500 vehicles lying at the bottom of the Mediterranean. This war is getting serious for us!"

"That it is, buddy," said the gunner. "Let's hope the same doesn't happen to us."

§

3
The Italian Campaign: July 1943 to End 1944

Empire and Tyranny

George Arrives in Sicily

In Sicily, George disembarked at Messina on Friday, 27 August, over a month after his Croydon departure. He had enough time to rejoin his regiment, readying for the invasion of the Italian mainland. He found the 1st Canadian Division and British 5th Infantry Division spread out around Messina and its surroundings with many other late-arriving divisional troops. Hundreds of units were busy cleaning up after the Sicily campaign and preparing for the next one.

Messina is the third-largest city on the island of Sicily, near the northeast corner of Sicily on the Strait of Messina, opposite Villa San Giovanni on the Italian mainland. The port is a large inlet, a natural haven for many centuries, opening on the western shore of the Strait. It allows for the access and docking of sizeable ships. In August 1943, the invading force had jammed it full of various military and other transport vessels, most loaded with vehicles and material for the campaign. It was a wild but well-organized hive of the military hustle and bustle. Allied planes were flying overhead to protect an otherwise vulnerable invasion army a mere three miles across the Strait from the enemy. The noise was almost deafening.

George approached some Military Police in the port. They directed him to the 2nd Field Regiment RCA HQ camp on the city's outskirts, and he hitched a ride with a truck heading in that direction. He immediately reported to Major Walker at the 2nd Field encampment.

Empire and Tyranny

"Welcome back, George," said the Major in response to George's salute while looking up from the pile of papers on his field desk. "You've missed our first action, but much more ahead of us. Did it go well with your wife and her birth?"

"Yes, Sir," said George, standing at attention. "Everything went well, and we now have a healthy 9-pound, 3-ounce baby boy. We named him Michael George. But here I am, Sir. Your driver is back with you and looking forward to my first action."

"Well done and at ease, gunner," said the major. "Sorry, but you won't be seeing them for a while. We are leaving soon for the mainland, where the Nazis are waiting for us. It's good to have my driver back. I exchanged my Ford Sedan for a new American Jeep. It's not as comfortable but is better suited for our road ahead. I hope you're OK with that. I need to do a few visits tomorrow. You are free to settle back in with your buddies. Report first thing in the morning after an early breakfast. Jones, please show George where his buddies are hanging out."

"Thank you, Sir. I'm glad to be back too, Sir. I drove Jeeps in England. No problem. I'll be here first thing tomorrow," George said to the major, then stood to attention again, saluted and turned to Jones.

"Come on, George. I'll show you the way," barked the bombardier, a corporal.

"Thanks, Bomb," said George, using the popular abbreviated form of address for bombardiers. A bombardier, or

'Bomb Aimer,' was also called 'Full Screw,' and they called a lance-bombardier a 'Lance Jack.'

"It's so good of you to join us in this war after your holiday in England, George," said the gruff bombardier as they walked. George already knew Jones for his obnoxious, ill-mannered demeanour and ignored it.

"We've lost many honourable men while you've been relaxing and avoiding the action," said the bombardier.

"Yes, I've heard," said George, not taking the bait. Then after a couple more snide comments from the bombardier, they arrived at his camp, and Full Screw led George to his tent.

Once there, he observed his companions seated on camp stools in a relaxed circle during their midday meal.

"George! Welcome back, buddy," someone called. "It's time you got here. You've missed all the action."

"Yup, I know, Guys," said George, finding an extra stool. "I had important things to attend to."

"Sure, sure, but there's a war on, buddy," said another.

"Oh, I know, and believe me, I wanted to be here," said George. "Give me a break. I couldn't leave my young bride alone at such an important time for us, could I? But please bring me up-to-date. I'm dying to know what has happened to you guys, eh?"

Full Screw glowered from the side until the buddies pulled George away from the belligerent bombardier. He was a coal miner from Sydney, Cape Breton Island, Nova Scotia, with a massive chip on his shoulder. He reflected on the short, curly-haired man of Welsh descent with a disagreeable nature and evaded him.

Jock McTavish said, "Yeah, well, the 2nd Field has lost thirteen killed and thirty-four wounded in Sicily. Most of these were three weeks ago when an American bomber hit by German flak crashed on the regimental command post and exploded. Seven of the 13 killed in this campaign, and 22 of the 34 injured, resulted from that disaster alone!"

"We weren't far from the command post," said Dave.

"It was a busy day and noisy enough. Then we heard the screaming sound of the bomber heading towards us. I saw it coming closer while the pilot, also visible to me, struggled to land the plane in a field near the command post. But he didn't make it, and we heard a massive explosion and saw the fireball rising into the sky over the HQ. We even felt the heat of the explosion."

"We ran to the site hoping to pull any survivors we could find out of the flames," said Jock.

"The fire was so fierce we had to stand well back until a fire-fighting unit arrived to put it out. Nobody in that plane or on the ground survived. I even saw two boys running out of the crash site on fire, but they didn't get very far, dropping to the ground as fireballs. It was horrific!"

"The CO, 2IC Major Walker, and several other senior officers weren't there," said Paddy. "1st Division headquarters had called them to a conference, which saved them."

"Wow! I just spoke to the major, and he didn't mention it," said George. "What a blow! But I'm so sorry I missed the start of this invasion, Guys. Tell me about it."

"Well," said Jock, "at the end of our sea voyage, we arrived at our destination off Malta and gathered with the others to invade Sicily. We joined a vast fleet of 2,600 merchant vessels, navy ships and assault craft waiting for the descent on Sicily on 9 July."

"You wouldn't have believed it, George," said Paddy. "There were ships and landing craft as far as you could see to the horizon!"

"Yeah, it was bloody impressive," said Dave. "When we arrived in Halifax, seeing our convoy in Bedford Basin was impressive enough. But Malta made it look like a kindergarten."

"Well, we're bloody lucky to be here," said Jean. "Look at our poor mates on the Devis, sunk by a German U-boat on the way here!"

"Yeah, that was unfortunate for those guys," said Dave. "They died for a good cause. I know who they were, too."

"Yeah, I knew a few of them, too," said Jean. "There were quite a few Montrealers in that group."

"I heard about that on the way here," said George. "Three ships, over 50 men, 40 guns and 500 vehicles now on the bottom of the Mediterranean. It ruined our journey since we were nervous and always watching out for U-boats."

Empire and Tyranny

The Fascist government of Benito Mussolini invited the Germans into Italy in the 1930s. But in July 1943, the few German soldiers left on the island were unaware of the plight soon to descend upon them.

"Many of the troops coming from North Africa and Malta made the voyage in landing craft," said Paddy. "The new amphibious Ducks[111] delivered the men and supplies to the beaches. The Allied airborne landings in Sicily took place late on 9 July in stormy weather."

"The joint British-Canadian-American landings on Sicily began the next day on 10 July," said Jock.

"It involved both amphibious and airborne landings at the Gulf of Gela and north of Syracuse on the south-eastern corner of Sicily."

Early on the 10th, the troops went ashore under a protective umbrella of planes strafing the enemy positions. The British Eighth Army came ashore on the right (Montgomery), the US Seventh Army (Patton) and the US II Corps on the left (Bradley). The untried 1st Canadian Division (Simonds) was in the centre.

The gunners of the 2nd Field were unloading their guns onto landing craft reserved for that purpose. George's buddies recalled the events of their landing.

---

[111] DUKWS, developed by General Motors. DUKW is a manufacturer's code based on D indicating the model year, 1942; U referring to the body style, utility (amphibious); K for all-wheel drive; and W for dual rear axles.

"Be careful with those guns, guys, and stay away from beneath them," called the Petty Officer in charge of the offloading. "Grab those stays and guide your gun into position."

"Shit," called Paddy, "easier said than done. The waves are moving us all over the place. Watch it, Jock. Pull her over to you, but make sure you keep your balance."

"I've got it under control," said Jock.

The guns and their transports were unloaded and shuttled to the beach one after the other. And they soon brought them into action, bombarding the remaining German units left behind on the shore.

German and Italian planes sank and damaged a few warships and transports in the invasion zone on 10 July, including a US destroyer. Later, on the 16th, an Italian torpedo plane damaged the carrier HMS Indomitable. Other than that, there was little resistance by the Italians and the few remaining Germans, and the Allies soon rebuffed any counterattacks the Germans mounted.

The Allies captured Syracuse on the 10th, and within three days, the British Eighth Army had cleared the southeast corner of Sicily. The 2nd and 3rd Field Regiments shared in the first significant firing of Canadian field guns in Sicily, an event on 14 July. While the Germans halted the 1st Canadian Division at Giarratana, the 51st (Highland) Division, coming in from the right, ten miles to the north, was nearing Vizzini, well inland. They sent the 2nd Field Regiment to support the Highlanders' attack on the town. The fire plan executed late that night succeeded, and the 51st Division occupied Vizzini with little opposition.

"Man, this is brilliant, Guys," shouted Dave. "Now we can put all our training to good use. Let's blast those bloody Jerries off this island."

"Fantastic," called Jock. "I love this!"

"A piece of piss," called Paddy. "You can see they're already on the run. And George is missing all the fun."

Still, in the excitement, German bullets marked for them were deflecting off their gun, making them duck, curse, and focus on the task without further comments.

As they moved inland, the Canadian artillery fired their first divisional concentration of mass fire on 18 July. Two 15th Panzer Grenadier Division battalions stopped the advance. They were exploiting the high natural strength of positions astride a narrow pass leading to a road junction southwest of Valguarnera to the full. This called for a "well-supported attack in strength." So Major-General Simonds issued orders committing the 2nd and 3rd Infantry Brigades supported by tanks and four artillery regiments. The 3rd Brigade sent the Royal 22nd Regiment to secure the narrow pass Portello Crottacalda. The Carleton and York Regiment and The West Nova Scotia Regiment moved to the flanks of the dominating high ground, a feature known as Monte Della Forma. Divisional artillery, machine guns, the Saskatoon Light Infantry mortars and The Three Rivers Regiment tanks supported them in scorching weather. The artillery concentrated 68 rounds per gun on selected targets around the pass, completed during the afternoon. By late afternoon, both infantry units were on their objectives. And by five o'clock, the road junction was in Canadian hands.

"That was incredible; our first concentration," said Paddy when it was over. "Incredible!"

"Yeah, that was a great fireworks display," said Jock.

"I wonder how many tanks we stopped and how many Jerries we killed in that one," said Dave.

"What a battle," said Paddy. "I sweated a bit but enjoyed that."

"Luckily, it was successful," said the Bombardier. "We blasted the shit out of them! But I could see that you need a lot more practice." The latter statement caused consternation among the gunners, who glanced at each other and grimaced. Later reports confirmed that the action killed 80 to 90 Germans and wounded many more.

Meanwhile, the Americans pushed north and north-west and captured Palermo on 22 July. By the end of July, the Allies held the entire island except for the northeastern corner, which included the Mount Etna volcano.

From Valguarnera, the Canadians advanced to Leonforte, then turned east towards Mount Etna through Nissoria, Agrira and Regalbuto to Adrano, at the foot of Mount Etna. On route, the 2nd Field Regiment suffered a crushing blow on 6 August. An American medium bomber hit by German flak while returning from a raid crashed on the regimental command post and exploded into a hail of metal and burning fragments. The toll of seven killed and 22 injured, most of them receiving severe burns, far exceeded the Regiment's losses in its fighting in Sicily up to that point.

On 17 August, American and British troops entered Messina and found it free of German forces. They had completed the conquest of Sicily in 38 days. By the end of the Sicilian Campaign, RCA casualties numbered three officers, thirty-one other ranks killed, and ten officers and 147 men wounded. Many of those losses were those of the 2nd Field Regiment, totalling thirteen dead and thirty-four injured, most from the crash of the American bomber. After its first three years of the war in England, the 1st Canadian Division had stood the test of Sicily. Now, a new action was in the offing.

On 17 August, Major-General Simonds issued his outline plan for the Canadian part in an assault crossing Reggio on the toe of the boot of Italy. [112] On a visit to the 1st Canadian Division on 20 August, General Bernard Montgomery praised the Canadians' achievements during the campaign that had just ended.

"When I say you did magnificently, I mean magnificently. I now consider you one of my veteran divisions."

---

[112] G.W.L Nicholson, The Gunners of Canada, The History of the RCA, 1919-1967, McClelland & Stewart, 1972

The next day, Major-General McNaughton, the First Canadian Army commander, arrived in Sicily for a six-day inspection tour. He visited most of the units in the 1st Canadian Division, offering his congratulations and gratitude for a job well done. [113] General McNaughton had commanded the 7th Field Battery at the beginning of the war, so he knew Major Walker well.

The Allies were victorious in this first stage of invading Italy, but they hadn't stopped the German and Italian evacuations from Sicily to the mainland. The Germans evacuated 52,000 soldiers, including 4,444 wounded, 14,105 vehicles, 47 tanks, 94 guns, 1,100 tons of ammunition, and 20,700 tons of gear and stores.

"Yeah, we missed the cowardly bastards," said Dave. "We'll catch up with them on the mainland."

George's intrepid little group of buddies in the 2nd Field Regiment gunners experienced their first taste of battle and felt pride in their performance.

"That was a bloody excellent job well done, boys," the sergeant called. "We came through our first proper test with honours."

"That was fun," said Dave. "I reckon we killed a good 100 or more Nazis. It's a pity George missed this action."

"Not bad," proclaimed Bombardier Jack Jones, known as JJ. "Still, we need much more practice to become a well-oiled team."

---

[113] Ibid

"Not bad," said Dave. "I'm sure we equalled any other 2nd Field detachments here."

"Well, thanks for that praise, JJ," said Paddy. "We'll work on it with your expert leadership. Dave, I'm sure George will catch up with us soon and see lots of action. We're only just getting started."

"Well, Lads, we are well into this war," announced Sergeant Peter Morgan. "You'd better get used to it. No more gallivanting around the English countryside for us."

And as the evening fell, the buddies dropped into a quiet memorial for their dead comrades. They reminisced over fond memories of their times together since the start of the war.

"Man, I'm bushed," said George. "It's been a hectic day."

And with that, everyone agreed, and they retired to their tents for a restless night's sleep.

§

During the campaign for Sicily, dramatic political developments took place in Italy. On 19 July 1943, 690 Allied bombers pounded Rome with 9,125 bombs, killing over 1,000 civilians. Most Italians saw this as further evidence that defeat was inevitable. [114] Then, because of the Allied invasion of Sicily and the crisis facing Italy, Mussolini agreed to meet with the Fascist Grand Council, the first meeting since 1939. Lasting

---

[114] http://www.historyinanhour.com/2013/09/12/the-rescue-of-mussolini-summary/

from 5 pm to 3 am on 24 and 25 July 1943, the conference centred on the resolution by Dino Grandi, Mussolini's former foreign minister. It concluded that Mussolini must leave power and King Victor Emmanuel III should replace the dictator as head of the armed forces. Mussolini delivered an impassioned two-hour speech, exhorting his fellow fascists to put up a fight. His plea fell on deaf ears, and after ten hours of heated discussion, the council voted 19 to 8, with three abstentions, in favour of Grandi's resolution.

The following day, Mussolini kept his regular audience with the King, believing the vote the evening before was neither constitutional nor binding. But he was very mistaken. Victor Emmanuel III dismissed the 59-year-old dictator. "My dear Duce, it's no longer any good. Italy has gone to pieces. The soldiers don't want to fight anymore. At this moment, you are the most hated man in Italy."

After Mussolini left the palace, the Carabinieri arrested him on the King's orders. His successor, Pietro Badoglio, appointed a new cabinet containing no Fascists. The Italian population rejoiced. Mussolini had been the first Fascist in Europe and became the first to fall!

A new Italian government, led by General Pietro Badoglio and Victor Emmanuel III, took over in Italy. Although they declared in public they would keep fighting alongside the Germans, the new Italian government began secret negotiations with the Allies to come over to the Allied side.

§

George had breakfast before sunrise the following day and hurried to Major Walker's tent to report for duty. The sun had risen at 6:30, and the camp was just waking. It was quiet compared to when George had arrived the previous day. Here and there, he heard semi-hushed voices as soldiers emerged from their tents. It was already warm, no breeze was stirring, and a chorus of birds caught George's attention.

"Good morning, George," said the major, who had just emerged from his tent, ready to start the day. "Let's get going. Lots to do today, starting with a meeting with General McNaughton. He's at the Hotel Residenza in town with all the other top brass."

"Good morning, Sir. I'm ready," said George. "Lovely morning, isn't it?"

"It is, George," said the major.

They were soon at the hotel, where the major vanished inside while George waited for him on the street. He wasn't alone. Parked outside the hotel were a half dozen other Jeeps, their drivers and two lieutenant-adjutants staying with them. So, the drivers came together, met each other, pulled out the cigarettes, and started a lively conversation.

"Where are you from, George?" asked another driver.

"Montreal," said George.

"Hey, me too. Whereabouts?" asked George's companion.

"Verdun," said George.

"Hey, man, me too. What a coincidence. My name is John," said the driver. "Where in Verdun?" asked John.

"Evelyn Street," said George.

"I know it. I see you're with the artillery," said John. "I'm with the Royal Canadian Regiment, Infantry. Joined up at Petawawa."

And so it went, as one after the other driver introduced himself. The officers initially remained aloof but joined the drivers when they overheard a discussion about who was in command. At that point, an officer came to the rescue and explained the chain of command.

"In November 1942, Allied Command appointed American General Dwight David Eisenhower as US Supreme Commander Allied Expeditionary Force of the North African Theatre of Operations," said the officer. "They designated the campaign for North Africa as Operation Torch, and the commanders planned it underground in caves within the Rock of Gibraltar. Eisenhower was the first non-British person to command Gibraltar in 200 years. From November 8 through 16, 1942, Operation Torch was a joint American and British invasion of French North Africa. They aimed to reduce pressure on Allied forces in Egypt and enable an invasion of southern Europe."

There was a flurry of reactions from the drivers. "Got it," one said. "I know we beat the Jerries in North Africa."

"Right, so that was the success of Torch and the capitulation of the last Axis forces by May 1943," continued the officer.

"Allied Command tasked Eisenhower to plan and invade Sicily as the kicking-off point for the Italian Campaign. Prime Minister Churchill called Italy 'the soft underbelly of Europe.' So, Operation Husky is what they have involved us in up to now."

"Yup, I've heard that name before now," said George to nods of the others.

"While preparing this invasion," continued the officer, "the Allies used a network of underground tunnels and chambers below the Lascaris Battery in Valletta, Malta. Known as the Lascaris War Rooms, they served as the advance headquarters of the Sicily campaign. In July 1943, General Eisenhower, Admiral Cunningham, General Montgomery, and Air Marshal Tedder occupied these war rooms. Earlier, the war rooms served as the British headquarters for the defence of Malta.

"Amazing," said John. "Is this top secret?"

"Not anymore," said the officer. "We've all moved on from those planning days. But genuine fun is about to start. The Allies agreed to invade Italy at the Trident Conference held in Washington from 12 to 25 May 1943. They instructed the Allied Commander-in-Chief, General Eisenhower, to remove Italy from the war and contain the greatest number of possible

German forces. We are to keep the German troops in Italy tied down and far away from the intended Allied invasion in the North. We are soon heading to the mainland and chasing the Nazis north and out of Italy—Canadians, British and The Yanks. But the Nazis know our plans and are ready and waiting for us."

"Wow. Very interesting," said George, echoed by the rest of the drivers outside the hotel. "Thank you for that explanation, Sir. You've given us a good understanding of our command and what we must do."

§

Allied Invasion of Mainland Italy

General Sir Harold Alexander's 15th Army Group comprised General Mark W. Clark's American Fifth Army and General Bernard Montgomery's British Eighth Army. Together, they were to carry out the Italian mainland landings codenamed "Operation Baytown" on 3 September 1943. This Army Group included Lieutenant-General Miles Dempsey's British XIII Corps, with the 1st Canadian Infantry Division (Major-General Guy Simonds) and the British 5th Infantry Division (Major-General Gerard C Bucknall). These landings were the preliminary step in the plan for the Eighth Army to leave the port of Messina and cross the Strait of Messina. Then, they would land near the tip of Calabria, the "toe" of Italy. The short distance from Sicily meant they could launch on landing craft instead of being carried by ship.

Allied intelligence staff expected no significant enemy resistance to the Baytown landings. A Canadian intelligence summary from 31 August estimated only two Italian platoons defended the landing beaches. They further determined that the German defence inland from the beaches comprised only two infantry battalions of the 29th Panzer Grenadier Division. [115]

The flotillas of landing craft carrying the assaulting infantry began their seven-mile journey across the Strait in the early morning of 3 September 1943. At the same time, an all-powerful bombardment burst from the Sicilian shore and from warships lying offshore. The US Seventh Army fired 410 field guns, and the Navy fired 120 medium guns in that bombardment. As the leading assault craft neared the Italian shore, a salvo of 792 five-inch rockets hurtled toward the beaches from the rocket craft behind each assault group.

"Man, what a display this is," shouted Dave to his companions as they neared the beach. "Here, we go again. Jerry, here we come, yahoo."

The 8th Army's XIII Corps, comprising the 1st Canadian and British 5th infantry divisions, under Lieutenant-General Sir Miles C. Dempsey, made the southern amphibious landings on mainland Italy. They landed between Villa San Giovanni and

---

[115] Ibid

Reggio Calabria opposite Messina at the end of the toe. The strength of this landing amounted to eight divisions of 10,000-15,000 men and two brigade-sized units of 1,500-3,500 men. They assaulted a 6,000-yard stretch north of Reggio with two brigades of the British 5th Division on the left and the 3rd Canadian Brigade on the right. [116]

On the same day, 3 September, the new Italian government signed a secret armistice with the Allies at Fairfield Camp in Sicily. With Mussolini out of the way, the Italians had withdrawn from the war and Axis.

The 2nd Field, supporting the 1st Brigade, landed the same evening of 3 September, with the 3rd Field crossing the Strait the next day. [117]

George and Major Walker were the first to drive their vehicle from the landing craft into the beach's shallow waters. Their transports pulled the guns, and their crews accompanied them. Hundreds of infantry soldiers leapt from their landing crafts and raced up the beach to the trees and shrubs lining the edge of the sand. They could see a hilly terrain rising to mountains behind the beach, with rocky cliffs jutting into the sea.

"My God, Guys, that was one hell of a bombardment, eh?" said Paddy. "Where are the Germans?"

---

[116] G.W.L Nicholson, *The Gunners of Canada, The History of the RCA, 1919-1967*, McClelland & Stewart, 1972
[117] Ibid

"Running north with their tails between their legs. It must have scared the shit out of the sons of bitches," said Dave. "I hope they don't run too far. I want my chance at blowing off a few of their heads!"

"Well, my buddies," said Jock, "Germans, or no Germans, we have the proper thing here. At last, we are on our way up the boot."

"Yeah, but looking at these hills so close to the beach, we will have a rough ride," said Paddy. "We don't know who's hiding in them."

After a few exchanges on the beach during the landing, the Canadians continued on their way inland. For the Canadian artillery, the next two weeks were a period of pushing forward from one battlefield of heavy fire to another.

"Here are the Germans," said Dave. "At last, a decent fight!"

"Yeah, but look at the mess they're leaving us," said Paddy.

"Yeah, leaving us gunners with a hell of a job," said the sergeant. "Let's put our backs to it, boys."

German demolition tactics extensively harmed roads, bridges, and railways. This frustrated any hope of the mechanized units catching up with the marching infantry. Engineers repaired as much of the damage as they could as fast as they could so that the artillery could catch up and offer cover to the infantry.

Empire and Tyranny

On the evening of 8 September, before the main US landings began in the Gulf of Salerno as part of Operation Avalanche, General Eisenhower announced the surrender of Italy.

Elements of the 1st British Airborne Division achieved an unopposed landing at Taranto at the top of the heel on the 9th. By 11 September, eight days after the first landing, the whole of the Italian toe and heel was in Allied hands. [118] It was a perfect invasion; the Allied landings met limited resistance since the Germans had withdrawn. Entire units of the Italian coastal division surrendered to XIII Corps intact. Prisoners captured in the first 24 hours numbered 3,000 Italians and three Germans.

By then, forward units of the 1st Canadian Division had advanced through the towering Aspromonte Mountains in the Province of Reggio Calabria. To allow his administrative tail to catch up, Lieutenant-General Sir Miles C. Dempsey halted his two divisions of XIII Corps at Catanzaro, known as the "City of the Two Seas." Only a narrow neck of land separates the eastern Gulf of Squillace from the western Gulf of Santa Eufemia at the top of the toe. This four-day breathing space allowed time for much-needed maintenance. Wide Mediterranean beaches and streams flowing from the hills allowed the Canadians to rid themselves of the dust they had accumulated on the way up from Reggio.

§

---

[118] Ibid

Rest in the Aspromonte Massif

The Aspromonte is a group of massif mountains running up the centre of the foot overlooking the Strait of Messina. It comprises 6,000-foot peaks dressed only by grasses and small shrubs, towering over deep gorges and valleys carved by the storm deluges of winter. Here and there, villages perched on the spines of ridges, built with solid outer walls to avoid falling into the canyons on either side. Life was harsh to the extreme for the inhabitants of these mountains. They made a living by herding goats or growing grapes for wine and olives for oil. While on the move, the soldiers saw lush valleys from time to time with green pastures and grain fields irrigated from the more robust streams and rivers. But the streams in these mountains were often dry in summer, providing no water for farming.

As XIII Corps marched through this range, the men looked out on its harsh, uninviting peaks and cliffs.

"How can people live in these mountains?" asked George of the Major.

"Beats me, George. It looks dry and unfarmable," said the Major.

"It sure does, Sir," said George. "We've seen these tiny villages perched atop some hills and cliffs. How do they survive?"

"They probably have wells," said the Major. "They have olive groves and vineyards below the cliffs. Olives, pasta, and wine make for good eating and drinking. I'm sure they have small vegetable gardens scattered around, too, not to mention the occasional pig or goat. Maybe that's what they are eating and drinking to survive."

"Hmmm, I think you are right, Sir," said George. "They are alive up there, so they must be eating something."

The going was slow since it often forced them to stop and wait while engineers repaired the road or a bridge they needed to cross. It seemed to take forever. XIII Corps found a wide area flat enough to stop in and lingered longer before continuing. The 2nd Field Regiment had struggled to keep up with the rough terrain and damaged roads, so they appreciated the break. It allowed them to carry out routine maintenance tasks. The gunners were weary from the rigours of the landings under the blistering sun of the Italian summer. So, they enjoyed the luxury of the refreshing pools of mountain water to frolic and wash their sweaty bodies. These pools seemed to defy their arid surroundings, welcoming the weary gunners.

"This is the life, my friends," said McTavish as the buddies languished in a pool shaded by the towering peaks of a high mountain,

"I like this, but I hope no Nazis are hiding up there in those villages!"

"We'll soon be in shit if they are, Gunner," said the Full Screw from the bank. "It wouldn't surprise me if they weren't watching us right now."

"No. You can't mean that," said McTavish. "Have you seen any?"

"Sure," said Full Screw. "Still, we've gotten rid of most of the Nazis."

The buddies laughed but became more vigilant of their environment after that.

"Tell us about yourself, George," asked Dave. "Tell us about your family back home, your work before joining the army, your love life and anything else important."

"OK. I was born in Montreal, like most of you," said George.

"My father is from Montreal, and my mother is in Niagara Falls. She was born near Hope Town in the Gaspe Peninsula. Does anybody know it? Her father was a farmer, and they moved to Niagara when he retired. Who knows how they met? But they did, married and had four children. I worked as a truck driver before I joined the Army. I worked for the same company, Drummond Transit, in Montreal for five years. And I liked it; I love driving and messing with vehicles, and it was an excellent company; a good bunch of guys."

"How did you learn to drive?" asked Dave.

"I started on a fruit and wine farm at Niagara in the summers before I left school. At harvest time, they taught me to drive the harvested fruit to the barn, where they sorted and packed them for the market. I loved my time at the farm, and it helped me to learn to drive when I was ten and could just reach the pedals. Niagara was great. I explored the falls with my buddies there."

"The Niagara Falls, George? Jeez, that must have been dangerous."

"Yup, sure was," said George. "A hell of a lot of fun! There weren't many tourists in those days. You couldn't do it now, and they wouldn't let you."

"Yeah, I drove early, too," said Jock. "I had a minor accident once, which ruined my driving for a while."

"Accidents happen," said George, "I've had a couple, but never my fault. My last accident was in England, do you remember? I was driving Major Walker in a Ford Sedan when the brakes failed, and the axle broke. It was hairy for a while as we careened down a hill, and the rear caught fire, but I stopped and extinguished the fire. So, the Major was OK. It was a fault on the car, so he understood."

"George and I worked together at Drummond Transit," said Paddy. "He was always being praised for his driving and hard work. Not me. I was always in trouble, haha."

"I still haven't learned to drive well," said Dave. "My father was a carter, so I learned how to ride his cart when I was small. But driving a tired old horse isn't too dangerous unless an idiot runs into you."

"Well, I'll give you lessons sometime," said George.

"Thanks, George. What did your father do?" asked Dave.

"As little as possible," said George with a grimace. "He was a lazy lout! My father left us when I was young. He just left my mother, three sisters, and me. He is a real bastard, a drunken womanizer. I have no time for him and haven't seen him for years."

"Sorry to hear that, George," said Dave, regretfully having asked the question. "My old man wasn't that great either."

"No problem," muttered George, "It taught me something. I have promised myself never to end up like him. I will be the best husband and father I can be to Dolly." Then, trying to change the conversation, reminded everyone, "Now we have another job to do, so let's get on with it!"

"Well, it hasn't been too tough so far," said Dave.

"A walk in the park," said Jock.

"Ha, sure," laughed Paddy. "A walk in the park. If you say so."

§

Heading north towards Potenza

Their brief sojourn in those remarkable mountains was too short. On the 15th of September, the 1st Canadian Division resumed its advance along the coast. On one long day, which ended at 1:50 am on the 17th, the 2nd Field Regiment drove 137 gruelling miles over potholed dirt roads. In this phase, the

Eighth Army's principal goal was Potenza, a vital highway and rail town midway between Taranto and Salerno in the middle of the boot ankle. The city of Potenza in the boot's heartland is the capital of the province and has the same name. It's the highest regional capital and one of the loftiest provincial capitals in Italy. It overlooks the River Basento valley in the Apennine Mountains of Lucania, east of Salerno.

General Dempsey ordered the 1st Canadian Division to capture Potenza. General Simonds ordered the 3rd Brigade to send forward an armed battalion group they called "Boforce." It took its name from Lieutenant-Colonel M. P. Bogert, the Commanding Officer of the West Nova Scotia Regiment, the infantry unit selected for the job. The task force moved forward from Villapiana on the afternoon of the 17th of September. But mines, blown bridges, and rubble-choked streets in towns and villages left as obstacles by the retreating Germans along the 100-mile route delayed progress. It was only at dusk on the 18th of September that the vanguard of the column reached the heights across the Basento Valley from Potenza. However, since the West Nova Scotia Infantry Regiment was moving into Potenza on the 20th, the field guns could only engage occasional targets for fear of hitting them. [119] After the 20th of September, there were only brief encounters with the enemy. As the bulk of the 1st Division moved into Potenza, the British

---

[119] Ibid

5th Army pulled abreast of Auletta, 20 miles west. By 21 September, the US 5th Army and the British 8th Army had joined and presented a continuous front line to the enemy. This line ran across the lower boot of Italy from Bari on the east coast to Salerno on the west coast. [120]

§

A private visit to Bari

During the halt at Potenza, Major Walker called George into his tent early one morning.

"Good morning, George," said the Major, "I want to take a trip to Bari today. A relative of mine lives there, and I've been able to contact her. So I want to make a visit while we are so close. Who knows if we will ever get back here?"

"Right, Sir," said George, "I'll get a map, and we can go as soon as you are ready."

"I have a map, George, and I'm ready. Let's get going right away. It may take a few hours to get there."

And with that, they were on their way. George found his way to a highway marked for Altamura, a town between Potenza and Bari on the coast. They travelled through the Altopiano delle Murge, the 'Plateau of the Murge.' This scenic region, which has few inhabitants, is a limestone karst plateau within the Apulia (Puglia) region and the sub-region known as

---

[120] Ibid

Murgia or Le Murge. This name stems from the Latin 'murex,' meaning 'sharp stone'.

Puglia, or Apulia, is the southern region forming the heel of Italy's boot, known for its whitewashed hill towns, centuries-old farms and hundreds of miles of Mediterranean coastline. After two hours of driving, they arrived at Altamura in the centre of the Murge plateau, known for its famous bread called Pane di Altamura. It was 28 miles southwest of Bari. Academic circles were interested in the city because of Altamura Man, the 130,000-year-old calcified fossil of a man discovered in the nearby limestone cave called Grotta di Lamalunga.

"Look at that church, Sir," said George. "It looks quite old."

"It's a cathedral, George," said the Major. "It's ancient, too."

Altamura's central landmark is the Romanesque cathedral, begun in 1232 by Frederick II, restored in 1330 and 1521, and untouched by the war. George and the Major, a religious man, stopped to visit it.

From Altamura, they followed the signs to the left towards Bari. Throughout Puglia, they noticed large olive groves and fields that, in summer, are full of durum wheat, the main ingredient of Pane di Altamura. But they were now barren because of winter.

After a quick drive of 30 miles, they arrived at Bari, the capital of Puglia, a vibrant port and university town. Once they had rid Puglia of the Germans, the ancient port of Bari had become an important supply centre for Allied forces fighting their way up the Italian Peninsula. Bari has a new section called "quartiere" or "quarters," developed in 1820, and an ancient one on a peninsula to the north. The old quarter has many magnificent antiquated Romanesque-Pugliese structures and churches, such as the Cathedral of San Sabino. It dates back to 1035. People founded the Basilica di San Nicola in 1087 to receive the relics of Saint Nicola.

They found the house where the Major's cousin lived in the harbour. George dropped him off and parked the car. He then enjoyed a few cigarettes while watching the hectic activities in the port.

After an hour-long visit with his cousin, a Canadian woman who had married an Italian from Bari, the Major emerged from their apartment overlooking the old port and invited George in for lunch. Their hosts treated them to a signature regional dish called Tiella con cozze, a casserole made with mussels, potatoes, rice, onion, olive oil and tomatoes. The Major enjoyed regional red wine with the meal, but George abstained, as a responsible driver should.

Then, after a dessert and a quick and robust coffee, George and the Major were on their way back to Potenza. They discussed the city, its sites and food until the Major drifted off for a nap in the back seat.

The army didn't allow soldiers to give any clues of where they were in letters, nor any other military descriptions not permitted by the censors. So George collected postcards from interesting stops he visited while travelling through Italy. He could show Dolly and the others once he was back in Croydon, as well as his grandparents and friends, on his return to Canada. He purchased the first of these cards at Bari from an antique shop for a few lire, a 'used' postcard showing a scene of the Corso Vittorio Emanuele. This was one of the two central boulevards of the 'new city' and the Teatro Margherita. They built the Teatro on pillars driven into the sea in the old port between 1912 and 1914. George and the Major stopped at the theatre on their way back and enjoyed the view along the long boulevard.

Back at camp, the Major thanked George for his excellent driving.

"I thank you, Sir," said George. "I enjoyed the day and found it most interesting. And I loved the casserole your cousin made us. Wonderful."

§

Maple Leaf City

By the 26th of September 1943, Canadian patrols had reached the Ofanto River north of Potenza, a distance of 320 miles in 23 days. The following day, the British 78th Division, also known as the Battle Axe Division, advancing westward from the Adriatic coast, entered Foggia, another primary goal. They formed the 78th Division in Scotland on 25 May 1942 as an assault formation for Operation Torch. After they toured North Africa, they landed at Bari on 22 and 23 September. Close to the 'spur' of the boot on the east coastline opposite Naples on the west, Foggia is the central city of a plain called Tavoliere delle Puglie. The area, translated as the 'Table of Apulias,' is known as the 'granary of Italy.'

Foggia was famous as a vital road and rail centre. However, because of the vast airfields on the surrounding plain, it served as a base for Axis bombers and fighters opposing the Allied advance. While under Axis control, the United States Army Air Force and Royal Air Force had bombed the airfields before the British Eighth Army seized them. So, It became a strategic victory.

Little by little, the Allied forces pushed the Germans back up the Italian Peninsula. The 1st Canadian Division's journey through the centre of Italy had been a real slog, made easier by the engineers clearing the way for them. But they reached and took command of each of their targets, Foggia among them.

They ordered the 1st Canadian Division to halt for a while at Foggia. George and his buddies requested leave to visit the city and many others, which the Army granted.

"Right. Let's see what this Italian city offers," said George.

"Yup. It's about time for a little R&R," said Paddy.

"What about the vino?" said Jock.

"What about the girls? I'm joining you guys," said Jean.

They hitched a ride with an army truck going into Foggia on an errand. Evidence of Allied bombing was everywhere as they drove into the town, particularly the railway yards and airport. The Germans had abandoned the city on 27 September, moving farther north. To their surprise, the citizens waved and called Grazie, Grazie, Benvenuto, and Benvenuto with enormous smiles as they drove by.

"Hey, this feels good," said Jock. "They are greeting us as liberators. How about that?"

"Amazing," said Paddy. "Some lovely young Italian ladies among them. This should be fun!"

The driver dropped them in the town centre and continued to his destination. So, the little band of Canadians stood looking about them and rubbing their hands together, keen to explore this old city. But they didn't get far. A group of enthusiastic citizens crowded around them, rapidly talking in Italian. None of the buddies understood Italian, but as luck would have it, an attractive dark-haired girl spoke fluent English.

"Please don't let us upset you," she said. "We are just so happy you have pushed the Germans away from our town."

"Well, we didn't do it alone," said George.

"What do you mean, George?" asked Jock, turning to the young lady. "You're welcome, my dear. What is your name?"

"Bianca," said the girl. "Are you American?"

"American?" they all said in unison. "No way! We are Canadian."

"Oh, I'm so sorry," she said. "We mostly know about America because many Italians went there."

"Well, we have a lot of Italians in Canada, too," said Paddy, pushing in to introduce himself.

"Meet my friends," said Bianca. "This is Carina, Eleonora and Bella."

The girls giggled and smiled as the men introduced themselves enthusiastically, but George stepped aside somewhat.

"What's the matter with your friend?" asked Bianca. "We don't bite, you know."

"George is a married man and a new father," said Jock. "So, he is a little, ah, reserved. But we are all single and thrilled to see you. Can we buy you all a drink at that café?"

"Yes, sure," said Bianca. "We'd like that very much."

With that, they walked across the square to a sidewalk café and behaved like perfect gentlemen while seating the ladies. They then called the waiter with more smiles and ordered a round of drinks. Lively conversation and sign language ensued between the bachelors and the young ladies while George took in the Piazza Cavour, which majesty stretched out before them. He could see an impressive fountain in a circle in the centre of the Piazza—the Fontana del Sele. Beyond that was an even more remarkable structure comprising many columns and the turreted Palazzo dell'Acquedotto building. Sadly, the Allies had damaged many buildings in the city centre through aerial and artillery bombardments.

"What is your name in English, Bianca?" asked Jock.

"Whiteness, or Pure," said Bianca. "Carina is 'Little Beloved One', Eleonora is 'Shining Light', and Bella is 'Beautiful'."

"Yes, she is, but you are all beautiful," said Jean, trying to earn some points.

When Bianca translated what Jean had said, they all giggled. The men were well on their way to a joyous afternoon.

But George excused himself after a glass of wine and wished his buddies and the girls well while walking alone through the ruined town, slowly returning to camp.

Throughout his time in Italy, George received regular letters from Dolly and wrote in return. The armed forces had a remarkable, dedicated, efficient postal service. Contact with loved ones was paramount for soldiers, and the army understood its importance. George's young wife kept him in the picture of life in Croydon and his son's and her family's progress. She inserted a photograph of Michael in every letter for his father, providing George with a running commentary and pictorial record of his son's growth. This he showed with pride to his gunner buddies, and other married men did the same.

Postal delivery was always a joyous occasion for the troops on the battlefield. George received news of a pregnant Peggy Rutherford's marriage to Jack Bass on 26 September 1943 in Croydon. Her child from Canadian soldier Bass was due at the end of December 1943. So young Michael could soon have a companion at 75 Cedar Road. Beattie Rutherford Simpson was also pregnant, expecting her first child in January. She and her husband Bill bought their own home in Croydon, which was made ready for the child. Besides letters from his wife, George corresponded with his Canadian relatives, his grandmother, Uncle Ernie, and Auntie Nellie in London.

§

The High Command ordered the 1st Canadian Division to resume its mission following the halt at Foggia. This time, the starting point for a westward advance along the convoluted Highway No. 17 was Lucera, ten miles northwest of Foggia. The German 3rd Parachute Regiment's machine gun and 88mm flak fire stopped the Allied advance from Lucera on October 1st. This happened at Motta Montecorvino, the first village they encountered in the hills west of Foggia. A late afternoon assault by the Royal Canadian Regiment (RCR) and tanks of the Calgary Regiment, supported by the 10th Battery RCA, failed.

Later, delayed by traffic congestion, the 2nd Field Regiment arrived. The 2nd Field then fired a concentration into

Motta, after which the RCR entered and secured the town. They awarded a Regimental Forward Observation Officer (FOO), Captain G. A. Eaton, the Military Cross. This was the first engagement of any size encountered by Canadian troops after a one-month, 350-mile-long slog up the mainland of Italy. But the German rear guards put up a determined and fierce resistance from positions of natural strength followed by rapid withdrawal to another dominant feature. For the Canadian artillery, it became a matter of using their guns "to convince the enemy that his resistance had lasted long enough".

Half a dozen miles as the crow flies west of Motta and a much longer distance by a wildly twisting road, the RCR launched an attack supported by divisional artillery. They attacked San Marco, a village on a prominent ridge above them. The battery prepared a timed program incorporating both barrages and concentrations. But when the infantry attacked up a rocky slope on the afternoon of 4 October, they benefited little from their expected artillery support. They ran straight into heavy enfilading German fire along their longest axis. This prompted the Commander Royal Artillery (CRA) to confine the fire plan to concentrations controlled by a superior observing officer closer to the Germans. [121]

So Major Walker jumped into the fray.

---

[121] Ibid

Empire and Tyranny

"Come, George, we've got an urgent job to do," called the Major. George leapt into his Jeep and drove to where the Major was standing.

"Get me as close as you can to the action, George," said the Major. They drove to a point close enough to the Germans for the Major to direct the fire as the Forward Observation Officer (FOO).

"Closer, George, let's get to that point over there higher up the valley," ordered the Major.

"I'll do my best, Sir," said George. "They mean these tracks for goats, donkeys and mules, not vehicles."

"Yes, but a Jeep is nothing more than a mechanical mule," the Major laughed. "Every bit as reliable."

They hung on for their lives as George pushed the vehicle as fast as he could over the rocky trail to reach their goal. Bullets were whizzing past as they drove, a few glancing off the sturdy metal body of the Jeep.

"That was bloody close," called the Major. "We've got to put those bastards out of action fast!"

"What about that spot over there, Sir," asked George.

"Ideal, Gunner," shouted the Major. "Get us there!"

They went bouncing and leaping from one point of the trails to another. In no time, George and the Major arrived at the spot the Major had selected.

"Bloody amazing vehicle, this, Sir, isn't it," called George. "I'm most impressed."

"What did I tell you?" asked the Major.

From this observation point, the Major grabbed his radio and positioned himself behind boulders to direct the firing. On his order, the firing started moments later.

"Too low," called the Major into his radio. "Too low. Move to the village and blast those bastards out of that castle before they get us. Good, now walk it up the mountain."

Darkness soon fell, and the Germans could no longer see George and his Major. But they had stopped firing at the 2nd Field since the intensity of the barrage distracted them. Late that night, another bombardment delivered by the 2nd Field silenced the Germans altogether, enabling the infantry to occupy the San Marco la Catola village without further trouble. It was the last barrage the Canadian guns fired for many weeks.

§

The Canadian advance continued inch by inch, mile by mile. That's how it was in this campaign—slow and treacherous. The winter rains had started, it was freezing, and manoeuvring was becoming more challenging. When they left the highway, the ground turned into a sticky, black sea of mud. Returning the guns to their routes from deployment demanded a monumental exertion. Jeeps were the only vehicles able to make genuine progress, and a few turned turtles. The carriers of the Forward Observation Officers became embedded in the mire, forcing their occupants to move forward on mules or, failing that, on foot. [122] Mined roads held up the artillery for three more days, during which the infantry pushed ahead to where only the medium or larger guns could cover them.

While waiting to move forward, a brief improvement in the weather enabled one artillery unit to see its first movie since leaving Scotland. The Auxiliary Services Officer had secured a newsreel of the Canadian division's activities in Sicily to supplement the feature film *That Lady Hamilton*. On a clear, chilly evening, hundreds of men sat on a hillside under the stars, watching the movies on a sheet hung on the side of an army truck. It was as odd a cinema as ever graced a spot only a few miles from the enemy positions, but it was a welcomed distraction for the tired soldiers. [123] The newsreel of their victory in Sicily amused the soldiers of the 1st Canadian Division, but it disappointed them when they didn't see themselves in the film. They enjoyed *That Hamilton Woman*, also known as *Lady Hamilton*, a 1941 movie starring Vivien Leigh, Laurence Olivier, and Alan Mowbray. It portrayed a story set during the Napoleonic Wars of courtesan and dance-hall girl Emma Hamilton, her relationships with Sir William Hamilton and Admiral Horatio Nelson and her rise and fall. The boys needed the right mix of romance and bravado on that crisp Italian autumn evening.

---

[122] Ibid
[123] Ibid

"I saw that movie in England," said George. "I could watch it many more times. It's lovely, and so moving."

"Yeah, I liked it too," said Jock McTavish. "It's a good historical movie, and it's such a pleasure to spend two hours that have nothing to do with this goddamned war!"

They thrust the 1st Canadians back into the battles the following day, moving along Route 17. They took the towns of Jelsi and Gildone between Gambatesa and Campobasso, one after the other, with brief resistance. Contemporary German records show that their heavy casualties had resulted in deepening respect for the Canadian artillery by the enemy. The German commanders often had the dilemma of having to decide between withdrawal or losses that their depleted formations could ill afford. At one point, the German 76th Corps Chief of Staff lamented, "My hair is turning grey!" ·

"You know, Guys," said George to his buddies that evening, "You've been doing a brilliant job, but I feel so sorry for these villagers. Look at these tiny villages. They look so peaceful. But these people have little money. And now, in this war, many lost their homes."

"It's not our fault, George," said Dave. "It's the fault of the goddamned Germans hiding in the villages. But I agree with you. It's hard on the villagers."

Such bombardments rewarded the skill and determination of the 1st Canadian Division gunners, who had successfully harried the enemy through the steep country west of the Foggia plain. But as George said, what about the Italian residents? The Division took its ultimate objectives in this phase with relative ease. Early on 14 October, the infantry of the 1st Canadian Brigade entered Campobasso unopposed.

During their advance, the Canadian artillery had the help of the C Flight, RAF 651st Air Observation Post (AOP) Squadron. They formed this squadron at Old Sarum, near Salisbury, Wiltshire, England, on 1 August 1941 to work with army units in artillery spotting and communicating. It began in November of that year during Operation Torch in North Africa. They were flying Taylorcraft Auster IV and V, British military liaison and observation monoplanes produced by Taylorcraft Aeroplanes (England). The RAF 651st was part of the RAF, but the pilots, drivers and signallers were from the Royal Artillery, while the RAF supplied the Adjutant, Engineer Officer and technicians. It was the premier Army Air Corps squadron. On 4 September 1943, it became the first AOP unit to cross the Strait of Messina to take part in the invasion of Italy. The 8th Army supported it again, using Auster IV and V planes. They deployed an officer with each field regiment to guide the aircraft. Pilots flew several sorties from their base at Lucera, 45 miles east of Campobasso, on reconnaissance and directing shoots for the Canadian guns daily. [124]

---

[124] Ibid

"This job is getting easier the farther north we get," said Jean. "Do you think the Jerries have given up?"

"I doubt it," said Dave. "They are just waiting for us further up the road."

"Still, we have reconnaissance planes flying around," said Jean. "Surely they can find them?"

"Yup, and that is just what they are doing," said Dave. "That is why we are winning."

With the Termoli-Campobasso line secured, the Eighth Army now paused until supply mechanisms were sufficient for continued movement and fighting. [125] Termoli is on Italy's Adriatic coast, and Campobasso is in the middle of the peninsula. This line was an important milestone for the British and Canadians in pursuing the Germans; they were making excellent progress. They were now 350 miles from their starting point at Reggio Calabria. For the next six weeks, most Canadian divisional artillery remained in positions around Campobasso. The anti-tank and anti-aircraft units joined the field regiments, giving defensive fire and carrying out counter-battery work.

Campobasso is the Molise region's capital in the high Biferno River basin, surrounded by the Sannio and Matese mountains. Like most Italian towns and cities, it has a historic centre with typical medieval features skirting and climbing the

---

[125] Ibid

hill to Monforte Castle. Since the 14th century or earlier, Campobasso has been renowned for making blades, including scissors and knives.

The battle between the German and Canadian troops to control the city destroyed many public buildings, including the City Hall and the valuable archives. They killed 38 civilians in the intensive bombardment, including the diocese bishop. And they injured an unknown number of citizens.

Once in their hands, the British XIII Corps used the town as an administrative and recreational centre. Auxiliary Services organized movies, stage shows, clubs, and other recreation facilities. Within a week of the German withdrawal, Auxiliary Services brought 4,000 officers and men from surrounding areas daily to enjoy these amenities. However, the surrounding region was still under hostile shelling. [126] The Allied soldiers gave Campobasso the nicknames Canada City and Maple Leaf City because of the number of Canadian troops bivouacked there.

Among the many movies shown in Campobasso was the just-released 1943 film *Hers to Hold*, featuring Joseph Cotton and Deanna Durbin, a singing actress from Winnipeg. This gorgeous Canadian singer stole many hearts that day, and most soldiers forgot the war for that moment of R&R. Other movies shown included the much loved *Gone with the Wind* and *King Kong*, with another Canadian actress, Fay Wray, born

---

[126] Ibid

in Alberta. Auxiliary Services provided many movies and stage shows featuring visiting stars; these were the favourite R&R escapes for the battle-weary soldiers.

George explored the city at Campobasso with his buddies while adding to his collection of postcards. One card he bought depicted a long boulevard named Corso Vittorio Emanuele lined with multi-story houses, trees, and cafés that the chums had enjoyed. George asked who this famous Vittorio Emanuele was. An informed officer told him, "Victor Emmanuel II was the King of Sardinia from 1849 until 1861, when he elevated himself by assuming the title King of Italy. He became the first and the best-loved King of a united Italy since the 6th century, a title he held until he died in 1878."

Another Campobasso card depicted the "Piazza della Vittoria" and the Caduti Monument. This memorial stood at the end of Corso Vittorio Emanuele II, celebrating the Fiery Sannita, who represented the Sannitian people who dared war with the mighty Rome between 343 and 290 BC. It is now known as the Monument to the Fallen of all wars. The Canadian buddies met a few girls hanging out there, too. Jock and Paddy had lingered with them there for a while, trying their hardest to make their acquaintance.

A third Campobasso postcard had a photo of the "Piazza Municipio" with its impressive town hall. And a fourth Campobasso postcard was a view of the Palazzo I.N.C.I.S. in the Piazza Savoia.

Empire and Tyranny

George and his buddies enjoyed a pleasant lunch at a street café at this Piazza. There, they had their introduction to pizza, a popular meal served at the café since this much-liked meal had not yet reached Canadian restaurants. They had whiled away the afternoon eating this delicious Italian dish and emptying a few carafes of red Italian wine.

"Is there a war on?" asked Jock. "Everybody is just doing their regular business, chatting and laughing as if nothing was wrong. And just look at these lovely signorinas, with their long locks of black hair!"

"I know. To think a few days ago, there might have been German soldiers enjoying a meal in this café, just like us now," said George.

"Crazy, isn't it? One minute, we're killing each other; the next, we're eating in their favourite cafes."

"I don't think the Italians care who is here," said Dave. "As long as the Germans paid and didn't bother them too much. But it's different with us Canadians, isn't it? I mean, we haven't pushed them around. I'm sure the Jerries did."

"Well, my friends, let's live it to the full," toasted Paddy. "We need to have fun again, for a change!"

The Canadians raised their glasses to each other and toasted Italians at the adjacent table, who grinned and returned the toast.

Just then, Sergeant Morgan and the Full Screw Jones wandered by the restaurant, stopping when they saw their crew.

Empire and Tyranny

"I see you guys are having an enjoyable time," said the sergeant, "that's fine, but just make sure you are back in camp on time."

"Yes, Sarge," the buddies said in unison. "Don't worry, we'll be there!"

"I'll be waiting for you," said the Full Screw. "God only help any of you who are late!"

"Don't worry, Bomb," they said with the slightest slur and giggles. "We won't be late."

It was a sunny autumn day, and despite a robust wind and the lack of leaves on the trees, the men had a very relaxing afternoon. Full Screw came up in their conversation.

"What is the story with that ornery bastard?" asked Jock.

"He's a real asshole," said Paddy. "He's a miner from Cape Breton Island with a huge chip on his shoulder. What the hell is he doing in our regiment? What was he doing in Montreal?"

"He was a cop until he got kicked out for roughing up the wrong person, a close relative of the mayor," said George with a chuckle. "That's what I heard."

"Nobody else will take him, so he ended up in our battery," Dave said disgustedly. "His only value is that he is an excellent No. 6 position in our troop!"

"Well, I'd love to hand him a few whacks with my fists in the dark one day," said Jock. "I can't afford to lose my leave right now. I'm having too much fun."

"His time will come," said George. "You can't keep treating people like shit and get away with it forever."

Then everyone except Jock and Paddy dragged themselves back to camp. They got the addresses of the girls they had met earlier and were getting closer to them when interrupted by duty.

Just before the end of the leave deadline at midnight, Jock and Paddy snuck into camp. The bombardier was waiting as promised. Disappointed that the entire team had arrived on time, he returned to bed. George was still awake and greeted them.

"Hey Guys, where have you been?" he asked.

"With Luciana, the sweetest thing since cotton candy," said Jock.

"Maria, the second sweetest thing since cotton candy," chuckled Paddy.

"Well, I hope you took precautions," said the ever-practical George.

"Of course," said Jock, "Whatever happens, I've got to see that girl again. That was the best lovemaking I've ever had. And although we can't understand each other too well, love makes the point. And we want to see more of each other." But how could he achieve that while on the move? He wasn't sure.

"Best lovemaking, Jock?" asked George. "Have you had that much, my friend?"

"Enough to know," said Jock. "She is fantastic! She taught me moves I didn't know existed."

"Well, my experience was the same," said Paddy. "These Italian girls know lovemaking. I love this country! I love Italian girls, and I love Italian food and Italian vino. If only we could get rid of these Nazis. Then life here could be perfect!"

At the end of October, the 1st Canadian Division relinquished its left flank along Route 17 to the British 5th Division. For the next week, patrols of the 1st Canadian Division and the 4th Canadian Reconnaissance Regiment ranged across the barren uplands. They were between the Biferno and the upper reaches of the River Trigno, ten miles to the northwest. The 2nd and 3rd field regiments provided what little artillery support these patrols needed, coming out of action again for a rest near Maple Leaf City.

Back within range of their sweethearts, Jock and Paddy disappeared into the heart of Campobasso as soon as they got their next leave of absence. [127]

Meanwhile, the Allies were preparing for the winter campaign. The capture of the Italian capital, with the strategic importance of securing its nearby weatherproof airfields, was paramount. It required that they continue the advance to ensure a stable defensive base north of Rome.

As for the enemy's plans, Hitler issued a directive on 4 October after meeting with Rommel and Kesselring at his Wolfschanze (Wolf's Lair) in East Prussia. It contained specific

---

[127] Ibid

orders for a German stand south of Rome. "Commander-in-Chief South will fight a delaying action only as far as the Gaeta-Ortona line. You must hold this line!" [128]

This line was the Gustav Line, which the Germans called a "string of pearls anchored by Monte Cassino."

Albert Kesselring was a notorious German Luftwaffe Generalfeldmarschall, the German Wehrmacht's highest regular general officer rank. He was the supreme commander of all German forces in Italy. In a military career that spanned both World Wars, Kesselring became one of Nazi Germany's most able commanders and one of the most decorated. He was one of only 27 soldiers awarded the Knight's Cross of the Iron Cross with Oak Leaves, Swords and Diamonds. Nicknamed Smiling Albert by the Allies and Onkel Albert by his troops, Kesselring was one of the most famous generals of WWII. He was popular with the German rank and file. Hitler knew he could rely on this able soldier. During the war, he won the respect of his Allied opponents for his military accomplishments.

§

Penetrating the German defensive lines.

In sixty-three days, a mere two months since landing on the mainland, the Eighth Army and 1st Canadian Division had covered 450 miles. The Germans under Generalfeldmarschall

---

[128] Ibid

Kesselring counted their strength equal to that of the Allies. With the advantage of the defence, they were to engage on the coast south of Monte Cassino on the Naples-Rome highway. The highway crossed the middle of Italy to Ortona on the Adriatic shore. The Allies knew winning Rome would be difficult, for they had to cross the fortified and German-occupied 'defensive lines.'

George was driving the Major to Campobasso when they stopped for a cup of tea, a sandwich and a smoke. George asked the Major to explain the German defensive lines.

"There's a lot of talk amongst the men about these so-called defensive lines, Sir," asked George. "What is that all about, and are they dangerous?"

"It's a little complicated, George," began the Major. "I'll do the best I can to explain them. After we invaded Italy in September, the German forces knew what was coming. They knew we would make our way up the peninsula, so they urgently started constructing a series of defensive lines across the middle of Italy. They designed these lines to stop or delay our advance towards the north and Rome. The German Army has been retreating north while we've been advancing. They are now dug in behind these lines to meet and defend them against our advances. Hitler himself gave orders to stop the invasion of the enemy at all costs. So, we must run the gauntlet through these lines to conquer Rome and the rest of Italy."

"What do they look like?"

"Our intelligence tells us they are lines of pill-boxes, guns, trenches and troops, dug in along each line preparing to fight us as we advance."

"How many are there, Sir?"

"Quite a few. I'll tell you about the ones I know of. The Volturno Line was the one we passed below Campobasso and the most southerly. They also call it the Viktor Line. It ran from Termoli in the east along the Biferno River and through the Apennine Mountains to the Volturno River in the west. The Volturno and Garigliano rivers formed natural barriers to delay the Allies' advance on this line.

"The *Barbara Line* is the second series of German military fortified hilltop positions ten to twenty miles north of and parallel to the Volturno Line. And it's the next one we have to get through.

"Then comes the *Winter Line,* another series of German military fortifications under Generalfeldmarschall Smiling Albert Kesselring himself. The Winter Line comprises three lines on the west, anchored by Monte Cassino. Two subsidiary lines, the Bernhardt Line and the Hitler Line, run from the Tyrrhenian Sea to just northeast of Cassino, merging into the *Gustav Line*. Once we break through that series of lines, the famous Highway 6 leads uninterrupted to Rome. The primary Gustav Line runs across Italy from just north of where the Garigliano River flows into the Tyrrhenian Sea in the west. It runs through Monte Cassino and the Apennine Mountains to the mouth of the Sangro River, just south of Ortona on the Adriatic coast in the east. That series of lines will be our most formidable challenge, I believe. But we'll get through it.

"After Rome, we must fight through the Caesar Line to reach the country's North. It extends from the west coast near Ostia, over the Alban Hills south of Rome, from Valmontone to Avezzano and then to Pescara on the Adriatic coast. Behind the western half of the Caesar Line is a subsidiary line called the *Roman Switch Line,* which takes a path north of Rome. This is a line of defence branching off the Caesar 'C' Line and running north of Rome towards the coast of the Tyrrhenian Sea."

"Good God, Sir. We have a lot of fighting ahead of us."

"We sure do, George. And that is not the end. Intelligence says they expect the Nazis to build more defensive lines once we have taken Rome. The effort and resources they put into constructing these many lines of defence are colossal. They are using commandeered Italian criminal prisoners to build them. So, to answer your question, yes, they are very dangerous. But we must fight our way through them. And we won't get the job done sitting around here. Get me to Campobasso, please, George."

"Yes, Sir," said George while starting the Jeep and pulling out into the army traffic plying the roads of Allied conquered territory. "Thank you for explaining that to me. I'll pass that on to my buddies, who are as perplexed about the defence lines as I was."

"You're welcome, George. On a lighter note, how's your wife and child?" asked the Major.

"Thank you for asking, Sir. They're fine," said George. "My little boy is growing, and London seems quiet, thank God. My wife sends me photos of Michael with every letter. So even though I am missing them in the flesh, I am watching him grow."

§

By October 1943, the Allies were through the Volturno and Barbara lines. They were moving towards the Bernhardt and Gustav lines and the German-occupied Monte Cassino Abbey. The River Sangro in the east and the River Garigliano in the west provided additional barriers for these lines. In the centre stood the immense heights of the Abruzzi Apennines, insurmountable barriers. This mountainous region includes the Gran Sasso, at 9,554 feet, the highest peak of the Apennines, and Mount Majella, at 9,163 feet.

The Allies planned operations to break through the Bernhardt Line in the east in successive phases. On the Adriatic flank, the British Eighth Army was to take the east end of the Via Flaminia. This Roman road ran from Rome to Pescara along the coast from a dozen miles beyond a town called Ortona. On the other side of Italy, the US Fifth Army was then to strike towards Rome through the Liri Valley between the mountains and the coast past Monte Cassino. General Montgomery's forces, coming from Avezzano, a town on Highway 5 at the centre of the peninsula, were to aid the Americans in this task.

The Eighth Army crossed the Sangro on 23 November 1943, the start of the Allied offensive on the Gustav Line defences east of the Apennines. When General Montgomery hit the enemy on 28 November in a "colossal crack," the 5th Corps had breached the Bernhardt Line on the coast. They captured the dominating heights north of the Sangro River flats. The Army Commander now called on the 1st Canadian Division to relieve the tired 78th Infantry Division. Then, with the 8th Indian Division on its left, the 1st Canadian Division was to lead the 5th Corps' advance up the coastal axis. They would then cross the Gustav Line to Ortona and Pescara. The New Zealand Division followed an inland route towards Orsogna and Chieti. They were to overcome the first obstacle, the Moro River.

After losing the Bernhardt Line, the command ordered the enemy to make a determined stand on the far bank of the Moro. The Germans quickly brought regiments of the 90th Panzer Grenadier Division south from Venice in early December to help stem the Allied advance, and they were facing the Canadians.

Empire and Tyranny

On 2 December, the command on the coast passed to Major General Chris Vokes when Maj.-Gen. Simonds left to command the 5th Canadian Armoured Division. The three Canadian field regiments crossed the Sangro on the 3rd. In a region in which the torrents plummeting from the Apennines had cut themselves deep gorges between the steep ridges of the coastal plateau. As a result, the areas suitable for field guns were most limited. Nor did the low-growing olive trees offer much cover. In their exposed positions, the Canadian batteries were under massive shelling by the Germans day and night, and casualties mounted.

"This river is in flood and moving fast," said George to the Major as they forded it under constant fire.

"Can we make it, George?" asked the Major as they inched forward, bouncing over large rocks on the river bed.

"The water's up to the axles, Sir," said George over the din. "If it doesn't get deeper, we shouldn't have a problem. They continued for a few yards when the Jeep suddenly dropped into a depression in the riverbed. Then, try as he might, George couldn't move the vehicle forward or backward, and water had entered its interior.

"Are you in trouble, George?" called a truck driver behind him.

"Yup," said George. "Stuck in a hole."

"OK, I'll move around you, and you can hook up your winch to my back bumper."

"Don't worry, Sir," said George to the Major. "We'll be out of here in no time."

With that, George leapt from his vehicle into the freezing waters of the mountain river. As the truck manoeuvred around the Jeep, George pulled the towline out of the winch and attached it to its rear bumper. Then he clambered back in his vehicle, signalling his readiness to the truck driver.

As they left the river with the rest of the battery, a hail of German shells hit them. The teams swung their guns into position and, with the Major's direction, started a return fire within a few minutes. After an hour and a few direct hits on the German batteries, the Germans turned tail and escaped into the hills.

"That was a close call, Sir," said George.

"Yup, sure was," said the Major. "I think we handled it well."

It wasn't the first such incident and wouldn't be the last. That night, the shelling continued. However, without shelter, they were sitting ducks. It was a stressful and uncomfortable night.

§

The next day, the Major heard the news of a terrible incident at Bari. On the night of 2 December, 105 German Junkers Ju 88 bombers attacked the port of Bari. They sank allied ships in the overcrowded harbour, including the US Liberty ship John Harvey, carrying mustard gas. They had mustard gas stacked on the quayside awaiting transport, too. The US intended the chemical agent for retaliation had the German forces used chemical warfare. They had kept this gas classified, and the US had not informed the British military authorities in the city of its existence. This increased the fatalities since British physicians did not know they were dealing with the effects of mustard gas. They prescribed treatment meant for those suffering from exposure and immersion, which often proved fatal. However, they were unaware of the mustard gas. The gas caused many more losses among the rescuers through contact with the contaminated skin and clothing of those more exposed to it. By the end of the month, 83 of the 628 hospitalized military victims had died. They thought the number of civilian casualties was even higher, but they couldn't verify it since most had left the city to seek shelter with relatives elsewhere.

During this catastrophic attack, the German planes sank 28 ships and damaged the harbour. They killed 1,000 military and merchant marine personnel and 1,000 civilians, including the Major's cousin and her husband. It hit the Major hard. The loss saddened George since he had found the couple to be the most welcoming and pleasant people. After the attack, the harbour was closed to operations for three weeks and did not return to capacity until February 1944.

§

Empire and Tyranny

The Moro River Campaign

The next major operation was the Moro River Campaign. Elements of the British Eighth Army and the German 10th Army's 76th Panzer Corps fought the Moro River Campaign from December 4th to 26th. This campaign was part of an offensive launched by General Sir Harold Alexander's Allied 15th Army Group to breach the German Army's Winter Line defences. They were to advance to Pescara and then on to Rome. On December 4, four infantry divisions attacked German positions along the Moro River. This assault involved four infantry divisions—one British, one Canadian, one Indian and one New Zealand—and two armoured brigades, one British and one Canadian. Fire came from the RCA's 2nd and 3rd field regiments, the Royal Artillery's 98th Army Field (SP) and the 4th and 70th Medium Regiments.

The first attack across the Moro occurred at midnight from 5 to 6 December. But the assault failed since strong German counterattacks forced the Canadian infantry to relinquish the tenuous footholds they had gained on the far side of the Moro. The action the following day brought the 2nd Field Regiment its first casualty and decoration in its new location. On 6 December, during a fierce firefight, a 2nd Field captain was acting as FOO with a company of the Seaforth Highlanders of Canada. They were attacking La Torre, and he was directing fire from a house in a well-advanced position. When the enemy counterattacked, they wounded him, but with his sub-machine-gun, he covered the withdrawal of the infantrymen. And as he left, he called fire onto his own position.

Major Walker, witnessing the incident, urgently ordered George to drive the Jeep to rescue the captain. He needed to get the captain to the medical tent before he died. George shot off over the rough terrain as commanded.

"Hello, Captain," he said as he entered the house to rescue him.

"Hello, soldier, so good to see you," said the captain. Thank you for coming to get me. George helped him out of his position and into the Jeep.

"Hold on as best you can, Sir," called George. The artillery was lobbing shells in their direction as ordered by the injured captain. Another soldier, who had helped George get the wounded officer into the Jeep, stayed with him to ensure he didn't fly out of the vehicle on the way back.

"Thanks for the lift, Gunner," said the officer, "I sure needed it!"

"Yes, Sir. The Major saw that," said George as he sped up the Jeep to reach medical care as fast as possible while keeping the vehicle from bouncing around too much. However, as they raced back to safety, shells flew over their heads, and a few bullets whizzed. They made it to the camp and field hospital well behind the front, where the orderlies helped the captain onto a stretcher and whisked him into the tent.

After they had dressed his wounds and his Company was preparing to fall back across the Moro, the Captain asked its commander to leave him there. He didn't want to risk the loss of more men by them trying to carry him. They immediately awarded him an MC; he was undoubtedly a hero. [129] The army only granted the Military Cross to officers at the time to recognize "an act, or acts, of exemplary gallantry during active operations against the enemy on land." They later included the lower ranks.

That night, the buddies discussed the day's events.

"That was a daring dash you did, George," said Jock. "You're lucky to still be alive!"

"You deserve a medal," said Paddy. "What an exciting episode."

"I'm lucky?" said George. "I'll tell you that Captain was much luckier. He was in shit until I pulled him out of there. He is a courageous man. And a caring officer for his men!"

"Well, George, you shouldn't be so modest, buddy. You risked your life trying to get him out. Well done," said the sergeant who had watched the entire episode, and his buddies shared that sentiment.

"That was one hell of a battle, Guys," said George. "I saw how hot your guns were."

"Yup, you are so right on that one," said Jock as more heads nodded in agreement.

---

[129] Ibid

The smallest artillery unit was the gun crew, known as the 'detachment' or 'troop,' and one of several within a battery. George's buddies were in Troop A, and their gun was a 25-pounder Howitzer ('25-pdr'), the primary British field gun during the Second World War with a 3.45-inch calibre. This weapon was separate-loading using howitzer variable-charge ammunition; the shell was loaded and rammed, and then they charged the cartridge in its brass case and closed the breech. They referred to the 25-pdr as quick-firing (QF) because the cartridge case provided fast loading compared with bag charges and auto-released when the breech opened.

In each gun detachment, there were six men numbered 1 to 6. The Commander of Troop A was Sergeant Peter Morgan in the No. 1 position to the rear, making left or right sweeps of the gun, known as traverses. He was a stocky, earnest, humourless man with dark, oily hair and greasy pock-marked facial skin. Jock was No. 2 position, holding the rammer that loaded the shells into the chamber and operating the breech lever while standing to the right of the gun. Dave immersed himself in his crucial No. 3 position, the 'Layer,' sitting on the wooden seat on the left-hand side of the cannon. He adjusted and used the sights, signalling adjustments to No. 1 in long traverses, with his finger on the trigger. Dave loved having his finger on the trigger. Paddy was in No. 4, the 'Loader,' with Jean in No. 5, passing the ammo to Paddy and checking the fuses. Bombardier (JJ) Jack Jones was No. 6 position (as Corporal

2IC to the sergeant). He set the fuses and charges and handled the movement and braking of the trailer. The team disliked JJ, an obnoxious, awkward, ill-mannered man, but he was very conscientious and good at his job. It was a recent game for the boys of the 2nd Field Regiment, but they were functioning well and improving with practice.

The sergeant and Full Screw overheard George and assessed the battle too.

"We're working well as a team now," said the sergeant. "I didn't see a single slip in that exercise."

"No. 3, Dave, could still improve his sighting," said Full Screw to everyone's annoyance, but Dave's in particular. "A few of our shots missed the target."

"Well, I didn't notice that, Bomb," retorted the sergeant. "I thought he did well under the circumstances. And we will continue improving with more practice, which I'm sure we will still be getting."

None of the buddies commented while the sergeant and Full Screw were still there, but once they left, the buddies broke into enthusiastic reactions.

"Bloody asshole," Dave blurted out. "What the hell does he know?"

"He always has to say something negative," said Paddy. "When was he ever in that position in wartime? He wasn't in the Great War."

"I'll punch the bastard in the face one of these days," said Jock. "Miserable prick!"

"Well, I'll tell you," said George, "I was watching you guys for a long time, and in my humble opinion, you sure looked good. And that was one hell of a battle!"

On the morning of 9 December, RCA Headquarters reported that since operations at the Moro had started, the divisional artillery had spent 65,000 rounds. The Canadians took San Leonardo on the opposite bank of the Moro on 9 December. But the enemy struck the 2nd Field Commanding Officer, Lieutenant-Colonel H. M. Hague, with an exploding shell, and he lost his arm. Command of the Regiment then passed to Lieutenant-Colonel E. W. Steuart-Jones. [130]

§

Christmas 1943—the Tragedy of Ortona

The Moro River Campaign continued and culminated with a fierce confrontation at Ortona, a small coastal town on the Adriatic Sea in the Italian region of Abruzzo. The elite German Fallschirmjäger (paratroopers) from the German 1st Parachute Division under Generalleutnant (Lieutenant-General) Richard Heidrich faced the Allies. The Allied assaulting Canadian troops were from the 1st Canadian Division under Major General Chris Vokes. This battle reached

---

[130] Ibid

---

the highest point of the fighting on the Adriatic front in Italy in December 1943.

Before the battle, Ortona was a lovely old seaside town steeped in history and perched on the cliffs above its tiny harbour. It is said the sailor Leone Acciaiuoli brought the relics of the Apostle Thomas to Ortona in 1258. They had since been resting in the town's Basilica di San Tommaso, built in the first half of the 15th century. After the Italians established the Kingdom of Italy in 1860, Ortona became one of its first sea resorts on the Adriatic Sea.

The Canadian 2nd Brigade's Loyal Edmonton Regiment, with elements of the Seaforth Highlanders of Canada, first attacked the town on 20 December. [131] Meanwhile, portions of the division's 3rd Infantry Brigade launched an offence to the west of Ortona to outflank and cut off communications from the rear. But both brigades made slow progress because of the rough terrain and a determined and skilful German defence.

The Germans had concealed various machine guns and anti-tank emplacements throughout the town, making movement by armour and infantry trickier. [132] House-to-house fighting was vicious, and the Canadians used a new tactic called "mouse-holing." This involved using weapons such as the PIAT, or even cumbersome anti-tank guns, to breach the

[131] Zuehlke, Mark, *Ortona: Canada's epic World War II battle*. Vancouver: Douglas & McIntyre, 1999.
[132] Bercuson, David, *Maple Leaf Against the Axis*. Red Deer Press, 2001.

walls of a building. [133] The Anti-Tank (PIAT) Mk I was a British man-portable anti-tank weapon designed in 1942 in response to the British Army's need for a more effective infantry anti-tank weapon.

Once they breached the walls, the soldiers threw in grenades and assaulted through the mouse holes, clearing the top floors and descending, both adversaries struggling in repeated close-quarters combat. [134] They used mouse-holing to pierce through walls into adjoining houses, sometimes catching enemy troops by surprise. They repeated the tactic over and over while assaulting through the streets. This intense fighting inflicted heavy casualties on both Canadian and German soldiers. Later, in one deadly incident, German Fallschirmjäger engineer Karl Bayerlein demolished an entire house packed with Canadian soldiers, with only one soldier surviving. [135] After six days of combat, the 2nd Brigade's third battalion, Princess Patricia's Canadian Light Infantry (PPCLI), joined the tanks of the 1st Canadian Armoured Brigade's Three Rivers Regiment.

However, on 25 December 1943, the fighting paused briefly while both sides celebrated the holiest day. The Canadians had been in the Italian Campaign for less than four

---

[133] Ibid.
[134] Zuehlke, Mark, *Ortona: Canada's epic World War II battle*. Vancouver: Douglas & McIntyre, 1999.
[135] Ibid

months, but it had been a tough slog. So, the Canadians celebrated this special day in fashion. They came together for Christmas in the ruins of Ortona. In the bombed-out church of Santa Maria di Costantinopoli, members of the Seaforth Highlanders gathered in shifts for a Christmas dinner a few blocks from the fighting. The soldiers had set up long field tables. They had scrounged the essentials for this celebratory meal: tablecloths, chinaware, beer, wine, roast pork, apple sauce, cauliflower, mashed potatoes, gravy, chocolate, oranges, nuts, beer, wine, and cigarettes. And the cooks whipped up a scrumptious feast. An organist played 'Silent Night' using the church's still intact organ. A hint of peace and normality returned briefly on Christmas Day as the soldiers sang these familiar words during a brutal war. There were two Christmas dinners served that day at the church. One was with Major Forin's Seaforths inside the church. They simultaneously served another mixed group of Highlanders and other soldiers at an enormous square table outside in the Oratory. And elsewhere in Ortona, soldiers gathered in groups wherever they could find shelter.

"Well, it's definitely the most exciting Christmas meal I've ever had," said the Major. The Major's old friend, Major Forin of the Seaforth Highlanders, had invited Major Walker and George to join the group to enjoy lunch under such precarious circumstances.

"That's for sure, Sir," said George. "I can't believe that we are here, eating our Christmas meal in a bombed-out church in a bombed-out town. This doesn't seem real." They laughed and agreed while passing more bottles of local red wine around the table. Little did George know then that an ancestor of his from his mother's side of the family was a Highland soldier. George was a descendant of Duncan McRae from Dundee, Scotland, of the 78th Frasers Highlanders at the Battle of the Plains of Abraham in Quebec in 1759.

Alas, even though it was not a dream, it soon ended. When the meal was over, the troops returned to the fighting. Sadly, that historic day was the last meal for a few Canadian soldiers.

The Germans withdrew two days after Christmas. The Canadians had achieved their goal but at a high cost. They had liberated Ortona, ending a month remembered in Canadian history as "Bloody December." It was the bloodiest month of the war in the Italian Campaign, with 213 Canadians dead during Christmas alone.

They captured both Ortona and the village of Villa Grande by the end of December. However, general exhaustion among the Allied forces prevented the capture of Orsogna and an advance to Pescara. When harsh winter weather set in, it became clear to the Allied commanders they would make no further progress, so General Alexander called off the offensive.

For the 1st Canadian Division, the December fighting, which began south of the River Moro and ended with the capture of Ortona, had been taxing. It had taken a heavy toll on men and equipment. On 3 January 1944, General Vokes reported to the General Officer Commanding (G.O.C.) 5th Corps that the month-long advance had cost his division 176 officers and 2,163 other ranks dead, wounded or taken prisoner. Of this total, the artillery had borne its proportion of losses. But the battle had moments of glory, too. Officers called for many awards for the heroism of the soldiers involved.

Sergeant Peter Morgan of the 2nd Field Troop A reported to his team that the divisional artillery had spent shells on an unprecedented scale.

"During December, the field batteries fired 3,000 rounds per gun," he reported. "Field guns supporting the 1st Division shot a quarter of a million rounds between 4 and 29 December. That's a lot of bloody shells!"

"We won that battle," said Dave. "Still, It wasn't easy!"

"I wonder how many more battles we will have before we push these Nazis out of Italy," said Jock.

"Many more, by the looks of things," said the sergeant.

The G.O.C. 1st Division summed up the results of the most intense fighting in which the division had yet been engaged. "We smashed the 90th Panzer Grenadier Division and gave the 1st German Parachute Division a mauling it will long remember." [136]

---

[136] Ibid

Brigadier Bruce Matthews, the Commander of the Royal Artillery, wrote in his personal Christmas message to the soldiers under his command. "The 1st Divisional Artillery has set a pace and an example to all other Canadian gunners. We also intend to increase the high-efficiency standard and maintain the excellent spirit of devotion to duty during the coming year.".

"We sure gave it to them Nazi bastards," said Dave!

"Yes, but not enough," said the Full Screw.

"What do you mean, Bomb?" asked Paddy. "How could we have done more?"

"You tell me," the Full Screw said, a reply that angered the rest of the crew. The buddies swore later to find a way of making him pay for his constant negative comments.

"I think you should back off, bombardier," said the sergeant, then turned to his troop. "You guys did an outstanding job."

The Battle of Ortona became known to those who fought it as the "Italian Stalingrad." The chaotic rubble of the bombarded town and the many booby traps used by both sides worsened the deadliness of its close-quarters fighting. War had turned a sleepy seaside resort into a living hell on Earth!

§

Meanwhile, back in Britain, the total evacuation of a zone near Portmahomack in Scotland began on 11 November 1943. They were preparing for a rehearsal of the planned Normandy or

'D-Day' Landings. No mention of these planned landings had leaked out, so there was much speculation as news of the evacuation circulated. Then, on the 16th of November, the complete evacuation of the village of Imber on the Salisbury Plain made way for US troop training. Removal of part of the South Hams of Devon began, too, making way for another rehearsal of the D-Day Landings. More rumours circulated. When the gunners heard these exercises' hints, they discussed them.

"Are we preparing for another invasion?" asked Paddy.

"So, it seems, Paddy," said George. "We may get help from the Yanks to free Europe from the Nazi grip."

"Yeah, and as I've said before, it's time," said Dave. "They are tough bastards, God knows, and we know. The only way to defeat them will be through overwhelming numbers."

"Yup, we've been here for a little over four months, and we've only just reached Ortona, 420 miles from Reggio Calabria," said the sergeant. "We're not even halfway up the boot and still haven't reached Rome. From our experiences over the last few months, we still face many challenges."

"Now that's a lovely thought," said Paddy.

"Isn't it, though?" said George.

"We're up to it, Goddamnit," said Dave.

"I'll second that," said Jock.

"Me too," said Jean. "Pas de problème!"

§

1944: Conquering the Soft Underbelly of Europe

George sent a military issue 1944 New Year's Greeting postcard to his grandparents in Montreal.

Front:

Greetings

From

Italy

Back:

Happy New Year

1944

To Gran & Grandpa

My Love & Kisses, and I hope this card finds you all in good health throughout the new year. Love to my No (1) Sweetheart & Grandpa.

Your Loving Grandson

George xxxx

D6618 Gnr. George
2nd Field Regt. RCA.
CMF CAO

Empire and Tyranny

For the Rutherfords, 1944 began with two new births within days of each other. On 16 January, Peggy gave birth to a boy she named Douglas, but the father, Jack Bass, was away with his unit in the war effort. On 19 January, Beattie gave birth to a girl whom they named Hazel. Hazel's father, Bill Simpson, was in attendance for her delivery since he had connections as a local businessman and serving with the Croydon stretcher service. The Rutherford family was growing, and Joe was a happy, proud, and caring grandfather.

But life in England was still precarious. The Baby Blitz, or "Operation Steinbock" (Capricorn), as the Germans called it, was a strategic bombing campaign by the German Luftwaffe in early 1944. In fact, they launched it in late 1943 in retaliation for the Allied Combined Bomber Offensive that had been gathering momentum against Germany. The Allied air forces were conducting a strategic bombing campaign day and night against German industrial cities. Adolf Hitler then ordered the Luftwaffe to prepare another bombing undertaking against Britain. This offensive served as propaganda value for the German public and domestic consumption. The German exercise ran parallel with the Allied Bomber Command's campaign against Berlin from November 1943 to March 1944, known as the Battle of Berlin. The German Air Fleet 3 assembled 474 bomber planes for their revenge offensive. It aimed at attacks in and around Greater London. In Britain, they called it the Baby Blitz because of the much smaller scale of operations compared to the 1940-41 Blitz. The bombings began in January and ended in May 1944. It achieved little, and the German Luftwaffe lost 329 planes during the five months of operations, an average of 77 per month before they abandoned it.

But Dolly mentioned it to George in a letter while it was on. George became distraught at the thought of Dolly and his six-month-old son being in the sights of the German bombers. He wrote to her immediately, appealing that she should leave London. But she thought she had nowhere to go. In fact, she could have gone north to her relatives on Tyneside. But Dolly didn't want to leave her familiar surroundings and fought against the idea.

"The Jerries are bombing London and Croydon again, for Christ's sake," called George to his buddies one night in camp. "Will they never bloody well stop?"

"Only when we've blasted them to hell, George," said Jock.

"We are busy doing just that," said another.

"It looks as if we still have a long way to go," said George.

"The Jerries are still in France, so when we've finished in Italy, we may have to go there, eh?"

"I've heard a rumour we're getting ready for another major invasion of Europe farther north," said another soldier. "France, maybe?"

"Rumours, rumours, so many rumours," said Jock. "When do we hear the facts, eh?"

"I guess when the big boys are ready," said George.

"Yeah, I suppose so," said Jock. "In the meantime, we have a big enough job right here!"

Full Screw arrived, and I couldn't resist getting in his comments.

"Well, you guys should dig in, work harder, and not just sit around chewing the fat," he said.

"Work at what?" Dave asked him. "We have cleaned and painted the gun and cleaned and looked after the camp. We are not fighting now, so what should we do?"

"Keep fit," said the bombardier. "so you are stronger when we need to fight."

The men just looked at each other and laughed. Full Screw resisted further comments, stomping off to the wild guffaws from the buddies.

"We've got to get rid of that moron," said Dave in disgust.

When the Baby Blitz passed, other senior Luftwaffe commanders were keen to use the German bomber force against the Western Allied invasion fleet. They predicted it would land in northern France in the spring or summer of 1944. Soon enough, the revenge attacks led to attempts to disrupt preparations for the impending Allied invasion, codenamed Operation Overlord. But Steinbock had depleted the offensive power of the Luftwaffe to the extent it could not mount any significant counterattacks when the Allied attack began. As a result, the Baby Blitz was the last large-scale bombing campaign against England using conventional planes. But the Germans had worse plans up their sleeves for England.

§

The Tragedy of Monte Cassino

In Italy, General Sir Harold Alexander's strategy was to force the enemy to commit the most significant number of their divisions when the cross-channel invasion of German-occupied Europe launched. In the six months since they had invaded Sicily, the Allies had been doing just that. After the hard-fought victory at Ortona, Rome was their next primary goal halfway up the Italian Peninsula.

However, to capture Rome, the Allies first had to cross the 'Gustav' and 'Adolf Hitler' lines. These defensive lines originated at the Tyrrhenian Sea coast of Southern Lazio in the west, cutting east inland across the Aurunci Mountains and the Liri Valley. The Allies intended to move along the direct route of the western coastal Via Appia, one of the ancient republic's earliest and most important Roman roads, to take Rome. They intended to outflank Monte Cassino inland but didn't do it fast enough. German forces had occupied Mounts Laziali and Lepini outside Rome along the old Via Latina, from which they rained shells on Anzio, 32 miles south of Rome. The Allies then started an initiative to reach Rome through the inland Liri Valley. This action began with the Battle of Monte Cassino, also known as the Battle for Rome or the Liri Valley Offensive, starting on 17 January. After that fight, the Allies planned to continue up the Liri Valley along Route 6 straight to the Italian capital.

The rugged mountain of Monte Cassino, with its ancient Benedictine monastery rising 1,500 feet above Cassino, dominated Highway 6 and the Liri Valley at its southern entrance. The old Benedictine sanctuary of Monte Cassino was a historic hilltop abbey founded in AD 529 by Saint Benedict of Nursia. It looked out over the village of Cassino below it and the entrances to the Liri and Rapido river valleys. In a protected historic zone, the Germans had left it unoccupied. Despite its excellent potential as an observation post, General Albert Kesselring ordered German units not to include it in their defensive positions because of the 1,400-year-old abbey's historical significance. He informed the Vatican and the Allies to that effect in December 1943. [137] But the Germans had entrenched themselves into the steep slopes below the abbey's walls. And they stood in the way of the Allies' intention to take Rome. Observation from there and from the peaks of several surrounding hills allowed the German defenders to detect Allied

---

[137] Hapgood, David; Richardson, David, *Monte Cassino: The Story of the Most Controversial Battle of World War II* (reprint ed.). Cambridge Mass.: Da Capo, 2002.

movement. They could then aim accurate artillery fire down on the Allies, preventing any northward advance.

The short, fast-flowing Rapido River ran across the Allied line, which rose in the central Apennine Mountains and flowed across the entrance to the Liri Valley through Cassino. The Liri Valley was a peaceful, wide, flat valley with tiny farms and villages. From a promontory overlooking the valley, one could imagine it as a patchwork quilt of various farming fields divided by neat rows of trees acting as hedges. The farm buildings had a red-tiled terracotta "baked earth" roof, a covering invented by the Romans two millennia earlier.

So, with its fortified mountain defences, challenging river crossings and the valley containing the only other route to Rome, Cassino formed a linchpin of the Gustav Line.

The 2nd Field Regiment arrived at the Liri Valley from the elevated ground on its eastern flank. The panorama they looked down onto afforded them another noteworthy sight on their forced tour of Italy. Being February, the patchwork quilt of small farms was not at its best, but it was an impressive vista. Then, they viewed the monumental Monte Cassino with its ancient abbey. It was remarkable, with hundreds of windows and a dome sitting on the summit in the late afternoon sun.

"Look at that," called Jean. "I wonder what it could be."

"Well, we've seen enough forts mounted on hills in this old country," said Jock. "Still, that one beats the lot!"

Empire and Tyranny

The sergeant said, "My map says it's Monte Cassino, with an old abbey on the top."

"I've read about that," said Jean. "It's an ancient Catholic monastery."

"Beautiful," said Jock.

George got the full story from the Major, "It's even more impressive than Saint Joseph's Oratory on Mount Royal in Montreal," said George

"That's for sure, George," said the Major. "It's much older. They built it in the sixth century, and it's the first house of the Benedictine Order, established by Benedict of Nursia himself. His room is in the oldest part of the abbey. There is a magnificent cathedral there too. I guess it is beneath that dome. It has 1,400 years of history and has seen many wars. Napoleon even came here with his army and caused damage to the abbey. Now it's potentially witnessing another."

"Still, these people are so poor," said George. "How did they build such an impressive building?"

"Funny you should ask that, George. I've just been reading about it. Wealthy rivals of the ancient Romans called the Volsci once ruled this region," said the Major. "They were heathens who first built a citadel on the summit of Monte Cassino, but the Romans defeated them in 312 BC. After that, the Roman Empire adopted Christianity. In AD 313, Emperor Constantine issued the Edict of Milan, which accepted Christianity; ten years later, it became the Roman Empire's official religion. The town became the seat of a bishop in the fifth century AD. By the time Benedict arrived in the sixth century AD, the barbarians had sacked the region. But much of that wealth was still here for the Christians to build this abbey. That wealth is long gone now."

"Wow. I didn't know you were so read up on history," said George.

"I love history and studied it at university," said the Major. "So wherever we go on this journey, I read up on the local history. It is interesting and helps me understand these people, including the Germans. Do you know the Germans were the Barbarians who defeated the Romans throughout Europe with the help of a few adversarial locals in the 5th century? And here we are now, fighting the Nazis for Rome."

"Well, it sure is beautiful," said George on the valley, the mountain and the abbey rising before them.

"Magnificent," said the Major. "How long will it stand with the abbey and the Germans blocking the way to Rome? We must take Rome and push the Germans out of Italy."

The Allies made the first assault on Monte Cassino on 17 January 1944. The British X Corps crossed the River Garigliano near the coast but came up against a reinforced German XIV Panzer Corps commanded by General von Senger. X Corps had 4,000 casualties during this first battle, a complete failure.

An attack by the US from 20 to 22 January 1944 became known as the Battle of Rapido River, despite the battle occurring on the Gari River. To break through the German defences of the Winter Line or Gustav Line, Lieutenant-General Mark Clark, commander of the United States Fifth Army, tried to cross the Gari River. He was south of Monte Cassino with two regiments of the US 36th Infantry Division, commanded by Major General Fred Walker. However, General Eberhard Rodt's 15th Panzer Grenadier Division counter-attacked. The Americans suffered very high losses, and after two days of fighting, the survivors retreated across the river. So, this US attack was a failure, too, with the 36th Division losing 2,100 men killed, wounded and missing in 48 hours.

By the 7th of February, a US battalion reached a hill below the Monte Cassino sanctuary. But machine-gun fire from the slopes stopped attempts to capture the mountain. Then, on 11 February, after a 3-day attack on Monastery Hill and Cassino town, the Americans pulled back the US II Corps, tired after two-and-a-half weeks of fighting. They lost 80% of their men in the infantry battalions, with 2,200 casualties. The Allies, by now, realized that defeating the Germans at Monte Cassino would not be a straightforward task.

On 15 February, the Second Battle of Monte Cassino began. 250 Allied bombers dropped 1,400 tons of high explosives on the abbey, one ton for every year of the abbey's existence!

"No," yelled Jean. "Why the hell are they doing that? Are they crazy? Merde!"

"To eliminate the Nazis up there, gunner," yelled the sergeant. "Focus on your job, LaFleur."

"We could knock the Nazis out below the abbey with our guns without destroying the abbey," yelled Jean to the sergeant. "Shit. It has stood for 1,400 years, and we want to destroy it?"

"Mind your business, gunner," said the sergeant. "The generals have made that decision. Who are we to question it?"

Jean became quiet at first while watching the ancient Catholic complex on the summit of Monte Cassino reduced by the American bombs to a mass of smoking rubble. [138] This profane desecration of the old monastery deeply offended him, a devout Catholic.

"Why the hell don't they give us a chance to bomb the shit out of the Jerries below the abbey?" called Dave. "We could do it without destroying that religious building."

"We'll get our chance soon enough, No. 3," said the sergeant.

Pope Pius XII was silent after the attack. But his Cardinal Secretary of State, Luigi Maglione, complained to the senior US diplomat to the Vatican, Harold Tittmann. He said the bombing was "a colossal blunder and a piece of gross stupidity."

---

[138] Manchester, William; Paul Reid (2012). *The Last Lion, Winston Spencer Churchill: Defender of the Realm 1940–1965* (1st ed.). Boston: Little, Brown.

Jean was furious, as was the other Catholic on the team, Paddy.

"A bloody, stupid shame," said Jean. "Why did they have to do that?"

"Because it's wartime, Jean. And we must beat the goddamned Nazis, sitting up there shooting at us," said the sergeant. "It is a shame—a terrible shame. But that's the way of war. Get over it. Blame it on the Nazis, not us."

That was just the start of the struggle for Rome. The Allied officers focussed their attention on the great Abbey of Monte Cassino. In their view, the monastery and its presumed use as a German artillery observation point prevented the breach of the Gustav Line. Fears escalated with the number of casualties, and despite a lack of evidence, it marked the ancient abbey for destruction.

The third battle began on 15 March. It started with another aerial bombardment of another 750 tons of 1,000-pound bombs with delayed action fuses lasting 3.5 hours from 08:30 am. Then, the New Zealanders advanced behind a creeping artillery barrage, firing from 746 artillery pieces, including those of the 2nd Field.

"Right, gunners, raise your hands when you are ready," ordered the Major through their radios as the batteries prepared for the creeping barrage action. George watched from the Jeep as he moved the Major from one gun to another.

Satisfied that they were ready, the Major ordered George to stop where he could see them all. George observed his buddies man their gun. Sergeant Peter Morgan, No. 1, called through each position:

2? Ready Sarge, called Jock;

3? Ready Sarge, called Dave;

4? Ready Sarge, called Paddy;

5? Ready Sarge, called Jean;

6? Ready Sarge, called JJ, the Full Screw bombardier.

The sergeant raised his hand, and the Major noted their readiness.

Then the bombardment started, all guns firing at once, an almighty rolling clap of thunder echoing off the mountains and around the Liri Valley. Immediately after the gun had fired, No. 2 Jock pulled on the breech lever, ejecting the spent shell still smoking from the barrel. Then, No. 4 Paddy instantly passed the next projectile to No. 5 Jean while checking the fuse, while No. 6 Bombardier set the fuse. Jock pushed the round into the breech with the rammer. No. 3 Dave adjusted the sights as required from his wooden seat, then signalled the adjustments to No. 1 Sergeant Peter Morgan, who gave the nod to Dave. Dave had his finger on the trigger to fire the next round. And so it continued for three and a half hours. To keep ahead of the New Zealanders as they moved up the mountain, the No. 1 position adjusted the height of the gun barrel as required.

George watched the entire show in wonder. The team was functioning like a well-practised machine, hour in and hour out, never missing a beat. It impressed him, and the Major also appeared satisfied with their performance. Success depended on taking advantage of the paralyzing effect of the bombing.

On 23 March, General Alexander met with his commanders. They weighed various opinions and options for probable victory, but the fighting had exhausted the Indian and New Zealand divisions. The 4th Indian Division had lost 3,000 men, and the 2nd New Zealand Division had 1,600 men killed, wounded and missing on Monte Cassino. [139] The German defenders had also paid a hefty price. Their War Diary for 23 March noted it left the battalions on the front line with strengths varying between only 40 and 120 men. They had started with 1,000 men each. [140] And the German 1st Parachute Division had taken a mauling but was holding.

Amidst all this lengthy and terrible destruction, spring had arrived in the Liri Valley. Because of the battle activities and wreckage, it was invisible for many of the soldiers battling for Monte Cassino. But it had come just as it always had through the centuries and millennia before this battle. Out of nowhere, poppies sprang from the trodden soil, just as they had in France and Belgium during the First World War. Here and there, almond and cherry trees blossomed, raising the hopes of a fruit harvest

---

[139] Majdalany, Fred, *Cassino: Portrait of a Battle*. London: Longmans, Green, 1957.
[140] Smith, E. D., *The Battles For Monte Cassino*. London: Ian Allan, 1975.

for the hapless inhabitants still surviving in the valley. The first leaves sprouted from the grapes vines the Romans introduced centuries ago. So, during a lull in the fighting, the gunners turned their attention to this transformation.

"Have you noticed the beauty around us guys?" asked Jock. "Look at these poppies here and the tree blossoms. Can you believe it? So many men have died in these fields. And these flowers are suddenly popping up just as they did in WW|. Do you remember the famous poem by Canadian Lieutenant-Colonel John McCrae, another artilleryman?

"*In Flanders fields, the poppies blow,*

Between the crosses, row on row.

"Thank you for that, Jock. You make an excellent point," said Jean. "Spring has arrived! And we are here with our guns, destroying everything in sight, to beat the bloody Nazis!"

"Can you imagine how this valley looks without us here blasting it?" asked George.

"Yeah, with the locals out working in the fields and vineyards," said Paddy. "Including those gorgeous Italian farm girls."

"Always thinking of the girls, Paddy?" said Jean.

"Bloody right, Jean," said Jock. "I just want this battle to end so I can return to Campobasso and Maria. My loins are aching!" To which everyone had a hearty guffaw.

"That's for real. I want to get back to Luciana," said Jock. "I'm in love with that girl."

"Yeah, and not wanting to repeat too often, I want to get back to my Dolly and my son," said George. "Never mind this battle; let's end this bloody war!"

On 5 May, General Alexander issued his operation order for the Allied offensive. It was to be a simultaneous frontal attack by both his armies on the night of 11 May. The British Eighth Army, now under the command of General Montgomery's replacement, General Oliver Leese, must enter the Liri Valley and advance up Highway 6 towards Valmontone. The US Fifth Army on the left was to break through the Aurunci Mountains and drive forward on a parallel axis. On General Leese's right, the British 5th Corps, under the direct command of H.Q. 15th Army Group, was to follow up on the expected German withdrawal. General Clark's forces on the Anzio front were to be ready by D-Day plus four to break out of the bridgehead and join the advance. The pursuit of the enemy north to the Trasimene Line from Rimini to Pisa was to follow the capture of Rome. [141]

By the evening of Thursday, 11 May, everything was ready for the fourth and the ultimate battle for Monte Cassino. Officers and men listened to the inspiring messages from General Leese and General Alexander that came to each unit. Alexander addressed his letter to the "Soldiers of the Allied Armies in Italy." It included the encouraging reminder that "in guns and tanks, we far outnumber the Germans."

---

[141] Ibid

Empire and Tyranny

The intelligence estimates of the number of German guns and nebelwerfers (smoke mortars) that the enemy had to support the infantry defences of the Gustav Line at 400. The British had 1,060 various Eighth Army guns deployed on its front, and the American Fifth Army had 600 weapons in action.

And then it went silent in the valley below Monte Cassino. Everything and everyone was ready. It was a balmy evening as the troops awaited their next big push towards the abbey and beyond. The 2nd Field was again at the ready, the men sitting around in small groups by their guns chatting quietly. They couldn't smoke either.

"I guess we'll blow the shit out of the Nazis tonight," said Jock. "It looks as if we have hundreds of guns out here."

"It sure looks that way," said George. "Things are bloody quiet right now. It's eerie."

A silence had pervaded the valley and surrounding mountains. Nothing stirred on that fateful night, not even the wind.

"Well, it's been long enough, Guys," said Paddy. "It's time we went to Rome!"

Everyone agreed with that sentiment for sure. The Canadians had been in Italy for almost a year of hard marching and battles. They needed a breakthrough.

"Rome, then Paris, and then Berlin, Lads," said Major Walker, who had arrived looking for George. "We will take Europe back from the Nazis soon enough, with your help."

"Yes, Sir, now you're talking!"

Rumours were circulating of a possible new and massive invasion of the European mainland. The men started placing bets. Belgium? Pas de Calais? Dunkirk? Normandy? Brittany? It was anybody's guess. But just the thought of getting more Allied support in Europe filled the Italian Campaign boys with comfort and bravado.

"What about Campobasso?" asked Paddy and Jock without a response.

At 11:00 pm, the massive counter-battery bombardment by the medium and heavy guns of the two Allied armies opened with an earth-shaking crash. The pounding of known or suspected hostile gun sites continued for forty minutes. Then, the program in the 13th Corps' sector switched to a barrage as the two infantry divisions launched their first assault boats in the fast-flowing river. It was a creeping cannonade, lifting 100 yards every six minutes from the guns of seventeen field regiments and two medium batteries. The gun teams of the 2nd Field were again in action. The remaining medium and heavy weapons kept up their efforts against the enemy's guns. [142]

On the morning of 12 May, they heard that the battle was going well, although not as well as they wished. At the end of the first 24 hours of fighting, the 8th Indian Division had made the best gains. Their bridgehead over the Gari was being enlarged with the help of Canadian tanks. On the 13th, most Canadian batteries remained in action, firing various targets on call. These

---

[142] Ibid

included helping to support the gigantic smokescreen designed to block German observers' view in the monastery's ruins. They gave the artillery orders to continue this smoking at a rate of 25,000 rounds a day until they had won the monastery.

Once again, George drove his Major to inspect the operations of each 2nd Field Regiment gun troop. Each of the weapons was firing six shots a minute at full tilt. George moved the Major from one position to the next. The Major leapt out of the Jeep and sidled next to each commander. He asked them whether everything was in order or whether they needed anything. One by one, they assured the Major that everything was in order and they were achieving their goals. Satisfied that this was the case, Major Walker moved on to the next.

The gun of his buddies, A Troop, interested George most as he watched their swift movements for each firing. They maintained their composure and were in high spirits while carrying out their repetitive duties, dressed in nothing but shorts in the heat of the late Italian spring. However, the team was so busy they didn't notice George watching them from behind, but it seemed extra efficient when the Major appeared beside the gun commander, Sergeant Peter Morgan. They were a competent team, executing every practised movement with speed and perfect precision. George felt a warm pride watching his buddies carry out their tasks. But a German barrage was getting closer and closer to their battery. Major Walker had signalled it was time to move to a new location when a shell exploded in a gun position two guns down from the buddies' weapon. Earth, rocks, and other shrapnel flew in every direction, laying a layer of rubble on the entire area, including his buddies' gun crew. Apart from a few scrapes and bruises, the blast injured nobody from A Troop. But when the smoke and dust cleared, they could see that the explosion had wiped out the entire D Troop team. All hell broke out as the Major ordered all detachments to stand down and move their guns at speed to a new position; he had chosen one farther up the hill. The Major also called up a reserve detachment to retrieve the shelled ordnance, which had survived intact. And he ordered a medical unit to recover the bodies of the dead gunners.

Across the entire Allied front, the tempo of the advance hastened. The battered Cassino stronghold was the only part of the Gustav Line still in German possession. That evening, on Kesselring's instructions, the Commander of the German 10th Army, Generaloberst Heinrich von Vietinghoff, gave orders for a general withdrawal to the Hitler Line. General Sir Oliver Leese directed the 1st Canadian Corps to relieve the 8th Indian Division and maintain the advance in the southern half of the valley. The 13th Corps joined the 2nd Polish Corps to isolate Cassino and Monastery Hill. Lt.-Gen. Burns ordered the 1st Canadian Division forward at once. At 1:00 am on the 16th, 1st and 2nd field regiments crossed the Gari to positions in the Liri Appendix. The Liri Appendix was the apex of land enclosed between the confluence of the Liri and Gari rivers, six miles south of Cassino.

In the early hours of 18 May, the British 78th Division and Polish II Corps linked up in the Liri valley two miles west of the town of Cassino. On the Cassino high ground, German forces battered the survivors of the second Polish offensive. "It took time to find men with enough strength to climb the few hundred yards to the summit." [143] A patrol of the 12th Podolian Polish Uhlan Regiment reached the heights and raised a Polish flag over the ruins. The only remnants of the defenders were a group of thirty wounded German soldiers who couldn't move. [144]

The Allies had won the Battle of Monte Cassino. However, the ancient Abbey, founded in 529 by Saint Benedict of Nursia with its 1,400 years of history, lay in total ruin.

American military historian Martin Blumenson summed it up and justified what happened there.

> "The Lombards ravaged it in the sixth century. Saracens pillaged it in the ninth. An earthquake damaged it in the fourteenth. French troops sacked it in the eighteenth. The Americans reduced it to rubble with bombs and shells in the twentieth. To many, the last act of destruction appeared as senseless and wanton as the others. Yet the men who levelled the sanctified walls believed they had

[143] Olson, Lynne; Cloud, Stanley (2003). *A Question of Honour*. Vintage.
[144] Molony, Brigadier C.J.C.; with Flynn, Captain F.C. (R.N.); Davies, Major-General H.L. & Gleave, Group Captain T.P. (2004) [1st. pub. HMSO:1984]. Butler, Sir James, ed. *The Mediterranean and Middle East*, Volume VI: *Victory in the Mediterranean*, Part 1 – 1st April to 4th June 1944. History of the Second World War, United Kingdom Military Series. Revised by Jackson, General Sir William. Uckfield, UK: Naval & Military Press.

compelling reasons. To save soldiers' lives, they felt they had to sacrifice an edifice representing one of the glorious traditions of a civilization they sought to preserve."

As the buddies met that evening, at the end of a long, hard day, talk revolved around the last four months of the Battle of Monte Cassino. Despite their exhaustion, it relieved them that the battle was over and that they were still alive.

"It's been one hell of a fight, Guys," opened George. "Four months we've been here. My God! I watched you in action today. You were amazing! I was much impressed."

"Shit, you can say that again," said Jock. "It was even worse than Ortona, if that's possible."

"What of our poor buddies in D troop on that gun?" asked Paddy. "Goddamned shame that!"

"Yes, they were a good bunch of guys," said George. "One minute, they were alive and doing their job, then snuffed out instantly! Just like that. And it could have happened to us."

"Hell, I was talking to those guys just last night," said Paddy. "I know two from my Montreal days. We worked together."

"Yeah, and even though we've seen a hell of a lot of dead soldiers in these few months, that's the closest to us anyone has ever died," said George.

"Four months, thousands are dead or injured," said Dave. "Thank God we are still alive. But did we beat the Nazis to hell? You're damn right we did!"

"It's a pity the Full Screw wasn't on that gun," said Jean. He seldom spoke out, but the bombardier had pissed him off too.

"Ha. Damn right, Jean," said Dave. "A great goddamned opportunity missed."

"I'm so sorry for the abbey, too," said Paddy, a Catholic. "It would still stand if the Germans hadn't held out there."

"Yeah, it's a bloody shame," said Jean. "They say it was an ancient abbey, a famous historical monument going back over 1,000 years, imagine. Now it's nothing but rock and dust."

"1,400 years old," said Paddy, "Started by Saint Benedict himself, a famous saint after whom they named the Benedictines."

"Yeah, but the Germans were watching everything we were doing from up there," said Jock. "What else could we do?"

Just then, Bombardier Jones appeared out of nowhere and had heard them talking from around a corner. "I'm sorry to have disappointed you, Jean, but I'm still alive," he sneered. "I will be on your ass, you little frog!"

Jean froze. Paddy moved closer to him in case the Full Screw got violent. Dave closed in on his other side.

"If you are on Jean's ass, you will have all of us to deal with," hissed Dave.

Paddy spat out, "Your shit attitude is getting on our nerves."

"Come on, Bomb," taunted Jock. "Make your move."

Then, the sergeant appeared from nowhere and called them out. "Vent your shit on the Germans," he yelled. "Stand down from the bombardier."

Then he turned to JJ and said, "What about you, Bombardier? Stop threatening these guys. What have they done to you? Take your frustrations out on the enemy. I want nothing to interfere with the morale and efficiency of my detachment. We have enough on our plate."

Everyone agreed and realized they had experienced the most brutal battle of their war so far. And it had taken as long to win as the primary campaign on the mainland from Salerno to Ortona to the Liri Valley. This prolonged and fierce struggle and the death of their artillery buddies had taxed their physical and mental strengths. It reinforced their relationships with one another, except for the Full Screw JJ, making their bonds even more robust. These bonds last a lifetime. But they were hell-bent on getting rid of JJ somehow.

§

Crossing the Adolf Hitler Line and Entering Rome

But the Italian Campaign and the World War were far from finished. On 23 May, five days after their victory at Monte Cassino, the next target in the Liri Valley was the Hitler Line. The Adolf Hitler Line was the German defensive line constructed just beyond Monte Cassino. In May 1944, the Germans renamed it the Senger Line on Hitler's insistence, not wanting his name sullied by another defeat. They named it in honour of General von Senger und Etterlin, a general commanding Axis forces in the area. On the same day, the US VI Corps broke out of the Anzio beachhead on the coast 32 miles south of Rome. Everyone's target was now the Italian capital.

At 5:45 am on 23 May, 1,500 Allied artillery pieces started a bombardment. Forty minutes later, the guns paused as close air support made attacks and then resumed as the infantry and armour moved forward. The first day's fighting was intense. 1st Armoured Division lost 100 tanks, and the 3rd Infantry Division suffered 955 casualties, the highest single-day figure for a US division during World War II. German units suffered, too, with the 362nd Infantry Division estimated to have lost 50% of its fighting strength. [145] The Allies broke through the Hitler, or Senger, Line on 24 May and continued their march on Rome.

The Caesar Line outside Rome collapsed on 2 June, and the German 14th Army began a fighting withdrawal from Rome. Hitler, fearing another Battle of Stalingrad, ordered Kesselring that there should be "no defence of Rome."

The Allies captured Rome on 4 June, two days before the Normandy invasion. The Gustav Line, though broken, had slowed the Allied advance for months between December 1943 and June 1944. The battles of Monte Cassino and Anzio alone resulted in 98,000 Allied and 60,000 Axis casualties. However, the Americans missed the opportunity to cut off and destroy

---

[145] Clark, Lloyd, Anzio: *The Friction of War. Italy and the Battle for Rome 1944.* Headline Publishing Group, London, 2006.

most of the German 10th Army, retreating from the Gustav Line between them and the Canadians. The German Tenth Army got away, and in the next few weeks, that same army doubled the Allied casualties farther north. The XIII Corps sent the Canadians through the city without stopping at 3:00 am the following day.

"The capital of the Romans, George," said the Major as they drove past the Colosseum. "Over 2,000 years of history."

"Amazing, Sir," said George. "What is that enormous building?"

"The largest amphitheatre ever built, completed by the Romans in AD 80," said the Major. "It held 50,000 to 80,000 spectators."

"Spectators for what?" asked George, who had never seen such an impressive monument.

"It was an entertainment arena for gladiatorial contests and other public shows such as mock sea battles, animal hunts and executions. They did reenactments of famous battles and dramas based on Roman mythology," said Major Walker.

"Unbelievable," said George. "I suppose it was like our largest sports events today."

"You must return when you can, George, to see the other historical sites of Rome as soon as you can," said the Major.

"That I will, Sir," said George. "That I will."

§

Empire and Tyranny

News of the D-Day Normandy invasion

Word of the Normandy Invasion on 6 June created extensive excitement among the men of the 1st Canadian Division in Italy. They no longer felt alone in the battle for Europe. News of the progress of the invading armies and the German defeats filtered through daily. With the announcements of every Allied victory, cheers went up among the Canadians.

"Now we're cooking," said Dave. "I'm sure the plan is now to put Hitler in a tight grip between the D-Day boys and us."

"Well, we still have a way to go before we can move towards Germany, Dave," said George. "I'm sure that's the plan. It can't come soon enough for me!"

"Don't forget the Soviets," said Paddy. "They are moving towards Germany from the east."

"They'll get their just punishment for this," proclaimed Dave. "We'll string Hitler up with the rest of the Nazis!"

But George was right; they still had a long way to go. And one week after D-Day, news came through of fresh attacks on London and Croydon, thought to be in revenge for the Normandy landings. The unfolding events in northern France pushed the Italian Campaign into the shadows. The 1st Canadian Division, known earlier in England as the "Forgotten Division," would become that again for a while.

§

Empire and Tyranny

News of V-1 Attacks on London & Croydon

"Those bloody Krauts are attacking London and Croydon again," George complained to his buddies one evening. "They are using new horrific flying bombs. My wife and son are in the middle of that bombing again! When will they bloody well stop bombing London?"

On 13 June 1944, a frightening and unfamiliar terror weapon rained from the skies on London and Croydon. Britons called it a flying bomb, a "buzz-bomb," or a "doodlebug" because of the strange intermittent buzzing noise the engine emitted. Its official name was the 'Vergeltungswaffe 1,' or the V-1 for short, meaning 'Revenge Weapon 1.'

Doodlebugs were small rockets that trailed a flame from the engine and had a loud and very distinctive noise from the device when they were flying. It emitted a strange putt-putt sound as with a two-stroke motorbike until the machine cut out, and the flying bomb fell to earth. Every citizen recognized the source of this noise, and they knew from the moment the sound stopped a massive explosion followed somewhere below and close. They knew the V-1s could destroy an entire city block, so their destructive power was mighty.

The first V-1 landed on the East End of London, killing seven people. The Germans launched 8,070 over the next four months, of which 2,300 evaded the defences and fell on Greater London. On Sunday, 18 June, a V-1 made a direct hit on the famous Guards Chapel at Wellington Barracks, near Buckingham Palace. Packed with worshippers, the death toll of 58 civilians and 63 servicemen shook the nation.

Of the London Boroughs, Croydon suffered the most, with properties suffering damage or complete destruction.

"They hit Croydon with more doodlebugs during the Blitz than anywhere else in the country," said George. "They were aiming at London, but they fell short." [146]

The widespread devastation was because of the range of the lateral blast. George developed deep anxiety over these attacks, worried they would kill his young wife and baby son.

His buddies were sympathetic since they, too, had developed relationships in London, Croydon and the surrounding areas.

"As I've said before, it'll end when we finish the bastards off," said Jock.

"Maybe," said George. "In the meantime, my little family is in danger again. And what bothers me is that I'm not there for them. It's eating me."

One day, the Rutherfords were doing their daily routine when they heard another buzz bomb approaching from the southeast. The engine stopped, and panic broke out. Everyone stopped what they were doing.

"It's on its way down," shouted Joe. "Get under the table."

---

[146] Brian Roote, a local historian, as quoted by Chris Baynes in the Sutton and Croydon Guardian, 16th December 2012

Empire and Tyranny

Someone grabbed one-year-old Michael and six-month-old Douglas and threw them under the dining table. The adults followed close behind and then waited in silence, except for the screaming of the terrified kids, for whatever may now happen. They heard a powerful explosion not too far away. It was close enough that they felt the house shake, followed by debris scattering around their neighbourhood and on their roof. Windows shattered from the shock wave, too. Outside, they could see a massive blaze and a cloud of black smoke rising into the sky.

"My God," said Dolly, sobbing. "Why are they bombing us again?"

"Because we are still at war with those Boche," said Joe, using the WW| name for Germans and noticeably shaking. "They won't stop until we've beaten them again."

After that incident, Joe insisted that Mary, Peggy and Dolly take their children to a safer place than Croydon. So they travelled north on 20 July to their aunt, Mary Rutherford's sister, Maggie Burgess Jowsey. She lived at 18 Trinity Street, North Shields, Northumberland, on the other side of the River Tyne from South Shields. Thirty-year-old Molly, unmarried and without children, stayed behind to look after her father. The mothers and their children spent a few weeks in the relative safety of the North East, where Michael celebrated his first birthday. They returned to the dangers of Croydon on 29 August.

A letter from Dolly in North Shields describing the incident horrified George. First, the Baby Blitz and then the V-1s were endangering his young family, and he became anxious about their safety. He had earlier written back, demanding that she stay with Aunt Maggie until the V-1 attacks had ended, but she had already left North Shields when the letter arrived. The danger persisted through the summer until the V-1 blitz ended.

As the jet-engine missiles packed with high explosives arrived in droves over the capital, the V-1s cost the lives of over 6,000 civilians, with another 18,000 injured.

§

R&R in Rome and the Amalfi Coast

During the next two months, various other formations of the British Eighth Army and US Fifth Army forces were fighting their way northward to Florence.

However, the gunner units of the Canadian Corps were recuperating and training. The army stationed them in a military zone well behind enemy lines, southeast of Rome and thirty-seven miles north of Naples in the Campania Region.

They directed the regiments to carry out maintenance on their guns and equipment. However, as far as was consistent with those instructions, they were to have as much rest and recreation as possible. Units dispatched their men for up to five days to Rome, Naples and Pompeii and week-long leaves at big recuperation camps established at Bari and Salerno. Officers enjoyed a brief time of relaxation at Amain and other places on the scenic Sorrento Peninsula. Visits to the "Orange Grove Club," a fun-filled spot in Naples run along American lines, were popular with gunnery officers. They arranged excursions to bathing beaches in Salerno Bay and the Gulf of Gaeta for unit groups. The 11th Army Field Regiment established its regimental rest camp at Torregaveta, on the north-western tip of the Gulf of Naples. "Holiday Inn" was a sizeable house overlooking the sea, providing amenities such as a writing room, games room, and a snack room. The soldiers could enjoy a decent grade of vino. A beach offered complete relaxation with excellent swimming in the constant sunshine of the Mediterranean summer. Those who wanted a change from army rations could climb the stairs of the Albergo at Gavento and eat steaks, chicken, spaghetti, fish and salad to their heart's content.

The Ancient Greeks colonized Campania, and during the Roman era, the region kept its Greco-Roman name as Magna Græcia—Great Greece. The capital city of Campania is Naples. It is a city rich in culture, gastronomy, music, architecture, and ancient archaeological sites such as Pompeii, Herculaneum, Paestum and Velia.

They derived the name of Campania from Latin. The Romans knew the region as Campania Felix, which translates into English as "happy" or "lucky" countryside, and the Romans valued it as a fertile region.

The vibrant natural sights of Campania make it relevant in the tourism industry, particularly on the Amalfi Coast, Mount Vesuvius, and the island of Capri. It was a region that the Canadian boys could explore at length, gathering precious memories.

Apart from Jock and Paddy, who scurried off to Campobasso, George and his buddies first went to Rome, which they had not seen while passing through earlier in the month. George bought a pictorial guidebook. A few pictures showed paintings of the old monuments and more recent photos of the various quarters of the ancient city. On the back of each page was a brief description of each site on the opposite side. The buddies visited the Colosseum, the Vatican with St. Peter's Square, St. Peter's Cathedral and the Apostolic Palace, including the Sistine Chapel. They did the rounds of Rome, including St. Angelo Castle, Piazza Navona, the Basilica of St. Paul, the Monument to St. Francis, and many other magnificent monuments and piazzas. They even saw the Mussolini Forum, where the Duce had officiated over 11,000 sportsmen and sportswomen on its inauguration in 1932.

"The Major explained to me that the Romans had grand spectacles at the Colosseum," said George to his companions. "The gladiators used to fight there and even had war shows, with ships and war machines."

"Sort of like a Military Tattoo, I guess," said Dave.

"For me, my friends, the highlight has been the Vatican," said Jean. "I never ever imagined that I would live to see it. Only the Pope was missing, but I understand that."

"Yeah, Paddy would have enjoyed that too," said George. "Maybe we can convince him to come here someday."

"I doubt it," said Dave. "Unless he can bring the love of his life."

The city drew them into a few cafés, bars and restaurants. The wine and food were inexpensive, very different, and tasty for the men from Montreal. So they felt obliged to experiment with as many pleasures as the friendly waiters could offer them. Dozens of appealing young Italian women greeted them, and apart from George, who abstained, the men arranged dates for later visits. The weather was hot and dry, and the summer days were long, so they could use every hour available. The soldiers of the 1st Canadian Division welcomed this period of R&R after the fierce battles they had experienced on the campaign thus far.

"Man, this is the life," said George as he enjoyed a beer at a sidewalk café. "I just wish I had my bride here with me."

"So, we're not good enough for you, are we?" asked Jean.

"Somehow, you are not quite the same," said George with a laugh, "I guess you must do."

"Let's have one of those pizza meals, like the ones we enjoyed at Campobasso," said Dave.

"Brilliant idea. Waiter," called George, "or whatever they call them here."

"Cameriere," called Jean while gesturing to his mouth. "Buongiorno. Menu, please? I don't know how to say that in Italian. I guess we should learn, eh?"

Mellowed after lunch, the buddies meandered through the streets of Rome, window shopping and admiring the passing smiling girls. Then they stood before a photo studio.

"Let's get our portrait taken," suggested George.

"Outstanding idea," said Dave and Jean, upon which they entered the shop.

The photographer welcomed them and could speak pidgin English.

"Buongiorno, my friends," he said. "What can I do for you today?" As if he didn't know.

"We'd like our portrait taken," said George.

"Bravo. Come over here, per favore. In what posture, sitting or standing? The photographer asked.

Then, George had his portrait taken with a pipe in his mouth against a neutral background. Jean did the same, and Dave had his taken standing with a view of the Amalfi cliffs and the sea in black and white as a backdrop. The photographer then asked them to wait for half an hour while he processed the photos. So, as luck would have it, there was another café next door, where they enjoyed a glass of wine while waiting.

"Guys, at moments like this, this war isn't so bad, is it?" said Jean.

"Nope. Not bad at all," said Dave, raising his glass as a toast.

"Well, maybe not," said George. "I'd rather be back in England with my bride and son."

They later collected a few copies of what they judged to be excellent likenesses of themselves in their casual uniforms, medal ribbons and all. The results delighted them, and they proudly sent the cards home to loved ones.

On other days, the army offered sponsored rides to Naples and the Amalfi Coast. They visited Saracena, where George bought a souvenir postcard of the old Castello Saraceno at Taormina. From the top of Taormina, they could see Mount Etna on the island of Sicily in the distance. They visited the Amalfi Cathedral, a 9th-century Roman Catholic cathedral in the Piazza del Duomo, where George bought another postcard. Another card he purchased was a view of the Amalfi Coast from the Hotel Cappuccini. They toured Naples at length, where George purchased a note with a photo of the Borgo Marinaresco in the historic quarter of Santa Lucia. In Naples, George found a Nazi belt buckle and uniform insignia in a memorabilia shop, which he bought as souvenirs. While the 1st Canadian Division fought at Monte Cassino, the active volcano Mount Vesuvius, a mere five miles from Naples, erupted, showering ash over the Amalfi Coast. That was from 17 to 23 March 1944,

George and his buddies, including Vesuvius and Pompeii, also visited that coast. They marvelled at being below an active volcano, a first for all.

"Look at this, Guys," called George. "Volcanic ash lying around everywhere. I will take some home." He collected a sample of ash, which he stored in a small bottle he found at the side of the road. And that became one of his prized mementoes from Italy. His buddies followed his example and did the same.

"Just so long as we don't get buried in ash like those poor people at Pompeii," said Dave.

This was the last time Vesuvius had a significant eruption. The United States Army Air Force (USAAF) based the 340th Bombardment Group at Pompeii Airfield near Terzigno, Italy, just a few miles from the eastern foot of the volcano. During the explosion, rock fragments and hot ash damaged the control surfaces, the engines, the Plexiglas windscreens and the gun turrets of the 340th's B-25 Mitchell medium bombers. Estimates of destroyed planes ranged from 78 to 88. This exceeds the damage inflicted on the 340th base at Alesani, Corsica, two months later, when the German Luftwaffe destroyed 75 aircraft. While Vesuvius claimed no military fatalities during the 1944 eruption, it killed 26 Italian civilians and displaced 12,000. Most died near Salerno, where heavy ashfall collapsed roofs. Falling volcanic rock killed three in Terzigno. In San Sebastiano, hot ash boiled a water tank, which exploded, killing two children.

The days off in June 1944 were a complete joy for the men of the 2nd Field Regiment. Everywhere they went, the locals greeted them with open arms. Few Italians could speak English or French, the only languages most Montrealers spoke, and none of their group could understand Italian. But they made themselves understood through gestures and expressions and the goodwill of the Italians, who saw the Allies as liberators. And apart from fellow Allied soldiers, there were few tourists. So, they had the Amalfi Coast to themselves! But alas, it ended too soon as leave allotments were over; the war was to restart for the men of the 2nd Field Regiment.

Once the army had suitable areas established for them, units began an active training program, bringing newly arrived recruits up to speed. Field regiments did their practice firing on a 25-pounder range on the shores of the Lago di Matese, southwest of Campobasso. The artillery staff at formation headquarters held study periods, which included a few of the problems encountered in the recent fighting. Regiments moved their guns to Cancello, north of Naples, for calibration supervised by the 1st Survey Regiment's G Troop and the 19th Canadian Meteorological Section. Tank and infantry officers attended course shootings using their respective field artillery regiments and batteries to better appreciate the problems confronting an artillery O.P. officer.

Reveille at 5 am made for a lengthy day. To avoid the oppressive heat of the afternoon, training began early each morning and stopped before midday. After the noon meal, volleyball or softball followed a prolonged siesta. The buddies patronize the unit canteen in the evenings. There, men who had become browned-off from training with no immediate prospect of a return to action vented their frustrations in vino Rosso and robust singing. When the stocks of native champagne or vino ran out, a quick trip into the next town replenished it. There, an obliging storekeeper stepped into a back room and whipped up another brew container in ten minutes. Those gunners with enough energy wandered off to a nearby village not out of bounds to fraternize with the inhabitants and indulged in 'plain and fancy courting'.

Jock and Paddy found their way several times to Campobasso, 57 miles away, where they spent as much time as possible with Luciana and Maria. They were getting earnest about these young ladies, and both were learning basic Italian.

"You guys have been missing the sights," said George one evening.

"True, but you've been missing women," said Jock.

"That's true for me, Jock," said George. "Our other friends have been enjoying the Italian girls of this region, but not always the same ones."

Empire and Tyranny

"I'm in love with this girl Luciana," said Jock, "I might marry her and take her back to Montreal after the war."

"Wow, that's serious," said Dave. "How are you two going to communicate?"

"I've been learning Italian, and she's been learning English," said Jock, "Amore—love; Abbracci e baci—Hugs and Kisses; Bellissimo—lovely; Fare l'amore—making love."

"Fantastic. We've been learning a few words too," said Dave, "Ristorante, Pizza, Spaghetti and Vino."

"Haha, well done," said Paddy. "That's important too!"

"What about you, Paddy," asked George. "Are you planning to marry Maria?"

"I'm not that far yet," said Paddy. "At the rate we're going, it may be a shotgun wedding. She is gorgeous, though, and she has said she wants to see America! She doesn't know Canada differs from America. They all know of America, meaning the US, not Canada. But there's enough time to work that out."

"Latin women make excellent wives," said Jean, "Italians, Spanish, French—wonderful!"

"They want to marry a Canuck or Yank and get to America," said Jock, "to get away from their boring lives here with these mindless farmers."

"Well, I'll tell you, the English girls are special too," said George. "I miss mine so much! It has been a year since I saw my wife and baby boy! You guys are lucky to see your women more often while we're here. I do not know when I'll see mine again. I suppose only when the war has ended. So we better get on with it, ending this war!"

"Canada will get lots of fresh blood once we head home with our war brides and babies," said Dave, "I need to get cracking and find one too."

On 31 July, the 1st Division had news of a special inspection by a distinguished senior officer, "General Collingwood." The visitor turned out to be King George VI.

His Majesty and the Supreme Allied Commander Mediterranean, General Sir Henry Maitland Wilson, came to Italy to decorate Major Mahony of the Westminster Regiment with his Victoria Cross. Mahony was one of only 16 Canadians awarded VCs during WWII. [147] This medal is the highest and most prestigious award, "for gallantry in the face of the enemy," which the army awards to the British and Commonwealth forces. On the same trip, his majesty knighted General Leese.

But JJ didn't show up for the parade. The sergeant asked the detachment whether anybody knew where he was, but nobody did. When he had still not appeared that evening, they declared him AWOL and notified the Military Police, who immediately began a search for the missing bombardier. On the sergeant's recommendation, the MPs questioned the regimental officers and each of the buddies. This revealed only that the bombardier was unpopular. Then soon enough, the Carabinieri

---

[147] Ibid

found the Full Screw's body at the bottom of a cliff near Amalfi. The coroner's report was inconclusive—he had died from head trauma when falling from the cliff, it said. They could draw no other conclusion, such as murder or suicide, so they declared the case an accident, and it was closed. None of the buddies ever discussed the man or his mysterious disappearance. Even the sergeant dropped the topic and found another well-practised bombardier to replace him—Pierre Tremblet from Trois-Rivières, Quebec. Pierre had joined the RCA instead of the Three Rivers Regiment. It was as if JJ had never existed. And the team was more representative of Montreal, with two French-speaking gunners.

And so ended a pleasant and reinvigorating R&R break in the Campania Region.

§

Crossing the Gothic Line, Operation Olive & the Battle of Rimini

On 18 July, the 1st Canadian Corps received orders from the Eighth Army to concentrate in secret near Perugia, Umbria, as a preliminary move towards a return to current operations. Perugia lay in the centre of Italy, 120 miles north of Rome. Two days later, General Burns learned that the Canadian Corps should continue the offensive against the enemy and break through the Gothic Line. The Gothic Line was the last of the German defensive lines.

Empire and Tyranny

The Germans anchored this formidable defensive line, which the Allied planners often referred to as the Pisa-Rimini Line, at Pesaro, 20 miles along the Adriatic coast from Rimini. It crossed the long spine of the Apennines 20 miles north of Florence. [148]

It was Field Marshal Albert Kesselring's last line of defence during the fighting retreat of the German forces in Italy. They were being chased by the Allied Armies commanded by General Sir Harold Alexander.

However, Adolf Hitler was concerned about preparing the Gothic Line. He feared the Allies could use amphibious landings to outflank its defences. To downgrade its importance in the eyes of both friend and foe, he ordered the name, with its historical connotations, changed. Hitler reasoned that if the Allies broke through, they could not use the more impressive title 'Gothic' to magnify their victory claims. In response to this order, Kesselring renamed it the 'Green Line' in June 1944. Not that the name change helped much—it was still the Gothic Line in everybody's mind, just as the Hitler Line had remained another historic defensive line.

By the first week of July 1944, the Allied pursuit west of the Apennines had closed to the enemy's Arezzo Line. The British Eighth Army, including the Canadians, was pushing north up the Tiber Valley from Rome, and the United States Fifth Army was driving northward closer to the sea. At this stage, the advance slowed. By the time Arezzo fell to XIII Corps

---

[148] Ibid

on 16 July, Kesselring had gained ten extra days to complete the defences of the Gothic Line. It was growing stronger daily through the work of hordes of Italian labourers conscripted by Hitler's representative in Italy. Kesselring received 2,000 more German soldiers to help him with his "recruiting."

With over 15,000 slave labourers, the Germans built 2,000 well-fortified machine-gun nests, casemates, bunkers, observation posts and artillery-fighting positions to repel any efforts to breach the Gothic Line. [149] The construction program called for them to protect the east and west coastal sectors with the same anti-tank defences used in the Hitler Line. They erected panther turrets on steel and concrete bases, supplemented by steel shelters and machine-gun posts. They then shielded the entire line with an anti-tank ditch, wire obstacles and extensive minefields. The defenders considered the central region's defences, even those on the mountain fronts, the most inaccessible. They included anti-tank trenches, casemates tunnelled out of the rock, tank gun turrets, and machine-gun pillboxes at every high pass in the Apennines.[150] "Stretching as an armour-toothed belt across Italy's upper thigh, the Gothic Line was the most fortified position the German army had yet thrown into the path of Allied forces." [151] It was Kesselring's last coast-to-coast defence line in Italy.

---

[149] Sterner, C.Douglas. (2008). *Go for Broke*. American Legacy Historical Press.
[150] G.W.L Nicholson, *The Gunners of Canada, The History of the RCA, 1919-1967*, McClelland & Stewart, 1972
[151] Mark Zuehlke, *The Gothic Line: Canada's Month of Hell in World War II Italy*, Douglas & McIntyre, 2003

Empire and Tyranny

Army command instructed units on 14 August to send a quota of gunners to the Corps Artillery to parade for a distinguished visitor the next day. Speculation that the VIP might be Prime Minister Churchill, who they believed to be in the country, proved wrong. It was Lieutenant-General Sir Oliver Leese who came to review the course of the war to date with the Canadians and to lift the curtain on what lay ahead. He praised the Canadian achievements in the campaign and promised that something big was in store for them. Concerning the war in Western Europe, he glanced at his watch and remarked: "You will hear of more landings in France soon." Sure enough, within a few minutes, the radios announced that "Operation Anvil," the Allied landing in southern France in August 1944, had started. They later renamed it "Operation Dragoon." That was where the British Prime Minister was—watching the naval bombardment from the deck of a British destroyer with much enthusiasm. The Army Commander's talk made an impression on the Canadian gunners. It left them with a happy feeling that the general was taking them into his confidence. They now had a better knowledge of future events.[152] The soldiers of the 1st Division received this news with enthusiasm.

"Now we're getting moving," said Dave.

"Yeehaw," said George. "We're moving in on you, Mr Hitler!"

---

[152] G.W.L Nicholson, *The Gunners of Canada, The History of the RCA, 1919-1967*, McClelland & Stewart, 1972

"Yup. That makes three invasions on the move towards Germany in the West," said Paddy. "No stopping us now!"

The US VI Corps landed on the beaches of the Côte d'Azur under the shield of a large naval task force. Several divisions of the French Army 'B' followed it. Close to 600,000 Allied troops landed in this invasion on 15 August 1944, so half the strength of the Normandy landings. 75,000 French Resistance fighters met and supported them.

There were 75,000-100,000 German troops on the beaches opposing them during the landings. But as they progressed inland, another 200,000 German soldiers fought to stop them. The Dragoon invasion resulted in 15,574 American casualties, including 7,301 killed. The French had over 10,000 dead and wounded. However, the war claimed 7,000 German troops' lives, injured 21,000, and captured 131,250, totalling 159,000 losses. The Allies then moved up the Rhone Valley and through Provence towards the Voges Mountains on the southern border between France and Germany. The tide was well and truly turning.

§

Friday, 25 August 1944, was hot, and except for the cicadas, a quiet day for the troops south of Rimini in the Marche, northern Italy. The silence as night fell behind the Canadian front contrasted with the rumble of traffic that had persisted uninterrupted on the earlier nights. The infantry moved forward with stealth under cover of darkness; Princess Patricia's Canadian Light Infantry timed to cross the Metauro River at 10:35 pm. The three other assault battalions passed during the next fifty minutes. They pulled socks over their army boots to muffle their progress, with muttered apologies to the knitters who had fashioned them lovingly. "Don't tell my grandmother," they joked. The leading companies waded into the shallow river three feet deep and groped up to the Via Flaminia. This ancient Roman road, from Rome over the Apennine Mountains to Rimini on the coast of the Adriatic Sea, was where they crouched to await their artillery support. Much to their surprise, they had yet to encounter any Germans. [153]

Troop A of the 2nd Field Regiment RCA was ready. Sergeant Morgan stood at the ready behind the gun, glancing at each of his detachment crew members crouching in the gloom. They had gone through this routine hundreds of times over the past year. George and Major Walker were farther back, waiting and watching in silence in their Jeep for the precise time to start the barrage. They allowed no one to even whisper or light a cigarette.

A single 25-pounder over-eagerly firing a split second early heralded the massive crash of the barrage at one minute to midnight. Behind the hail of steel, the infantry charged up the rising ground unopposed. The Canadians were to occupy the villages of Saltara and Serrungarina and secure their assigned positions on the perimeter of the bridgehead. They learned

---

[153] Ibid

from locals and enemy prisoners that just before the assault, the German 71st Division was pulling back north. They headed to a chain of hills, including the 1,600-foot Monte della Matera, which marked the height of land between the Metauro and Foglia Rivers. Dead Germans on the ground were grim proof of the heavy casualties inflicted on the enemy as artillery fire caught them in the open.

The 2nd Field followed the infantry as they progressed, lobbing the shots over their heads towards the retreating Germans. Troop A executed every movement with reliability and precision. Reports were coming from the Observation Post that they were hitting their mark. They needed no command. Each well-practised man knew and carried out his role as an automaton, the whole detachment operating like a well-oiled and lethal machine. Everything was functioning as it should.

"Keep it up, men," the No. 1 sergeant called as they moved through their well-practised routine.

"We're on it," said No. 6, the bombardier Pierre.

"We're on the mark, Sarge," called No. 3 Dave, the "Layer," back, his finger quivering on the trigger.

"Keep the ammo coming," called No. 5 Jean as he passed each round to No. 4 Paddy, the loader.

"Next round ready, Dave," called No. 2 Jock, the "rammer," as he locked the breech.

That shot fired, and the team ran through their routine again and again and again. The men were oblivious to their surroundings, sweating with only occasional grunts in the heat of that night. They were too busy and consumed with their tasks to appreciate their perfect performance. But the enemy did!

§

25 August 1944 became an important historical day for another Allied victory farther north. The "Liberation of Paris," or "Battle for Paris," was a military action from 19 August 1944 until the German garrison surrendered the French capital on the 25th.

The liberation of Southern France began when the French Forces of the Interior, comprising the French Resistance, staged an uprising against the German garrison. On the night of the 24th, General Philippe Leclerc's 2nd French Armoured Division made their way to Paris and arrived at the Hôtel de Ville just before midnight. The following day, the 25th, the bulk of the 2nd Armoured Division and US 4th Infantry Division entered the city. Dietrich von Choltitz, the German garrison commander and the Paris military governor, surrendered to the French at the Hôtel Meurice, the just-established French headquarters. General Charles de Gaulle arrived to assume control of the city as head of the Provisional Government of the French Republic.

When news of the defeat of the Germans in Paris reached the boys in Italy that day, a tremendous cheer arose from the Allied soldiers in Italy as elsewhere.

"We've taken back Paris," called George from the Jeep where he had heard the news on his radio. "Our troops are heading to the southern German border."

"We'll be there soon, too," shouted Dave while punching his fists into the air.

"Moi aussi," called out Jean. "I want to find me a lovely little French girl or two...."

However, the 1st Canadian Division still had to finish its work in Italy. It resumed its advance towards the Foglia River, the northernmost river of the Marche region of Italy, at 7:30 am on 26 August. They were approaching the top of the boot east of Florence. During that day, the four field regiments under Brigadier Ziegler's command moved across the Metauro River farther south. The artillery could not follow any set fire plan in this battle phase. Instead, they decentralized fire control to make continuous and rapid support available as required by the infantry. They kept field regiments as far forward as the infantry's progress allowed. They chose gun areas from aerial photographs. As soon as the artillery representative with a brigade declared a sector safe, regiments dispatched their recce parties to select gun positions. Despite difficulties of movement over the rough, narrow roads, in many places gapped or blocked by enemy demolitions, regiments got their weapons forward with commendable speed. They completed a move and had their guns in action within two to five hours, leap-frogging ahead two at a time. By the evening of 29 August, the four field regiments had surmounted the heights. They were now on the flats south of the Foglia River. They positioned them to support the deliberate, timed attack on the primary defences of the Gothic Line.

In the 1st Brigade's advance on the right, the 48th Highlanders of Canada ran into trouble when they came up against the last enemy outposts defending the Foglia. The Famous 48th was a distinguished regiment out of Toronto with a lengthy history and the motto Dileas Gu Brath ("Faithful Forever"). Founded in 1891, it fought in the Boer War in South Africa and WWI. Their battle honours read like a history of those two conflicts, battle by battle. But the Germans trapped one of its companies in a few houses early on 28 August. They were coming under small arms and mortar fire from elements of the 4th Parachute Regiment entrenched on Point 146, a hill east of the village of Ginestreto. With the Highlanders was Major Conrad Harrington of the 2nd Field, who would work with the battalion more often than any other artillery officer. The 48th Highlanders had their own particular name for Con Harrington. It originated in an incident on the static Ortona front when higher authority had imposed strict rationing of 25-pounder ammunition. They reported Harrington struggled to dissociate himself from top-level artillery policy.

"Hell," he said. "The men of the 2nd Field are stealing shells and hiding them in barns just in case you footsloggers get into real trouble."

Under intense pressure from the battalion for artillery support, he ordered five more rounds fired, incurring a stern lecture from the rear for wasting shells. From that day until he called in the last projectile for the 4th Highlanders at the war's end, they knew him by the nickname "Five-rounds Harrington."

On Major Walker's call, George drove him to join Major Harrington to give him moral support in this challenging exercise.

"Could you use an extra four eyes, Con?" asked Major Walker.

"Always welcome, GM. As you can see, I have excellent support here," said Harrington while waving his hand towards a group of spotters with him, "I can always use more."

Just then, the enemy opened a relentless and extended barrage creeping towards Harrington and his team.

"Come, Lads, time to move on," commanded the FOO. "We need to get to another unobserved observation spot."

And with that, they gathered up their equipment and threw it into George's Jeep while the Major jumped in for the drive to another observation point. But as he thrust forward, shrapnel struck a gunner in his Jeep. He raced ahead as fast as he could over rough terrain to deposit the FOO and his team at a new observation spot.

"Thanks, George," said Major Harrington, "You had better take our man back to sick bay on the double and the Major back to HQ."

"Aye, aye, Sir," said George as he launched off with the injured man and one other to pick up Major Walker before retreating to HQ.

But a bullet hit the uninjured man as they careened over the rough terrain. He slumped over but held on. But it soon became clear he was losing consciousness as George screeched to a halt outside the field hospital.

"Two injured," yelled George to the orderlies standing there.

"Got it," one of them yelled as he leapt into action.

"This one is serious," the orderly called to other orderlies standing there. "Get us stretchers, fast! And oxygen."

Soon, the injured men and orderlies had disappeared into the hospital, freeing up George to return to the Major.

"How is the injured man?" asked Major Harrington.

So, George explained what happened.

"Well, hopefully, the Germans didn't injure them too badly," said Harrington. "We need them. Oh, and I think your Major Walker is ready to return to HQ."

During that rough day, when the infantry waited for the tanks to reach them, Harrington called in the fire on Point 146. To quote the Highlanders' regimental history, "his guns scored many valuable hits, on those points which harassed the Highlanders from threatening positions in particular." Towards nightfall, a radio intercept betrayed paratroopers were forming up for a counterattack. Divisional headquarters lay on a series of concentrations of field, medium, and heavy guns. That ended the German threat. As reports came of an enemy withdrawal over the Foglia, fire from Canadian guns hit the most likely crossing places. By the morning of the 29th, the Canadian Infantry held the high ground on the nearby bank.

"That was a tough day," said Paddy. "It looks as if we pushed the bastards back."

"Yeah, it was great working with Major Harrington," said Jock, "I liked him."

"Five rounds, Harrington," said Dave. "What about you, George? Looks as if you had a busy day, too."

"I sure did. I'm sorry for that poor bugger that collected a chunk of shrapnel," said George, "Not sure he will make it. And my other passenger collected a German bullet. But they are both in excellent care now. But you guys did well again."

"The new Full Screw did well, too," said Paddy. "It looks as if he's had lots of practice."

They didn't bring JJ up in their discussions for a while, but it was as if his evil spirit was still hovering over them.

On 2 September, on orders from Kesselring's headquarters, the Germans pulled back behind the Conca River in the Marche and Emilia-Romagna regions. Early the following morning, units of the 1st Canadian Brigade crossed the riverbed, dried from the scorching summer. This river was part of the Gothic Line, which the Allies had now breached. They had successfully completed the third phase of operations planned by

General Burns. They had achieved the breakthrough of the Gothic Line with more ease than they had expected, and Phase IV could now begin.

§

"Operation Olive" was the British action led by Lieutenant General Sir Oliver Leese's 8th Army to break through the German defences of the "Gotenstellung" (Gothic Line). It called for the Eighth Army to attack up the Adriatic coast toward Rimini and pull the German reserves from the centre of the country into the battle. Clark's Fifth Army was then to attack the weakened central Apennines north of Florence toward Bologna with the British XIII Corps. The latter was on the right wing of the offensive, fanning toward the coast to create a pincer with the Eighth Army advance. This meant that as a preparatory move, they had to transfer the bulk of the Eighth Army from the centre of Italy to the Adriatic coast. However, it took two valuable weeks before Olive could move against the German 10th and 14th Armies. In the interim, they started a new intelligence deception plan called "Operation Ulster" to convince Kesselring that they had planned to attack the centre.

They have described Operation Olive, including the battle for Rimini, as the most significant battle of materials ever fought in Italy. Over 1,200,000 men took part in the fight. Rimini, a city Allied air raids had hit, had 1,470,000 rounds fired against it by Allied gunners. Lieutenant-General Sir Oliver Leese commented,

"The battle of Rimini was one of the hardest battles of the Eighth Army. The fighting was comparable to El Alamein, Mareth and the Gustav Line (Monte Cassino)."

Just south of Rimini, attached to the 1st Canadian Division, was the 3rd Greek Mountain Brigade commanded by Colonel Thrasyvoulos Tsakalotos. The Greek government was in exile and formed this mountain infantry unit on 1 July 1944 in Lebanon. Near the village of Cattolica, they pushed back two powerful German attacks on 8 and 10 September. On 13 September, the brigade launched a counterattack to take Rimini. The joint armour and infantry of B Squadron, 20th New Zealand Armoured Regiment and 22nd New Zealand Motor Battalion from the 2nd New Zealand Division supported it. The brigade also received help from infantry, mortars, and machine guns belonging to the Canadian Saskatoon Light Infantry (SLI) and the New Zealand 33rd Anti-tank Battery, which had 17-pdr weapons.

Rimini, ten miles up the coast, was the next goal, and the coastal highway offered a likely axis of advance. The battle to oust the Germans from this Rimini Line took three weeks of the bitterest fighting Canadians had experienced in Italy. [154] On the morning of 21 September, the 2nd Greek Battalion reached

---

[154] G.W.L Nicholson, *The Gunners of Canada, The History of the RCA, 1919-1967*, McClelland & Stewart, 1972

the city via the Ausa River and raised the Greek flag on the balcony of the municipal building. At 7:45 am on 21 September, the mayor surrendered the city without conditions to the 3rd Greek Mountain Brigade with an official protocol written in Greek, English and Italian.[155]

The actions of the Greek brigade during the battle earned it the honorific title Rimini Brigade (Ταξιαρχία Ρίμινι).[156]

At the end of Olive, a signal came from the Army Commander to Brigadier Plow, congratulating him on the satisfactory performance of their guns throughout our recent operations. He relayed the message to the Royal Canadian Artillery, New Zealand Artillery and Greek Artillery fighting under his command.

General Leese testified to the effectiveness of the artillery as shown "by the numbers of the enemy found dead and the demoralization of prisoners captured." Later, the Eighth Army News cited the Army's expenditure of ammunition from 8 to 2 September as 1,470,000 rounds, weighing 14,000 tons, of which they fired 1,200,000 shots with 25-pounders.

In the 2nd Field camp, the buddies celebrated another victory over a few beers.

"Guys, that has to be the highlight of our artillery careers," said Dave. "What a battle!"

---

[155] Ibid
[156] https://en.wikipedia.org/wiki/Battle_of_Rimini_(1944)

"One and a half million rounds," said Paddy. "That has to be one of the greatest barrages of the war. Maybe of all time? Unbelievable!"

"We were part of it," said Jean. "Did you watch us, George?"

"I did, guys," said George. "You were fantastic, as always."

"We were exhausted, too," said Jock. "Two full weeks of hard work. Every muscle in my body is aching."

"Surely, we've reached the end of fighting in Italy?" asked George.

"Who knows?" said Jean. "As far as I know, we've only finished one part of northern Italy. But let's hope the war will soon end."

"I'm praying for just that," said George. "I want us to finish the job as soon as possible so I can return to my family."

But the war was far from over, and George soon received disconcerting news from home that caused him more anxiety.

§

News of V-2 Attacks on London & Croydon

Farther north in Europe, London and other cities were again under attack, but this time by a horrific new German weapon—the V-2. The Vergeltungswaffe 2, or V-2, was the world's first long-range guided ballistic missile designed by a team under Wernher von Braun, technical director at the

Peenemünde Army Research Center. The Germans founded this Centre, known as the Heeresversuchsanstalt Peenemünde (HVP) in 1937, as one of five military research centres under the German Army Weapons Office (Heereswaffenamt). With a liquid-propellant rocket engine, they developed the missile as a 'vengeance weapon' for attacking Allied cities as retaliation for the Allied bombings of German towns. By that stage of the war, they had bombed virtually every major German city to a greater or lesser extent. They had suffered between 20% to 80% destruction. The Allies also attacked many smaller towns with industrial facilities.

So, beginning in September 1944, the German military launched the V-2s towards Allied targets, first London and later Antwerp and Liège. [157] British intelligence sent false reports via their Double-Cross System, implying that the rockets were over-shooting their London target by ten to twenty miles. This tactic worked; over half of the V-2s aimed at London landed outside the London Civil Defence Region. [158] Most landed on less-heavily populated areas in Kent because of erroneous recalibration. But Croydon was on the border between Surrey and Kent, so they could hear those explosions and received a few rockets, too. For the rest of the war, British intelligence kept up the ruse. They sent many false reports implying that the missiles were now striking the British capital with massive loss of life.

[157] https://en.wikipedia.org/wiki/V-2_rocket
[158] Jones RV; *Most Secret War*, Hutchinson, 1978

"I can't believe these bloody Jerries are attacking London again," complained George one evening to his buddies. "We thought they were on their knees, but not entirely, it seems."

"Desperate measures in desperate times," said Paddy, "I hear those are serious weapons!"

"Yes. I've heard the V-2 explosions are massive, sometimes wiping out entire city blocks, and the sound of them carried for many miles," said George.

§

Battles in the Romagna

On 11 October, the 1st Canadian Division returned to the line while the 5th Division went into reserve. For three weeks, the Canadians fought in the water-logged Romagna Region, which included the cities of Ravenna, Rimini and San Marino. They breached the formidable defences of the Savio River, but the Germans counter-attacked to throw the Canadians back. Then, the Army withdrew the Canadian Corps into the reserve, where they could recuperate from the ten weeks of continuous fighting and train for the battles ahead. Meanwhile, the 1st Armoured Brigade continued with the Americans and British north of Florence.

For most of November, the Canadian gunners in Italy relaxed while doing maintenance and training. They stayed in billets in Riccione and the Cattolica Naval Barracks on the windswept shore of the Adriatic just south of Rimini. [159] Cattolica started life as a Roman settlement on the Via Flaminia. Later, it was a resting place for pilgrims who travelled the Bologna-Ancona-Rome route to Loreto's sanctuary or St. Peter's in Rome. In 1500, it counted over 20 taverns and inns despite its small permanent population. "Cattolica," wrote the Seaforth Highlanders of Canada war diarist, "was proving, perhaps, the best rest area the battalion had ever enjoyed."

In a region unmarked by war, every gun sub-section had a house to live in, and every Command Post was in an elegant 'casa.' Extras for the mess were plentiful. Chickens and geese abounded, and their owners would let the men have a proper meal for a change. The gunners got on well with the civilian population, who were anti-Fascist. The Partisans of the Italian resistance movement, who were belligerent towards the Germans to the extreme, had organized themselves there. A few Canadians spoke with awe of the Partisan nurses, equipped with first aid kits, Red Cross armbands and a long knife. They also had a Sten gun and a supply of grenades dangling from each belt by their pins.

"Now, those are fearsome women," said Dave. "Equipped to kill, but caring for our wounded too."

---

[159] G.W.L Nicholson, *The Gunners of Canada, The History of the RCA, 1919-1967*, McClelland & Stewart, 1972

"This place is The First Class," said Jean. "We have our own house, which they call a villa, with comfortable beds and clean linen. How's that, eh?"

"We have a private beach," said Paddy with a glint in his eye. "OK, it's November, but the beach isn't that bad on sunny days. The Messerschmitts are a nuisance, but I guess that's the price we must pay to beat them. So far, they have caught none of us on the run off the beach."

"The food is great," said Jock. "How about those nurses? They are something else. But I must say, nowhere near as lovely as my Luciana."

"Or my Maria," said Paddy.

Although the Germans had mined the beach, engineers had cleared paths through the German defensive barriers. They lifted the mines in places so that the soldiers could swim and laze on the soft sand. The Seaforth Highlanders war diarist declared:

"It's an ideal place for swimming. The Adriatic is appealing, the sand's lovely, and the entire district is free of German troops. Every man gets his own villa. Luxury for a day!"

"Watch the minefields, Guys," said George as A-Troop sauntered onto the beach. "This sand is wonderful. And just look at the colour of that sea."

"Yeah, let's soak up some sun and rest while we can," said Paddy. "We'll be back to the grind and war soon enough."

"Right on," said Jock. "Pass the vino."

"I'd rather have some Italian beer," said Dave. "It's grown on me, even though it's not as good as our Canadian brew."

"Yesterday killing and being killed," said the sergeant. "Today, we're lolling on the sand, swimming, and lounging. As you said, Jean, First Class. This is a crazy war."

The gunners of the 2nd Field began the demanding task of restoring their equipment to the condition they were in before the last two months of active use. They stripped, cleaned, and painted their guns. They scoured and overhauled the vehicles and checked their signal equipment. George took advantage of the time to provide his Jeep with thorough service. The batteries took their weapons for calibration at a coastal range south of Bellaria in the province of Rimini. Training began, too, in the gun drill "by the book" and gun-laying practice.

"Just to keep you guys on your toes," said the sergeant.

"Just look at our gun, Sarg," said Jock. "Isn't she a beauty?"

"You've done an impressive job, Guys," the No. 1 sergeant said. "I can't fault you on anything."

And the Major congratulated George for his outstanding job on the Jeep, too.

"From top to bottom, Sir," said George. "I also gave the engine a thorough work over."

"Excellent, Gunner," said the Major. "So, no excuses for breakdowns, eh?"

"No, Sir. There won't be any breakdowns," said George.

At a more elevated level, senior officers and their staff spent much of early November preparing for the Corps Artillery Discussion on artillery orders. This event took place in the Theatre Dante in Riccione on the 10th.

Privilege leaves for Rome and Florence started, too, although the thick snow in the Apennines made the trip across the mountains tedious and dangerous. Lower ranks preferred Rome, where the Canada Club and the rest centre outside the city looked after them. Most officers headed for the famous Hotel Macdonald in Florence. Those not on leave patronized cinemas, clubs and recreation centres organized by the Auxiliary Services in Riccione, Cervia and Urbino. Two detachments of the Canadian Army Show, a musical revue first produced for radio by the Canadian Army, played to large and appreciative audiences. [160] Among the cast were comedians Johnny Wayne and Frank Shuster, who wrote much of the material, and the singers Jimmie Shields and Raymonde Maranda. Geoffrey Waddington conducted the orchestra and chorus. The Canadian Army Radio Show's success resulted in a touring stage version to entertain the troops. It promoted recruitment by enhancing the army's image and aimed to increase the sale of war bonds and bolster civilian morale.

"These people are so pleasant and so generous," said Jean. "They won't allow us to pay for anything."

---

[160] Ibid

"They are so happy we got rid of the Jerries," said Dave while eying a passing Signorina.

"That's so true, Dave," said George. "They've welcomed us everywhere we've been on this tour. They love us, and we love them. And they are such wonderful people!"

"That's for sure," said Jock. "They make us feel so special. It makes it all worthwhile."

Relations with the local inhabitants were friendly in the smaller centres. The Mayor of Fossombrone held an official reception for the officers, which, despite language difficulties, was a grand success "owing to fine pre-war liquors." The following Sunday, the Regiment reciprocated with a musical program in the Officers' Mess. The unit war diary recorded, "The officers and many pleasing chaperoned signorinas enjoyed it. The party ended with the lovely signorinas wending their way homeward—still chaperoned." Members of the Survey Regiment appear to have made better time in Cesenatico, where they used the Queen's Inn for dances. "It went well until the local girls wore out their shoes, fresh ones being unobtainable." [161]

They arranged other festivities, with wine and food, for the gunners. The buddies, including George, took part in these fun activities, and Dave and Jean could start relationships with two signorinas of Fossombrone.

---

[161] Ibid

Empire and Tyranny

But as soon as the Army granted Jock and Paddy leave, they went to Campobasso as always. They endured the 250 miles along the coast and inland to revisit their sweethearts by hitchhiking with military vehicles.

George and his other remaining companions resumed sightseeing, visiting Rimini after the victory. The buddies loved the town, and George collected another two used postcards from a book and antique shop as mementoes. One was of the Templo Malatestiano, and the other was of the Grand Hotel 1908. This majestic and elegant hotel, designed by the South American architect Paolo Somazzi, faced a park on the beachfront. There, George insisted on seeing the sights first. The buddies then spent two pleasant hours at the hotel's sidewalk bar sipping cocktails and munching on delicate canapes while admiring the beach, the Adriatic Sea and the signorinas.

"You know," said Dave. "We would never have seen all these places and sights without a war."

"That's true," said Georg. "I wouldn't have met my Dolly."

"So, the war has been good?" asked Jean. "I don't think so."

"No, definitely not," said Dave. "I'm just saying we would never have seen England, Scotland and Italy without a war. We would never have left Montreal."

"You've got an excellent point there," said Jean. "We could never have afforded such a trip. But we've put our lives on the line for it. What would it have cost if they had killed us? And they can still kill us. This war isn't over yet."

"Well, I'm not planning on getting killed," said George. "That would be too high a price. We are young. We've got our entire lives ahead of us. Let's stay safe and get home together when it's over."

"I'll second that, George," said Dave.

"Ditto," said Jean.

When their Campobasso buddies returned, there was important news. Jock announced he was a married man and expectant father of a half-Italian child together with Luciana.

"Hey, Jock," called George. "Congratulations, times two!"

"I don't believe it, Jock," said Dave. "You're trying to catch up with George here. Well done."

"Félicitations," said Jean. "Some more Latin blood in our small team family will be splendid. And you, Paddy? When are you going to get married, eh?"

"Don't pressure me," said Paddy. "I'm thinking about it."

At that comment, the others roared with laughter.

"Well," said Dave. "You'll have a fatherless child if you don't hurry."

Paddy was still single but was now an expectant father-to-be. Although he was under heavy pressure from her family, he hadn't yet worked up enough courage to marry Maria. He got away with a promise to return and marry her, which appeared to placate the large Italian working-class family for the time being.

These significant events further strengthened the bonds between Jock and Paddy and the others on the team. They now often talked about marriage, children, and the safety of their young wives. How war and women can change fighting men!

Then George got more distressing news from Dave.

"I heard of a terrible V-2 explosion in New Cross on 25 November, George," said Dave. "There were over 160 deaths and 108 injured at Woolworths and neighbouring stores."

"Shit! That's ten miles from East Croydon," cried George, "Bastards! They're driving me crazy!"

This incident and the many others they had heard of drove George into severe anxiety. It worried him that after everything they had gone through in this war, he might not have a family to take home to Canada. He had been slipping into mild depression as the war and its horrors progressed, not because of himself but because of his young family. His buddies had noticed it, and even Major Walker, who knew him well, had watched his driver slip from the ever-cheerful and helpful gunner-driver into a nervous wreck. The Major had even considered having George committed for examination but decided that such drastic action could push him over the brink. Instead, he attempted to give George as much positive news and diversions as possible.

§

The Canadians returned to battle on 1 December 1944 when the Eighth Army made one last try to break through into the Lombardy Plain of Italy. Several Alpine passes converged there, a much-coveted and often invaded region for centuries. They were closing in on complete control of the Italian Peninsula. They fought through to the Senio River in a bloody month of river crossings, which resulted in heavy casualties. There, the Germans, desperate in their resistance, drew reinforcements from their western flank and, aided by the land's weather and lie, stopped the Eighth Army.

§

Christmas 1944

Along the short Senio River, the Canadians settled into their second winter halt of the campaign. The troops had to contend with the bleak Italian winter, which brought fog, rain, and frigid east winds from the Adriatic. This wind dropped a blanket of snow that soon turned the ground to mud. However, there were rectifying factors to help maintain morale. At last, long-service rotation leave to Canada had started; for those who did not yet qualify, the lull in hostilities allowed a generous quota of visits to Rome or Florence. [162]

---

[162] G.W.L Nicholson, *The Gunners of Canada, The History of the RCA, 1919-1967*, McClelland & Stewart, 1972

Empire and Tyranny

Before engaging in the two last operations to tidy up the Corps flanks, Canadian gunners had done as good a job celebrating Christmas as circumstances allowed. Regimental histories and war diaries show the "thoughtfulness" of units in "rescuing turkeys and chickens from the hazards of shellfire." And from all accounts, the region had no shortage of vino. It was a gruelling time for regimental commanders. One anti-tank unit recorded that on Boxing Day, the Commanding Officer "visited every troop by noon, starting at 6 am. He ended up inebriated at the Regimental HQ dinner, having celebrated with most of the 700-odd men under his command." For better observance of Christmas Day, they planned for every man to have 24 hours off duty if possible.

With the knowledge the worst of the fighting in Italy was over, the men were much more relaxed. They sensed that the end of hostilities in Italy was near, and they had an enjoyable Christmas Day, ate well, and drank lots of vino.

"It's been a full year since we celebrated Christmas at Ortona, Guys. Do you remember that?" asked George.

"Remember it?" said Jock. "How could we forget Ortona?"

"My God, we've been through a hell of a year," said Dave. "Ortona, Cassino, Rimini, and the many other battles in which we've taken part. But the Jerries have been through hell, too and are on the run. That's what we have worked so hard to achieve. And I am proud of that and of my minor part in it."

"I couldn't agree with you more, Dave. It's been a marvellous year for me too. I got married and am now a father of a handsome Italian-Canadian boy," said Jock. "We're alive! Alive! After what we've endured. I've heard we will get leave soon, and I can't wait to see them. "

"Hey, that goes for me too," said Paddy, "I'm a father too, but not married yet. But I will fix that on my next leave."

"Hey, Paddy," said George. "That's fantastic news!"

"Rumours are we will end our stay in Italy soon and head to northern Europe to help finish the war," said Dave.

"That's when I hope to see my little English family again," said George. "I can't wait!"

"I can't wait to kill the last bloody Jerry," hissed Dave.

Then something came up they had not yet discussed as a group since the Full Screw JJ had vanished and the police found him dead.

"We lost that shit bombardier near Amalfi, remember?" Dave asked, "I wonder whatever happened to him. I, for one, didn't cry over his end."

"I wonder," pondered George. "Was it murder, suicide or accident? The Carabinieri concluded it was an accident, but JJ was cautious. How could he have fallen off that cliff? But he had lots of enemies within the regiment."

"Slipped on a pile of cow shit?" asked Jock.

"Ha, unlikely," said Paddy, laughing. "No cow goes that near the edge of such a high cliff. They aren't that stupid."

"You may be right, Paddy," said George. "Still, it's a mystery!"

"Yup," said Dave, not the least bit remorseful. "Good riddance and a Merry Christmas! Everybody disliked him, so I suppose anybody could have put him out of his misery!"

The buddies had a Merry Christmas buoyed by the knowledge that the war was approaching its end and they would soon go home. They had experienced many deaths and injuries over the past eighteen months. But the mystery of JJ's death lingered in their thoughts.

On 30 December, Field Marshal Alexander issued orders for the 15th Army Group "to go on the defensive and concentrate on making a genuine success of our Spring Offensive."

A few days later, Joe received a letter from Dolly and more news of the V-2 bombings in Croydon. He passed on the information to his buddies.

"Dolly said one landed in South Croydon and did a lot of damage," he said. "One fell behind Undercliff at the Conduit Lane and Croham Valley Road junction. That was a few days ago, on 29 December, not a mile from the Rutherfords. I've been to Undercliff with Dolly to visit a friend of hers. I hope her friend is alright. Other V-2s have fallen just north of Croydon between Thornton Heath and Bromley and at Elmers End, Beckenham. We bivouacked there earlier in the war, remember? And my father-in-law works at a factory at Elmers

End. I'm worried about Dolly, Michael and the Rutherfords! My father-in-law's shaking is much worse during these massive V-2 attacks. My mother-in-law and the rest of the family are more concerned about him. But true to form, the old boy insists they should not worry."

§

4
The Endgame: January to May 1945

1945 January: Winding Down in Northern Italy

The Royal Canadian Artillery regiments welcomed the New Year with a salvo fired at midnight. Later that first day of 1945, they reported traffic between the messes to be heavier than usual. [163]

The buddies were no exception and took part in the lively New Year celebrations. They made the rounds of the infantry units they had supported over the past year and received a roaring welcome as heroes everywhere. Beer, vino and superior-quality Canadian Rye Whiskey flowed in every mess, and many snacks lined their stomachs. Even before midnight, they were well enough oiled to take part in the singing along the way with enthusiasm.

It disappointed them that there were so few women in the messes. They were nursing sisters and officers, more or less out of bounds for lower ranks. But they celebrated New Year at midnight in grand style with a round of warm and robust hugs among the troops and even a few tears.

After that, the buddies returned to camp and collapsed into their bunks for a good night's rest, but before crashing.

---

[163] G.W.L Nicholson, *The Gunners of Canada, The History of the RCA, 1919-1967*, McClelland & Stewart, 1972

George, Paddy and Jock lingered for a few minutes outside to gather themselves over a parting drink of whiskey.

Paddy asked, "Whatever happened to that shit, JJ?"

"Why do you keep bringing that up, Paddy?" asked Jock.

"Because I want to know," he said.

"Do you think someone pushed him?" asked George. "If so, who?"

"Anybody could have pushed that piece of shit over the edge," said Paddy. "He had enough enemies."

"Enemies in our little group?" asked George.

"Maybe," said Jock. "I didn't do it for sure, but I could have many times."

"I know you guys too well," said George. "I rule both of you out for murder."

"OK, so who then?" asked Paddy.

"Dave, Jean, the sergeant?" asked Jock.

"The sergeant didn't do it either," said George. "He considered JJ a valuable team member, and you know his team was the most important thing in his life!"

"Well, it could have been someone from another team that JJ had pissed off," said Paddy. "Or even someone outside the Regiment we don't know?"

"Whoever," said Jock, slumping to the floor before catching himself, "Or nobody. Maybe he just slipped."

And with that, the buddies surrendered to their bunks.

The Army soon granted the men leave again, and Jock and Paddy hurriedly left for Campobasso. George and his other buddies grabbed this opportunity to revisit Rome, Florence, Rimini, and Ravenna. In Rome, George had another excellent photographic portrait of himself in army uniform. He wore a Canada Voluntary Service Medal ribbon with a metal maple leaf on his chest and held a pipe in his mouth. Two weeks later, he sent his grandparents a postcard of this photo.

Rome, Jan 14/45

This is really me, and Boy, do I look fat. I had a good time and saw all the sights.

Love & kisses

Your loving Grandson George xxxx

At the start of 1945, the Allies had confidence they were entering the "End Game."

Victory in sight, the Allied leaders met from the 4th to the 11th of February 1945 at the Yalta Conference, codenamed the "Argonaut Conference."

It included the heads of government of the United States, the United Kingdom and the Soviet Union. The countries were reprise represented by President Franklin D. Roosevelt, Prime Minister Winston Churchill and Premier Joseph Stalin.

The conference convened in the Livadia Palace, a summer retreat of the last Russian tsar, Nicholas II, and his family in Livadiya near Yalta, Crimea, Soviet Union. They were to discuss Europe's post-war "reorganization." It aimed to shape a post-war peace that provided a plan to give self-determination to the liberated peoples. It was also to discuss and agree upon re-establishing the nations of a war-torn post-Nazi Europe.

In Italy, the 1st Canadian Division held the Senio Line until mid-February; artillery fire remained minimal. Canadian field regiments cut their ammunition allowance to four rounds per gun per day, and each infantry brigade's firing battery registered only defensive fire tasks. They beat off small-scale enemy raids and carried out air bursting over the German lines with rounds filled with propaganda leaflets. [164]

§

On the 10th of February, General Foster took over responsibility for the 27 miles of Canadian front on the Senio River. The Eighth Army, including the 1st Canadian Corps, prepared to "move into Army Group Reserve, to train for operations in the spring."

But the Canadian Corps soon discovered it was the start of "Operation Goldflake." This was the codename for the move to Northwest Europe to join the First Canadian Army. For the

[164] G.W.L Nicholson, *The Gunners of Canada, The History of the RCA, 1919-1967*, McClelland & Stewart, 1972

field gunners, the army had allotted comfortable billets in the 1st Division's campgrounds around Fermo in the middle of Italy. They stayed there for a week, enjoying as much rest as possible within a varied maintenance, training, celebrations, and packing program.

Jock and Paddy got two days' Leave of Absence and hitched rides for the 170 miles to Campobasso to see their sweethearts and children before leaving Italy. Paddy had written to Maria asking her to marry him, and she had agreed, so they planned an Italian wedding for his visit.

They left camp early in the morning, but it had taken them a while to get the first ride in the darkness of that early winter morning. They got a ride with a jolly, rotund Italian farmer who spoke little English but talked and laughed the entire time with them and even offered them his vino. They declined since they needed to be alert at the start of proceedings that evening. They feigned understanding of what the farmer was saying and laughed when he laughed. After ten hours of rides interspersed with quick walks to stretch and relieve themselves, they arrived at Luciana's home in Campobasso. They dressed in their best uniforms, which Luciana had pressed for them. Then they marched as fast as they could, Luciana and the baby in tow, to the Church of San Bartolomeo, a Romanesque limestone building dating back to the 11th century.

Mama and Papa were relieved the wedding was over. The whole family rejoiced, though Paddy suspected some cousins, judging by their attire, might be connected to the Mafia. But Maria assured him later they weren't. Jock was the Best Man at his friend's wedding, so he and his bride were guests of honour.

Maria was at home with her mother, aunts and sisters, dressing for the ceremony. When ready, the ladies led her to the church. They entered the frigid, rough-hewn stone interior with three aisles lined with rows of baseless columns with geometric capitals joined by arches and a wooden ceiling. Maria's father greeted them. Then he led Maria into the church, where the wedding march played. The music included organ, violin, and accordion. The Canadian soldiers stood at attention to the side of the aisle before the altar, not daring to move or risk a sideways glance. And then, the bride, dressed in a simple but gorgeous white wedding dress and veil, sidled up next to her fiancé. Only then did Paddy risk a glance and look into the lovely face of his pregnant bride. Maria gave him a shy smile, then turned to face the priest before them.

The ceremony was brief out of sheer practicality, even though it seemed an eternity to Paddy. As it was a Catholic wedding, the priest conducted it in Latin, which made Paddy comfortable as a Catholic. There was an exchange of rings, and the priest pronounced them man and wife in Italian with his blessing. There was an embrace and a passionate kiss, and their lives in Canada stretched before them. Then, the assembled family and friends broke into a cheer, laughed, and clapped for the couple while congratulating each other for this addition to their extended family.

They then vacated the church with family and friends, showering them with rice, and made their way to Maria's family home. There, the family had prepared a wartime feast and assembled the best wines they could find, augmented by wine brought by their guests. There was another entrance march around the large dining room with the bride and groom at its head. The violin and accordion again accompanied them, and a party began that lasted the entire night.

"Allora, la mia Sposa," said Paddy to his recent wife. "Ti Amo!"

"I love you too," said Maria. "With all my heart!"

"What do you have under that bump?" asked Paddy.

"Un maschietto, my love," she said. "A baby boy."

"What will we call him?" Paddy asked.

"Michelangelo," she said.

"Bravo," said Paddy. "I love that name. And if it's a girl, we will call her Maria."

"Sì, certamente," laughed Paddy's young bride. Then, they danced Italian dances well into the night. When it was over, Maria led Paddy to her house.

"That was a grand wedding," said Paddy to his bride. "Gran matrimonio!"

She nodded with a gigantic smile, kissed him and pushed him into her bedroom.

Before dawn, Maria's father introduced Paddy and Jock to a friendly driver, a relative who had offered to take them back to camp for the price of the fuel. The Canadians then said their goodbyes to everyone and told their wives they'd be seeing them again in Montreal with the help of the Canadian Army. They added that they'd return to Italy often to visit them to calm the parents.

The round trip took up most of the two days. However, they were at least able to see their loved ones for an evening event, the night and an early breakfast before they had to return to base. And that was enough for Paddy to marry a pregnant Maria and enjoy his first Italian celebration.

§

Back at camp, two MPs arrived at the detachment. The Major introduced the MPs, who told the men they were still investigating JJ's death and had more questions for each of them. Despite the hundreds of casualties they had experienced during this war, this one continued to haunt them. One by one, they put the buddies through another grilling.

"When had they seen the bombardier last?"

"What did they believe had happened to him?"

"Were they not surprised that a healthy, fit and sober soldier could slip and fall off a cliff to his death?"

"Where were you when it happened?"

"Who was with you?"

"Was the bombardier murdered, and who do you think could have done it?"

The MPs spent an hour with each team member, except for the new Bombardier Tremblet. They spent less time with him and wanted to know whether he had picked up any suspicious clues. Tremblet said he had picked up chatter amongst a few team members, such as Dave and Jean. He told the MPs he understood they had hated the deceased bombardier and had displayed no remorse at JJ's death.

The buddies heard the MPs had called Dave and Jean into a room together. Then they questioned them at length, asking why the two had "hated the deceased so much." The buddies declared in front of the new bombardier they hated the dead Full Screw because he was so belligerent towards everybody. But they both said they didn't hate him enough to kill him.

So once again, the MPs could draw no definitive conclusions from their questioning, leaving them frustrated again. But they suspected Jean may have been the most likely suspect because of the exchanges between him and Full Screw before they went to Amalfi. But there was no proof, so they had to let it drop. "Just another one of the many unsolved and mysterious deaths of obnoxious individuals in wartime," one of them mumbled to the Major as they left.

§

1945 February: Transfer from Leghorn, Italy, to the Netherlands

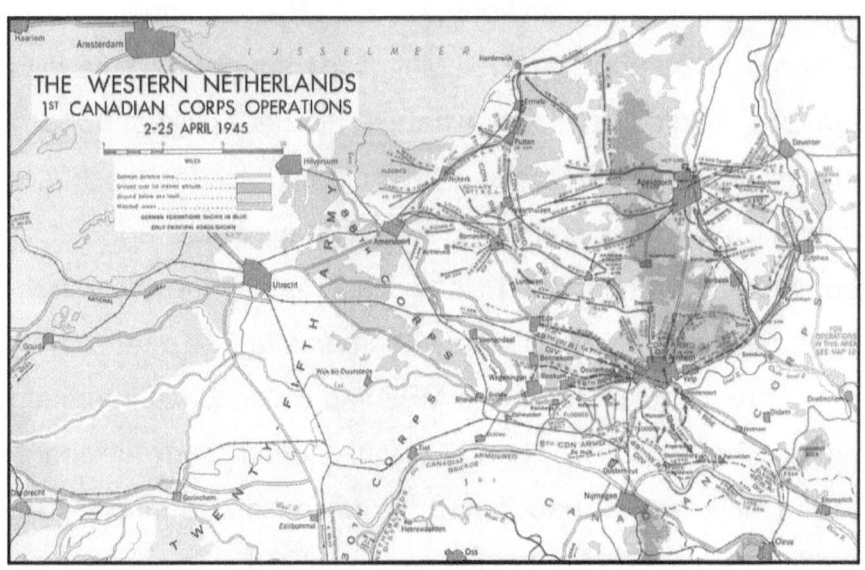

Operation Goldflake

On the 25th of February, rumours of leaving for northern Europe became a reality for the men of the 2nd Field Regiment. On that day, they abandoned the Senio line for the last time. They moved south along the Adriatic coast, then crossed Italy through Tuscany to Livorno south of Pisa. The troops at the time knew it as 'Leghorn,' after a breed of chicken originating in Tuscany. These well-known birds were first exported to North America in 1828 from the Tuscan port city of Livorno. Livorno suffered extensive damage during World War II. Ally bombs preceding the invasion destroyed many historic sites and buildings, including the cathedral and synagogue of Livorno.

The 2nd Field, including George and his buddies, boarded the landing craft on 7 March for Marseille, France, where they disembarked on the 9th. When they arrived in Marseille, the army had strung miles-long convoys of vehicles of the Canadian Corps out along the highway heading north.

Regarding the fighting on the Italian mainland, the Royal Canadian Artillery sustained losses of 35 officers and 296 other ranks killed. The casualties included JJ, plus 115 officers and 1,404 men wounded, and five officers and 17 men taken prisoner. This was nine percent of the total Canadian battle casualties on the Italian peninsula. From the beaches of Pachino to the flood banks of the Senio, Canadian gunners fought in all major phases of the Italian campaign. Their contribution to the successes gained in those operations had been significant. Now, as they prepared to join their comrades in the First Canadian Army in the North West Europe Campaign. They had earned a well-deserved reputation as valued representatives of their arm of the service.

§

For Operation Goldflake in the south of France, it was spring. The almond blossoms bloomed, and the rapeseed fields showed a slight yellow blush. The lavender and artichoke fields were a quilt of distinct shades of green but still without flowers.

"My God, look at this," called Jean. "They are out to cheer us."

Empire and Tyranny

Everywhere, the farmers and their helpers working in the fields, olive groves, and vineyards waved to the Canadian soldiers as they made their way north. Liberated citizens lined the highways, cheering them on, handing them bottles of local wine, bread and cheese, the girls blowing kisses.

"Man, I love this," said Dave. "We have been through hell and back, but such moments make it all worth it."

They had won the fight in Italy, so the troops were celebratory. They were leaving behind a traumatic period of war in Italy and swelling with the pride of a well-done job. And they knew that the war was nearing its end. They were on their way to help deliver the final blow to the Nazis in Northern Europe before going home.

It took five days to complete the 674-mile journey through France to the distribution base at Renaix (Ronse) in East Flanders south of Ghent, Belgium. From this point, dispatchers redirected them to the final battlegrounds of the war. Canadian formations were still arriving from Italy when, on 15 March, General Foulkes' Headquarters became operational again north of Nijmegen. They handled the left wing of the 21st Army Group. This Group comprised the British Second Army, the First Canadian Army, and other supporting units. They completed the transfer of the Canadian artillery from Italy three weeks later.

The buddies were in high spirits. Apart from the distances between them and their Italian sweethearts and acquaintances, they knew it would soon be over, so they could get on with their lives. The waving, cheering people of Italy and France exhilarated them as they made their way north. They were receiving the same reception from the citizens of Belgium.

"Can you believe this, Guys?" asked George. "They love us too! The Italians, the French, the Belgians. They all love us. What a welcome, one after the other. They see us as heroes."

"Mais oui," said Jean, so excited by being somewhere where he could use his own language. "We are their liberators, their rescuers, their sauveteurs! They have had German masters for too long. And now they are free. We have helped them become free!"

Jean was so overcome with the moment's joy that tears welled in his eyes. And he wasn't alone. His buddies surrounding him, bursting with pride and emotion, cheered, "Now they are free."

"It's not over yet," said Sergeant Morgan in his usual seriousness, devoid of emotion. "We haven't finished the job. There's still the Netherlands to liberate!"

"Yeah, and Germany to invade and punish," said Dave, rubbing his hands together. "I can't wait to see their bloody faces and look into their eyes when we get there and blow their heads off in their own country!"

§

Empire and Tyranny

The Allies in North-West Europe

In the last months of WWII, they gave Canadian forces the prestigious and deadly task of liberating the Netherlands from Nazi occupation. British, Canadian and American troops first entered the southern Netherlands in early September 1944, three months after the D-Day landings in Normandy. In mid-September, the Allies launched Operation Market Garden, a massive campaign to secure bridges across the Maas, Waal and Rhine rivers. Allied forces launched a massive airborne assault on the Dutch town of Arnhem, hoping for a quick route into Germany by crossing the Rhine River there. But the Arnhem attack failed and delayed the Allied advance. [165] Then, Operation Market Garden was unsuccessful because of poor intelligence, leaving most of the Netherlands under further German control.

Many Allied units reinforced the First Canadian Army in North West Europe. For the first time in history, two Canadian army corps, the 1st and 2nd Canadian Corps, fought together. The 1st Canadian Division was part of the 1st Canadian Corps, and the 2nd Field Regiment, RCA, was still part of the 1st Canadian Division. With an international strength of over 450,000 men, the 'First Canadians,' as they became known, had become the most extensive army ever commanded by a Canadian officer. [166]

---

[165] http://www.thecanadianencyclopedia.ca/en/article/*liberation-of-holland/*
[166] http://www.thecanadianencyclopedia.ca/en/article/*liberation-of-holland/*

As the Allies looked for another way into Germany, they needed a large harbour to ship supplies to their advancing armies. The Allies had liberated the Belgian city of Antwerp, one of Europe's biggest ports. However, the Germans still held the 45-mile-long estuary of the Scheldt River, which connected Antwerp to the North Sea. They also assigned the First Canadian Army to rid the Scheldt of enemy forces. From September 1944 to April 1945, the First Canadian Army fought the desperate German troops on the Scheldt estuary, opening the port of Antwerp for Allied use. [167] They had spent the winter patrolling its section of the front line in the Netherlands and France—skirmishing with the enemy.

The American forces in Belgium fought against Germany's surprise attack from the east into the Ardennes Forest, a forested region extending into Luxembourg, France and Germany. This decisive battle from 16 December 1944 to 25 January 1945 became known as the 'Battle of the Bulge.' The German counterattack created a salient as they pushed back into Belgium. It cost the Americans 89,500 casualties, including 19,000 killed, 62,500 wounded and 23,500 captured or missing. The Germans destroyed 733 US tanks, tank destroyers, and assault guns, and the Americans lost over 1,000 planes in this last desperate German attack. But the Yanks had won the fight. Most importantly, it depleted the

---

[167] Ibid

German resources on the Western Front. They wiped out the last German army reserves, destroyed the Luftwaffe, and pushed back the remaining German forces to defend the Siegfried Line along their country's border. [168]

In February 1945, the Allied advance in northwest Europe resumed, with a massive offensive to drive the enemy back across the Rhine River. [169] They fought the Battle of the Rhineland, as it became known, from 8 February to 10 March 1945. The First Canadian Army, including the British XXX Corps under their command and the US Ninth Army, forced the Germans back to the Rhine River. The Canadians attacked over the flooded Rhine plain from 8 February to 11 March. This fight became known as 'Operation Veritable,' or the Battle of the Reichswald. In the second phase, from 26 February to 10 March, known as "Operation Blockbuster," the Canadians fought against stubborn opposition through the Hochwald Forest to Uedem, Germany. This fight became known as the Battle of the Hochwald Gap, where the Germans defended German territory.

Poor weather didn't allow Allied tactical air support throughout the month, while mud often immobilized their armoured forces. But they cleared the West Bank of the Rhine as far south as Düsseldorf in bitter fighting. Allied casualties totalled 23,000, including 5,300 Canadians. The Germans lost

---

[168] https://en.wikipedia.org/wiki/Battle_of_the_Bulge#Result
[169] http://www.thecanadianencyclopedia.ca/en/article/*liberation-of-holland*/

90,000 men, including 52,000 taken prisoner. Many of the German 'men' were boys as young as twelve. They either volunteered or were "recruited" to protect the Fatherland. By 23 March 1945, the Allies covered the entire 300 miles of the west bank of the Rhine. They stood ready to cross the river and attack Germany from Strasbourg, France, in the south to Nijmegen, Netherlands, in the north.

Field Marshal Montgomery concluded his message to the officers and men of the 21st Army Group a few hours before "Operation Plunder" began on the evening of 23 March:

"May the Lord mighty in battle give us the victory in this our latest undertaking, as He has done in all our battles since we landed in Normandy on D-Day." [170]

A 20-mile-wide assault, spearheaded by the US Ninth Army (right flank) and the Second British Army (left flank), crossed the river. The attack stretched downstream from Rheinberg toward Duisburg and Düsseldorf. The First Canadian Army held the Rhine and Maas/Meuse River line from Emmerich west to the sea. They also had to secure the Nijmegen bridgehead over the Waal River.

As other Allied armies crossed the Rhine into Germany, the First Canadian Army removed German forces in the rest of the Netherlands. The broken roads, bridges, and other infrastructure destroyed by the fleeing Germans slowed the

---

[170] G.W.L Nicholson, *The Gunners of Canada, The History of the RCA, 1919-1967*, McClelland & Stewart, 1972

Canadians, who faced hard fighting in some areas. The Nazi army blew up a few dykes in the western Netherlands, too, flooding vast areas of the countryside.

The Dutch again greeted Canadians as heroes as they liberated smaller towns and major cities, including Amsterdam, Rotterdam, and The Hague. Millions of Dutch had suffered during the harsh 'hunger winter' of 1945. Canadian troops facilitated food, fuel, and other aid supplies to a population to avoid starvation, so they were heroes to the Dutch.

§

George Gets Marital Leave

By early April, when the 2nd Field arrived in the Netherlands, the battle for the Netherlands was all but finished. Events of the war were drawing to a close. The 2nd Field was not needed in a few of the worst battles in April. So, Major Walker gave George permission to take marital leave on the 6th. He crossed the channel on a landing craft made available for the troops to visit Britain. He then took a train to Croydon, where his wife and toddler son were waiting for him.

A soldier's first wartime homecoming to his young bride and infant son, after two years apart, is difficult to describe. George took the train from London, Victoria Station, to East Croydon. Dolly and Michael waited for him at the station. He couldn't believe his eyes. Dolly was as lovely as he remembered her, but she had grown into a genuine woman and was no longer the innocent teenage girl he had once known. But Michael, dressed in his finery for the occasion, his locks of bleached blonde hair waving in the breeze flowing through the station, his son! George rushed to them, dropped his bag on the platform and, throwing his arms around them, gave his wife a long and passionate kiss. He then stood back and laughed with joy at the sight of his son while looking into the child's eyes. This commotion was too much for a child not yet two years old, and he burst into tears. "Who was this strange man? What was he doing to his mother? Why is he laughing so loud at me?" No! It was too weird and frightening for the child!

Dolly calmed him and gestured to George that he had other familiar faces waiting for him. He turned to see Joe, Mary, Molly, Peggy (with Douglas), Beattie and Bill (with Hazel), and Violet and Trevor (with Brian and Sally). John and Mabel were there with their four children, too. "Wow, the entire family is here to meet me?" With that, there were more excited greetings and hugs. Then, they all left the station together and headed to 75 Cedar Road, a short walk away.

On their arrival, the ladies, except Dolly, rushed to the kitchen to prepare tea. It was a Saturday, but their employers had given everyone the afternoon off to welcome their returning Canadian soldier. And despite not being a Sunday, Mary and her daughters had prepared a high tea. They sat to enjoy a rare occasion and celebration, then questioned George about his experiences in Italy.

"Yes, I'll take you through that," said George. "First, I want to know you are OK after the terrible bombing you had to suffer."

"Yes, we've had a few frightening moments," said Bill. "It has been harrowing, but we're safe and sound now."

Bill was a businessperson and always matter-of-fact in his communications. But emotion filled him as he described the worst bombings nearest them. He also told of the V-1 and V-2 attacks that levelled parts of Croydon. His stretcher team had conveyed many injured from the bomb sites to ambulances through those attacks. The ladies piped in, mentioning friends they had lost and other pertinent information, the while making sure George had enough tea and cake. Yes, cake! How they had done it, he dared not ask. But it was such a wonderful homecoming.

"We once had to throw Michael and Douglas under the dining table when we heard a doodlebug engine cut out," said Dolly.

"Yes, we didn't impress the boys," said Peggy, laughing. "Still, you can't be too cautious with doodlebugs!"

"You know, we heard of the V-1s and V-2s in Italy, and it terrified me that something horrible could happen to you," said George. "I'm so glad that everyone is OK."

Empire and Tyranny

"We are so thrilled that you have made it this far, George," said John. "It must have been far worse where you have been!"

"Yes, it was horrific at times," said George. "At Ortona, Monte Cassino and Rimini in particular, the fighting was severe. It killed or injured so many of our men. I was lucky. A shell landed a few feet from where I had parked my Jeep once. It killed the entire crew of a 25-pounder gun, but the rest of us were OK, thank God. That was the closest I came to meeting the Maker."

"It has been a terrible war," said Beattie. "We have the Germans to thank for that."

"Yes," said George. "We are on their doorstep now, and they are on the run. We will soon end this war as we did the last."

It filled Dolly with admiration and love for her warrior man in uniform, home from battle and looking handsome and mature. They couldn't take their eyes off each other. The children were playing in the backyard under the watchful eyes of their guardian, Aunt Molly. Soon enough, John, Violet, Beattie, and their families had left, and George and Dolly were alone. Dolly told him the family had arranged a bedroom for them alone for the few nights he was there, much to George's delight.

George then spent an enjoyable few days making up for lost time with Dolly, who had taken leave from the factory where she worked. He also had time with his son, who got to know his father. It was a sunny April, so George and Dolly spent much time in Shirley Hills with their son.

"He's a grand little lad, Dolly," said George one day.

"He is, George," she said. "Smart too and talking." They both decided that Michael should say 'Daddy' before George returned to his regiment.

George elaborated on his thinking on their life in Canada. Over the past two years in Italy, he had laid out his plans for how he wanted to live when they returned to Montreal. As George had told her, his goal was to own his own trucking business one day. Sure, he couldn't do that right away. He needed to work for somebody else first but wanted to start his company as soon as possible. Dolly found this thought exciting. "Bill wants to do the same," she told him. "As a real estate agency."

"I went to the Canadian Army headquarters, darling," she said. "They sent me to the Canadian Wives' Bureau to arrange for our trip to Canada. So I registered with them, and they told me everything was ready to move when the war ended. They told me I must prepare myself to leave at a moment's notice!"

"Good," said George. "It's still too dangerous now because of the German U-boats. But as soon as the war is over, it should be OK. I have written to my grandmother and Aunt Bea in Montreal, and they have told me that even if I come later, they will look after you and Michael." That put Dolly's mind at rest.

One day during the week, they travelled by train to London to visit Uncle Ernie and Auntie Nellie and enjoy the city's sights. The Jenkins had volunteered to be Michael's godparents, so seeing them was essential so they could meet their godson. Michael loved the train ride and the bus rides through London. Auntie Nellie cooked a superb meal for them, and they spent a pleasant afternoon walking around Kensington and Hyde Park.

But the week was over too soon, and George had to return to his regiment. He left on Saturday to make sure he got there by Sunday, but before departure, he gave Dolly his present for her twentieth birthday on 19 April. George said his goodbyes to everyone and went to the East Croydon station with Dolly and Michael, who, relaxed by now with his father, threw his arms around him with a "Daddy" as they said their goodbyes. "My darling, the next time we see each other will be in Montreal," said George as he mounted the train. "It won't be long now. How exciting is that?"

As George returned to his regiment on 15 April, WWII in Europe was drawing to a close!

§

They Solve JJ's Murder Mystery

When George got back with his buddies, they greeted him as always.

"Welcome back, George, you lucky bugger," called Paddy. "How was your leave?"

"Fantastic, Paddy," said George. "I had a wonderful week with my gorgeous wife. And my son called me 'Daddy'!"

"Oh, I'm so glad for you," Paddy said. "Have you heard the news?"

"The big news in camp is on what is happening in the German capital," said Jock before George could answer.

"The Russians have surrounded Berlin, George," called Paddy. "We've numbered Mr Hitler's days."

"It's about bloody time, too," said George. "We are pressuring the Germans from the west, and the Russians are doing the same from the east. The vice is closing on those bloody Nazis, and the war must soon end."

"It's only a matter of days now," said Jock. "Oh, and the Major told us that the police in Italy have arrested a woman in Amalfi for JJ's death."

"What?" said George. "Tell me more."

"Well," said Paddy, "they found out that JJ was seeing a woman in Amalfi."

"No. JJ seeing a woman?" said George. "She must have been a tough cookie to put up with that man."

"Yeah, well, the police found a witness who saw them arguing on the cliffs, and the witness saw her push him over the edge."

"Pushed him over the cliffs?" asked George in shock. "How many others wanted to do just that, including us?"

"Yup," said Paddy. "He met his match at last—with a woman. Incredible! And that woman is now in jail in Amalfi awaiting trial."

§

1945 May: Victory in Europe

Days later, the men on the Western Front heard the news about Benito Mussolini's execution.

"They got that Italian Fascist at last," said Paddy. "Maybe now Italy can relax and recover from this insane war. But what happened?"

"I've heard the Partisans executed him in the village of Giulino di Mezzegra in northern Italy on 28 April," said Dave. "The people strung him and his girlfriend by their feet in a village square."

"Hurrah," cheered Jock. "One big nasty guy dead, and the Russians are closing in on the other!"

Two days later, the world heard the news of Hitler's death.

"The Führer shot himself on 30 April 1945 in his Führerbunker in Berlin," said Dave. "His wife Eva Braun committed suicide before him by taking cyanide."

"Well, Guys, that's it. Number one has fallen," said George. "First Mussolini and now Hitler. So, let's now wrap up this bloody war."

"Hey, we're with you on that," said Paddy. "Let's finish the job and go home."

For the artillery of the 1st Canadian Division in the western Netherlands, active operations had stopped by the third week in April, at the end of the drive westward from the River IJssel to the Grebbe Line. As with the rest of the formations under the command of the 1st Canadian Corps, they marked time and enjoyed a period of comparative ease and relaxation as they waited for hostilities to end. The army concentrated units of the 1st Divisional Artillery around Barneveld, nine miles east of Amersfoort.

As boredom set in among the buddies, the dominant topic of conversation in the messes was the "good old days with the 8th Army in Italy."

"I can't believe that it's over," said George.

"Yup, nothing left except to go home," said Paddy.

"Home for you Guys," said Dave. "I'm not ready for that yet. I think I might hang out here for a while longer. Who knows what I'll find out there in peacetime?"

"Agreed," said Jean. "I'm not ready to go back to Canada just yet. But I might like to go back to Italy."

"I can't blame you for that," said Jock. "You've got to love those Italian girls. But mine will be on her way to Canada soon."

"I'm proud of what we achieved in Italy," said Paddy. "That was one hell of a fight, but we had magnificent times there too."

On 28 April, a truce went into effect to allow shipments of food for the starving civilians to move through the German lines. The Corps Commander Royal Artillery (C.C.R.A.), Brigadier H. A. Sparling, declared a policy of no firing except for defence. On 2 May, the 2nd Field Regiment delivered one last retaliatory regimental salvo. Those were the last shots fired in anger by the 2nd Field in WWII.

At last, the period of impatient waiting ended. On 2 May, word of the mass capitulation of the remaining German forces in Italy arrived. At 6:30 pm on 4 May, a German delegation at Field Marshal Montgomery's headquarters signed an "Instrument of Surrender" covering German armed forces in the Netherlands, north-west Germany, and Denmark, to take effect from 8 am the next day.

"They persuaded me to drink champagne at dinner tonight," the abstemious 21st Army Group Commander later confessed to Field Marshal Sir Alan Brooke.

From General Crerar's headquarters at Delden, they relayed notification of the end of hostilities to every formation of the First Canadian Army. The Supreme Allied Commander accepted the capitulation of German forces on 7 May, and they ratified the surrender in Berlin just before midnight on the 8th.

Over 7,600 Canadian soldiers, sailors and airmen died fighting in the Netherlands' last days of the war. They buried them in official war cemeteries across the country. Groesbeek Canadian War Cemetery, the largest near Nijmegen, holds the graves of over 2,300 Canadians.

The Dutch remembered the Canadians fondly as liberators and saviours who rescued millions from sickness and starvation in 1945. The joyous "Canadian summer" that followed forged deep and long-lasting bonds of friendship between the two countries. Every year since the war, the Netherlands has sent thousands of tulips to Ottawa to appreciate Canada's sacrifice. Canada provided a safe harbour for the Dutch royal family, who lived in exile in Canada during the war. The Dutch celebrate the Canadian-Dutch bond every summer during the Nijmegen Marches, an annual international military marching competition. During this event, they remember the liberation of the Netherlands by Canadian soldiers with warmth and gratitude.

For the beleaguered people of Europe, Britain and the Commonwealth of Nations, a great sigh of relief went up on 8 May 1945. They could go home, reconstruct their homes or rebuild their lives on the strengths that had flowed from this grand victory and the end of another horrific war.

Empire and Tyranny

The victorious nations occupied Germany and divided it into sectors governed by each of the Allies in Europe: the British, Canadian, American, French and Soviet "Zones." The Allied powers occupied the German Capital of Berlin and subdivided the city into four sectors. General Eisenhower became the "Governor of the American Zone of Occupied Germany" from May 1945 to November, then became the 16th Chief of Staff of the American Army from November 1945.

There was now only one overwhelming need by survivors of the conflict, whether as combatants or displaced civilians.

"Let's go home and find peace!"

§

Conclusion

The War Brides Migrate to New Pastures

On 10 May 1945, two days after VE Day, Dolly and her infant son began their journey to George's country of birth, Canada. The authorities contacted Dolly even before VE Day. They issued her a Canadian Travel Certificate (No. 6301 dated 3 April), valid for a single journey to Canada directly or via the United States of America. The Passport and Permit Office stamped her passport with Exit Permit No. 155239x - Valid for departure before 10 July 1945 and for one journey only. The Foreign Office counter-stamped it on 10 April. Everything was in place. Then, on 8 May, she received a telegram confirming when and where she and her child should report for emigration within two days.

Dolly was not alone. Close to 48,000 British war brides sailed to Canada, accompanied by 22,000 children at the war's end. Since the Canadian Army had stationed most Canadian forces in Britain from 1939, 94% of the war brides arriving in Canada were British. But another 3,000 war brides came from the Netherlands, Belgium, Italy, and France. Most Canadian war brides landed at Pier 21 in Halifax, Nova Scotia, on troop and hospital ships such as the Britannic, Queen Mary, Lady Nelson, Letitia, Mauretania, and Île de France. Pier 21 was the Canadian equivalent of the American Ellis Island from 1928 onwards. There, they welcomed and processed over one million immigrants to Canada during the age of steamship travel to the Americas.

Since most Canadian servicemen lived in Britain during the war, many of their young families had forgotten that, in time, they were to leave with their husbands. There were heart-wrenching scenes as women said goodbye to their old-world families. In Dolly's case, the entire Rutherford family turned up for her departure. She left Croydon by train, compliments of the Army, and arranged by the Canadian Wives' Bureau, arriving the next day at Liverpool. There, they embarked on R.M.S. Britannic, the ship for the voyage to Canada on 11 May. Dolly and Michael sailed The First Class, Deck A, Cabin A 27, berths 5 and 6. They arrived in Halifax at Pier 21, where the Canadian Immigration Agency stamped them into Canada on 23 May.

Railway passenger platforms on both sides of the Pier 21 annexe served five long tracks to accommodate passenger and express trains for departure to the rest of Canada. Dolly and Michael embarked on a train to Montreal the same day they arrived in Halifax. George's Montreal family met them at Montreal's C.N.R. Central Station. There, she met her husband's grandmother, Sarah, step-grandfather William Jenkins, aunt Bea Martin, Sarah's daughter, and her husband, John Martin, with their three children, Joan, Beverly and Fred.

At first, Dolly and Michael lived with Aunt Bea, Uncle John, and their children at 3359 Wellington Street, Verdun. A few days after her arrival, she visited George's grandmother,

Sarah and grandfather, Bill, at 3884 Evelyn Street in Verdun, within walking distance of the Martins' apartment. It was a small apartment, having less space than 75 Cedar Road, but George's grandparents had offered to leave so he could move in with his budding family. She saw that 3884 Evelyn Street was adequate for their little family. When George returned from Europe, his growing family took over the Evelyn Street apartment and began their new lives there. But that's another story.

§

Victory Celebrations

Back in North West Europe and throughout the Canadian artillery formations, it was natural that the war's end should call for special celebrations. VE Day had been a series of festive welcomes for those units on the march on 8 May. The citizens hailed them as heroes in every Dutch village they passed through. On the evening of VE Day, 8 May 1945, they celebrated the long-awaited event in time-honoured fashion in headquarters and the regimental messes throughout Europe.

In the following days, the Dutch people expressed their joy at liberation by staging dozens of festivities to entertain the Canadian troops, whose partying stamina they put through rigorous tests. "The endless rounds of celebrations," recorded the historian of HQ RCA 1st Canadian Corps, "left everyone with fatigue and languor explicable only by the long separation from such peacetime activities."

"Man, I'm battling to keep up with all this partying," said George.

"Yeah, me too," said Paddy. "What the hell. We've suffered long enough. It's time to celebrate our victory and party, party, party."

"Yup. Soon enough, it will all be over," said Jock. "We'll be back on our old grind back in Canada."

"You are right, Jock, but I'm not returning to the old grind. I'm excited about working towards starting my company in Montreal," said George.

As the enormous task of repatriating the Canadian Army Overseas began, the Army supported the morale of over 280,000 soldiers serving in the UK or Europe on VE Day. The military authorities regarded the welfare of troops awaiting reallocation in Europe or return to Canada as a prime concern.[171] They expected a lengthy relocation process. So, they organized a vast and varied program of recreational activities to help fill the growing spare hours that became available to the troops as their duties diminished. With athletics replacing training, there was widespread participation in organized sports, interest being stimulated by inter-unit and inter-formation competitions. When off duty, soldiers could relax

---

[171] Ibid

in clubs and other establishments set up by the Army. Most clubs were in troop concentration centres such as Utrecht, Hilversum, Amersfoort, Apeldoorn and Groningen. Officers visited the Park Plaza Hotel or the Country Club in Apeldoorn. Warrant officers and senior NCOs frequented the Park Lane Club. Junior NCOs and other ranks hung out at the Kit Kat Club, the Moonlight Gardens and the Bluenose Swimming Pool. In Barneveld, there was the Red Patch Theatre, and similar establishments functioned at Arnhem and Hilversum. They introduced regular sports programs, and there were frequent competitions within and between Canadian formations during the summer.

The Canadian Auxiliary Services looked after the recreational needs of the Canadian troops on occupation duties in north-western Germany. They operated clubs, theatres, swimming pools and sports fields in Aurich and Oldenburg, Germany. A few field artillery regiments set up their own Gunners' Club, requisitioning a local inn or other building to serve as a wet or dry canteen for the unit. Divisional artilleries sponsored rest centres, which provided excellent accommodation for officers and men. Leave allotments were generous enough to give each man a visit once a month to various towns and hotels in the Netherlands and Germany. There, he could spend his 72 hours enjoying sea bathing, tennis, sailing, and dancing every night.

George and his buddies visited Amsterdam over a weekend and marvelled at its uniqueness.

"Have you ever seen anything like this city?" asked Dave. "There are canals everywhere! Everyone lives on a canal and has a boat, I guess. But there are also a hell of a lot of bicycles!"

"Well, we saw something like it in Venice, you remember," said George. "This place is beautiful."

"So many blond beauties," said Jean. "I love their costumes. I must meet one or two. Do you think they speak English or French?"

"Few of those we've met so far spoke English or French," said Dave. "What the hell? Who needs to talk?"

The buddies laughed at the conversation between Dave and Jean and left them to their devices.

"Don't get into any trouble," called George. "We'll meet you back here at 6 pm."

They didn't know they had left those two in the famous De Wallen district, the medieval city centre, with canals and narrow alleys lined with bars and brothels.

"Do you see that, Dave?" said Jean. "I think we are in the brothel district. Look at those girls hanging out of the windows and doors. They are beautiful, and they are looking for some business."

"I think you're right, Jean," said Dave. "So, what the hell, let's oblige them."

§

Repatriation, Reallocation and Disbandment

There was little doubt that the most critical factor affecting a soldier's morale was where he fitted into the army's plans for repatriation and reallocation. The Canadian Army learned that lesson at the end of World War I. They gave details of these schemes three days after VE Day in the Canadian Military Newspaper—*The Maple Leaf* - which reprinted a special pamphlet called 'After Victory in Europe.' They devised a point-score system of repatriation based on the principle of 'first in, first out,' subject to limitations. There was a need to keep qualified personnel to support the administrative framework of the Army. Forming a service contingent for the Far East was pressing, as was the redistribution of officers and men for German assignments.

A questionnaire distributed to the troops determined each soldier's preference between three options:

1. Serving with the Canadian Far East Force (CFEF) in the ongoing Pacific War,
2. Serving with the Canadian Army Occupation Force in Europe,
3. Taking his discharge from the service.

The army assured the men who selected the first alternative that the army would first return them to Canada for 30 days' leave. After that, they were to report to the CFEF for duty in the Pacific War.

Empire and Tyranny

Jean LaFleur hadn't soldiered enough, so he took the army's offer to go to the Far East Theatre of the war. That war was still raging, but it was also in its last months. Dave Smith stayed with the Occupation Force. The freshly married family men, George, Jock and Paddy, returned to Canada as soon as possible.

"What did you choose, Jean?" asked George.

"I have applied to the Pacific War," said Jean. "I want to see more of this world before I leave the army and return to Montreal."

"What about you, Dave?" asked George.

"I'm staying with the Occupation Force," said Dave.

"I want to experience a peaceful Germany while getting to know the Germans better, the women in particular, who I've heard can make wonderful wives."

"Well, us married men are heading home," said George, "We want to start our new lives with our families."

§

The field regiment gunners reached "a new high in social life" with a "vicious round of dances, movies, shows, parties and hospitality," with many new Dutch-based romances blossoming.

The 2nd Field Regiment organized an open-air street dance. The unit's Auxiliary Services Supervisor, seeking to speed up a slow start in the evening's festivities, offered a chocolate bar to any girl who danced with a Canadian.

"Whether it was the chocolate bars or the charm of the Canucks is uncertain," reported the unit history. "Still, the dance livened up, and everyone had a rollicking time." [172]

The buddies took part in most of these celebrations with enthusiasm.

"These Dutch girls are gorgeous," said Jean. "I might just change my mind about the best bride. I love these girls."

George, Paddy and Jock also attended many festivities but remained faithful to the women in their lives. For them, there was only one more goal to achieve: to get to Canada to rejoin their young brides.

In early June, the Canadian forces in Europe started disbanding. The last parades for the 1st Canadian Division field regiments were before they relinquished their guns. One of the most impressive of these was the final divisional show held by the 1st Canadian Division in Rotterdam on 10 June, with General Crerar taking the salute. The artillery units performed splendidly, with every vehicle and gun painted and gleaming in the bright sunshine. They drove past the reviewing stand at four miles an hour in a double-column formation. The senior man in each vehicle stood, and the rest sat at attention. It was an outstanding display for the division's C.R.A., Brigadier Ziegler.

Then, with mixed feelings, Canadian artillery units bid their guns farewell. [173]

---

[172] Ibid
[173] Ibid

"It's heartbreaking," said Paddy. "We've looked after these babies for so long. And they have held up to the punishment we gave them during so many battles. I, for one, am attached to our gun."

"They, we, did an impressive job," said Dave. "We hammered the bloody Nazis and helped win the war with the help of our gun. I agree, Paddy. It's hard to be leaving them."

"Yup, and I will miss my Jeep," said George. "What a vehicle it is—tougher than a mule! But I will not miss this war. It's time to get my little family to Canada and to start life afresh."

§

After a pleasant summer crossing of the Atlantic, George and his buddies arrived at Pier 21 in Halifax. They had granted Dave and Jean extended leave before returning to service at their respective destinations, so they sailed with their friends. They followed the typical route home by train to Montreal Central Station and were in Montreal with their wives and children by the end of July. Their families were out in force to meet them, including recent wives, children, and all.

For George, who had left Montreal in December 1939, his arrival in this magnificent city was an absolute pleasure. His entire family was there to meet and honour him. The Martin children showered him with rose petals, and his wife Dolly threw her arms around him and gave him a long, passionate kiss.

Dolly delighted in seeing him again and in the prospect of moving from the cramped Martin apartment into their own home. Michael, who had seen his father four months earlier, charged him with a gigantic smile and called "Daddy" as he fell into his father's arms. George had brought a duffle bag full of little gifts from Italy and the Netherlands, including small wooden toys for the other children. When they walked out of the station into the city's heart, George stopped and took a huge breath. He was savouring the old familiar scents and sounds of his loved mother city. George was home! This was where he belonged after what he had seen in Great Britain and Europe!

Later that evening, George and Dolly found a few moments alone before a large family gathering and meal at the Martins'.

"I'm pregnant again, darling," she informed her husband.

"Fantastic," said George. "Our family is growing, and I hope this will be a girl."

"You got home just in time for Michael's second birthday," said Dolly. "I will bake him a cake. Do you have any presents left?"

"No," said George. "Don't worry. Let's buy him something together. He is talking so much more, Dolly. And have you noticed he is always calling me Daddy? I love that! I'm so looking forward to our life together as a family."

He set everything in motion immediately to get a job and move his little family into 3884 Evelyn Street, Verdun. He was on a mission.

The army gave George an honourable discharge on 4 August 1945, at No 4 District Depot, Canadian Army, Montreal South, after four months of service in Canada (Sept-Dec 1939). He served 66 months overseas in the UK, Sicily, mainland Italy, France, Belgium, the Netherlands and Germany.

/George had served his country with the 2nd Field Regiment of the Royal Canadian Artillery throughout the war as a talented driver mechanic group B. It was a job he enjoyed and at which he excelled. He had joined at the innocent age of 21 and had seen a good chunk of the world. Now 27 years old, he was much wiser.

§

The army awarded Gunner George Alexander, D6618, 2nd Field Regt RCA, the following medals in order of precedence: the 1939-45 Star, the Italy Star, the France-Germany Star, the Defence Medal, the CVSM (Canadian Volunteers Service Medal) & Clasp (Overseas Service) and the War Medal 1939-45.

§